THE CRAVING IN SLUMBER

M.L. PHILPITT

The Craving in Slumber (Fractured Ever Afters #2)
Copyright © 2023 by M.L. Philpitt

ISBN: 978-1-990611-15-5

Warning: This book contains mature content. Reader discretion is advised.

Cover Designer: Cat Imb, TRC Designs
Editing and Proofreading: Rebecca Barney, Fairest Reviews Editing Services
Formatting: M.L. Philpitt

AUTHOR'S NOTE

The Craving in Slumber is book 2 of The Fractured Ever Afters series. While this can be read as a standalone, there is an overarching plot so it is recommended to read the books in order. Start with The Hunt in Elusion

This book has content some people may find triggering. You can read the content warning list on the last page.

This book uses Canadian spelling. This means words will have U's in them, "re", or double LL's. (colour vs color, centre vs center, signalling vs signaling, etc.) These are not typos.

PLAYLIST

"Butterflies" by Zendaya

"Marionette" by Antonia

"Devil in Her Eyes" by Bryce Savage

"I Hate Everything About You" by Three Days Grace

"My Type (Little Attitude)" by Bryce Savage

"Addicted" by Saving Abel

"Better Than Me" by Hinder

"I'll Make You Love Me" by Kat Leon

"like that" by Bea Miller

"Earned It" The Weeknd

"I Did Something Bad" by Taylor Swift

"Can You Hold Me" by NF & Britt Nicole

"Change (In the House of Flies)" by Deftones

"Sacrifice" by Black Atlass & Jessie Reyez

"i'm yours" by Isabel LaRosa

"Devotion" by Tullia Benedicta

"Soldier" by Samantha Jade

"Can't Help Falling in Love" by Hayley Reinhart

“Can’t Help Falling in Love - DARK” by Tommee Profitt &
brooke
“Chills - Dark Version” by Mickey Valen & Joey Myron

For the brats

1

ROSEN

Visiting Dad always brings me peace. For a little while, I'm not the head soldier of the Corsetti family, but simply a son. A regular person dropping by to see a family member.

The black, rusted, beat-up Jeep parked in the driveway confirms he's home, so I knock on the front door. I hadn't mentioned I'd be coming by, in case I got called away last minute.

Feet shuffle on the other side almost immediately, and the door I've walked through countless times growing up, swings open, revealing my father. His outfit of choice, a colourful wool cardigan, sweats, and slippers, always throws me, considering growing up, he was almost always dressed in clothing mirroring my own—all black and tactile.

"Rosen!" he exclaims. "My boy, how are you?" His arms come up to hug me, which I return, using the moment to check the strength of his aging body.

Dad retired a couple years ago, around the time Nico was made the underboss of the Corsetti family. After serving

Lorenzo, Nico's father, for so long, being in a highly-trusted position, the doctor said he'd be struggling to keep up with the demands of the Corsetti lifestyle if he kept going. So Lorenzo authorized an early retirement with a full pension in Dad's name.

Dad releases me and backs into the house, waving me forward. After a quick, habitual scan of the quiet Outremont neighbourhood, checking for anything amiss, I shut the door, kick off my shoes, and follow him into the living room.

I drop onto the faded blue couch along one wall, examining the moderately-sized living room. Dad hasn't changed much in this place from how Mom had it before she died a few years ago. Breast cancer took her from us much too soon. Dad's determined to keep the environment the same, which means a house so tidy, it's like living in a museum.

"It's been a few weeks since you last visited," Dad comments, lifting a mug up from the table beside him. "How's the Corsettis been?"

"Well—" I grimace, thinking about the whirlwind of drama that fell upon Nico's shoulders in such a short amount of time. First, his father demanding he find a fiancée worthy of the Corsetti name, and then our enemy's stepdaughter, Della, trying to lure him to his death, who, despite everything, will soon be his wife. His younger sister is also coming home in a few days for the first time since being sent away when she was six-years-old. "That's basically why I'm here. It might be a while until I can visit again."

"Nico sending you away on a job?"

"Not away. I'll be in the city. They're bringing Aurora home and have asked me to be her personal bodyguard until her engagement in the coming months."

Over his mug, Dad's brows rise. "That's huge, Rosen. I'm proud of you."

Of course, he is. Dad's entire life has been about protecting the Corsettis. In hindsight, I have no idea how Mom managed it.

"That poor girl," Dad muses. "I mean, that entire situation was a lot on the family. First with Hawke's kidnapping and—" He stops, cutting himself off from detailing the abuse Nico's older brother experienced. "And then him leaving. As a father, I can understand Lorenzo and Caterina's fears about wanting to keep Aurora safe, but also," his expression pinches, as though in physical pain for disagreeing with the family he holds in such high regard, "forgetting your child in an entire other province is a bit much. Even for me."

At least we agree on that point. Even Nico does, which is why the moment he became underboss, he was determined to bring her home.

Fifteen years ago, Aurora Corsetti, who was six at the time, was sent to a private boarding school at a convent after Nico's oldest brother, Hawke, was kidnapped and raped by men who wanted to bring the Corsettis to their knees. When her parents sent her away, they were determined to hide her from the world, but she's never returned. Now, she's a twenty-year-old woman, still stuck at the school, two years after graduating.

I hardly remember her, barely interacted with her back then because my time was spent learning how to fight. Being around Nico and Rafael's age, and with Dad's role as Caterina's personal guard, I grew up with the Corsettis knowing one day I'd be inducted as a soldier as well. When Nico and Rafael trained, as well as Hawke before he left, I trained with them. In a way, it helped me become a better soldier; I'll not only die for them because of the oaths I have taken, but also because they're genuine friends to me.

"It's gonna be a long year," I murmur, blowing out a breath. Leaning back into the couch's cushion, I position an arm across the back and kick up one leg over the other, attempting to relax the gnawing making my muscles tight.

"It's an honour," Dad counters. "You know, during those dark days when Lorenzo stole Caterina away from her wedding, I was the soldier they had guard her door to ensure she didn't go anywhere. Lorenzo trusted me with her, and Nico feels the same about you with his sister. This is a good thing."

"Except, it's coming at an inconvenient time. Something's happening in the family." I don't say what because, with Dad's retirement, he's no longer privy to this information. "I should be working on that situation instead of babysitting." My tone turns harsher as I attempt to tamp down the growing frustrations expanding in my chest.

Dad tilts his head to the side. "Is that what you see it as? Look at it as a respected position, son. It's a sign of ultimate trust. Anyone could run around with a gun and get whoever's threatening the family, but only *you* can protect Aurora."

I should have known how this conversation would go. He's not wrong, I guess, if I wanted to look at it like that, but still...I throw a grunt into the silent air in response. "I guess. But you know me; I'd rather be in the field than following her on shopping trips."

Since Nico gave me the order a few weeks ago, it's all I've been considering. The girl grew up secluded from the outside world, with only younger children and damn nuns as her company. She's bound to be the meekest, most boring woman now, only interested in what this life has to offer her. Which means being around her will prove to be a very mind-numbing time.

Dad shrugs, showing no sympathy. "Well, this was your order. Besides, the months will pass quickly. Visit when you can, but don't stress yourself out trying to come here. I understand your job and what it requires. Aurora Corsetti comes before me." He pauses before adding, "Besides, think about *her* and what this means. She'll be brought back to a life she barely knows, let alone understands. Don't be an ass to the poor girl and make her life more miserable. You'll be the one constant around her, so play nice."

Again, Dad with his great advice, except he's forgotten one major thing: my role doesn't demand emotional support. Aurora Corsetti will have to search inside her family for that.

I'm guarding her. Nothing more.

"Be sure to visit Poppy in the hospital before you start this task," Dad suggests. "I'm sure they'd appreciate a visit from you."

"They're next on my list. Enough of all that. How have you been, Dad?"

After visiting my sister and nephew, I return to the Corsetti mansion, heading straight to Nico's office, instead of down to my room. He's in his usual place behind his desk, with Rafael reclining in one of the two chairs across from him.

"How's your dad?" Rafael asks the moment I shut the door.

"Good." I drop into the free chair, focusing on Nico. "You wanted to see me."

Nico leans back, nodding slowly, the look of a man who has a lot going on. "I have the jet scheduled for takeoff at nine in the morning tomorrow. You'll fly to Toronto, pick her up from the convent, and then return to the jet right away. By mid-afternoon, you'll both be home."

I give Nico the nod of agreement he's looking for while my heart burns with empathy for the Corsetti princess. After speaking with Dad, my annoyance over the task hasn't lessened, but I suppose I understand why I was chosen for this job.

There's a lot of changes coming to Aurora's life very soon, and mine as well. All my focus will be on a single individual. My other tasks are secondary to keeping her safe. I'm not even sure how to act around her. Most of my time is spent around Nico and Rafael, and the other men, where it's easy to be myself, but Aurora might require something else.

"Della had the idea of moving up our engagement party and wedding," Nico continues, "to get Aurora used to us quicker. Rather than having a welcome-back party with all the attention on her, Aurora might feel more comfortable sharing it. So she'll be re-introduced to society then."

Days ago, he became engaged to Della Lambert, Stefano De Falco's stepdaughter and the woman who was sent to infiltrate Nico's life. She managed to almost win, but stole his heart in the process, the same he did to her. She was forgiven when revealing the purpose behind her actions—protecting her younger sister, Ariella. I won't admit it, but I'm a bit afraid of a woman with so much ability within her small frame.

"That all sounds like it'll go south, Nic, if I'm being honest. You really think Aurora will enjoy being thrown into the thick of things?" Rafael asks, skeptical.

"And," Nico adds, completely ignoring his brother, "the Rossis are also invited to the wedding. Rossi and Aurora will not be engaged for many more months, but this is a time for them to meet."

Erico Rossi, Underboss of the New York *Famiglia* is a smart alliance for Nico to make. They're a ruthless crime family I can't help but admire from afar. Aurora will want for nothing by his side. Besides, the quicker this engagement happens, the sooner my babysitting duty will end.

A strange noise comes from Rafael's throat before he

speaks. "Day one of her being home and she'll already despise you. You're asking for bloodshed at this point."

Nico's eyes shift from me to his younger brother, hardening in a cold look of contempt. "She'll learn. Mother and Father made a mistake by sending her away, considering Hawke's assailants had been dealt with at the time. She's been there too long, and it's time for her to claim her place."

All I see is the picture Nico showed me the other month when he first gave me this task. Amidst the noisy club, that picture captured the entirety of my focus. The way she was looking dismissively off to the side, like she couldn't be bothered to glance at the camera, the wind catching her blonde curls and waving them around, even in the still image.

Rafael laughs, leaning over, and sending a slap to my forearm. "Fuck, do I ever pity you, Rosen. Remember, she's a Corsetti. Raised apart from us or not, our stubborn-ass blood runs through her veins. She'll be interesting on the trip home."

"She knows what's expected of her," Nico cuts in. "She'll be fine."

Not that I'd admit it, but I side with Rafael in this. No person would be "fine" with being raised away from her true life and family, dragged home by a guard, and then shoved back into the life she was forced to leave, expected to be pleasant during it all. Not that I want to deal with her attitude, but I'd get why she'd have one if she did.

I also wonder if she's aware of her upcoming realities. Rossi isn't a *bad* man necessarily; I haven't heard of him abusing women or anything of the sort, but he is a Made Man, and the New York mafia is known to be more violent. He's the best of the worst, if anything.

"I'll handle it," I reassure them both—as well as myself. In the end, my empathy toward her is secondary to the vows I made to her family. I'll get her home, even if I must hogtie her to do so.

"Thank you, Rosen," Nico says, pushing himself further into his leather desk chair with the deep sigh of a man who carries too much weight on his shoulders.

Rafael shakes his head at his brother. "Dude, you're insane to be moving these celebrations up. Even you can't pull off the last-minute planning they'll require. Money won't make this happen, sorry to inform you."

Nico lifts his chin a fraction. "A wedding planner's coming here tomorrow. Mother, Della, and Ariella will be meeting with her. But that's beside the point because there's more." He glances at me for a long, bated second, and then his brother. "Della insisted I reach out to Hawke and invite him to the wedding...so I did."

"Shit!" Rafael and I both curse at the same time. Rafael slides to the end of his chair, his hands tightly gripping the edges of his seat. Of everyone, he was the one who took Hawke leaving the hardest.

"He's agreed to come."

What?

"What?" Rafael verbalizes, this time lifting to his feet. He almost falls forward, his hands landing on the desk's surface as he leans toward his brother. "Nic, you better not be fuckin' with me. This isn't a joke."

Without breaking eye contact, Nico reaches into his desk drawer and pulls out a folded-up piece of paper. "I wouldn't joke about something like this." He slides the sheet of paper toward us, gesturing for Rafael to take it. "He had very clear stipulations, which is where you," his eyes flick to me, "come in. We do this right; we might get *both* our siblings back. Him and Aurora."

I reach for the paper that Rafael hands me after he's done

reading over it and skim Hawke's response, answering the question I was about to ask.

"Protect his girlfriend." I toss the sheet back onto the desk in front of me. "Easy."

"He's killed for her, remember. He's made it known; he'll do it again if he feels he must. Rosen, you know I want you there as a guest. Job title or not, you're one of us. I don't want you working the same way everyone else will be, but watch out for Aurora, and Hawke and his girlfriend. Keep people away from them. If Hawke's coming here, we play by *his* rules. No one says shit to them, whether it be a cousin, my father, or the fucking staff, we shut it down."

In all my years of working here, Nico never bows down to others. The lengths he's going to ensure Hawke will not regret visiting speaks volumes as to what this means to him.

I nod. "Done, Nico."

"I can't..." Nico trails off, speaking lower than before, with less force. He slumps back in his seat and his arms drop, limply, onto his armrests. "We can't lose this opportunity. This is a miracle I never believed we'd get." He focuses on Rafael, who I'm not sure has blinked since reading the letter. "When he asked for help, it was different. But the expression he had when telling me goodbye said everything. He's determined to *not* be us."

While I don't have as large of a stake in Hawke's visit as Nico and Rafael, once I trained alongside him, and the idea of seeing him again is exciting. Last I knew him, he was a scrawny kid who threw skillful punches.

"Are you telling Aurora about Hawke?" Rafael asks. "Personally, I don't think we should shock her at the ceremony when he's there. She'll have enough to deal with."

Nico slowly nods as his brother makes his point. "No, yeah,

maybe. I don't know. That's a big thing to wrap her mind around."

"Our parents?"

Nico points to the letter. "You read what he wrote. Hawke's adamant I don't inform them. I think he hopes to slip in and out and not even alert them to his arrival. But, you know what? We're respecting that request because if he can get away without our parents knowing they're here, good. It'll avoid a fucking scene—because they'll certainly cause one—and at the end of the day, the wedding is for Della and me. I won't take that from her, so for the sake of everyone's sanity, no, I'm not telling them."

If Lorenzo and Caterina were to ever find out we all kept this from them, none of us would be safe. Heads would roll. Lorenzo Corsetti is ruthless, right from the moment his own father was killed, and he kidnapped Caterina in response. If he were to learn of Hawke being there, I can't even imagine his reaction.

"It sounds like these next few weeks will be a shitshow," Rafael breaks the heaviness lingering in the room, "between the wedding and all that's involved, Aurora's re-arrival, Hawke's appearance...Fuck, bro. You can't do simple."

"Let's not forget De Falco," I comment, adding the final straw to that messy pile of hay he's listed out. "No idea where he is at this moment, and with so much happening, he's bound to use this opportunity."

"To get farther away or to attack is the question," Rafael finishes.

Silently, Nico grabs his glass and then his brother's, and stands, heading for the small bar he keeps on the far side of his office. He uncorks the glass bottle of bourbon and refills the two glasses before adding a third to the mix. Then he returns to distribute them before retaking his chair.

"No, I don't do simple," he comments on his brother's previous statement. "I don't because I know this family lives by the oaths we take. Here's to us making it through the next few weeks."

He tosses back his drink, and I do the same, reflecting on the meaning behind that oath.

Unisciti a leale. Muori leale

Join loyal. Die loyal.

2

AURORA

"And that's how Sleeping Beauty found her prince and her happy ending," I conclude, shutting the book and standing from my chair between the two rows of beds.

Ten curious faces with the largest eyes and smallest button noses peer up at me from their dorm-room beds. They blink, sleepiness falling over them, but youthful determination has most leaping onto their knees, some going as far as crawling to the end.

"Can you read it again?" Miranda asks, her smile large and eager. She's practically bouncing from where she's kneeling on the bed closest to me. One bounce too hard and I imagine her tiny form would fall from the bed.

I tuck the book beneath my arm, shaking my head. "Sorry, you know I have to follow the rules. If I keep you up any later than you already are, I'll be the one to get in trouble." Not that I haven't done that before. Especially since I have only a short time left here.

A chorus of *Awws* carry through the room, and every syllable from their tiny lungs is a knife to my heart. One more slice, and they'll see me be a blubbering mess. I never believed I'd be hesitant to leave the convent since, for the longest time, it was all I dreamed about. But this place has become home, and these kids are the lifeline for my sanity.

"S-sorry, girls," I push out through the growing pain in my chest, which makes it more difficult to breathe. "Tomorrow, I'll choose a new fairy tale for you."

"What about the one where the girl falls in love with the beast and becomes a princess?" Carrie calls out. Her hands fold dramatically against her chest as she gushes, "That one's my favourite."

I chuckle. "Didn't we do that one the other night?"

"So?" Another girl, Lily, shrugs with her question, backing up Carrie's choice.

"All right." I scan the room, catching all their excitedly expectant gazes. "Anyone *not* want to read that story again?"

For the first time ever in this dorm room, there are absolute crickets amongst the girls.

"You got it," I conclude after a couple of seconds when there's no disagreement. "For now, sleep, all of you."

I complete my standard goodnight process by going around the entire room, hugging each child goodnight and tucking them in. Life here without these kids would be so different, and while each one of us has a story before ending up here—one I would change for them if I could—I can never describe the gratitude I have for all of us being stuck together. If it takes a damn story each night for these children to feel loved, then I'll read them a million.

I wish someone did that for me twelve years ago.

No one deserves to be abandoned by their family, forced to

grow up around strangers, creating a second family due to circumstance. We've come to rely on each other. Not that the nuns don't do their part, but they're also our teachers and guardians. Birthdays, holidays, any major life events, we only have each other to celebrate with. Being removed from regular society means we lose out on a lot of regular childhood experiences we should otherwise be having.

Which is why *I* love these kids. As they grow, my activities change, as I'm frequently doing crafts and sports with the middle grade students, the kids who used to sleep in this dorm before they aged out. No one did that for me when I was in their place, so over the years here, I've become determined to care for them until their biological families remember them. Every night in the elementary wing, I read the girls a bedtime story, and I spend breakfast with the boys, giving them the attention they all deserve.

After waving my final goodbye, I head for the door, shutting it behind me. Leaving them causes my heart to break all over again because any one of these nights could be my final visit.

What's worse about being taken away from the kids is the limbo I'm currently in. The Sisters haven't been able to give me a set date because my family hasn't provided one, which is beyond inconsiderate.

The storybook of Sleeping Beauty feels heavier in my grip and I'm half tempted to throw it away, except the girls enjoy the stupid tale too much, so I won't. Everyone knows the story, of course. Girl sent away for her own safety when the villain threatens her with death. Raised by her three fairy godmothers, away from her royal family until they call her back.

It's like my parents used the damned fictional story as a fucking manual for my actual life.

I am Aurora Corsetti, of the Corsetti mafia family who

rules Quebec. Princess of the mafia, daughter to the boss, sister to the underboss—based on the reports I've gotten from the Sisters here. Sent away for my protection when my mother had a breakdown after my oldest brother, Hawke, was harmed.

Or, that's what I've been told at least.

It wasn't even a full week after Hawke's rescue when my own bags were packed. My brother's kidnappers were rightfully murdered by our father, but that didn't seem to ease my parents' psychotic worries.

Imagine being six, beyond confused and scared, brought to a boarding school—sorry, *convent*—where strangers expected you to immediately fall in line and accept your new reality. Where older students sent pitying stares your way. Imagine growing up with only pictures of your family. Never a phone call or even a fucking letter from them. Absolutely no contact whatsoever because, apparently, they had the insane idea it would be safer. Fast forward fifteen years later, and the only thing I really know about my family is that we share the same last name.

This whole scenario is all fucking bullshit if you ask me.

Walking down the hallway, there's a lone table with a row of candles for décor by a window. I abandon the stupid book on it, annoyed I chose that one today, when it hits so close to home.

Am I a tad pissed off at this entire situation? Just a "tad."

I make it back to my bedroom, undisturbed. Bedroom. Home. Pick a term. This is the room I've had since I was twelve, when the nuns move children from shared dorms to individual spaces. The walls are still decorated with the unicorn lights I once enjoyed. The bedspread has been updated with more muted shades of green, changing out the bright one I used to have. The small desk across from the bed houses a laptop, which is locked down, only authorized to reach certain programs and websites to complete my school work.

Even now, having graduated over two years ago, they still don't allow me the freedom I should have. Something about my safety—and probably orders from my family, so I don't search them up.

Wandering through the small space, I go to the attached bathroom to shower and wash my face before climbing into bed after a typical boring day. Hanging out with the younger kids is my only entertainment, since I no longer have classes to occupy me, let alone any of my other friends.

Children from prominent families often end up here to remain safe during their schooling. It's a small group, but there's enough of us—a few dozen. There are no rules with how long a stay can be; a family can place their child here for a short time, or longer. This place is hidden in a small neighbourhood in Toronto, where, despite the bustling city down the road, people won't look for us. Heavily-secured, cameras at every angle, we're protected from everything but the monsters that lurk under the bed and inside our heads.

Over the years, I've watched more and more of my friends get to return to their families, while I've been forced to remain here. Perhaps it's why I connect with the younger kids so much. Besides the nuns, they're my only constant. At least for a few years before they're taken home.

With my head on my pillow, I'm able to see the bedroom window above my head, and the moon shining through it. So large, so bold. A sign of endless possibilities. I imagine that other people my age are out partying beneath the moonlight. Enjoying life. Enjoying their freedom.

While I'm dreading the moment mine finally begins after so long of nothing.

Since the Sisters told me "soon" a few days ago, I've been a bundle of mixed emotions. On one hand, I'm pleased to *finally* go home, even if there are other sentiments alongside it: fear of being thrown into a new world where people will expect shit from me; anxiety of a litany of unknowns that I won't understand; stress of living up to my last name. On the other hand, I'm being forced to leave what's been home for so long as well as the kids, knowing there's no one my age who'll read to them, who'll be a comforting older sibling for them.

Soon. What's "soon?" A year. I mean, after *fifteen* of them, one year could be considered soon in comparison. Or is it a matter of days?

I sigh, the sound heavy in my silent, cramped room.

Corsetti.

A name that's meant nothing to me for years, but will soon consume my entire being. I don't know what I'm supposed to be to these people. Mafia princess. Daughter. Baby sister to three older brothers—Hawke, who I know escaped this life before I was sent off; Nico, who became the heir; and Rafael, the middle child.

If what I've heard is true, there might be one other title attached to me soon. That brief notion has my hands knotting in the blanket with trepidation and rage.

Wife.

The nuns were always honest about my family and their lifestyle. Arranged marriages are commonly used as a way to fuse families together and make strong alliances. I'm sole Corsetti female; the only daughter of Lorenzo and Caterina Corsetti. Sister to the current underboss. The nuns haven't directly stated it, but they've inferred what's to happen to me. I'll be a desired connection, but worse than that...I'll be *used*.

A pawn. A game piece they sent away and returned only when I was essential.

"Fucking bullshit," I whisper into the empty room. "If they think I'll fall in line and become someone's fucking wife, they're going to find out who they're dealing with."

I am a product of their own mistakes. They sent me away. Didn't raise me as a Corsetti; therefore, they don't get a trained pet to parade around now.

Take me from the only life I've known—fine.

Force me to be who they need me to be—not happening.

Suddenly, I can't *wait* for them to come for me.

3
ROSEN

"**F**ucking hate this city," I grumble as I weave the Coupe Nico had waiting for me on the tarmac through the neighbourhood where the convent is located. I've been able to avoid the traffic-heavy areas of Toronto, but there's a chaotic vibe in this place my skin itches to get away from.

As I approach the wrought-iron gates of the convent, I poke my head out the window I rolled down, tipping my head up toward the camera positioned there and waiting for them to grant me entrance. Nico had already sent them my picture this morning, so they'd know who to be expecting.

As anticipated, the gates open with a loud crank, and I drive straight up the gravel driveway, parking off to the side of it, by the grass line. I get out and do a visual sweep of the area, spotting all the cameras on the building. This place should be secure, considering the people—children—living within its walls.

I stride to the old-style, large wooden doors, but before I can knock, it swings open, an older woman dressed in a habit standing there. She smiles at my approach and gestures for me to enter.

"Please come in, Mr. Carrigan."

"Thanks." I step inside, my hands immediately brushing against the weapons I'm carrying: a gun in my waistband and a knife strapped to my side. A force of habit when entering unfamiliar places, even if there should be nothing evil in this place. Children and nuns. Can't get much safer than that.

And a Corsetti princess who'll despise you.

"My name is Sister Mary Weather, but please, call me Sister Mary. Pleased to meet your acquaintance. This way." She begins walking down the connected hallway. "She's out in the garden, where I've asked her to wait. Figured it's a better place for her to yell at you than inside, where the other children can overhear." Sister Mary throws a smirk over her shoulder.

Huh. A nun with a sense of humour.

"What's she like?" I find myself asking. Not sure why. Maybe so I can bring back new information to Nico.

Not because I pity the girl whatsoever.

Sister Mary's steps slow, falling in line with mine. Her hands weave together in front of her habit as she muses, "She's a quiet girl when she wants to be, but certainly a handful." She pauses, rolling her lips together, and I can tell she's attempting to formulate more details.

"What aren't you saying?" *Oh, fuck, why do I suddenly get the feeling I'm not being paid enough for this shit?*

The Sister's steps halt. "A couple months ago, we caught her sneaking off the property. The first time, we stopped her the moment she left the compound, but the second time," she shrugs, seeming now unbothered by this traitorous admittance, "we let her go. I had someone trail her, to ensure her safety."

A mix of awe and annoyance swirl in my gut. Slipping out of a place we're told has top security measures is impressive, but there's also a litany of reasons her being away from here is a bad idea.

"Have you told the Corsettis?" Nico mentioned being told she tried to sneak away, but not about a successful instance.

"No." She picks up her steps again, this time much slower.

"Why allow something against their rules and yours?"

"To speak plainly: we do what we can for everyone here, but ultimately, we're not their true family. Aurora has spent most of her life here. Longer than most, and longer than anyone who's come before her. She's tenacious, so it doesn't surprise me she found the single blind spot that we had. That's been fixed since her initial attempt, but we still let her out because I sympathized with her." She sighs, gesturing toward the walls. "Aurora is more than a student here, especially in these last two years. She cares for the younger children, helps tend to the garden, and continuously decorates these walls with the artwork her and the children create." She motions her hands at the walls, hung with paper banners, painted canvases, and other crafty creations.

There's a sense of admiration on the woman's face, drawing me to conclude, "You care for her."

"We all do," she murmurs, nodding her head slowly. "She's a good person, and I understand the realities of her role. By the time she turned eighteen and no one retrieved her," her sharp gaze cuts to me, blame evident, "it made sense she wanted to explore the outside world. She's restless here. When we realized she wasn't doing anything indecent or going anywhere of importance, it became apparent she wanted, even needed, a small sliver of freedom. She believes we never knew, so we haven't said otherwise."

"Where did she go?" I ask, mentally preparing to have to report her response to Nico. He and his parents will be pissed to learn the place they paid extremely high amounts of money to, to keep Aurora locked inside and safe, allowed her to wander the busy streets of Toronto.

"Around." Sister Mary gestures, indicating the neighbourhood beyond. "We kept expecting her to head for downtown, even if that's quite far by foot, but she never did. She walked around the community close by. It was always in the evening and only for an hour or so at most."

It's not *okay* what Aurora did by any means, but at least there's no harm done. Still, the Sisters broke their own rules—rules the Corsettis expected them to abide by.

"You realize what you say could get you killed, right?"

Sister Mary's steps don't even falter. "You'd murder a nun? You realize that could earn your eternal damnation, right?"

She's fucking with me, surely, but opting not to test that theory I follow her out of the back door we finally reach. She opens the glass door and steps into a small courtyard.

Almost every inch of the space is covered with a plant of some sort. As she leads me through the shrubbery and toward the centre, I nudge a low-hanging tree out of my way, pushing aside branches that could tear at my clothes. Sister Mary seems to weave through the space easily, knowing exactly the path to take, but I get snagged on every damn rose bush, tree, and flower patch I seem to pass.

"Aurora?" Sister Mary calls. "Your guest is here."

"Is he a guest if he's unwanted?"

Sister turns to me with raised eyebrows that asks, *You ready for this?*

But all I'm thinking about is her voice. Husky, but feminine. The voice of a woman who'd gift the most delicious moans when she's in the throes of sex. And then her choice of words. Lined with an attitude I can't help but appreciate, even if her brashness agitates something inside me before I remind myself *who* is talking.

Sister Mary goes around the plants, toward the other side, and I trail behind her slowly, suddenly very interested in seeing the girl from the picture come to life.

"Aurora," she warns, "we've talked about this. You've known for days now of his arrival."

"That doesn't mean I should invite him in for tea and conversation. Oh, wait, that's exactly what it means! That's how you fucking trained me to be, after all. A *woman*," she snarls in a tone that implies being a woman is a negative fact, "a future wife. They're the *mafia*, Sister. How long do you think it'll be before you're reading about my wedding in the papers?"

A year or less. That's Nico's plan anyway.

I hang back, letting the women finish their conversation.

"They're your family," Sister Mary replies softly.

"Are they?" Aurora retorts sharply.

Maybe Raf was right. Maybe she will be trouble. Bracing myself, I step out from behind the plants and into view.

Nico might have shown me a semi-recent photo of her, but nothing prepared me for the real version. Long blonde hair curls down her back, nearly to her waist. It frames what seems like the softest face, which I ache to touch, with green eyes that are narrowed on me. Full lips curl into an unhappy sneer, but still, the overwhelming craving to take those lips with my own hits me, no matter the inappropriateness of that fantasy.

She's fucking beautiful.

Forbidden fruit, but beautiful.

Shaking off the momentary, unwelcome thoughts, I stride forward, my hand out toward her, where she's seated on a stone bench. "Aurora Corsetti. An honour. My name is Rosen Carrigan. I work for your brother, and I've come to take you home."

4

AURORA

It pains me to admit this, but my future captor is fucking *hot*.

Yes, future captor. *Future*, as in, within the next hour when he drags me away from here. *Captor* because that's his job. Instantly, I hate him for two reasons: for my family sending him instead of coming themselves, and simply because he's one of *them*—a monster from the same world that hasn't acknowledged my existence in many years.

He's larger than any man I've been around—not that that list is particularly long. Standing, he'd easily tower over me, and if I'm honest, would probably break me the moment he touches me. Dark hair and a handsome face. A strong jaw, which I've never understood the appeal of, but seeing him, I can appreciate the feature. He's older than me, by a few years, that I can tell. Mid-twenties, perhaps?

Even his stance exudes power, and as much as I hate to admit it, I wouldn't mind being overpowered by him. He stands with his back straight and his legs slightly spread. One hand is stretched toward me, while the other is by his side, resting on his hip. I assume there's a weapon there.

When he speaks, it's with the most delicious, deep rumble. The kind of voice I've imagined in my head in the past, with my fingers stroking between my legs.

"Aurora Corsetti. An honour. My name is Rosen Carrigan. I work for your brother, and I've come to take you home."

Rosen, huh.

I recline in my seat, looping my interlocked hands over my knee as I peer up toward the towering man. "That so? Because that's your *job*, right? To come kidnap the woman who's never known her family and drag her home."

A muscle in Rosen's cheek twitches, but it's the only sign of annoyance he reveals. "Precisely, so please come, so I may do that very job. Your family is waiting."

My family is waiting...Waiting. So have I.

"I don't have a family. They left me here many years ago."

"For your own safety," he snaps, an edge to his tone. "Come, *princesse.*"

Come. Amidst the annoyance I feel toward this stranger already, and the appreciation for what he looks like, my insides clench with that simple word.

Princess. Worse—princess in the French language. My family is from Quebec, so of course the Sisters were insistent I learn the language. I've always struggle with rolling my Rs correctly and the smoothness French demands, but it's effortless from his lips, almost like a sexy purr...Mentally, I groan, imagining him giving that very order in another situation. A situation involving his cock. He looks like someone with big-dick energy.

"Aurora," Sister Mary begins, her voice soft, a direct contrast to his, "we've spoken about this. You're prepared. You know this."

Do I? Yes, we've spoken about it. Yes, my bags may be packed and by the front door. But am I prepared?

Not even a little bit.

To Rosen, she states, "I have someone loading her bags into your vehicle now. You'll be able to be on your way soon. I know how much Mr. Corsetti and the entire family eagerly await her arrival."

"Thank you, Sister," he replies, all without looking away from me. His brow does a half-cocked thing, saying, *See?*

They're speaking like I'm not right in front of them. As if I'll be standing any moment and taking the steps to complete this inane plan.

"I will carry you, Miss Corsetti," Rosen threatens, surprising me with the sudden shift in his demeanor. "I don't have time to be hanging around here longer than I need to be. You have no idea the kind of people you're dealing with, and this bratty thing you're doing right now won't fly once we're with your family. You have a role. I'm sure you've been kept well-informed as to what that role is, so it's time you do it."

I might hate Rosen being here, but it's clear he isn't a fan of his new role either. I can't figure out if I feel better by this notion, or worse. Makes taking my anger out on someone easier because, after that spiel, I'm sure he'll take the bait.

Although he wasn't talking to Sister Mary, she angles herself toward him. "Yes, she has been. Aurora is aware of the kind of family she has and what's expected of her upon re-entry into the home. She's simply anxious, I believe."

So many assumptions about me. For half-a-second, I'm happy to be gone from here. But then, I look behind them and up the side of the stone building that's been home for so long. I pause on the windows where I know the girls' dorms are, picturing the final story I read them last night. *Sleeping Beauty* again, because it's appropriate, but I never made it to the end because I was crying too much. This morning, saying goodbye to the boys at the final breakfast I shared with them, and then later, doing my rounds with the older kids. Kids who'll only have each other after today.

My throat feels thick and my eyes burn, but I flick them toward the right, into the sunlight. *Don't cry. Don't let him see you cry.*

Rosen catches my movements. His cocky brows lower with confusion and he slowly turns, following my gaze to the windows. He doesn't know the love within those rooms, but whatever he presumes is enough to have him reaching for me again, this time, his tone less harsh.

"I know this is difficult, Miss Corsetti. I promise you, it's for the best. You should never have been here in the first place."

"Don't call me that. Use my fucking name," I snap right away. "And yeah, I shouldn't have ever been here." Thinking about all the kids up there has me taking hold of Rosen's large hand. How many of them are peering outside, watching this moment? How many of them are using me as an example? I must be strong and follow-through.

Rosen helps me to my feet and releases me the second I'm steady. "Good," I hear him rumble softly, and then he turns back toward the convent, heading for the entrance.

Sister Mary cuts in front and heads to the side of the building, to a wrought-iron gate. "This way. No need to walk through the house again."

No need. My heart shatters right there. Right on the stone walkway, surrounded by nature, and observed by innocent children above. No need to walk through, one last time, the place that's been my home for so many years. No need to risk me having a panic attack in the lobby or for the kids to fight not to let me go. A clean break. That's what she's doing. I've seen it done with others, with old friends, and now, it's my turn.

I don't even know how, but Rosen spots my pending breakdown. He falls in step beside me, the warmth of his skin radiating over my own. "It's okay, Miss—Aurora. This is how it was supposed to be."

For once, I have no response. Sister Mary leads us around the front of the building, where there's a row of staff waiting by a vehicle, which I guess to be Rosen's. The two other nuns, Sister Florence and Sister Shawna, who run this place with Sister Mary, are closest to us. The women who became my stand-in mothers, older sisters, staff, and teachers. Beside them are the other staff and teachers who work here.

I said my goodbyes to them earlier this morning, but I hug them all again. With each final goodbye, it becomes harder and harder to release the person I'm holding until I reach the last one.

Sister Mary takes me into her arms for a long embrace. Her fingers stroke over my cheek, wiping away stray tears. "You are strong, Aurora. One day you too will be leading a household, and you're going to be great at it. But you will never be forgotten here."

Thank you. I want to say those two words, but they're locked in my throat, stuck amidst the emotion clogging it. Instead, I manage a nod and back away toward the car, which Rosen waits by with the passenger door open.

Without looking at him, I slide inside and buckle up, trying to recall the last time I was in a car. Occasionally, we have outings, but they're heavily-guarded and meticulously orchestrated for our protection.

Rosen climbs into the driver's seat and starts the vehicle. It rolls away from what I've been considering home, from the kids, from the Sisters, and I watch in the side mirror as the place grows more distant, the line of waving nuns becoming a single blob before we turn out of sight entirely.

A piece of my heart remains there and will forever. I glance up at the sky again, using the sun to burn away more tears that threaten to come.

"Ready?" Rosen asks after a moment.

"Not even a little."

"You'll manage."

I give him my full attention, my face scrunched in a sneer. "How do you know?"

"You were strong enough to withstand being raised without your true family. You'll survive going home."

"Huh," is all I can manage as Rosen drives us through Toronto, presumably to the airport. "Quite insightful for a guy who's known me for all of two seconds."

He shrugs, seemingly indifferent, not sparing me a glance. "I'm observant, that's all."

I'd believe that. He must be decently high in the ranks, considering it's him they've chosen to come fetch me, not even having the decency to do it themselves. Which means, he's likely proficient at his job, and I suspect, being observant is simply one part of it.

"So, who *are* you?" All he said in the garden was his name and we never got around to sharing further details when I hesitated in leaving. "Like what do you do in my family?"

"I'm a soldier," he responds right away.

Not only a soldier, I'm certain. The Sisters once told me my parents have a mini army behind them, and they wouldn't send just anyone.

"I'm assuming you're pretty high in the ranks, considering you're the one they sent to fetch me."

That muscle in his cheek twitches and he looks away from the road to me. "Now look who's insightful. Yes. I work closely with your brothers. They place a lot of trust in me, and it's a highly-valued position."

I study him, searching through decades of memories, trying to find a younger version of him in my mind.

"Would I have known you before?" I don't define, 'before,' because we both know what it means.

At the next red light, his eyes cut to me. "Known me, no. But I was around, yeah."

"I don't remember you."

"You were six. It was a different time for both of us."

When the car moves again, I fall silent. How strange to be getting picked up by a guy who once would have been around me as a child, and yet, neither of us has any memory of it. How many other soldiers and staff in my family's home remember the child version of me? It's bizarre that people I have no recollection of remember me.

Like my brothers. Faces in a child's mind. People who are about to look at me, expecting me to remember everything about them when I don't.

Rosen drives the car down a small hill, and my breath stalls, but it has nothing to do with the direction of the vehicle. Breathing gets heavier, pain flashing across my sternum. My hands curl in my lap, digging into my legs, trying to use the pain as a distractor.

"You okay?"

Somehow—some fucking how—he knew. He knew without even knowing. I don't think I was obvious, but maybe I was. Either way, his gentle probing returns air to my lungs, allowing me to breathe normally again, his tone something else for me to focus on.

Anger flashes right over where the pain was. How dare someone, who's known me for less than an hour, help me? *Fix* me? He has no right to this. He's one of *them*.

"I'm fine." Crossing my arms, I twist my form toward him.

"If you work closely with my brothers, you must be aware of what my future looks like."

His lips twitch, fighting a smile. "I do, but telling you isn't a part of my job description. Sorry."

His apology is hollow at best, and the fact that he even tries should bring positive feelings, but instead, it annoys me. He's trying to placate me in the same manner my family, no doubt, will upon my arrival.

"Aren't I ranked higher than you because of my last name, which means I'm your boss? Which means you have to do as I order."

At a stop sign, he stomps on the brakes a bit harder than what's comfortable. "*Princesse,* you are not my boss. Your brother is. Between you and me, *one* will be giving the orders, and that won't be you."

Yep. Like I thought earlier, big-dick energy. It's been confirmed.

I smile because once again, that icy exterior cracks a little bit. If my family sent Rosen to retrieve me, it means they trust him and won't appreciate me being a dick to him. But he makes it too easy.

I lean over the console, practically on my knees, getting close enough I hope to make him uncomfortable. Propping my chin on a fist, I slowly grin, letting my gaze rove over his body.

"Yeah. And what kind of orders would you give me?"

He does exactly as I want and takes the bait. His nostrils flare, but it's the only sign of me affecting him whatsoever, since he presses the gas again and takes us through the intersection. "I'd command you to sit the fuck down. If you haven't noticed, I'm trying to get through Toronto traffic, heading toward one of the busiest airports in the country, and that takes quite a bit of focus."

Fine. While the convent's outings were far and few, the

streets were always packed with thick traffic, no matter what time of day we went out. I suppose I appreciate his necessity for focus and not wanting to get us killed.

I sit normal again but still comment on his previous statement. "That's not a fun command."

"Then what kind would you want me to give you?"

Why do I feel as if the tables have turned?

"That's what I thought," he adds in a haughty tone after I don't respond.

Frowning, I tell him, "You're not very nice for someone who serves my family. Or is that the power that comes from being my brothers' right-hand?"

"I'm plenty nice," he counters. "When I want to be. It's a two-way street, *princesse*."

I ignore the jab, my mind locking on the nickname he continues to use. "Why do you keep calling me princess? In French, at that."

As Rosen maneuvers the vehicle onto the off-ramp toward the airport, he peeks over at me. "Because that's what you are. The mafia princess. As for the language, get used to it. You'll soon learn your family speaks in all three languages—English, French, and Italian. The outcome of a French-Italian family living in an English-French country."

I don't respond, tipping my head back onto the headrest as I study the airport and the numerous people parking cars in the lot, unloading their bags, and waving goodbye to family.

"When was the last time you left the school?" Rosen asks randomly.

Last week. "The latest outing was about a month ago."

Rosen rolls his neck, turning his face toward me with an expression of clear disbelief, his mouth pulling up on one side. "Let's try that again, Aurora. When was the last time?"

I stare at him for a moment, deciphering his words, his

knowing look. "You know?" Wait—that means *they* knew. The Sisters knew what I was doing but never said anything. My heart beats faster in my chest with this new information, fearful of how this will ultimately play out. If he tells my family, what will they do? What *can* they do?

"Yes."

Fuck.

"I see no reason your parents or brothers should know."

I do a double take. Surprise ripples through me, slowing the fear my heart was enduring. "I don't believe you."

When Rosen takes one of the airport's back exits, heading away from the main building entirely, I realize we're not heading inside, like the rest of the public. We pass signs pointing our way to a private airfield. Of course, my family doesn't fly commercial.

"Believe me, Aurora, I *should* be, and if the secret I hid this from them was ever revealed, my ass would be on the line, so I'd appreciate it if this remained between us."

"Obviously, but that doesn't answer why."

Rosen is a Corsetti soldier. He's a monster. He's a part of the group of people who've brought hell and pain to my life. So why is he being nice? It doesn't align with what—who—I need him to be. I've been grouping my family into little compartments of evil, and he must be in there with them, for my own mental processing.

He doesn't respond for the longest ten seconds, his eyes focused on the smooth, paved road in front of us, which winds around the airfield. Far off, dozens upon dozens of airplanes of different sizes are parked, waiting to be used. The last time I was in a plane was when I was six and arriving in Toronto, but I remember nothing of that trip.

"Because," he finally speaks, "you didn't do anything. The Sisters had staff trail you. After your first attempt, they fixed the blind spot you discovered, but they still let you go when they noticed all you wanted to do was walk around the area."

A new wave of appreciation for the Sisters hits me and I long to go back there and thank them all. Venturing farther, to explore Toronto the way it should be experienced, was a consideration every single time, but found I was content to be away. As if the air outside of school was different and ignited new vitality every trip I risked outside the walls.

"Why'd you sneak out?"

"Ever been locked away in a place almost your entire life?" I snort, continuing without waiting for him to respond, "That's what I assumed. Until you spend your entire life restricted, you won't get it."

He's silent again, as the car rolls to a stop beside a white private plane with a single black strip on the wing. I reach for the car's handle, pausing. This plane is supposed to be a sign of independence, so then why do I feel less free than I ever have? I should be excited to go home. Nervous to see everyone again after all these years. Instead, a crippling unknown threatens to consume me.

Rosen climbs out of the vehicle and comes around the front to open my door. The few times I've been in a car, I've never had someone open my door for me so it isn't until he reaches for me, that I move, resting my palm in his. His strength helps me to my feet as my eyes take in the huge expanse of airfield around us.

"Freedom."

My attention flies back to the hulking figure inches from me, my hand still wrapped in his. "Huh?"

"Freedom," he repeats. "That's why you left, right? To gain a little bit of freedom that *you* were in control of. No one else."

"E-exactly." That was *exactly* the reason and Rosen picked

up on it so easily. It's alarming to have my emotions so bare and obvious to another.

His hand around mine tightens a fraction and I wonder if he even realizes he's done it. "It's okay to be nervous, Aurora."

"How do you know I am?"

"Told you, I'm insightful."

It's interesting, considering the Sisters frequently told me I hide my emotions well. That my poker face is strong, and they praised me, saying it would be useful one day. Being vulnerable in front of a stranger is both alarming, and a bit welcoming. Like I already have at least one person on my side.

Rosen drops my hand and gestures for me to head toward the plane closest to us, and to the man—the pilot, I assume, based on his attire—who waits at the bottom of the metal stairs. The pilot tips his head when I approach but says nothing.

After another glance around the airfield, I suck in a large gulp of that wide-open air and use it to lift me up the stairs.

To take me home.

Despite the fresh air, every step up the stairs makes my body feel completely weighted down by the reality of my situation.

At the doorway, I pause, studying the private jet, one of the wonders of my new life. White leather sofas and recliners, a bar and a table in the back. Everything is smooth and spacious and not at all like what I've seen planes as being in movies.

"Sit anywhere," Rosen commands from behind me.

"I'd rather stand." I don't know why I'm fighting him but sitting means this trip begins, that I'll soon see my family. Standing puts the entire thing on pause. For all the years I've spent dreaming of this moment...I'm not sure I want it anymore.

You've already made it this far.

"Sit." To emphasize his order, Rosen's two hands land on

my shoulders and he presses weight into them, encouraging my legs to buckle under me and I land on the couch.

"Better." He takes the sofa across from me, kicking one leg up over the other and pulling out his phone. "Ride will be an hour. Rest."

"And then?"

"Then we get to the Corsetti mansion."

"And then?"

Dark brows furrow. "And then you meet the people who have been very eager to see you."

Noises come from the front of the plane, assuming the pilot is preparing for take-off, but I pay him little attention, looking again at the man across from me. It's easier to taunt Rosen than focus on what happens in an hour. Easier to see him as a Corsetti monster, rather than the stranger who somehow recognized a breakdown in its early stages and who understood my requirement for freedom when it came to sneaking out.

"What comes after? You can't tell me I'm being brought home, so I can live inside that house and what, be the princess you all claim me to be?"

"Already said, I'm not revealing anything about your future."

I try another tactic, pouting as my shoulders slump with fake depression. "Why won't you tell me?"

"I'm not *not* telling you. I simply think it's better for you to hear it from the person making these decisions."

"Nico."

My older brother is basically a mystery to me, but I was taught a bit about the mafia lifestyle. They protect their own. Woman are treated as dolls. Meant for social situations, arranged marriages, and baby-producing. Men are the soldiers, leaders, and caretakers.

And I'm new to all this, which means my family won't leave me unprotected, which means my freedom is a thing of the past.

That's when it hits me. There's more to Rosen's presence than simply being a trusted soldier. Anyone could have retrieved me but *him* being chosen is purposeful.

"You have to guard me." My smile spreads slowly with the deduction. "Nico wouldn't leave me unprotected, considering I'm so new to this whole mafia thing, which means he's giving me my own personal bodyguard. You."

Which means Rosen and I will get to spend *a lot* of time together.

Let the games begin.

5
ROSEN

The mischievous expression on her face makes me curse.

She's a Corsetti for fucking sure. If there was any doubt before, it's one thousand percent gone now. She has the brain of her brothers.

I've already done way too fucking much for this woman. I have no requirement to be keeping secrets from her family, considering my loyalty lies with them. I'm not even sure why I am. Sister Mary claims they had eyes on her the entire time, but what if that was a lie? What if she went places? Her virginity could be questioned. Nico certainly doesn't need that stress. The New York *Famiglia* is as traditional as they come, and if they learned she'd been out on the streets of Toronto, only supervised from afar, they'd have a fit.

But perhaps it's the other things Sister Mary had said, about granting her the little bit of freedom before she's forced into mob life. Maybe it's the look Aurora got when speaking about it in the car earlier.

Which is also why I don't bother lying to Aurora. Nico

never indicated if he wanted me to let her know the truth of my role, but she deserves a bit of truth.

"Yes, Aurora. I am your personal guard."

That fucking smile grows and it looks so damn sexy. I'd love to take her over my knee and show her what being cocky around a man like me could cost her—if she wasn't forbidden.

"Which means, earlier, when I said I'm a higher rank, that's certainly the case. You must do as I say. Bring me where I want to go. The list goes on." She flips her hair.

I pin my arms to my sides as I recite *Corsetti, Corsetti, Corsetti* in my mind a few hundred times until it sticks as to who this girl is.

"It means I protect you with my dying breath. When I took the vow of your family, *Unisciti a leale. Muori leale*, I took it seriously. Whether it's Nico, your mother, or you, I am loyally bound, which means being near you to ensure no one assassinates Montreal's newest *princesse*."

Did I add a bit toward the end there, making my statement more dramatic than it calls for? Sure did, but it works, because she straightens slowly, lifting her head from her fist as the cocky grin fades into something else. Resignation. Nerves.

She reclines into the couch, making herself comfortable, and shifts her attention toward the cabin. By now, they have the door shut and locked and the pilot is readying for takeoff. The engines turn on, the cabin filling with a loud grumble as the plane begins its taxiing.

"Your safety isn't a game, Aurora," I continue, feeling the urge to further explain and make her understand. "Fifteen years ago, it wasn't, and while what happened may seem extreme to you, they did it to keep you safe. Bringing you home is appropriate, but they won't if they believe someone could harm you. You'll be doing a lot of navigating, trying to figure out upper-class society"—*and your fiancé*— "so having me there as your protector is only for your benefit. I'm not a dog you can order around."

Finally, fucking *finally*, I get through to her because her only retort is a quick nod. Then she peeks over her shoulder, catching the ground speeding by her as the plane is lifted into the air, tipped at an angle she's obviously not used to, based on the flash of panic consuming her expression. I bite my lip to keep from chuckling, certain Aurora wouldn't appreciate it.

Within moments, the plane is straightened, so I take out my phone again and open a gaming app for something to do to pass the time.

"I suggest you sleep," I advise, without looking at her.

"You do, eh? That an *order*?"

She's attempting to bait me, and I'll admit, it's taking more self-control than it should not to react. Women of her status are typically calmer, trained to be reserved, but Aurora's refreshing. I can almost picture her at Nico's engagement party, brash and colourful amongst all the other dull women, and I smile at the image. Being a bodyguard might not be the task I want, but at least she won't be boring, like I initially assumed. From the very second she fought Sister Mary in the garden about leaving, I realized how utterly incorrect my assumptions about her were.

"That's a suggestion. Today will be mentally and emotionally draining, so why not rest when you can. It'll be a good way to make the trip go by faster."

"Or I can get to know you, since we're apparently spending so much time together."

Bad idea. The only way a strong relationship between any soldier and a member of the family works is with distance. Boundaries. Aurora doesn't understand that yet, which means I should be the one to set them.

But I do wonder, "Does having a bodyguard bother you?"

"Not sure yet. Depends how *restrictive* you'll be."

The double meaning in her words, once again, has me tightening my fist around my phone, while my traitorous mind imagines it being her throat as I hold her still for her punishment. She's very forward for a virgin.

"I'll keep you safe. Now sleep, Aurora. I'm done talking because I'm exhausted from retrieving your ass." *Your beautiful, shapely ass.*

Some-fucking-how, I get through to her because she lies down and hooks an arm beneath her head, acting as a pillow. It doesn't seem the most comfortable or functional, so I stand and head for a back closet I know has a few extra blankets and pillows for such an occasion. A recent addition after Nico used this plane to find Della hiding in Edmonton.

I return, handing her the items. "You'll hurt your neck sleeping how you were."

Aurora takes the pillow with a tight smile. "Thanks," she murmurs as she settles back into position. Once she relaxes, I toss the blanket over her.

"Gets cold up in the air. Temperature is much different than below. You'll want this."

She tugs it over her shoulder, peering up at me. Her long, black eyelashes blink slowly, words formulating on her parted lips, but she doesn't speak, instead snuggling further into the cushion and shutting her eyes.

I retreat to my seat, feeling an odd sense of...of *something*... in my chest. It felt *good* to care for someone else. I'll admit, I like my women bratty and teasing, but nothing's better than when I get to reward them with praise and attention. My relationships have never been long-term because so many women struggle to understand the career I've chosen.

Over my phone, I observe the sleeping woman. There's so much fight, so much determination within her small form, it's easy to see the Corsetti in her. She truly will succeed. Once she gets over the initial round of anger regarding her pending engagement, which I suspect will be there, she'll master being queen of the New York *Famiglia* too. One day, she'll look back on all this and will question why she was even scared in the first place.

When the plane hits turbulence, Aurora rolls over, but her hair doesn't completely follow, causing a handful of it to land right on top of her face. I itch to remove the strands because it can't be that comfortable, but touching her is a bad idea for both of us.

I don't know why she annoys me so much. This girl I met literally an hour ago, who, for all her snarky comments, *is* my boss. She's a Corsetti, and I took vows to their entire family. The moment she thinks she can order me around like her lap dog is the moment my self-restraint *may* break and—

I shut down that wayward idea, brushing a hand over my face. Aurora Corsetti is a fucking *Corsetti*, and an engaged one at that. Not someone for me to get involved with. Her brothers would kill me and that's not an exaggeration. Being chosen for this task, as she guessed earlier, speaks to their trust in me, and the thoughts I'm having about their baby sister are *anything* but trustworthy. The eight-year age gap alone should be enough to deter me because she's brand new to adulthood, and I'm not.

For the remainder of the short flight, I return to the game on my phone, ignoring Aurora until the plane begins its descent. The change in elevation wakes her up and she blinks into the afternoon light.

"Hey." Her sleep-riddled voice is huskier than normal, and I can't help but appreciate it.

"Hey, we're landing soon."

She lifts herself into a sitting position, her arms stretching above her head and her back arching with her movements. Her breasts become more noticeable in the blouse she's wearing, pulling my attention to them.

"And then?"

"We drive to your home. It's about a half-hour away from the airport."

She nods, now seeming more serious. Tucking her legs up to her chest, she stares out the window as the plane takes us to the ground. At landing, I spot her hand curl into the chair beneath her, gripping it tightly. That small motion being the only sign of her uncertainty or fear.

"You handled your first airplane ride well," I comment as we slow down on the airstrip, wanting to praise her in any way I can to see her light up.

She shrugs, glancing at me before she answers, "Not really scary, to be honest. As long as they remain in the sky, that's all I care about."

"Still impressive."

The plane comes to a complete stop, and within minutes, the door is opened and Quebec sunlight streams through. I stand, pocketing my phone and begin heading for the stairs, motioning my head toward Aurora for her to follow.

She trails behind without argument, which surprises me. She even thanks the pilot on her way past the cockpit. At the base of the stairs, a car waits, a driver positioned in front. I recognize him as Sam, Nico's main driver.

He gets out upon seeing us and heads for the back door to open it. I nearly wave him away but decide a show of such privilege will be good for Aurora to experience.

"You first," I tell her, stepping aside.

She pauses, glancing at Sam first, and then at me. I spot genuine anxiety in the way her eyes pinch in the corners, and she bites down on her bottom lip. Her chest rises and then slowly falls as she takes a deep breath before moving again, sliding into the car. She shuffles across the bench, pressing herself to the other side, peering out the window. Her reaction reminds me of inside the car, when she started breathing heavily. I couldn't understand the abrupt change in her demeanour, but I'm pleased it passed quickly.

I follow her and then Sam shuts the door before taking his own seat behind the wheel.

"It's okay," I murmur loud enough for only her. Then, compelled to care for the girl, and annoyed at myself for even being concerned about her comforts, I hold the button that raises the divider between Sam and us. "One less person to deal with."

"Thanks."

The woman beside me isn't the one who was in the passenger seat when I was driving to the airport in Toronto, and while she was annoying and full of attitude that made me want to punish her, I prefer that version of her. This meek, fearful one isn't quite the same. I haven't known her past a few hours, but docile doesn't seem to be Aurora at all.

For the entire thirty minutes, Aurora makes no noise. She's completely silent; she hasn't even shifted an inch, which tells me she's probably getting stiff. It's not until the mansion comes into view as Sam turns onto the long tree-lined road that leads to her future home that she makes any noise.

A squeak.

Her head spins, her eyes widening as she looks at me.

"Welcome home," I tell her with a small smile, but it doesn't seem to help. Pulling out my phone, I throw a quick warning text Nico's way. "Same place you were born into, Aurora. Building hasn't changed."

"I don't remember it being so huge."

She continues to watch out the windows as we pass her lands, until finally, Sam parks in the roundabout driveway. He gets out and opens the back door for us. I exit immediately but remain by the car door, should she want help.

Aurora slides to the edge and props one foot out onto the ground, before pausing and skimming the side of the massive house. It's impressive, but for someone who hasn't seen it since being a child, I imagine it's a bit more impactful.

Then something flicks inside Aurora. Something that removes all her anxiety and replaces it with rage. Pure rage. And by the time she's on her feet, she's practically bristling, her nose scrunched, her teeth bare as she speaks.

"*This* is where my family lives. *This* was too unsafe to allow me to stay? *This?*"

Unsure if she's speaking to me or ranting in general, I gesture toward the staircase. "They're all waiting for you, Aurora."

"Then let them wait! I've waited *years* for them. The least bit of decency they can have is to allow me five fucking minutes to breathe. To take this all in. It's not easy, you know. Also, they care about me *so much* that they can't even fucking greet me outside?"

I sigh at the sudden change in her attitude, while hiding the fact that I understand her point. Seeing the stronghold of the Corsetti mansion would have me questioning the purpose in being sent away too, had I been in her position.

I turn toward the large front steps. "Follow me. Sam will unload your bags and will bring everything to your room. Once you arrive at your suite later, all your items and clothing will be ready for you."

"Don't," she snaps back, her attention sliding to Sam. "In my room but don't unpack them. I'm not an imbecile; I can do that much."

Sam glances at me, his expression obviously questioning which order to follow. I tip my head a fraction toward Aurora, indicating hers. If Aurora being able to unpack her own stuff makes her more comfortable, then so be it.

I start up the stairs, fully aware of the possibility of needing to return for her in case she doesn't follow.

"The Sisters underplayed their worth," she comments.

"*Your* worth."

"Then wouldn't it have been better to hire a dozen guards to protect me for my entire life rather than send me away? Just sayin'..."

Perhaps the Corsettis should have done it differently, but the past is the past and Aurora ought to face the future now, even if I appreciate her for being angry.

"This is such bullshit and I'll be sure to tell them that too. All the etiquette training the Sisters put me through is about to go right out the window. I *won't* be calm about how cold-hearted these monsters really are. So eager to see me, they can't even meet me outside," she grumbles. "Seriously, Rosen, what do you think about all this? Wouldn't it hurt you that your family waited so many fucking years to bring you home and then didn't have the decency to greet you when you arrived?"

Yes. But I won't admit how harsh I find the treatment. Not my place to decide how the family conducts business. It almost feels like she's challenging me to be on her side, and despite my feelings on the matter, I can't let her know that I am.

"Well?" she demands.

"Your family is waiting. They love you and that's all that matters."

"Can you have any more of a non-answer, dick?"

"Just because they're not out here, I'm sure they are close by, which means they can already hear you, if that means something."

"Not funny, dick."

That word again. My hands clench and unclench into fists,

frustrations prickling my spine. "You can stop referring to me as that now, when I'm only doing my job."

"I doubt the comments are a part of the job description."

"Neither is dealing with a bratty mafia *princesse*, but here we are." I think about the numerous other, more useful tasks I could be doing.

Eight front steps have never felt so long because her tirade continues: "I swear to fuck, they better be on the other side of this door! Because if they don't even have the fucking decency to meet me at the door—"

I tune the rest of her rant out, reaching by her for the large front door. I don't know what Nico's planned for her re-arrival, but for everyone's sake, I hope they're waiting in the entrance.

I enter first, peering in, instantly relieved at the line of Corsettis. Lorenzo and Caterina are closest to the door, gripping onto each other, their eager eyes immediately landing on me with slight disappointment. Caterina lifts onto her toes, trying to become taller than the heels already allow her to be, to see around me.

Rafael leans on the farthest wall, his arms crossed over his chest, his typical nonchalant expression not at all a surprise to find. Beside him and across from the front door, I throw a *Good luck* expression toward Nico, giving him some kind of indication what this day's already been like.

At his side, Della smiles tentatively at me. Probably the only one here not trying to look around my shoulder. Beside her, her sister, Ariella stands, her lips pursed. After her sister's recent engagement to Nico, the mute woman found herself in a whole lot of family drama.

I step aside, letting Aurora enter beside me, revealing her to the entire Corsetti family.

6

AURORA

One. Two. Three. Four. Five. Six.

There are six strangers staring me down.

Six people expecting me to say something.

Six family members who should love me, but instead, abandoned me in Ontario, a long way from them.

Six people I can't decide what to feel about.

Six plus one soldier—Rosen. The only one who's been genuine with me so far. My entire life, the Sisters have raised everyone at the school to understand we're children of social royalty. Even with rules and a strict life to follow, we weren't as free as regular kids were.

The Sisters never responded to my attitude. Every single time I tried to get a rise from them, they all brushed it aside as my personality. As me being "strong-willed."

Rosen is the first not to treat me like I'm glass. When I gave attitude, he handed it back. When I tried to get a rise from him, he gave me none. He remained calm. Poised. My urge to piss him off, simply grouping him with the people in front of me, quickly went away when my taunts felt too natural and easy.

I search for him, looking to the left to where he stands, his back to the wall, his hands in front of him. Gone is the man who brought me here, the one I need; instead, I find an expression without emotion as he silently observes.

Fuck. If not him, then who else can help me? What other person will support my mental breakdown? Not the people causing it, that's for certain. The fact I even *want* his help throws my insides into a tailspin that makes no sense.

"Aurora."

I search for the feminine voice who called my name. A tall woman steps forward, her hands reaching for me, even as her steps falter. It's like looking into a mirror. An older mirror. Same hair, same figure, same face.

Mommy.

My actual mother.

My mother who used to read me bedtime stories, who would tuck me in, who held me when I was scared of the dark. Who insisted, even though staff could assist her, doing so much of it alone.

"Mommy," I whisper the last name I ever referred to her as. The name I yelled as the car drove me away from here, when I last looked at this entranceway through a child's eyes.

I want to go to her. Want to hug her and feel her arms around me again. Feel her love, her care.

The same love that sending me away was based on. For my safety, when all I craved was her to continue to love and protect me. It's all *any* child needs. I think about all the kids I left behind in Toronto. It's what they all want too.

My mother makes a whimpering noise but doesn't approach, and I realize, everyone is waiting for me to make a move.

I want to, but something keeps my feet frozen.

A man steps up beside her, wrapping his arm around her

waist. Even with age, my father looks the same as what I remember him to be. His green eyes focus on me, bright, anxious.

"Aurora, we've missed you."

Daddy. But this word, I can't speak aloud. My father was Boss even then. He ruled the family, but still allowed me to go away. He's as much at fault as my mother.

I continue scanning the room, searching for the faces I know had no say in sending me away. Across the room, leaning on a wall as though he has no care in the world, I find the person I still dream about as he watched from the steps as I was loaded into a car.

Rafael is only four years older than me. I shouldn't be able to recall the child version of him as well as I do, but that's the interesting thing about childhood trauma—things can stick even when you don't expect them to.

With my attention, he kicks off the wall but doesn't approach. His expression is impassive, unlike my parents, and I'm dying to hear him speak, to do anything, and am disappointed when there's nothing.

Maybe he's giving me space. Like my mother, he's waiting for me to make the first move. But, like, what do they expect from me right now?

I continue my survey around the wide entranceway, landing on my other older brother, Nico. Now the "first-born" with Hawke's absence. He stands front and centre, looking so much like our father in the way he holds himself, staring at me with dark-green eyes. Like Rafael, his expression is blank: a trained poker face.

Beside him are two women, neither of whom I recognize. One with striking dark red hair. Her smile is only a hint of being there. Between her and my brother is another woman. Her blonde hair is done up in a bun, and her white blouse billows around leggings. She looks so normal, so average, not being made up to the nines. On her left hand, a shiny diamond ring sits on her fourth finger and given how close she stands to Nico, I draw a conclusion.

Oh.

My siblings grew up. Met people. Got into relationships. Became their role in the family.

While I...

...Did nothing.

I was raised in a partial school, partial convent simply for being a girl. My brothers got to remain here, to grow up normally. Have teenage lives and enter adulthood with our parents' influence to guide them. I was treated like a little girl for my entire life and the only freedom I experienced was when I snuck out and stole it for myself.

I look at Rafael again and feel a shred of relief easing my nerves when I spot his bare left hand. No woman in his life. At least, there's that.

I glance at mine, picturing a large diamond on it, as the Sisters claimed I'd eventually have to accept. Mafia families rely on unions, and I wonder at what point of my re-arrival will I be tossed into one.

That won't be a conversation I let go by easily.

"Aurora," my mother—because even my brain can't use the term *Mom*—repeats, taking another paced step, treating me as a scared creature that'll run away.

Wouldn't you, if you could? my inner voice asks, leaving me without the answer.

I should speak, to say something. Anything.

"H-hi."

She makes a gasping sound and throws her hand to her mouth, covering her parted O. She twists into my father's shoulder for a moment as she composes herself before lifting her head and managing, "You sound so grown-up."

"That's what happens when you drop a kid off and don't look in on them for many years."

Shots. Fired. And I won't apologize for it.

My family's expressions are a mixture of shock and disbelief, and I can't help but look to Rosen, maybe seeking some sense of agreement. He's still staring at the floor, but I spot the tiny smirk lifting one corner of his mouth, showing me, despite his brush-offs outside, he doesn't agree with their actions.

My mother brushes my words aside. "You're right, Aurora. It's inexcusable what we did, but you're home now, so the past is the past."

Just like that, huh? Move on like none of it happened.

My father approaches too, his hand held out toward me. "Can we please hug you? We've missed our little girl."

Should have thought of that.

What do *I* want? On one hand, I do miss being held by them, but on the other, it'd be like hugging strangers. Worse, because these strangers shouldn't be unfamiliar.

"I-I don't think I can," I reply with a gentle shake of my head.

He blinks and my mother flinches, making me feel a bit shitty. Maybe it's all it'll take. If my feet can move, maybe—just maybe—I can begin the process they want me to.

But I don't.

Nico gestures behind him, into the expanse of the house. "Come. Why don't we get out of the foyer? You've had a long day." Then his gaze goes to the left of me, and he says, "Thank you. I'll text you when we're done here."

"Sir." The familiar grumble comes from behind me. I hear his shoes echo on the shiny floors with his steps and turn in time to catch him escaping through the front door. My stomach lurches, a silent plea coursing through my head to follow him, propelling my feet backwards.

No! Rosen might be even more of a stranger than these people, but I need him here. Need to know I'm not the only one stuck in this hellish charade. Need him to see what losing a family can do to a person.

I almost say it out loud too because I'm sure Nico wouldn't deprive me of it. Instead, I don't, shutting my mouth as Rosen closes the door behind him.

Leaving me alone in the lion's den.

Fuck. On shaky legs, I stride past my parents, without glancing at them, and wander farther down the hallway, eyes greedily devouring every inch of this magnificent house. The vast entranceway, the ornate floors I can see my own blurred reflection through. The long hallways, where Nico slips by me, directing us all down one.

I want to inquire where we're going, but don't. The last thing I wish is to seem eager. Behind me, I feel my parents' gazes poking into my back. At my side, Rafael trails close, winking when he catches me looking.

Nico opens the first door in the hallway, flicking on the light as I enter behind him, taking in the old-fashioned sitting room. A rich bar on one side, leather couches and chairs in the centre, in a semi-circular pattern. The kind of sitting room you see in movies and shows depicting historical times.

"Please sit, Aurora." Nico gestures to the seating area as everyone else enters the room, standing back to see which place I claim.

I steal the one farthest from the door, and one of the few single chairs, ensuring no one can sit beside me. Pain flashes once again through my mother's eyes , but she and my father take the couch directly across from me. Rafael sits in the other single seat nearby, while Nico's fiancée and the redheaded woman snag another couch. Nico remains standing between our parents and his fiancée.

"I'll admit, Aurora," my brother starts, "I think we were all hoping for a bit of a warmer welcome, but I do understand how angry you are. Our parents did what was best back then, and look at you now, grown-up and safe. Home and we're all so pleased for the chance to get to know you."

I cross my arms. "You say 'best back then,' but what do you think about the choice they made?"

The only sign Nico gives me is the twitch of a lip. Like Rosen, his poker face is strong. Must be a Made Man thing. It's enough to show me he's either amused or appreciates my question.

"I wasn't in a role of power then, so my feelings toward the choice are irrelevant. However, I *am* the underboss now, and Father is our Boss, and *you* are a member of this family."

Which means doing what the women do. Shop and get married to produce future heirs.

"When's my engagement then?"

My comment is meant to be a bit of a snarky farce, a fake belief that I've guessed his master plan, but then the joke's on me when he doesn't laugh. When his lips purse for the briefest of seconds and his eyes shift a fraction—the sign of a liar. For an underboss, he apparently still has elements of that poker face to perfect.

*No...*Now. Already? As in...

I can't breathe. It's happening again and my hands curl around my sternum, digging into my own body. Anything to hide the impending panic attack quickly making my breaths speed up, my head go light.

I need out of here.

I stand, no longer wanting to be around any of these people. I planned, mentally prepared, to be forced to eventually wed, but to already have my entire life mapped out before I even came back is something else entirely.

"No." I back up a few steps, eyes skimming everyone, head wildly shaking. Seeking someone to be on my side. Nico's fiancée looks away, staring down at the floor by her feet. She's the only one to show compassion. Rafael doesn't falter in his stare and my parents simply observe. They're all waiting for me to fall in line.

"Nico—" our mother starts.

"What?" he snaps in response. "You want me to lie to my sister? Tell her she's not engaged and then shock her with that surprise in a week? If she's guessed correctly, there's no point in hiding it."

A week? My throat feels so thick, it steals my breath. That's what I would have gotten. A motherfucking *week* to settle in.

"This wasn't how I wanted you to learn it, Aurora. You will have time before getting the introductions underway."

I hold up my hand, stopping him from spewing further bullshit. "Here's the thing. You already had a plan. You fucking *planned* for me to be wed. Is that the only reason I'm here?" I scan them all, seeking a crack in any of their exteriors that will reveal their deception.

"Of course not," my mother cries at the same time Nico answers, "Not the only one, no. Your place is here. Rafael and I have missed our sister. Our parents have been without their child for a long time. You are back because you are one of us, but I'm sorry, your place also comes with a job. As do any of ours. *That's* what it's like to be in this life, Aurora. Even if you weren't sent to Toronto, Father would already have had plans in place by now. Either way, your engagement is a reality."

I glance at our father, eager to see his feelings, but he only gives me a small reaffirming nod, agreeing with Nico.

"Wow," is all I manage. "Fucking *wow*. Way to allow a girl to breathe." I cross my arms again, rage building to an extreme point, I can't tie down the questions that burst from me. "What's his name? Which family is he from? Where will I be expected to live the rest of my life? How long will I be here before you ship me off again? Does he know about me? Does—"

This time, it's Nico who holds up his hand, commanding, "Silence, Aurora. We do not have to discuss those details right now, but to ease your mind, it won't be for a year."

"Before the engagement," I check, even when the disturbing feeling in my stomach tells me I'm wrong.

"Before you're wed."

Again, not entirely surprised.

My father stands. "Nico, I think we've done enough for today. Aurora began her day in an entirely other province, and has now met everyone, and still has to get settled into her suite. We can pick this up tomorrow." To me, he adds, "I love you, Aurora. I realize it'll take a lot for you to understand that, but we'll start with today, okay?"

Am I supposed to respond to that? "Sure." Whatever to get them off my back.

"I can take you to your room," our mother offers. Her hands do a strange fluttery thing, like she's excited, but I'm shaking my head, shattering all her blooming hopes.

She can't take me because then she'll be *there*. Her and me. Alone. And I'll be forced to speak with her.

"It's okay. Thanks." I toss a weak smile that I don't totally mean their way. "I'll find it myself. I only need directions."

The flash of hurt once more in her gaze pains my chest with guilt, but she quickly shoves it aside with a small smile before moving to the side of the room, toward the bar. Her hands come up to her eyes in a wiping motion.

Shit.

Nico's watching the exchange, his mouth turned down into a frown. After a beat, he digs out his phone from his pocket. "I'll have Rosen take you up. If he hasn't already told you, I've assigned him to be your personal bodyguard for the time being. It's standard for us all to have protection, and given how new you are to us, I'm sure a lot of people will be curious about you. He's one of my best and will keep you safe."

I already know this, but at least *this* fact he informs me of. I force my lips to stretch into a smile and nod, taking small steps around everyone, toward the door. Six people watch me, but I don't focus on any of them.

"I'll go out into the hall then," I tell them, offering no room for them to take that as an invitation. "Beautiful home. Must have been nice to grow up here."

"We're having supper later, if you would like to join us," my father calls as I reach the door.

"Thanks, but no, I'm tired. It was good to meet you all, I guess."

The knob in my hand makes my muscles work properly for the first time since I've entered the room. Turning it, I back out quickly, letting go of the breath trapped in my lungs.

"Holy fuck."

A deep gravelly voice comes from behind me. "Went that well, huh?"

7
ROSEN

Nico may have texted me, requesting I return for Aurora, but I never really went far to begin with. Something compelled me to remain close by, almost like I suspected their conversation wouldn't last long and she wouldn't entertain any of her family showing the way to her room.

The door to the sitting room Nico let me know they're in opens, and Aurora backs out, keeping her family in sight. Like she has so little trust in them, she won't give them her back yet.

Appreciation of the fact she's not so trusting that she'd immediately fall into the place her family demands of her runs through me. She should, but it conveys tenacity that she doesn't just do as they say.

The moment her feet pass the threshold and the door swings shut behind her, her shoulders slump. "Holy fuck," she whispers, and it's in that word, I realize how painful the interaction was for her.

I clear my throat and say, "Went that well, huh?"

She gasps and spins around, shoving her backside against

the door as her eyes focus on me. She wipes at them. Blinking those addictive long lashes twice before exclaiming, "Shit, Rosen, where the hell did you come from?"

"Never really left." I kick off the wall, scanning her, my gaze landing on her reddened cheeks, stomach churning at the sign of her heartbreak. "You okay, *princesse*?"

It's no more than a question I'd ask her brothers if I witnessed them upset, but I find myself more eager for her response than I would theirs.

Aurora's expression doesn't falter, like she didn't hear me, until she blinks again and laughs. Not a feminine laugh either, but one of disbelief that has her shaking her head too.

Before she can comment on something that will hurt her family's feelings, I turn and guide her away, heading down the hallway and toward the staircase that leads up to the family's suites.

"Do you know, you're the first person to ask me that? And you're a *soldier*," she spits the word like it's poison, "which I think is even more sad. Staff have checked in on my feelings but not them." She gestures behind us, back toward the way we came.

"They're as anxious as you, Miss Corsetti. You see them at fault, but they are humans, and humans make mistakes."

It's a big mistake, but, hey.

At the base of the staircase, I start ascending, with her following. "The suites are up here."

"'Miss Corsetti'? Remember what I said earlier?"

"We're in a mansion with many ears," I tell her, peeking over my shoulder, catching her subtle frown. "It's a title of respect, and one you'll need to get used to."

"Except no one's around."

"Nico asked the staff to be scarce for the day."

At the top of the stairs, I take a sharp right, heading toward a series of bedrooms and stopping at the first one, which is also one door down from the room Nico gave Ariella when she moved in here. Pushing open the white door, I step aside and allow Aurora through.

"This is your room."

She pauses at the entryway, hardly even through the doorframe. Her expression falters, all the anger and hardness present a moment ago shifting into the hints of softness I found earlier in the car and then on the plane. Like her entire being isn't sure of which attitude to consistently portray. The openness she's showing around me is—

I shut the thought down, not allowing my mind to finish, while watching her study the room, which was recently redone to transform the space into something more suited for a twenty-year-old. The walls were repainted to an off-white, the Queen-sized bedspread a deep green, contrasting with the grey carpet. Muted tones throughout the bedroom and sitting room area, and for some reason, I enjoy the fact her mother opted for a green theme. It reminds me of Aurora's eyes.

"It's changed."

"Go inside," I urge.

She does immediately, wandering through, her gaze touching every inch of the room. Her bags wait at the base of her bed, resting on a cushioned bench I imagine her one day using as she dresses or prepares for bed.

I've brought her to her room, which means my task is over and I can leave, but I'm compelled to stay, to watch her get reacquainted with her old room even if I have no business in being here. Propping myself against the doorframe, I watch her wander through the space, peeking inside the bathroom, which I assume has been stocked for her arrival.

"A cell phone has been set up for you." I gesture toward where the box sits beside her bag. "Code is your birthday, so I recommend you change it. Set up Face ID too because it's a safe way to ensure no one can access your phone."

She lifts the new phone, intently perusing the whole thing, flipping it around in her hands, which makes me feel like a moron. All these instructions on changing passwords and adding her face metrics into the Face ID section, and she's likely never held a cellphone.

I push off the doorway and enter the room, coming up behind her when I should be leaving. "I can help with all that if you'd like." An offer I certainly shouldn't be making when there are numerous other people who could help her.

Without question, she hands it over, intently watching as I unlock it with the passcode the Corsettis' IT guy set it up with the other day. I scroll through the settings until I find the pass-word options, click what I need to, and turn the phone toward her, placing it back in her hand.

"Follow the instructions on the screen. Turn your head as it requires."

She does, and a moment later, all is programmed in. She tries to hand the device back to me, but I block her, shaking my head.

"You're done. Good to go."

"Yeah..." Her lip curls beneath her teeth. "I-I...There were cell phones to use. Some of the kids got to call home, but," she shifts her feet, eyes diving to the phone in her hand, "I never did. So I never actually learned how to use one." She scoffs, shaking her head. "Stupid, eh? I've been brought back to 'take my place' and yet, I don't even know how to use basic technology."

"It's not stupid," I instantly counter, despising the misplaced way she criticizes herself. "It makes sense, given your circumstances. The Sisters should have taught you, knowing where you were coming back to."

Aurora's frown is still in place, and I want to see her smile again. I'll even take her snarky grin. I shouldn't have any opinion about her expression, but I do. She looks so fucking lost; it makes me really miss the brat from earlier.

Beneath long lashes, she tentatively glances up at me, barely tipping her head. "Can you teach me?"

Tempting. So fucking tempting to sit by her and teach her how to use a phone. But Aurora has many people available to help.

"I think we should ask your brothers or parents."

She crosses her arms, her brows dipping in determination, and her mouth flattening until she reminds me of the girl from the car—the abrupt shift from pacifying to assertive. "Why not you? So far, you're the only one to not treat me with kid gloves. If I admitted to any of them about my limited knowledge of tech, they'd try to coddle me more than they already are. I don't want that."

There are many reasons why I shouldn't. Why I should turn away and leave her be, but I can't fight the lightness coursing through my chest at her pleading look. Of all the people now in her life, she's chosen me to help her. She trusts me enough to reveal what she believes is a weakness, and my heart beats faster with that knowledge. It's fucked up to feel like I'm winning a competition against her family when neither team—them and me—is aware we're playing.

"Fine," I agree, and then have to taper down my dick's response to the way she lights up. "One lesson and that's it. It'll stay between us."

She heads for a couple of the chairs across the room, pulling one closer to the other, for me to take.

I spend the next hour showing her how to text, add contacts, call people, record her voicemail message, and be able to check it, download apps, change settings, and anything else she ought to know. I program my number in, so she has an easy way to get a hold of me.

In that hour, I also ignore how close she's sitting to me. How her scent invades my every sense and how her little comments and giggles as she takes in the lesson has me feeling content. How, with the hour passing, eventually food is bound to be delivered here or her family will finally give up waiting and come to find her.

"And that's it." I slide the phone back into her hand after checking to ensure all the apps have been updated. I stand, brushing my hands against my pants, and immediately move away from Aurora, creating distance we should have had from the second I brought her here.

She also stands, abandoning the phone on her seat as she trails behind me. "Hey, thanks a lot, Rosen. Seriously. You didn't have to do that, but you did."

Don't call me nice, princesse. I'm not nice. Not when I want to show you how impolite I can be.

And maybe, if she were any other woman, that's what I'd do.

But I respond with, "No problem. It's my job."

"But it's not, is it? Guarding me is. You said that already. So therefore, thanks."

"We'll chalk it up as a one-time thing."

Before I can turn again, her hand darts out, landing on my arm. So warm, so tiny, so able to freeze my entire form in ways no one ever has before.

"You said you knew what my future holds, so you know I'm already engaged then?"

Oh. No wonder she left the sitting room pissed-off. What a welcome home present, but I'm also not entirely surprised. I have massive respect for Nico and his decisions because they're always focused on bettering us, but I sympathize with Aurora in that no one would want to be engaged to a stranger so soon.

"Yes."

"I should be angry you kept that from me, but I get it. You're on their side. What else do I expect?" She huffs, shaking her head, and I wonder if she's talking more to herself than me.

Either way, I respond with, "Exactly." I'm loyal to her brothers and her family name and telling her such things about her engagement is beyond what my role demands of me. It certainly isn't my business what they do with her future, given I'm an outsider to the politics mob families endure.

"Do you know who my fiancé will be?"

I hesitate before responding, "Yes."

Her next question is bound to be who he is, not that she'd really know who I'm talking about. Instead, she wonders, "Is he a good man?"

Deny. It's the only way to get out of here without accidentally giving away shit I shouldn't. "I can't say, *princesse.*"

"Please," she begs, her voice rising to a near-panic. Her nails curl into my skin, her calm restraint slipping. "I want to know if I'm going to hate my life or not."

So you can run away? "Aurora, no. I'm sorry, but it's the final thing I'll say on the matter."

Her hand slides away from my arm and I hate how much I already miss her touch. She pouts, looking way cuter than she should. "Fine. I get it."

She's not pleased, but she's letting it go. I manage to get through her door and barely into the hallway when she speaks again.

"Where will you be?"

"Around," I reply, keeping my answer vague. "If you want to go somewhere, text me."

"Okay."

"Goodnight, Miss Corsetti," I say, giving her the final word. "Good to have you home safe." A respectable farewell, and one no less than I'd give any other member of her family.

When I shut the door, I imagine her bunking down for the night. Crawling into a bed she's never slept in before. In a room she has vague memories of, if any. Surrounded by a new life that already irritates her.

Does it matter? my mind probes. How Aurora manages to get through the night is none of my business, and she shouldn't even be a consideration on my mind.

I leave the grand wing, lined with a few bedrooms—Aurora's, Ariella's, Rafael's old one he only uses when he spends the night, and the one Nico used growing up before moving in the opposite wing and taking over his parent's room. As I head downstairs, a text comes through my phone.

> NICO
>
> She's not going to adapt easily. Please keep me updated if you get any inclinations about her doing something she shouldn't.

Why do I get the sense that Aurora will be giving me a run for my money?

8

AURORA

The cell phone feels strange in my hand. I haven't been so sheltered that I've never seen one before, but certainly, I've never *owned* one.

Or used one. I think back to moments ago when Rosen was in the chair beside me, going through the menus, educating me about things I should probably already know. For two extra years after graduating, I hung around the convent, and no one contemplated teaching me the other life lessons that would be of a benefit.

I open the contacts app and scroll through the names and numbers preprogrammed in there: Mom, Dad, Nico, Rafael, Rosen, and Della. When I asked Rosen about that last one, he explained she's Nico's fiancée, the woman who was by his side earlier.

There's a phone number missing, but I haven't considered asking Rosen for it until now. He probably doesn't have it, but he might. I swipe away the contacts app for the messaging app, returning to the conversation he started with me, where we practiced sending each other texts.

Fingers over the keypad, I'm ready to type out my question, but hesitate. He likely doesn't know, and even if he does, I doubt he'd hand it over without checking with my brother. Nico seems to be in control here, despite the title my father still holds, and I'm getting the idea, after the sitting-room conversation earlier, Nico wouldn't entertain my request, since he's all about me being in the present and not the past.

Which means the goodbye I shared with Sister Mary will be it. No further contact and the notion has me dropping the cellphone like it's on fire and quickly escaping to the gleaming, connected bathroom.

The thing's huge, much more excessive than I believed a bathroom could or should be, and it's stocked with everything I already use. Clearly, there has been communication between the Sisters and my family, even if I was never in on it.

With everything changing today, at least my shampoo brand remains the same.

After undressing, I step into the glass-walled shower and turn it on, immersing myself in the steaming water. After twenty minutes, I have to drag myself away from this spa-like wondrous creation. Never have I had so many settings on a showerhead, and I'll admit to having tested all of them. .

Finally exiting the steaming bathroom, I go straight to bed instead of dressing in anything. No doubt, the closet is massive and packed with items I honestly don't even want to look at. I'd half expect to find a wedding dress in there that has already been pre-picked for me.

The bed is larger than I've ever had, and when I slide toward the middle of the soft mattress and stare at the white-painted ceiling, it becomes more obvious than ever I'm no longer at the convent.

Day one.

Sleep doesn't come easily. Or at all. Considering how heavenly the bed is and how long of a day I had, sleep should have hit me nearly instantly, but instead, I toss and turn, watching as the time on my new phone ticks away.

Three in the morning.

For fuck's sake. Rolling over with a deep breath, or, more like a puff, I stare at the white ceiling.

An hour ago, I opened the large curtains to allow the moonlight to shine through the room. A patch lands on the end of my bed, right by my feet. My room in Toronto had a small window over the bed, and each night I went to bed with the nighttime streaming through, so I hoped a bit of that would feel the same and help me sleep.

It didn't.

What do other people do when they can't sleep? I've never had sleep issues before, typically falling asleep quickly each night, so this is a new and unwelcome experience.

On the bedside table, I retrieve my cell phone from the charger, which was already plugged in and set up even before Rosen dropped me off. Clearly, there's nothing in this place that won't be done for me. I imagine other people would relish the idea of having staff around to do everything, but already, it's strange. The Sisters were always very firm in ensuring everyone did their own chores, which often included maintaining our rooms and cleaning up after dinner each night.

I unlock the device, swiping up at the same time the metrics scan my face, even through the room's darkness, which is kind of cool. Rosen helped me download a couple of gaming apps, claiming they're useful for when there's a few minutes of spare time when I could be bored.

While my finger hovers over the small group of them,

scanning each icon and determining which one to choose, none of them call to me. Instead, I open the messaging app again, finding our thread of random messages from earlier.

There's *no* way he'd be awake at this time of night. Maybe once, I imagine, but if his new role is really to be by my side, I doubt he's staying up all night.

This is silly.

I should place my phone back on the nightstand and try to sleep again. Count sheep, meditate, stare out the huge windows —anything but what I'm doing.

Besides, there's no way he'll respond, even if he is awake. And it's not like speaking with him will change anything other than letting him know I'm struggling to sleep. This isn't his issue.

Yet, my fingers still click the corresponding letters. Slowly, because every movement is clumsy and strange. Earlier, Rosen's fingers were speeding over the screen and I wonder if I'll ever reach that point.

ME

Hey.

This isn't going to work.

He's not going to answer.

He's asleep.

His job doesn't require him to entertain me.

But then the little text beneath my message switches from *delivered* to *read*, and my heart leaps.

ROSEN

Hey. You're up late.

Smiling, I grip the phone a little tighter and push into a sitting position, leaning back against the mound of pillows this bed was stocked with. Very different than the mere two I had at school, but a welcome change.

ME

So are you.

ROSEN

I was sleeping. I'm a light sleeper.

Probably a source of training. I read his message again, realization setting in, making me sink lower into the bed. *Shit.*

ME

I'm so sorry. Fuck. Sorry. I'll go.

If he didn't respond so quickly, I'd likely have the phone back in its place. My message woke him up, which wasn't at all what I wanted.

ROSEN

No worries. You obviously messaged for a reason.

I smile, unable to help it. I woke the guy up and yet he's still concerned for me.

Don't read more into that. He's simply doing his job.

It doesn't stop me from responding.

ME

I can't sleep.

ROSEN

So keeping me from mine was your solution?

That's a joke, by the way.

ME

I can go. I don't even know why I reached
out. Something to do while I'm trying to
sleep, I guess.

ROSEN

I'm sure this is natural. A bed you're not
used to. A room you're unaccustomed to.

ME

New people.

ROSEN

They're not new. They're your family. I'M the
new one and here we are.

Is he pointing out the fact that of everyone I could have
reached out to, he was the only one I considered?

ME

Like I said before, when you were walking
me here, you're the only one to show me
any kind of empathy so far.

ROSEN

They're trying. Besides, you're not who I
expected to pick up today.

Intrigue runs through me.

ME

Is the bodyguard handing out compliments?
Who did you expect to pick up?

ROSEN

I already have complimented you, but
obviously you've already forgotten, so it's
not that memorable.

Every second of today has been memorable, all moments
with him included.

ME

> You told me I was strong because I grew up away from here, so I'd survive coming home.

Survive seems like a stretch now because if every night is as sleepless as this one is, I won't be living much longer. Despite the dramatic thought, I laugh. It's a little maniacal but removes some of the weight on my chest.

ROSEN

Exactly.

After a full minute and no additional message from him comes in, I wonder if this is his way of ending the conversation. It doesn't stop me from selfishly probing.

ME

> ...I'm waiting.

His response comes in right away, telling me he was waiting for me to message first.

ROSEN

...what?

ME

> Not funny, dick. You didn't answer my question. Who'd you expect to find today?

I laugh when I refer to him by the name I had earlier, but then wonder if I've made a mistake, since it's a full minute without a response. Anxiety builds until I'm about to type out another message when my phone pings with his newest.

ROSEN

I'm not sure I should say. I've already spoken out of turn.

ME

No, I refuse to allow you to be boring. That's
an order, by the way. We're not playing this
game.

ROSEN

Game?

ME

Being proper and shit. My last name might
be Corsetti but so far, as I've said MULTIPLE
times, you've been nicer to me than
everyone here. Therefore, exactly how I
asked you not to call me Miss Corsetti,
we're not doing this whole boundary thing.

The rant pours out and then I realize what a mistake that message was. What if he takes it one way I didn't mean? Does he think this is my plea for friendship or something? Will it only make him pull back further? What happens if he shows it to Nico? Will he tell Nico about these messages?

Questions roll through my mind. The moment I formulate one, another takes its place, stacking the pile of curiosity so high until it topples.

ROSEN

Well. As for the boundary thing, too bad.
They stay whether you like it or not because
it's your reality. Everything you said in your
previous message is an example of you
being opposite of what I expected. Honestly,
I assumed you'd be meek and boring. You
were raised by nuns, taught to eventually
rejoin your place here. I expected a prim and
proper literal princess. Instead, I got you.

I. Got. You. Not sure why, but those three simple words make me tingle in a pleasurable way.

ME

Is that a bad thing? That I'm not what you were expecting.

ROSEN

No. You wanted honesty, that's the most honest I can be. Corsettis are a colourful bunch, and you'll fit right in, even if you don't believe it right now. You were a complete brat earlier...but it was refreshing.

I reread that last statement again, my finger tracing over the words.

ME

Returning to the boundary thing: am I allowed to be messaging you?

Like this.

ROSEN

I shouldn't be the person you reach out to for a normal conversation, no. But I'll forgive you for tonight.

Does that mean he won't be showing this to Nico?

ME

Even though I interrupted your sleep?

I think I'm flirting, but don't mean to. I hadn't expected a conversation with him to go on this long. I assumed he would have ignored me, been asleep, or told me to go to bed.

ROSEN

Even then.

ME

Well, I should let you get back to it.

Regret makes the phone heavy. I glance up from the screen and out the window. I wonder if his bedroom has a window in it and if we're looking at the same moon. The ping pulls my attention back down, my stomach lurching in a pleasant way at his next response.

ROSEN

What'll help you sleep?

ME

No idea. Still don't know why I felt talking
would be helpful, but thanks for responding.

ROSEN

Anytime. What did you do in Toronto when
you couldn't sleep?

ME

Never happened.

And the one time it did, I went for a walk through the halls. But I'm *not* doing that here. Who knows who I'd run into and what kinds of forced conversations I'd be having.

ROSEN

Huh. I'm sorry. I'm not good at this stuff. I'm
typically so tired from the day, I also don't
have issues falling asleep. You must be tired
now? It's nearly 3:30.

Even reading that statement has my mouth widening in an involuntary yawn, followed by a chuckle for my body's reaction.

ME

Yes. I've been yawning all night but can't
seem to settle enough. I guess this is
anxiety?

ROSEN

Probably. Let's think about this: right now,
you're anxious for numerous reasons, I bet,
but your whole focus should be shutting
your eyes and sleeping. Nothing else. Not
the morning. Not next week. Not your family.
Only sleeping.

Makes sense because he's correct about that point. As I've tossed and turned all night, all I could picture was facing my family again. After the way I left them earlier in the sitting room, I can't deal with any more conversations about my future.

About my fiancé. I shudder, sinking deeper into the pillows. At least in this bedroom, it's safe. I'm unbothered.

ME

I'll try that. Such an obvious method and
one I never came up with. Thanks.

ROSEN

You're welcome. Anything else I can help
with?

I don't know why, but his latest message causes me to slide deeper into the bed, pulling my knees up as I read it over and over.

ME

Not right now. Go back to sleep. Again,
sorry to bother you but thanks.

ROSEN

Anytime. Try to sleep. Goodnight, Aurora.

I place the phone back on its charger and snuggle back beneath the blankets as I gaze at the moon: big and round, shining over the Corsetti lands. I vow to one day sit beneath that moon, but for now, I shut my eyes and block out any theories about tomorrow.

Sleep, I mentally command myself.

Only, it's not my voice I hear in my head. It's one gruffer, more commanding, attached to a soldier who I had no business taunting how I did today, or messaging in the middle of the night.

9
ROSEN

After wishing Aurora a goodnight, I rest my phone back in its spot on the bedside table and roll the opposite way, facing the wall instead.

I don't know why I responded to her when I caught her name lighting up my phone. The small *ping* woke me instantly. Given the time of night, there's no way she expected a response, and I nearly used that to my advantage to ignore her.

Before I could stop myself though, I responded to her and then jumped into a complete conversation, that, as it ended, has me more awake now. Chuckling, I roll over onto my back, staring at the ceiling.

Somewhere above me, Aurora is lying in bed too, struggling to sleep. For her sake, I hope she's clearing her mind and is dozing off, but I completely understand her challenges. If my entire life was changed within just a few hours, sleep would be the last thing my body would be able to manage too.

Three in the morning and she reaches out to me. Those boundaries I must set begin now. She can't be doing that every night. I *can't* be her safety net. Responding tonight was to help ease her and because, after earlier, it's natural for her not to want to connect with her family about her struggles.

But tomorrow and every night after this one, she'll have to find a new support system. Not that our conversation was inappropriate by any means, but it's unique, and one she can't get used to. Messaging staff when she's a Corsetti isn't right.

My hand rubs over my heart and my single tattoo. A small part of me enjoys being her safe person for the time being. Of everyone here, for some reason, she's seeing me as someone on her side.

Even if I *can't* be on her side. Or at least, show I'm on her side.

Boundaries.

Tomorrow, we'll set boundaries, and it'll be for her benefit. Consider it practice for when she's shipped off to New York.

A tomorrow problem.

∼

Boundaries include only receiving text messages from her when she needs to go somewhere, but by noon on the next day I'm the first to break the restriction when no one's heard from her.

I join Nico for lunch, but it's less eating for him and more glaring at the doorway until he finally snaps, "Why is she not out of her room?"

She might still be sleeping, considering going to bed after three-thirty doesn't exactly scream a seven a.m. wakeup, but I don't tell him that. Setting those limitations are my job at this point, not his. She doesn't deserve getting in trouble for reaching out to one of the few people she knows.

Given it's almost noon means she's hopefully gotten nine hours of sleep, if she went to bed by four, but I doubt she's slept in that much, considering Lorenzo and Caterina have been taking rounds outside her door, trying to get her to come out.

"She must be hungry," he argues. "She skipped dinner last night, and now breakfast. Her last meal was at the convent. If she thinks starving herself will save her in any way, she's sorely mistaken."

At that second, two figures enter the room. Della goes straight for Nico, draping her arms around his shoulders as she leans over him and presses her lips to his cheek.

"Hey. Wedding planner just left. She's heading out to inquire about churches and what openings they have in the next month for us."

With the family this planner was hired to work for, she'll make it happen because that's how it is.

Della slides away from Nico and takes up the first chair on his left, beside the one Ariella has claimed. Ariella leans forward for a couple of the sandwiches on the tray in the centre of the table. She meets my gaze briefly but looks away just as quickly.

"Have my parents gone yet or are they still trolling the halls?" Nico asks Della.

She chuckles. "Your mother met with the planner for a few minutes and mentioned they both had to run out."

He blows out a long breath, tapping his fingers against the table. "She's not going to leave her room if they're stalking her."

"I can go up and knock if you'd like," Della offers. "She never answered your mother's knocks, so I doubt she'd respond to me, but I can try."

Nico tosses his phone onto the table by my hand, nodding to it. "Look at that. She's doing this on purpose. This is ridiculous."

I lift the phone, reading the one-sided text thread he's opened with Aurora. The dozen or so messages he's sent her, varying from polite, morning greetings to inquiries about her status of leaving the room—not an *if* but more of a *when*—and finally demands.

"She's probably anxious," I comment, handing his phone back to him,

"Impossible. She had no trouble standing up to every one of us yesterday, but suddenly, she's nervous?"

Isn't that how anxiety works? Certain things trigger and certain don't. One-on-one with me in the vehicle, that could have been a defense mechanism, or simply less emotions to deal with, but when arriving, she was faced with the entire Corsetti clan.

"Maybe, maybe not." Della voices my thoughts. "Why don't we give her time—the day—and see what comes from it."

Nico growls his agreement and judging by the loving expression he gives his bride-to-be, he won't argue the point further.

The soup I was working through goes cold, so I push away from the table, excusing myself on the guise of heading to my room. Which I suppose I am, my gait slow as I pull out my phone and open the messages from last night, breaking the very boundaries I put in place.

For good reason though. Checking on her well-being.

ME

Planning on emerging sometime today?

If she hasn't responded to Nico's texts or any of their knocks, I doubt she'll answer me, but almost instantly, the message's status changes, and her typing bubbles come up.

AURORA

Oh, god, did they send you to do their dirty
work?

So different from the apologetic girl from last night. Her
attitude changes are fascinating.

ME

Not at all. Simply worried about you.

AURORA

Why?

Why indeed?

ME

Because it's not normal for someone to live
in their room. Because no one here has
witnessed you eating yet, and you must be
starving.

Her response doesn't come right away.

AURORA

I am.

I pause in the middle of the hall, glancing behind me. I
should return to Nico and show him these messages, so he can
see she's willing to eat and he can do with that information
what he wants, but if Della's getting her way, they'll leave her
alone until Aurora's ready.

That doesn't mean she should starve though.

ME

I can bring you food.

AURORA

Isn't that above and beyond your role? In
the plane you said you're my protector, not
my lapdog.

I said that so she doesn't think I'm someone she can demand random tasks from. I'm not a lackey, but this is different.

ME

Bringing you food = protecting you. Can't
have you dying of starvation on your first
day home.

AURORA

Just my second, right?

My laugh travels through the hallway, as I head for the kitchens. Realistically, I can have one of the other staff bring food up to her, but *I* offered, therefore I'm determined to be the person she opens the door for.

ME

Exactly. Glad that humour's back.

AURORA

It never left.

In the kitchen, I wave down the main chef, requesting a tray of food I can bring up to her. Within minutes, he has more of what was served in the main dining room—soup and sand-wiches—on a tray and is handing it to me before adding two water bottles to it as well. Good. Hydration.

Nico's bound to be done eating by now, so before he spots me in the hall and questions me, I quickly head up the stairs as fast as I can with the food in my hand and stop in front of Aurora's bedroom door, rapping on it with the corner of the tray.

"It's me."

The door opens almost instantly, and I'm struck by the sight. Aurora, in the tiniest shorts known to human, showing off smooth legs that'll get me shot simply for looking a beat too long. She's in an oversized plain, black hoodie, her blonde curls on top of her head in a messy bun.

She looks so...*normal*. Once again, the *princesse* isn't the princess I pictured her being because no Corsetti would be caught dead wearing what she is, even when their plans are to remain in bed all day.

She steps aside, gesturing me in before quickly poking her head out the door then slamming it shut. "Good, you're alone."

I enter farther into the bedroom, setting the tray on the small table by the chairs we occupied yesterday for her phone lesson. "Expected this to be a trick to get your family through the door?"

"Never know with you people." But her next words are softer, less irate. "I hoped I could continue trusting you to do the right thing." Those fucking large, emerald eyes of her bat up at me as she claims the same spot she had yesterday.

"Della actually," I explain, hoping to bridge some of the animosity between her and the others. "She told your brother to calm down."

"And you?" She lifts the spoon, using it to point at me. "You tell him you got through to me?"

"I didn't, but you could respond to his messages. What's keeping you in here?" The numerous answers are guessable, but I'd prefer her to admit it the actual reason, so there's certainty.

"Them." The skin around her nose wrinkles. "You're not stupid, Rosen, but you honestly believed I'd be all merry and shit and leave my room so easily? To do, what—*hang out* with those people."

"They're your family. Now that you're here, Nico has plans for you."

"Oh, I know his plans," she shoots back, all snarky, before taking a bite of one of the sandwiches on the accompanying plate. After swallowing her first bite, she mumbles, "They can't force me down the aisle if I never leave my room."

They can and will. They won't allow her to hide forever, and as much as I'd enjoy alerting her to this fact, for her own benefit, I don't. I simply turn away, remembering those boundaries I set for myself. Why she's in her room isn't my concern. She's alive and is now eating, so my job is done.

"Hey," she calls out after me, "where are you going?"

I don't break my stride when I answer, "Away. What you do isn't my business, Miss Corsetti. I'll be around the moment you choose to leave the mansion." Based on so far today, I doubt that'll be anytime soon, which makes this task even more tedious than I initially believed.

"Can you do me one more favour?" she asks as I make it to the door.

My hand is on the knob, so close to escape, but her demand halts me, curious to hear what she could possibly be asking for.

When I don't leave, she continues, "Can I have the phone number to the convent."

I have no idea what I imagined her asking for, but that wasn't it. A simple request tinged with childish hope I would love nothing more to grant her. It's obvious why she wants it: to have the ability to reconnect with the only family she's known since she was six.

Then I hate Nico for giving me the number. It's programmed into my phone in case there were any issues or major delays yesterday. It makes denying her more challenging.

"Aurora," I turn to face her, noticing that she stood from

her seat in the time I walked away, "I'm sorry but that's something you should talk to—"

"I'm not talking to Nico about this," she interrupts, taking quick strides toward me, stopping inches from me, her makeup-free face peering up with the same determined look she gave me yesterday on the drive to the airport. "Please, Rosen. I want to speak with Sister Mary, at least once more."

Please, Rosen.

There's no logical reason for my dick jumping in my pants, but fuck me, if I don't imagine her saying those words under different circumstances.

Boundaries.

"Aurora—"

"Rosen," she cuts me off again, her hands going to her hips. She looks fucking adorable in the large hoodie, not at all menacing. *"Please."*

What the fuck is this girl doing to me? Keeping secrets from her family about her excursions, our conversation last night, and now, not informing Nico I managed to contact her when he couldn't.

Beneath the determined set of her eyes and her flat mouth, her plea is there. The softness peeking out again that compels me to pull my phone from my back pocket and open the contacts app.

"I'm saying the digits once, so be sure to get these down."

Eager, she rushes across the room, snatching her phone from where it's lying on the edge of her bed, which is still unmade from her restless night's sleep. She's focused as she swipes through the menus, presumably bringing up her contacts app. She's using her phone correctly, and a sense of pride fills me.

When she looks expectantly at me, I rattle off the convent's phone number once, exactly as I said I would, but my speech is paced, giving her the chance to get them down.

"Stays between us," I rumble. Only because I don't think Nico would approve.

She nods enthusiastically, grinning up at me as she hugs the phone to her chest. Something so simple, but now, it's worth it to see her smile like this. The next few days will be hard on Aurora as she gets used to her family, and then experiences her first major event, and if it takes a small act of kindness to make her more comfortable, so be it. If anything, this speaks to my loyalty to her family. I'm helping them and their relationship with her by helping her.

That's what I tell myself anyway, as I back out of her bedroom without another word.

10

AURORA

The second the time on my phone flicks to read five o'clock, feet approach the other side of my door, almost like they're working on a schedule. When the knocks finally ended this morning, I was pleased, but now, they're back. Clearly, my mother doesn't understand the concept of space.

"Aurora," she calls through the door, "I'd really enjoy seeing you."

I would have enjoyed seeing you my entire life.

"I'm sorry, honey, but can you come down to eat dinner?"

"No." From my spot in the centre of my very comfortable bed, my voice should travel to her, but I'm not spending extra energy to exert my vocal cords to make it happen either.

"I'll send up food."

Sure. I don't bother to say it aloud because she'll do it anyway. Food, a tray at my door, I'll accept. When I finished eating the lunch Rosen brought hours ago, I laid the tray outside my door for someone to take away. I assumed the staff informed Nico I ate, and he's bound to wonder why, and I'm curious to know what Rosen told him.

I don't hear my mother leave, but she must, since she stops talking. I shut my eyes and wait for the knock announcing food to arrive. I dislike being waited on like this, but it's the lesser of two evils, knowing who's prowling on the other side of the door.

The monsters my family is made up of.

When a person approaches my door, it's not my mother's voice who speaks, but my father's.

"Aurora, you're upsetting your mother. Please come out."

Oh, that's fucking hilarious. I'm *upsetting* her. *Hm, wonder how it feels for family to hurt another member.*

"No."

"I am the Boss of this family. You realize how easy it would be to break this door down?"

Turning my head until the door's in sight, I glare through it, imagining my father beyond it.

"Do it then." *And watch me hate you even more.*

I've called his bluff because he doesn't do it. All I know is I can't handle this another day, so swinging my legs to the side of the bed, I stand and head for the door, yanking it open, finding both my parents on the other side.

My mother steps forward the moment she sees me, but this isn't an invitation. My father's leaning on the doorframe, his palm holding him up, but he straightens upon seeing me.

Hooking my hand around the door and my other against the wall opposite of the door, I keep my feet in spot as I lean toward them, baring my teeth with my speech. "Fuck. Off."

"You're angry—"

"At least you have enough parental instincts within your cold bones to recognize that emotion." I cut my father's pointless explanation off. "Now, go back a few years and apply it to our relationship and then maybe we won't be here."

My mother opens her mouth, but it's my father who speaks. "Aurora—"

"Do you honestly believe you deserve any of my attention?" My gaze darts between them, seeking an answer from either one. "You got *rid of me*, like I was fucking *garbage*. I made my own home in Toronto because you never came to get me. *Fifteen fucking years*, all for you to yank me from the happiness I was forced to create for myself, and you, what—expected me to walk in with open arms and call you Mom and Dad? Not. Fucking. Happening." My mother flinches, but I'm finished with them and this conversation, so I begin inching the door shut, right as further points come to mind. "Oh, and my favourite: when you *finally* come for me, it wasn't even you two. You sent a soldier." Who's shown more heart than these two, which is fucked up because he shouldn't be the one being the most sympathetic to me. "You sent someone else to retrieve me like I was a package from a mailbox and *then* no one met me outside of this monstrosity of a house, which, you could have very easily kept me here with an army to protect me instead of discarding me. Yesterday, *I* came to *you*, which, if you think about it, is pretty fucked up."

"Aur—"

My father doesn't even have my name out of his mouth before I'm cutting him off. "Then I return to find out my entire future has already been decided for me in the form of a pending engagement, so excuse me, if I demand time and space. In fact, why don't I treat this place," I wave to the room at my back, "like the convent. When you're ready for me to walk down the aisle, I'll be here. So, another fifteen years sound right?"

And then I slam the door shut on their faces, daring them to attempt to enter. Pressing my back against the door, I quell my racing heart with my palm over it, trying to use the force of my hand to press down on it. It doesn't really work, and only when I hear them leave, does the adrenaline that made my argument possible begin dissipating.

With the anger gone, sadness creeps up, and my body becomes weighted. I slide to the floor, my knees drawn up, back still to the door. My eyes feel heavy, like they have tears building, but I don't want to cry about these people. They don't deserve it.

From my hoodie's pocket, I pull out my cell phone and unlock it, swiping away the game I was playing earlier. Turns out, it was useful for Rosen to download some because the problem of hiding from one's family is utter boredom.

I immediately send Rosen a message, knowing he'll understand.

ME

I hate them.

Almost instantly, the status changes, and I expect the typing bubbles to follow, but none come. A full three minutes pass of me staring, breath bated, waiting for his response.

ME

My parents came here demanding I come
out. I might have screamed at them a little.

Still nothing, even after the message is read.

ME

You ignoring me?

Nothing. Huffing, I shut the conversation away, my annoyance prickling for him again. Obviously, he's taking a side, and it's not mine. Which tells me everything from this morning and all his understanding yesterday was a sham.

91

Dick.

A dick who gave me the contact number I wanted. Since lunch, I've been waiting for the day to turn into the evening because I know the Sisters have more time to chat than in the daytime, when they're busy managing the convent.

Five's late enough. I tap the number programmed into my contacts, watching as it opens the calling app and dials the number.

The call is answered on the second ring. "Hello?"

"Sister Mary," I breathe, the sound of her voice instantly bringing my anxiety down. I relax against the door, calmer than I have been since Rosen brought me here yesterday. She's always had that about her; she's able to do for me what my mother should have done.

"Aurora?" She pauses. "My dear, how did you get this—"

"They gave it to me," I interrupt, responding to her question. "You didn't think I would leave and never reach out again, did you?"

"Well, Aurora," I picture her rubbing at her chin, an action she does habitually when she's lost for words, "yeah, that's often how it goes. You're with your family now, so we're in the past. How is it there?"

Sure, I've lied to her about a lot of things in the past—sneaking out, amongst others—but in this I tell the truth.

"Sister." It comes out more broken than I mean it to sound, more of a gasp than anything. "I-I...I don't know what they want from me." *Well, I do.* "I'm already engaged. This is ridiculous. I don't know what to do, who to be. Two nights ago, I was reading books to kids for fun, and today...today, I have a family who wants me to adopt a new identity, as if the last decade and a half never happened. Am I supposed to forget everything they've done and be like my mother? I don't know how to do any of this. Also, I might have made that known, like, twenty minutes ago when they came to my door, demanding I leave my room. I'm so...*angry* at them," my hand tightens in my lap, "but I don't want to be, you know? I despise them, but how many times have I mentioned wanting to be here? I'm so confused, Sister. Help me."

At the end of my rambles, Sister Mary asks one question: "Do you remember your strategies for what to do when things get challenging?"

When my panic attacks hit. I think back to when I was around twelve and the first one happened. I recall struggling through a math test, unable to grasp the equations and concepts. My grip was so tight around the pencil, while my other hand was in a tense ball on my lap, nails digging into my palms from how jagged they were from me chewing on them so much. Then things went black, and I no longer saw the paper in front of me. I didn't hear my teacher call my name. Or anything else really.

They happen when the stress gets too much to handle. Two threatened me yesterday. One in the car on the way to the airport, which Rosen talking quickly saved me from, and the other in the sitting room.

In the meantime, the Sisters worked hard to give me other strategies, for when exiting a situation isn't an option.

"To breathe deeply," I respond, albeit reluctantly. When I called her, I was seeking sympathy, not a reminder of what I already know. My legs straighten, stretching out in front of me, crossing at the ankles.

"Precisely. My dear, it's completely normal to feel how you do. You are literally being shoved into a life you know little about. It won't be an easy change, but I promise, in the end, it'll be better. Now, breathe with me," she commands in her authoritative tone. "We'll practice box breathing because I know you like that one. Ready?"

I grunt in response, mentally holding up a finger. As a child, I traced the air, but growing up, I learned to do it mentally, so no one knows what's in my head.

"In. One, two, three," she instructs.

With her count, I breathe in, filling my lungs with new air as I imagine a dot growing into a straight upward line.

"Hold. One, two, three."

I trap the air in my lungs, the line gaining a new addition to the right.

"Out. One, two, three."

With her count, I breathe out and mentally draw a line down.

"Hold. One, two, three."

With her count, I don't breathe at all and my mental box shuts, the final line being drawn.

"And again. In. One, two, three."

We complete another round, and by the time the second one is finishing, I straighten in the chair.

"All right, yes, Sister. I breathed."

"Do you feel better? More calm at least."

No. But yes. For the moment, yes, because, somehow, her breathing trick is fucking magical, but I know tomorrow, my anxiety will spike again.

"What do I do, Sister? You told me marriage would be part of my future, and I get it, but obviously, they want me to be ready for that. How do I fit into this world?"

"Whatever you did here, do there."

I scoff. "Funny. I don't exactly have a brood of children around to read to."

"Then find some. Women of the mafia don't work, but I believe some do charity work. Things to keep them busy, rather than sitting at home. You're in Montreal; there's bound to be an orphanage, or library reading group, or pick one of the hundred schools. Children are everywhere. Talk to your brother and inquire about volunteering somewhere. Make your mark as a Corsetti, Aurora, by showing the world and your family that you're more than a woman to be married off. You have hobbies and activities you enjoy, things you'd like to continue. Slowly, open up to your parents. My advice: start with breakfast tomorrow. Let it be awkward because the sooner it is, the sooner it will fade and you can all move forward. Play the game, my dear. That's all anyone can do."

That's...helpful. My mouth snaps shut. Volunteering with children, I can do that. The children won't be *mine* from school, but it'll be something like what I'm used to. At the very least, it'll get me out of the house. That should appease them, me leaving my room, but on my own terms.

"I guess I could do that."

"Do that, my dear. And talk with your mother. Plan a lunch or something soon. The more involved you become, the quicker your negative feelings will resolve themselves."

Lunch might be pushing it, but still, I agree with, "Okay."

"Good night, Aurora. Enjoy your life in what I'm certain is a lovely room."

She's not wrong. The sheer size of my room is triple what I had at the convent. I don't really recall the décor I had in here as a child, but I assume it's not this. This is elegant, in a dark forest manner.

"Thank you, Sister. Oh! Also, thanks for letting me take those occasional evening walks." I smile into the phone, biting down on my lip and hoping that she's able to conclude that Rosen told me of her secret-keeping.

Sister Mary chuckles. "My pleasure, my girl. Good night." She hangs up and the phone goes silent, and while the urge to call her right back and talk about anything to clear my mind is strong, I don't. Because the conversation I had with her did enough.

It gave me direction.

Hope.

Play the game. Play the game of life. Of *this* life.

Which means connecting with my family. Having a body-guard. Getting married in a year.

"Tomorrow will be better," I convince myself.

It has to be.

11

ROSEN

Ignoring Aurora's text messages earlier today was for both our benefit. Her angry yells travelled farther than she believed, and Nico and I heard everything, even before her mother rushed down the stairs and right outside, Lorenzo following at her heels with barely a glance toward us.

Sure, I could be sympathetic to her parents, but if my feelings picked a side, it's hers. Everything she said came from a place of pent-up rage, one that she's been building for countless years. She said what she had out of necessity, and her parents had to experience her wrath.

But then her messages came through almost right away and I ignored her, no matter how much it pained me to turn away from her as she was seeking support. Aurora needs to start relying on her brothers, or even Della, for support. Not her bodyguard.

Boundaries.

But when I'm walking my way back to my room and it's close to ten at night, the ping of my phone alerts me to another one of her texts. I hope it's Nico or Rafael, but I know even before taking out my phone, it's not.

AURORA

Am I allowed to leave?

ME

Princesse, that's all anyone's wanted today.

AURORA

I don't want anyone to know. And I meant more than leaving my room. I'd like to go outside. You're who I talk to about that, right? Jailor.

Despite the snarky question, I smirk as I type in my response.

ME

When do you want to go?

AURORA

Now. And we don't have to leave the land. Outside, in the yard, will do.

Probably for the best anyway. Aurora's first outing off the Corsetti property shouldn't be at nighttime.

ME

Be right there.

Spinning on my heel, I retrace my steps backwards, past Nico's office. I should let him know she's about to leave her bedroom, but she asked me not to, and I suspect it has to do with the family descending on her.

Again, for their benefit, I keep her secrets. If she leaves now and trusts that no one demanded attention, then maybe she'll repeat this tomorrow. In the daytime. When her family is around.

At her bedroom, I knock once and wait, propping myself against the doorjamb until I hear the knob turning. She smiles tentatively at seeing me. Aurora is dressed in a similar outfit as this morning; only, she's swapped the shorts for skin-tight, black leggings and added shoes to her feet.

Her head pokes out of the doorway and she scans up and down the hallway, making me chuckle.

"Nico's in his office. Not sure where Della is. Ariella's in her room. No one else is here."

Relief lightens her eyes, and she steps into the hall, pulling her door shut behind her. I lead her down the hallway and toward the large staircase.

"Seems silly to involve a guard when I'm only going to the backyard."

From my place two steps lower from her, which puts me around the same height as her, I glance over my shoulder. "Seems so, but sometimes the places we feel the most safe are actually the most unsafe."

"That's insightful."

That was the warning Dad always fed Poppy and me growing up, and given my position was once his, his outlook makes sense.

I lead the way down to the main floor, past the sitting room she learned about her engagement in, noticing how she glares at the innocent oak door, past the library and games room, and right to the end.

"Holy shit," she breathes when I step aside, holding the glass door for her to enter the small greenhouse. "This is so pretty."

"This is a place your father had made for your mother a few years before you were born."

Her gaze cuts sharply to me, an accusation there, which I

ignore as I walk her to the opposite end, to the door leading to the outdoors.

"Every other exit in the house, and you chose this one?" One brow lifts as she walks through the second door I open for her.

"It's the one closest to us. There," I say when we're both outside, immersed into the warm, summer night air. "Like you wanted. We're outside."

As she moves forward, her feet gliding against the grass, her head tips back, her face up to the waning moon. Nature takes over and her arms spread wide. She spins away from me and I catch the hint of a smile.

Is this what she was like before I found her? Free, as much as she could be within her cage. And here, now trapped within another cage. All the Corsetti mansion is, is a holding case; a temporary place before she's handed to her new handler—Erico Rossi.

While she enjoys her outing, I prop myself against the side of the mansion, watching her. My eyes skip over the lands, so much of the distance darkened. We've never had an attack directly on the land, for as long as I've been inducted anyway, and I don't anticipate anything happening tonight, but it's good Aurora remembered the rules placed around her. The one that says she must be accompanied when leaving.

She makes it about ten feet away before her twirling ends, her smile dying when she notices the distance between us.

"Hey," she calls. "You coming?"

"No. You don't require so much protection I have to follow you step for step."

Her head tips, that messy bun of hers threatening to topple to the side. Gravity shouldn't even be possible at this point. "What if I run away?"

"Then I'll chase you."

She thumbs toward the forest in the distance, her smile growing with her taunt. "What if I hide?"

"Then I'll chase you and find you and drag you back here. And might have to tell your brother that you tried to run away."

Her smirk drops into a frown, her lips pursed. "Dick. You're no fun."

I'm plenty fun, but not for you.

Boundaries.

"Stay close, Aurora, and you'll be okay."

The order is barely out of my mouth before her wicked grin returns and she backs up. One step, and then two, her body shifting to turn and run.

She can have her amusement, but I'm not playing with her. Not like this because the level of inappropriateness is too much for either of us to handle.

"Aurora," I growl low, commanding—a test. See how she manages an affirmative tone, and certainly one I shouldn't be using on the *princesse*. "Don't do it. Or we go back inside. I can't protect you if you're too far away."

"That's the point." She spins on her heel and hightails it away.

I move, pushing off the wall, using pure leg muscle, strength, and agility—over a decade of training—to easily catch up with her. She's only made it a few strides by the time I do. My one stride equating to three of hers.

I pass her by a single step and whirl, throwing my body in her path. She runs right into me, her small body against my hard one, her hands flying to my shirt, which she grasps, holding herself upright.

"Shit." She's panting, her shoulders rising and falling, her chest heaving beneath her hoodie. "You're fast."

"Warned you." I step into her, forcing her backwards. And again. And again, until she finally comprehends she's lost. She's still holding my shirt as she walks backwards and I'm uncertain if she realizes she is, and I stupidly don't push her away.

"Yeah, but," she peeks behind her, "you were all the way over there."

"And?"

"You're fast."

Bearing down on her, I form a tower over her, and I don't let up until we're closer to the house. Then I step to the side, forcing her to release my shirt.

"Don't do that again." I head for the wall again, taking up the same spot I was earlier.

Aurora pouts but doesn't go anywhere. Thankfully, she lowers herself onto the ground, crossing her legs as she leans back on her arms positioning behind her and stares at me.

"Who pissed in your Cheerios?"

The mouth on this girl... "It's called safety, *princesse*. There's a reason I said don't run away. Your family won't be pleased if I have to tell them you tried to take off."

She scoffs, shaking her head. "Trust me, that wasn't running away. You'd know if I was. Gonna stay over there the entire time or join me down here?" She gestures to the space beside her.

"Yes. We're out here for you to get fresh air. Not to spend time together."

"Ouch." She crinkles her nose, which looks sexier than I'd care to admit. "What's with you? You're different than you were earlier."

"Boundaries, Aurora, that's how relationships between the family and the soldiers work. I'm not meant to be your friend." A lump builds in my throat at the words, but it'll be for her own benefit.

Hurt flashes in her eyes so quick, she glances to the moon and back, in the same manner she used the sun yesterday to burn away her sadness when leaving the convent.

"If we're not supposed to be friends, then why stay up with me last night and answer my messages."

Given we're only a few windows beneath Nico's office, instinct drives me to peek up the side of the mansion, checking that he's not staring out of it, even if I know him to frequently have his curtains shut, especially at this time of night.

"I said we're not meant to be friends. Not that I don't want to."

Shit. No. That's not what I was supposed to say, but the fucking admittance slipped out before I could stop myself.

Beneath the moonlight, Aurora's smirk looks even more forbidden. She falls back onto the ground, dramatically throwing her hands in the air. When she speaks, it's to the sky, the stars and the moon, rather than me.

"I see the confusion, Rosen. Back to my original statement then. Come sit."

"You forget I don't obey your orders."

Her hands push into the ground and she props herself up by her elbows. "Too bad. Or else I'd order you to get the stick out of your ass."

*Princesse...*I look away from her, staring into the forest beyond, waiting until my dick calms down. She's such a goddamn brat. Nico owes me a raise after this.

As tempting as it is to reply, I don't, instead watching her stare at the sky. Her expression is pensive, and while I'd love to know what's in her head, I remain stoic where I stand, meaning every word I said. We're not supposed to be friends, and while I understand she wants one, it shouldn't be me.

After a few minutes of silence, of only the night wind coasting over us, she speaks again in a voice so low, it's nearly swallowed up by the breeze.

"You didn't answer my texts. I guess now I see why."

Regret weighs my tone down when I respond. "If you're

pissed at your family, it's an internal issue, Aurora, and one I shouldn't be privy of." Even if I wasn't around, it seems like something Nico would later share with me, but I don't admit that to her.

"I hate them," she states, repeating the first text she sent after the screaming had stopped. "They want me to instantly fall into line, but it's fucked up to want that. I mean, they got rid of me. They don't deserve this kindness."

"You made your stance abundantly clear." My response is short and to the point because she can't believe I'm on her side. Plus, while we're not loud out here, we're not exactly hidden and anyone could easily overhear.

Her long sigh mingles into the night air, finding its way up to the sky and becoming part of it. "After I yelled at them, I called Sister Mary."

Not a surprise. When I gave her the number, I didn't imagine it'd be long before she made the call.

"She suggested I *try*," Aurora spits the word like poison. "That I make a connection with them by attending breakfast tomorrow."

"Not a bad idea."

She lifts her head, finding me still in the same spot. She doesn't speak, only stares, until shaking her head with an annoyed huff and dropping back to the grass.

"Of course you'd say that," I think she grumbles, but it's swallowed up by distance. "Still not gonna join me? Is it so bad to want to get to know my bodyguard, since we're going to spend *so* much time together?"

Yes. Yes, because already, I've kept secrets for you when I shouldn't have. Have made a connection with you that only your family should be experiencing.

"It's not done," I manage, no matter how much I wish it

could because Aurora Corsetti intrigues me in a way no one else has.

Spitfire attitude, a brat, but beneath it all, an anxious woman who wants a connection but on her own terms. She flip-flops her attitudes so quickly, it'd be exhausting for anyone else, but I revel in the challenge keeping up with her requires.

That's not even counting how fucking sexy she is. The moment Nico showed me the image of her a month ago, it was a fleeting opinion, but the living version is temptation in the flesh. Full lips that spew attitude, mischievous emerald eyes, a golden waterfall of hair and curves my hands ache to hold.

I once wondered how long this year would be, and I firmly still believe it, only now for different reasons.

Which is why boundaries are really fucking useful.

"Whatever," she finally responds, flippantly. "How long until you drag me inside and lock me in my room again?"

"Miss Corsetti," I use the name she dislikes, "you were the one locking yourself away. Until tomorrow, I take it." With this revelation, I should tell Nico, to ensure he gets the entire family over here, but it'll be strange telling him how I know this.

"Yes." She groans. "Life was so much simpler before yesterday."

"But more lonely." Suddenly, I want to know her true feelings on being back. For all her hatred and anger, there's a small fragment of her at least happy she's home. "Do you wish you could go back to Toronto? That I never came for you?"

She's silent, and only the movement of her eyelids tells me she hasn't fallen asleep yet. Deliberating the answer or how much to admit, I'm not sure, but a full two minutes pass before I hear her murmur, "No. All I dreamed of growing up was coming home. It sucks, you know?" She pushes to a sitting position, all impish behaviour gone for the sombre Aurora to reveal herself again.

"They claim they're pleased to have me home, but Nico's marrying me off the first chance he gets. My parents think I'm still a child, and they didn't come for me themselves. No offense."

"None taken."

She sighs, scanning the side of the mansion, and then the sky before repositioning her hands to stand. I don't move until she approaches, stopping inches from me. Heat from her body warms mine, inviting, compelling, and I step away, heading back for the greenhouse's door.

"You spoke so calmly," I comment, leading her through the tiny floral space, past the water fountain in the centre, and back inside the main part of the house. "About your emotions toward them and why the anger. Try saying it like that to your family."

"Easier said than done." She snorts.

I know but the fact you're speaking so open with me can be dangerous, princesse.

She remains silent until I return her to her bedroom. Just like leaving earlier, we pass no one. At her room, I twist the knob and open her door for her, stepping aside to let her through.

She doesn't enter right away, but pauses and rests her hand on my forearm, the same way she did last night when I taught her how to use her phone. I wouldn't have if I'd foreseen she'd be using it to speak with me about her family.

"That was nice. Needed, I think. A bit of fresh air before the shitshow of tomorrow morning."

"You'll be fine," I reassure her, pulling my arm away before her touch brands me more than it has. "Goodnight, Aurora."

Every step away from her door, I count, and when I reach eight, she shuts the door.

12

AURORA

The next morning is one hundred percent better already. Maybe it was getting out of this bedroom last night and sitting outside for the short while, or maybe it was speaking with Sister Mary yesterday.

Either way, Sister Mary's point about finding children to volunteer with sticks with me late into the next morning, as I dress inside the closet that's easily the size of my old room. For the numerous items in here, there's a strong theme of dresses, but after a lot of searching, I find jeans and a dark tank, which I cover with a grey cardigan.

I exit my room, and like old memories have been dredged up, I find the dining room quickly. The arched entryway used to be my favourite for the "unique."—at least to a six-year-old— shape. Through it, there's a long table filled with colourful breakfast foods of all sorts of scents and a row of people sitting on either side.

Fuck. I expected this, but still, I'm unprepared. Returning to hide in my room again and yell at my parents through the door seems like a better idea, but now I'm here and I'm unable to leave as every single person turns at my arrival.

My mother's eyes light up from across the table, while my father's hand lands on top of hers, as if holding her down. After yesterday, I wouldn't be surprised if they *weren't* eager to see me in attendance, but clearly, they're trying.

At the head of the table, Nico watches me intently, his expression blank, while the woman beside him smiles gently, clearly trying to ease me. Della, if I remember what Rosen said her name is. Across from her, that redheaded girl barely spares me any attention before returning to her bowl. Rafael turns around from his place beside Della and winks, gesturing to the open chair beside him.

"Sis. Come sit."

Sis. Such an offhanded nickname. So normal. Something that shouldn't bother me at all.

Go sit, Aurora. My inner voice commands until I walk stiffly to the chair beside Rafael.

"Good morning," Nico greets politely. "Glad you left your bedroom. Have you been sleeping well?"

The first night, no, not at all. Last night, after Rosen dropped me off at my room, I was passed out within the hour. The mattress is softer than I've ever had, and I know that's really what he's asking.

"Yes. The room is beautiful."

"We had it redone," my mother chimes in. "We spoke with the Sisters, who said you preferred natural colours."

"I do." A better method would have been speaking to *me* about my preferences, but hey...

Della stretches her arm over Rafael's plate toward me. "I'm Della, Nico's fiancée. I'm sorry we didn't officially meet earlier."

I don't bother admitting that Rosen already told me who

she was, simply grateful to have her care enough to make her own introductions.

She's an outsider. Immediately, I feel more comfortable with her than any of them. Della knows what it's like to be thrown into this family, which means she's on the outs. We could have formed our own merry band of misfits, if she wasn't already aligned with my brother due to the sparkling engagement ring on her finger.

"Hi." I take her hand, shaking it once, awkwardly. "Nice to meet you."

"You too. This is my sister, Ariella." She gestures across from her to the redhead.

Ariella glances up from her bowl again and shoots me a gentle smile, before looking right back down. I get it. I wish I could do the same honestly. To be the sister of the in-law means Ariella doesn't have to behave a certain way. She's granted the freedom to ignore the rest of us, exactly what I'd die to do.

Della frowns at her sister but quickly masks her disappointment with a smile she sends back my way before returning to her own plate.

"Hungry?" my mother asks. "There's a lot to choose from." She gestures toward the spread, like it isn't right in front of my face.

Don't be rude.

"Thanks," I manage to mutter, and reach for the food closest to me. The butter croissant is warm, soft, and makes my mouth instantly water, reminding me I skipped dinner last night.

Rafael nudges over a bowl of fruit salad. "Do yourself a favour and eat more than that. As you can see, the chefs put out enough to feed an army and then some."

"Thanks." I scoop a moderate-sized amount of fruit onto my plate beside my croissant.

I'm two grapes in when I realize almost everyone is staring at me. Everyone, but Della and Ariella. Ariella is still slumped in her seat, quietly eating, while Della is attempting to engage my brother in small talk, but instead, Nico watches me. Rafael is shooting side-eye looks as he slices into his homemade waffles covered in more whip cream than necessary, while my parents outright watch me to the point it's getting creepy.

And they wonder why I didn't want to leave my room yesterday. Hell, if I didn't call Sister Mary, this probably wouldn't be happening. I'd happily be hiding away, angry at them, refusing to start the healing process, or however Sister put it.

I shuffle and do the impossible—begin a conversation.

"So," I focus on Nico, since he seems to be the decision-maker, "where's the nearest library? Or a community centre? Somewhere I can volunteer with children."

Nico's brows dive inward, while across the table my father coughs into his coffee. "Excuse me?"

What is their problem?

"You heard me. I want to volunteer."

For all Sister Mary's advice, I hardly hear her voice in my head anymore. It's gone, replaced by another rant, similar to the one cast toward my parents yesterday. Beneath the tablecloth, my hand forms a fist. With every deep breath I wish I could take, I tighten my hand, squeezing out my frustrations—another strategy to manage my anxiety.

"At the convent, I'd gotten close to the younger kids there. Once I graduated and no one came for me," I don't bother hiding the bitterness in my tone, but I do clench my fist even tighter for five seconds, counting every one, until my tone returns to neutral, "I had nothing better to do than make those children feel less lonely. I became the older sister none of them had." I focus solely on Rafael and Nico. "You two may have lost me, but you had each other. I watched the people I grew up with leave, while I was *still* there for an unknown length of time. Those young ones became everything to me. It was so difficult leaving them yesterday, knowing I'll never see them again." Tears threaten my eyes, but I blink them away, not wanting them to interrupt my tirade. "Nothing will replace those children because simply being with them made me happy. Made me feel productive. I don't want to die of boredom around here and I suspect that's what'll happen." I scan the table, seeking any sign of compassion in these people, finding it so far only from Della and her sister, who looked up again. "It'll help me feel better about being home. A bit of my old life mixed in here because," I pause on Nico and our father, "as much as you all expect me to come home and live the life you've all been versed in, *I* can't. It doesn't work like that. People don't easily switch themselves on and off. I'd like a job, so to speak. Somewhere I can go and feel like I'm making a difference in kids' lives."

I pause, but no one speaks. They all stare at me with varying expressions of shock. I count to five and when no response comes, the bubbling emotions within my chest won't allow me to be still any longer.

I stand, throwing my cloth napkin onto the table as more tears fill my eyes. Tears for another reason this time. Tears because not one of them even fucking responded to the heartbreak I dished out.

"You took me away from my family," I say coldly, shoving my chair back. "No one deserves being abandoned. Me. Them. No one."

Without another look at any of them, I turn away and rush down the hall as the tears consume my eyes, blurring my vision.

~

The wind blows warm air over my face, making my tear stains more noticeable. It curls over the Corsetti land, catching on the massive yard that stretches far beyond what an average backyard would be, and right toward the trees that line the background.

Through the silence of the wind, the peace I've found being alone out here dissipates as footsteps quietly approach. When leather shoes appear in my vision, I nearly leave, not wanting to be around any of my family. I tried for a peaceful breakfast, but that failed. Apparently, I had some pent-up shit to get released, even if I didn't realize it at first.

It's not Nico or my father. Rafael flops down beside me onto the stone bench I've discovered on the side of the house. He stretches his legs out leisurely, crossing them at the ankles as his hands slide into his pockets: the picture of ease, contrasting my own stiffness.

"Pulled the short straw?"

"On the contrary, I volunteered. I should be offended you think so little of me, but I understand why you do."

"You do?"

"Oh, yeah. You're right, you know." He shrugs. "Nico and I always had each other. We had our parents. But you didn't get any of that. Your life changed in every way possible. So yeah, I understand. I might not be able to completely comprehend what you went through, but I can empathize."

Such simple words but so impactful, especially that last statement. Even when saying he understands, he claims not to know how *I* felt. It's all I've wanted from any of them. A true acknowledgement of what happened—what's happen*ing*. So far, the only one to show a sentiment like that one has been Rosen, and it's still fucked up a soldier did before my own family.

"Thanks."

Rafael smiles crookedly, nudging my shoulder. "You'll learn soon, I'm the fun brother. Our other one is always locked away in his office."

Somehow, I'm not surprised by this. "What do you do then?"

"I run a club."

My ears perk. A club. I've seen them on movies. They look like fun, with the music, the lights, the massive amount of drunk people enjoying life and forgetting their worries.

"What's it called?"

"Eden."

That's an intriguing name for a club. "Why Eden?"

"Because...er...No matter. You'll never get a chance to visit it."

Because this family will control my every move, if they get their way.

"Anyway." Rafael sits forward as he pulls something from his pocket. It's a piece of paper, which he slips into my palm. "The Sisters mentioned you enjoyed gardening when you were there, so this might interest you. It's a community garden with a program for underprivileged kids. A place they get to play in the dirt, tend to plants and grow food, and simply be kids. I already called the owner, told her who you are, and that you want to volunteer. She's completely for it."

I take the paper, reading the scribbled name written on it. "Just like that?"

He winks. "She knows our family. That's all there is to it. I've passed the address onto Rosen, so whenever you'd like to visit, you'll be good to go."

Rafael did more than listen to me. He respected me. Went out of his way to get me what I wanted.

"I think you might be edging for favourite sibling," I tease.

"I mean, my competition is Nico," he hikes a thumb over his shoulder, "so if that's saying anything..."

I laugh, and it feels damn good for my chest to hurt from feeling light and airy rather than heavy and packed.

"Thanks, Rafael. At least someone here is nice."

He leans forward with a long breath and dangles his hands between his legs. He scans the land when he answers, "Again, I get why you feel as you do, but our parents were terrified, Aurora. Hawke had his innocence ripped from him, and they lost a son as a result."

"And a daughter."

He turns his head, his lips pursed. "Do you actually believe that? Because I don't think you do, or else you would have tried to run away by now. You're here because a part of you wants to be. You want us as much as we want you. Now comes the healing on both sides. They need to acknowledge what they did, but you need to forgive."

Forgive? That might be taking it too far.

"Except they're marrying me off so soon. Can't be that eager to have me home."

Rafael holds up two hands, palms out. "Hey, don't blame me for that. That's all Nico, and I made it known how much I guessed you'd despise it. He's doing what he thinks is right, and there's a lot of instability right now."

"Instability?"

He waves me off. "Don't worry about it. Point is, he's trying to do his job. It's not only you, don't worry. Any day now, I'm sure he's going to insist I get married too."

"Della," I refer to Nico's own marriage. "We should all be following him then?"

"Exactly." He chuckles, and with a heaving breath, pushes to his feet and offers his hand for me to take. "Let's go find Rosen and get you out of here."

Without a second thought, I take his hand. "Why are you being so nice to me?" I ask as we begin walking toward the side entrance.

"Because I'm your brother and that's what we do. You cared for the kids back at your school. Consider me doing the same." We reach the door and he opens it, waving me in first. "Besides, I told you. I'm angling to be the better brother."

You already are.

13
ROSEN

Since Rafael gave me the name of the community garden and mentioned how likely it is for Aurora to want to visit today, it's no surprise I receive a text from her within the hour.

Very demanding. Even reading it has my hand twitching with the craving to teach her how manners work. Hard to believe this is the same woman who thanked me in such a gentle voice last night. She's like that story, *Jekyll and Hyde*.

Instead, I don't reply, and drive one of Corsettis' many vehicles from the multi-car garage that is on the side of the mansion toward the front entrance. There is a driver the family shares, but I decide not to bother Sam today, since being in the front seat will ensure my hands have something to hold onto that isn't her neck.

Her delicate neck. A neck to nibble as I thrust into her...
Whoa, wake up, Rosen. No.

Did I see her forbidden body in my dreams last night? Yes. Did I wake up, drenched in sweat, cursing Nico all over for making her my problem? Also, yes. I know every reason I should never consider Aurora in any way past being my charge, recounted every single one of them when I stood outside with her last night, and yet, my stupid subconscious pictured her in my sleep.

Parking in the front of the house, I get out and wait for her, leaning on the hood. The sun shines brightly, which is appropriate for where we're headed. I tug the sunglasses that are poised on the top of my head over my eyes, shielding them from the rays.

While I wait, I input the garden's name into my phone's map app, determining the most efficient way to get there. It's on the other side of the city: a thirty-minute drive, most of it on the Décarie Interchange, which means I'll be so busy monitoring the hectic traffic, I won't have to worry about accidentally looking too long at Aurora.

AURORA

Well? Are you there?

Impatient minx. I have to take three deep breaths before I type out a half-respectable response.

ME

If you look out the window, you'll see the only one waiting is me.

Okay, so maybe less than half-respectable.

AURORA

Next time, answer me. I'll be right down.

Within minutes, Aurora exits the front of the house. She walks down the steps in tight jeans that show off her every forbidden curve, and a low tank, which unwittingly draws my attention to her chest. Sunglasses are perched on her head and she has a small black purse strapped diagonally over her shoulder. So different from the woman in a baggy hoodie and a messy bun from yesterday. While she looks sexy like this, I can't help but miss her casual attire.

"Next time, tell me you're ready," she shouts, coming to a stop in front of me. Her hip cocks to the side, her head following too, but her show of assertiveness only makes me smile. "No need to be a dick, *dick*."

It takes all my years of training to brush off her comment. How is it that I've had people curse me, my family, my life, anything they can think of while they're screaming bloody murder for mercy, and yet this tiny girl pisses me off so damn much?

Yet, I'm also pleased that the playful exterior has returned, and not the sad version of her. I long to ask her about breakfast this morning, even when I already got the details from Rafael and Nico in two separate accounts. I want her version, and the only reason I don't ask, is what I told her last night: boundaries.

I open the back door of the car and gesture for her to get inside. "We'll leave right away."

Aurora strides by me, her chin lifting in defiance, and her smirk tells me she fucking knows it too. She opens the front passenger door and gets in slowly, reaching for the door, which I grasp the top of, halting her. She can't sit there. Not with the multiple sets of eyes that could be watching us from inside.

Boundaries. Did she not comprehend what I told her last night?

"What the hell do you think you're doing?"

Her eyes flick to me and then the console and back and forth before she shrugs innocently. "Sitting. Waiting for you to get in."

"In the back."

"I'd rather be up here with you."

"If I asked a driver to take us, you'd be in the back. It's not typical for a member of the family to sit with the staff. Therefore, back seat." *I personally don't typically care where Corsettis sit, but it'll be easier to focus if she's not right beside me.*

Her smirk grows into a wicked, sexy grin. "So, you *do* think of yourself as staff. Which means, I have authority over you."

As much as I despise letting her win, if it's what this takes… "Sure, whatever. Get in the back seat, *princesse.*"

She removes her purse and drops it at her feet before making a show of settling into the leather seat and locking herself in with the seat belt. The gentle *click*, which feels obnoxiously louder than usual, masks the sound of my teeth grinding together.

"Aurora, I'll move you to the back myself. You want to fit into this family? Act proper." Well, what they deem proper, at least.

"We've ridden in a car together before, so I don't see how this is any different."

"It was a Coupe. Two doors. There's barely a back seat for you to get into," I counter, thinking about the car Nico had Toronto Pearson lend us yesterday.

"And? Picture this having two doors if it'll make you happy."

My grip tightens around her door and it's all I can do to exhibit the level of frustration this girl makes me feel. Releasing it, I slam it harder than I mean to, and with a set jaw and nerves that are seconds away from snapping, I get in the driver's seat, noticing that in the time it's taken me to get to my side, she's kicked off her shoes and has her feet propped on the dash.

"Comfy?" I ask, sarcasm in my tone.

"Very. Thanks for asking."

I turn the car on and pull away from the house as I mutter, "It wasn't meant to be polite."

As we drive down the tree-lined road to leave the Corsetti property, I plug my phone into the vehicle, waiting the couple seconds until the screen flashes with the directions I pre-setup. Aurora remains quiet as I do so, only speaking once I turn onto the main road.

"Why don't you like me?"

"I don't hate you," I immediately counter. "Do you not remember everything I said to you last night? We can't be friends, Aurora."

"But you don't like me," she continues, skipping over every point I've made. "You seem very annoyed by my presence."

Because you're so fucking good at annoying me. I merely shrug. "You enjoy being a brat," I mutter, instantly despising myself for using that term. It's out between us now, too late to be snatched back.

Thankfully, she seems to move right past it. "You're easy to rile up."

"Well, one day you'll be collared. And if he's smart, muzzled too."

It's when I'm getting us into the thick of Montreal traffic that she speaks. "Still won't tell me anything about *him*?"

"Nope. I'd like to keep my job, thanks. It's certainly not my place to be telling you those things. The only reason I know is because of the long-standing trust your brother has in me."

"And friendship," she adds. "What if I promise not to say anything?"

"Even then."

The look of utter disappointment on her face makes my stomach churn, so for the next few minutes, I conduct more mirror checks than usual, subtly peeking at her, simply so I can curb my apprehension for making her feel bad.

Especially since she's merely concerned. Her probing comes from a place of anxiousness, I'm assuming, and rightfully so. How I fucking wish I can be the one to smooth those worry lines from her face, but instead, I grip the wheel tighter and remind myself of the differences between her last name and mine.

So tight, I'm sure I lose my fucking mind because my next words are coated with a sigh. "I'll make you a deal: when your family tells you who your fiancé is, I'll give you my report on him. My *limited* report," I emphasize, so she knows not to expect a novel on Rossi.

Out of the corner of my eye, I watch her lips purse before nodding once. "Thanks, Rosen."

For the remainder of the drive, she remains silent and watches the city pass by. I wonder how different it is from Toronto, and how much of Toronto she got to see. Any major part of the city we pass, I try to point it out to her, even if she doesn't respond.

Eventually, we break through to the other side of the city and off onto a long road that stretches into an urban neighbour-hood. I park in front of the single, small house surrounded by a vast, flat yard. The two-story home has seen better days, based on the peeling, yellow—or perhaps, stained—siding, dusted windows, and crooked front steps.

Real nice, Rafael.

While the grass stretches far and wide on either side of the house, a piece of it has been fenced-off. With the angle I'm at, only the side is visible, but it's clear, we're in the right place at least.

Despite the broken-down appearance, Aurora gushes, "Thanks, Rosen, for driving me here. I'm really excited about this. I don't know if Sister Mary mentioned, but I used to spend a lot of free time with the kids, and well..." her head lowers, "I miss them. Miss being a support for children. I'm hoping this will give me the same sense."

Her genuineness has returned and I'm struggling to determine which I prefer: her playful brat behaviours or the moments of real emotion she reveals.

The second I switch off the vehicle, Aurora jams her feet into her shoes, grabs her purse, and hops out of the vehicle.

"Jesus fuck." Excitement or not, she can't jump into things like this. I take off after her, my gaze scanning every inch of the property. The Corsettis have a history with this place, but still, training demands me to check out everything and verify its safety. With De Falco out there, I'd rather be extra cautious.

I shove in front of Aurora, my hand landing on my hip, untucking my holster from my shirt, for the Glock stored there.

"Shit, Rosen!" She yanks on my elbow, trying to pull my hand away from my hip. "Rosen, there's kids here. Put the damn gun away."

"Your safety comes first." I growl.

"The children won't hurt me, *god*. Put it away!"

Only when feeling satisfactory that the wide-open area doesn't provide much of a chance for attacking, I fold my shirt back over the weapon. Once she's mollified that I listened to her, she heads for those rickety front steps, and I follow close behind.

We make it two steps before she throws her heels into the dirt, and I nearly bump into her with her sudden stop. Peering over her shoulder, her annoyance is back in her unyielding gaze.

"*I'm* the one they're expecting."

"You think your brother gave you a bodyguard like I'm some sort of accessory?" I step by her, taking the lead. "I have a job to do, Aurora, and you make it very challenging."

She grumbles her next words, but I'm finding myself getting

so attuned to her, it's easy to hear her, no matter how hard she tries not to be heard. "Says the guy who doesn't even want this."

I ignore the jab, and knock on the door, my hand instinctively floating to my hip again. She lets out a dramatic, aggravated noise, which I also ignore, until an elderly lady fills the doorway. She instantly beams, wiping the back of her hand against her forehead, clearing the sweat away. Then she wipes her hand on her dirt-smudged overalls, making me question the effectiveness of her cleaning methods.

"Ms. Laurent?" I use the name Rafael provided.

"I'm her. Clarisse, please." She steps aside, gesturing for us to enter. "Come in. Aurora, I assume." Clarisse peeks over my shoulder to where Aurora is extremely close behind me.

I step aside, allowing Aurora in, while I study the small foyer. A coat hook to my right, a mirror to my left and a large carpet with a few pairs of shoes strewn around. By the time I turn back around, Aurora is shaking Clarisse's hand.

"Hi, yes. Thank you for having me."

"I'll admit, I was surprised to get your brother's call, but come on, let's chat in my office." She leads us down the short hall, right into an attached room.

I enter first. It's small and cramped, with stacks of paperwork all over the wooden desk. In front, two plastic chairs are positioned, one also filled with stacks of papers. The old, off-white walls are peppered with colourful artwork by varying degrees of talent.

Clarisse shuts the door behind us, though I wonder why, since we should be the only ones in the house. Either way, I position my back to it while Aurora sits in the only available chair.

"Welcome back to the city, Miss Corsetti. Your brother requested I keep your visits discreet." She stretches her arms to the side, gesturing to the space. "It's only me here. Me, the children who enjoy the program, and the few volunteers who help out, but we can book you on the days they're not here if you'd like."

"Aurora," Aurora immediately corrects. "Those were Rafael's requests, sure, but I don't mind if your other volunteers are here. It'll be nice to meet people outside my family."

The moment she finishes speaking, she whirls around, catching me in her daring gaze. I don't respond because if it's people she wants to meet...well, in two days' time, she'll be meeting a whole lot of them at an engagement party.

"After all," she continues in a sugary-sweet tone, a brow lifting in a challenge, "how else can I immerse myself with the public if I never see anyone?"

"O-okay." Clarisse cuts through the tension with her gentle tone. Rubbing her hands along her overalls, she glances over Aurora's head, toward me. "If it'll make the Corsettis feel more at ease, I can provide a list of names of the volunteers working here, as well as their clear police checks. Since it's children we serve, the program demands that all volunteers come with a clean background check." Her gaze lowers to Aurora. "Your paperwork, of course, has already been taken care of."

I roll my lips together, answering Clarisse, but staring at Aurora when I respond, "I'll mention it to your brothers and see if that's what they want. For now, we'll skip that part." Given their connection to this place, Rafael might have already done that.

"Great!" Clarisse exclaims, garnering Aurora's attention once more. "So I have an idea, how often would you like to come by? I mean, stop by on your schedule, if that's what you choose," she quickly backtracks, her hands waving dramatically in the air, "but I like having a heads-up for planning purposes. If possible. But it's okay if not."

"Every day," Aurora responds right away.

For fuck's sake.

"Miss Corsetti," I grit, "remember your other responsibilities."

"What? You mean shopping? Parties? Lounging around that huge house? Yeah," she scoffs, "I'm sure *that's* more important than giving children a bit of attention and love." Her hard gaze softens for a beat, and she has the exact expression from the car earlier, when she was mentioning her anticipation over working here. But as fast as she blinks, it's gone.

Every muscle in me constricts to the point of pain and I curse Nico for the billionth time for making Aurora my problem. Because that's what she's becoming. A huge fucking problem. A pain in the ass who ought to be taught a lesson on how to check her attitude. All those considerations about her genuineness when we first arrived—gone.

"Those are a few, yes. Your upcoming engagement for another."

She stiffens, her back going rigid, telling me I've reached her patience's limit, so I lower my tone for my next point.

"Your role will pick up, Aur—Miss Corsetti, and you can't overschedule yourself. Can I make a recommendation?"

"If I say no, I suspect you still will, so sure, why the hell not."

"Agree to weekly, and if you can do more, then you can adjust your schedule."

"When I'm in the mood to come, as long as it's not every day," she counters, going stiff like she's preparing for a longer fight.

I picture every possible way her plan will go south, but once again, her excitement at arriving slips into my head again. The emotion in her tone when she spoke about leaving the kids in Toronto behind, and about being a support to the ones here. It's getting increasingly difficult to deny her.

"That could work too."

Her eyes brighten and she smiles before turning back around, but I felt every inch of that smile inside my gut. A little bargain, and she's an entirely other girl.

"Is that okay?" she checks with Clarisse, who won't deny her because Aurora isn't a regular volunteer.

"Of course. If you come around three, that's when some of the kids start showing up. I've partnered with local schools, so buses drop them off here right after, and then parents retrieve them later in the evening, before the sun goes down. During the day, we have a lot less visitors, since most of our kiddos are in school."

"Got it. Whatever and whenever. Thank you."

Clarisse smiles gently and begins lifting to her feet, with an ease a woman her age doesn't seem like she should have. "We appreciate you, Aurora. Would you like to see the property? No one's here yet, and they won't be," she glances at a clock on the far wall, "for another four hours. You can stay if you'd like."

Four hours is a long damn time to wait around, but thankfully, Aurora shakes her head. "Thanks, but I'll come back another day to meet them. I'll take the tour." She springs to her feet and immediately follows Clarisse to the door.

I step aside, squishing myself against a shelf, so Clarisse can open the door. She exits with Aurora following, and I trail behind them both.

I'm barely out of the office when Aurora spins around, finger jutted in my face. "You can stay here."

And leave her to wander a place that hasn't been inspected yet? Nico would kill me. "Not happening."

She puts her hands onto her cocked hips and the argument is so ready, it's practically visible on her mouth, but she clamps her lips shut and glances back at the waiting woman.

"Give me a moment, please, Clarisse. Thank you."

Clarisse shoots a worried look at me, but wisely doesn't question Aurora and wanders deeper through the house, making herself busy, as Aurora backs me into the office, shutting the door behind her. With the shelf at my back and the door at hers, we're only inches from one another and she's forced to tip her head up.

"Children, Rosen. We talked about this. You—with your huge fucking size," she waves her hand up and down the length of my body, "and the gun shouldn't be around children."

"There's no children here," I remind her. "Clarisse said she's alone right now."

She opens and shuts her mouth three times, trying to create an effective counterargument. Every time she gives up, her expression pinches a fraction more, until I'm biting on my tongue to prevent from laughing at her.

"Still," she finally spits out, "not required. My own brother recommended this place. Why would he do that if he thought it could be dangerous?"

"It's a wide-open area and anyone could be hiding out, watching us. You have no idea who you are, *princesse*, and what your family is dealing with right now. Your safety is important. Seeing the layout of the land, so if anything happens—and I'm not saying it will, but *if*—I'll know what to expect. You want to be here? You need to let me do *my* job."

Her mouth snaps shut and the skin between her eyes furrows in annoyance. "Just stay. Okay? Sit." She points to the nearest chair, the one she recently occupied. "There. Sit. Wait."

So good at giving commands like I'm a fucking dog...

My teeth sink down on the inside of my mouth, stopping the reaction I certainly shouldn't be having—the desire to command her instead. To show how talking to me like that has consequences.

But then she just *has* to fucking continue...

"I'll have Rafael ask for the blueprints of this place to send to you. And then you can stay up all night and fucking study them for all I care. Hell, jerk off to them! Maybe then, you can also take the stick that's shoved so far up your ass and—"

I. Can't. Fucking. Help. It.

She asked for it.

Begged for it.

And I enjoy granting pleasure to those who beg.

I move before levelheadedness can alert me with its red alarms. My hand is around her throat, not tight, but enough to keep her still, her back slammed against the door before her gasp registers in my mind, exactly how bad of an idea this is.

Not only do I have a Corsetti, the family I've taken oaths for, pinned helplessly against a wall, but I'm leaning into her, revelling in the way her eyes get wide and hopeful, the way her throat moves against my palm.

Her lips part and I drink in the most luscious aroma I probably ever have or ever will. Fear and lust mingle together, making her limp and mine for the taking.

No, not mine.

Seeing her like this replicates those damn dreams that invaded my mind last night. She gazed at me with the same green fire as she is now. Only last night, I touched her. Had my hands on her. My tongue licking the seam of her mouth—

No. What the fuck is wrong with me? What did I do?

My hand doesn't move. It's a vise around her neck, unable to unclasp from its position without the proper mechanism.

There's no way this could be worse, but then it does, when she smirks up at me, those full fucking lips of hers curling at the edges. Her shoulders push against the doorway, arching her back enough that I'm able to perfectly see down her tank and into the valley between her breasts.

Fuck, no. I unwillingly yank my gaze away.

"You look a little wound up."

I'm not 'wound up.' That's not me. I'm calm and poised, trained should the worst happen. Even if I was never prepared for the complexity of this girl.

When I should be pulling away, my thumb strokes over her pulse, feeling it thump beneath my touch. A rapid beat matching her shallow breaths.

But ordering me around like that pisses me off. More so, it enrages me with an unknown fear because if she spoke to Erico Rossi like she had me—I shut the thought down, the sight of blood—*her* blood—evading my position. The *Famiglia* won't play as nice as merely gripping her neck.

"I'm *wound up*," I emphasize her word choice, "because you're a fucking brat. Life lesson, *princesse*: your fiancé will not take kindly to such behaviour. You want to survive the life you're being tossed into, then consider me your fucking practice." My hand tightens a fraction, enough to make my point without harming her. "Here's that hint about your future husband that you're dying to know. If you talk back, his family will expect you to be punished. The life seems glamourous, but reality is, outside your parents and brothers, it's grim. There are worse out there, that I'll promise you. Not everyone would hesitate to hit a woman."

Being a soldier doesn't always mean it's only men I've fought. Sometimes women are the biggest snakes, which is something Nico recently learned with Della.

When her pulse double taps against my thumb, I determine she's gotten enough of a hint, and my fingers manage to release her, one at a time, unpeeling from her skin as the horror sets in.

My mood got the best of me. Her sharp tongue and bitchy commands were no reason for me to react how I did. If Caterina spoke to me like that, I would have obeyed her easily and willingly and ignored the difference between the women because Caterina has respect for everyone in this life, not only her immediate family, which means this opportunity would never have happened.

"Fucking Christ."

Reaching past her, I can't grab the doorknob fast enough. Aurora, not finished with her show apparently, slides in front of it, leaning against my hand, as if trying to knock me away. Ignoring her weak attempts, I yank open the door, barely missing hitting her. The demand for escape drives my clumsy movements, the urge to get away from her growing with every passing second.

Boundaries. This is why they exist. I've been so wrapped up in ensuring she knows them, I've forgotten myself. Wrapping my fingers around the fragile neck of Aurora Corsetti is everything opposite of said boundary in place.

Insanity must be the explanation because there's no other that makes sense. No real purpose for this woman being able to strike my nerves in a way no one has before.

Once I'm safely into the hallway, breathing in air that isn't packed with Aurora's tempting aroma, and she's stepping out of the room behind me, my head clears. Clarisse spots us, her expression brightening with our approach, reminding me why Aurora and I were alone in her office at all.

"I'm checking this place out whether you like it or not."

14

AURORA

What the hell just happened?

As Clarisse leads Rosen and me down the hallway, I'm not listening to her talk about the centre, pointing out the kitchen and the spare room she and the kids sometimes do art in, using plants in their craft making, because my mind is too attuned on minutes ago when I experienced something I didn't think I ever would.

Rosen reacting. Rosen unravelling.

He's easy to be myself around, and who I am is a bitch. I'm aware of my own faults. When one doesn't have parents, and the stand-in family they gained is so busy managing dozens of other children, all at different life stages themselves, it means my attitude goes unchecked sometimes. My temper shorter; my demands sharper.

While I appreciate Rosen's secret-keeping and kindness the past two nights, and I'm finding it easy to be free around him, when he pulls shit like he had, he pisses me off. Demanding he check this place out—okay, I *get* it, but by the time I understood his reasonings, we were too far gone in the fight. But I *never* assumed our battle would end like that.

As Clarisse talks, I'm recalling the feel of his fingers at my throat. His grip firm enough I couldn't fight it if I wanted to, but gentle enough not to rob me of breath. He was...dominating, and not purely in his hold, but his attitude. His very being. The way he stared down at me, his eyes saying one thing, his mind obviously struggling with another. The subtle look he gave my mouth.

His steps following close behind me are all I hear. His gaze prickling down my spine is all I feel. My mind conjures up his annoyed expression, becoming all I see. His scent—cologne and leather—all I smell.

"Watch it," he hisses suddenly. A heavy hand darts out, branding my hip where he grabs to redirect me away from accidentally walking into the nearest doorframe because my attention isn't on my surroundings at all.

Clarisse holds open a back entrance, before stepping aside, and revealing the most colourful garden I've ever seen. Even more so than the one I cared for back in Toronto.

"Wow," I breathe, walking down the two wooden steps and right into paradise, the instant burst of scents and colours temporarily erasing thoughts of Rosen.

Trees taller than the house square off an acre of land, creating something like walls lining the garden. It's split into defined sections, with one side being rose bushes, small lilac trees, and every other colourful flower bush one could imagine. To my left, planter boxes, each with different food, appropriate for this time of the year. I catch the distinct sight of strawberries, raspberries, and blueberries.

"Some of the trees produce apples," Clarisse explains, gesturing to them. "And if you see between them, that far-off patch of land," she points to a darkened area, much different than the green expanse surrounding it, "that's where we plant pumpkins. At the end of the season, the kids are allowed to take home the food they contribute to growing and, in the fall, the pumpkins they cultivate. Of course, I always plant extra in case one child's pumpkin doesn't develop correctly. It teaches them about the fruits of their labour, pun not intended."

"Wow," I repeat. Are there better words to describe the feeling expanding inside my chest? Maybe. But I can't think of any. Being able to work with plants again, *and* children, and watch them have a sense of pride in their hard work. To take home the things they have created...

Rafael officially made brother of the year for this one.

I glance back to Rosen, catching him studying the far-off tree line on the other side of the property. He must feel me watching him because he quickly changes focus, from the trees to me, and for everything that happened inside, when he smiles at me, I feel a chip fall from my heart for an entirely other reason.

Thank you, I mouth to him, hoping he'll see now why this is so important to me.

His response is a slight head nod before he looks away, but I catch a hint of a smile still present.

"This is perfect," I tell Clarisse. "You have a heart of gold to run this for these kids."

Her wrinkle-lined cheeks grow a deeper shade of pink and she shrugs. "It's nothing. Merely what I enjoy. I used to work in the city, in an orphanage. Once I retired, I realized that I own this large chunk of land that sits unused when it could be put to better use. Once I had a plan, I initiated the program and part-nered with schools, orphanages, and social services, who links underprivileged families to me. That was five years ago, and I've never looked back."

Wow. Once again...wow.

"I, um, used to work with children," I start, wondering how best to explain being abandoned in another province. "Like, I lived with a lot of them that didn't have their own families at the time. So I guess I took on a big sister role," I shrug, "and... yeah. I read to them. Crafts. Meals. That kinda stuff. Activities to show them they're loved."

Clarisse pats my arm with a fond smile. "You're kind, Aurora. You certainly are a Corsetti."

"How so?" I ask, almost in a demanding tone. So far, everything I've seen and heard about my family has been the exact opposite of kindness.

She tilts her head, her lips slightly parting. "Your brother didn't say? Your family is one of the reasons I was able to get this program up and running. They donated to the orphanage I worked at—well, still do. And then helped with this venture."

What? Maybe I form the word. Maybe I don't. Maybe I can't because the ground gets rocky, the feeling of falling right through preventing me. My family donates to orphanages. *My* family? She must be mistaken.

"It's no secret the illegal activities the Corsettis are involved in." Her gaze darts to the side, to Rosen, who appears every bit a Made Man can look. "But who am I to complain about people doing a good thing? Many might fear them, but I see them only having generous hearts."

Then she walks away, heading toward the side with the fruit bushels, ending the conversation. The revelation.

The fact that they *donate.* To kids. To community gardens. To orphanages.

When Rosen comes up behind me, I can't move. I can't look at him. Instead, I'm stuck gaping at the land they helped bring to fruition.

"You knew?"

"Yes," he replies, his tone gruffer than usual.

"You didn't tell me."

"Does it change anything?"

Yes. Bad people don't support children.

I mean, no. No, because they're still dicks who pay to make children's lives better while leaving their own without a family.

"I'm done here. Let me go thank Clarisse and then I'd like you to take me home."

"Of course, *princesse.*"

15
ROSEN

The moment we arrive back to the mansion, Nico texts me.

"Your brother wants to see you," I relay to Aurora, reading over the message as I open the front passenger door, where she insisted on riding *again*, much to my chagrin. But after what happened in Clarisse's office, I lost the energy to fight. "He's in his office."

"Fantastic," she utters in a tone implying it's not at all fantastic. Besides breakfast this morning and her introduction the other day, she's barely been around Nico.

This time, I agree with her. It'll be the first instance having to look my underboss in the eye hours after pinning his sister to a door—after betraying him in ways no one of my position should. I had my hands on a Corsetti that didn't involve protecting her. No matter how it's spun, it doesn't look good.

I lead the way, straight toward Nico's office before knocking once and entering with Aurora. Nico looks up from his laptop at our entry, nodding to me once in acknowledgement before focusing on his sister.

"How was it? I'm sure they were happy to have you."

When she hesitates, I'm almost positive she's about to comment on what she had learned about where some of this family's money goes. A small fraction because she doesn't even know the rest yet. The part involving my own sister and nephew.

"She is," she replies, her smile tight, skipping right over her revelation. "At least Clarisse appreciates what I'm doing."

Nico breathes out a long sigh and lifts to his feet, buttoning his jacket as he strides around to the front of his desk, where he props himself against it. "Well, circumstances are different, Aurora. I'm trying to look out for you."

"By marrying me off."

His smooth expression doesn't shift. "Precisely. This life chooses how we live it." His eyes dart to the side, and while the flash is so quick, I doubt Aurora would catch it, but I do. It's the same depressed look he had the other month when we took shots in a club, the night before the party held to find him a wife. Also, the night he gave me the task of protecting Aurora.

"Whatever," she mutters flippantly, crossing her arms. "Heard you wanted to see me."

"You met Della this morning. She and I have decided to move up our wedding, which means in two days, we're having our engagement party here. In a week, the wedding."

Aurora's shoulders lower a fraction. "Are all mafia ceremonies so quick?" I get the sense she's also inquiring for her own eventual future.

"We've expedited things."

"Why?" Her tone is low, uncertain, and while I'm standing far behind her, I can almost picture the nervous expression she's battling to hide. The way her feet shift side to side and her shoulders move beneath her cardigan, working out the tightness I'm sure she's experiencing.

"The why doesn't matter," Nico states. "The *who* does. These events will be an opportunity for you to meet many of our business associates. The wives and daughters of the men we're aligned with, or work with. Your future husband and his parents are also invited, so I suggest you take the chance to get to know them."

Three...two...one.

Right on time and in a tone harsher than I've ever heard from her. Even when she was commanding me to sit and stay in Clarisse's office, she didn't have this edge. "Uninvite him, Nico. Until you force me down the aisle, there's no point in me playing nice."

Nico leans forward, keeping a firm grip on the side of his desk as he gets in her face. "That's the point, Aurora. You must be ready. Meet him so you can see what you're so determined to fight and realize how pointless your battle is. Besides, does it really make a difference?" Nico's brow lifts, daring her to challenge him. "Now or a few months from now. This alliance is desired from both sides. Get to know him with the understanding we're all behind you. That you and he are doing a service to us all."

Ouch. Even I recognize how many thoughtless statements Nico tossed her way.

"Users," she spits, shaking her head. "Fuck you all."

"We do use," Nico remarks plainly, without missing a beat. "Everyone under this roof uses Father for leadership, me for direction, Rafael to lead our soldiers. We use them to protect us. We use each other for alliances. And if, deep down, you didn't want this, you'd have tried to run away already."

"Wanting a family is much different, Nico. What kind of fucked-up logic do you live by? Besides," she jerks her thumb in my direction, "this one watches me too closely. Couldn't run if I tried."

Last night being the example of how easy it'd be to catch her if she did.

Nico straightens, pushing off the side of his desk. He brushes his hand along the front of his suit jacket, his expression turning neutral. I've seen this look time and time again when he's dealing with people who bother him. Wordlessly, he strides to the side of the room and pours himself a large glass of liquor before calmly returning to his desk, retaking his seat. The entire thing is a production, leaving Aurora to seethe in silence.

After a single sip, he rests the glass on the edge of his desk. "Then leave, Aurora. You're determined to hate us that much? Go." Two fingers lift from the glass, gesturing to the door beside me as he speaks. "Be free of us. No one will stop you."

For half a second, the room turns deadly silent, and I expect her to take him up on his offer. Instead, she almost falls forward, her palms slamming into his desk as she leans over it.

"What kind of reverse psychology bullshit is that, *brother*? You want to challenge me? Fine. Challenge fucking accepted! I'll attend your little party. I'll become the princess you all so clearly want me to be, and I'll even meet my future ball-and-chain. But if you think I'll be pleasant, ha!" She barks out a single laugh. "That's where you're wrong. *So* wrong."

In the same breath, she spins on her heel and stalks right down the length of the office. She spares me a half-second glance before slamming the door shut behind her.

The moment she's gone, Nico's shoulders slump and he takes a large sip from his glass. I wander closer, chuckling.

"Was that smart?" I ask, dancing on the edge of speaking out of turn. "Considering today's the first day she's left her room since arriving"—*well...*— "to remind her of all the reasons she should go back into hiding."

Nico merely rubs at his forehead, groaning. "I know, I know, you sound like Della. She must understand the situation and family she's in. If only Mother and Father hadn't hesitated in bringing her home. We wouldn't be having these issues if she was younger."

In my mind, I picture the woman from last night, lounging on the grass just beyond the window across from me. When she spoke about hating her parents for abandoning her and Nico for making this arrangement so soon but still not denying her desire to be here.

"I think she's looking for a genuine connection," I tell him, thinking out every word before speaking. "A friend amongst the family, but no one's given her that." *And I can't be the one to, so if this conversation helps the boundaries between Aurora and me, even better.*

"Maybe if she left her fucking room from the beginning. Stopped yelling at our parents."

"If you were in her position, you'd do the same."

"Probably." He smirks. "How is she around you? Because if she's anything like that," he gestures to where she stood last, "to Erico, the Rossis won't play nice. And her attitude will *not* get her out of this arrangement."

Earlier, in the worst possible method I could have done this with, I presented an outcome regarding the Rossis' reaction to her bratty behaviour. She'll be an underboss's wife, expected to act a certain way, dress a certain way, *be* a certain way, and his family could demand her to be reminded of her own place in the New York *Famiglia's* hierarchy. With the limited reports on Erico, he could respond favourably toward her, in which she gets to continue her little games. Or he won't.

"Once they're married, she'll become a Rossi. Which means, we won't be able to help her. Being gentle around her now would only be a disservice." Nico taps his finger along his glass as he speaks.

Aurora Rossi. The name blisters my mind, reminding me

who she *will* be, even when it makes my stomach churn. Aurora deserves someone who enjoys her attitude but enjoys putting her in her place more.

"Yes," I agree, only half paying attention to what he said.

"Well, now it's a matter of her not slaughtering him at the party." He chuckles, staring past me at the door. "That girl has no idea how much she's one of us. Her tenacity speaks volumes."

"Show her that," I suggest. "Prove to her you care for her. Then maybe she won't kill Rossi." Switching subjects, I wonder, "Any leads on De Falco?"

"None. Rafael has his men scouring the city and beyond, scanning phone towers for any signals leading his way. I have soldiers stationed in rotations at his house in case he returns."

"And his daughters?" Della's ex-stepsisters.

"Also missing. They've been absent at all the places they're known to frequent. I can't find anything on them either. Still," fingers drumming against his glass, "I feel like we're missing something. Like he's right fucking *here*."

"We'll catch them, boss."

"And then he'll pay."

16

AURORA

I know Sister Mary and I had discussed "playing this game," and I did that. Well, I tried to. Volunteering at the community garden will show them I'm a person with interests.

It should be enough. Learning what I had—that they have hearts buried somewhere beneath the icebergs—*far* down, I imagine. But it's not enough. Not even close. Because every time one of them opens their mouth and reminds me of that engagement—every time they refer to how eager they are to get rid of me—the anger can't dissipate, no matter how many deep breaths I remind myself to take. No matter how many times I tightly clench my fists.

The festering anger wanting to burst from my chest, to explode, wiping them all out with it. The emotions I can't tie down, no matter how much I want to.

Maybe it was Nico's shitty timing. I felt *good* returning home. Learning what I had sent my heart into confusing loops I still can't make sense of, but my brother ruined that the moment he brought up the party.

I glance at the time on my phone, noting how in only two more hours, the kids would be arriving at the community garden. It'd be easy to get Rosen to drive me back, to escape from this place for the rest of the day, to meet people who could see me as a friend rather than a pawn.

It's tempting, but when I turn the next corner of the house, I, instead, walk into my mother. Literally, walk into her. Her hands come up, catching my shoulders, preventing my fall.

"Ah, Aurora, I was coming to look for you. Figured Nico would be finished speaking with you by now."

Is there nowhere in this house I can walk without someone tracking me?

"Not sure why you're looking for me. I've already made my stance known." Without sparing her a single glance, I sidestep her, continuing down the hall.

Persistent, she trails, but I force my strides to be quick. The end of the hallway is my focus, the staircase leading to the upper floor where I can lock myself in my room and away from this conversation.

"Aurora, stop, honey! Aurora! Please!"

"I'm not ready for this." I'm not sure I ever will be. Sister Mary's voice echoes in my mind, telling me to go for lunch or to spend any quality time with her, but I can't stomach such an idea yet. Maybe soon but not today.

At the staircase, I rush up them two at a time, building as much distance between her and me as possible. In her heels, I doubt she can keep up, and when I'm at the top, I find she hasn't even bothered trying. Dismay isn't hidden in her expression, one hand leaning against the post, her fingers clenching tightly as she watches me turn away from her.

Inside my bedroom, I slam the door shut, keeping my back to it in case she decides to come anyway. After a few minutes, I hear no one, but don't move from the spot. The carpet beneath my ass is comfortable, and this position is safe.

He probably won't respond, but regardless, I reach out.

ME

Why do they all suck? I've tried. Breakfast. Nico's office. My mother just chased me down the hall.

ROSEN

They're trying in the only ways they know how to. Your brother wants you to be comfortable here quicker.

ME

By throwing me to the wolves?

ROSEN

He'll be your husband.

Eww. No. *Gag.* No. Simply reading that word sends red, flashy, blaringly loud alarms off in my head.

ROSEN

If you need to talk, I suggest you reach out to Della.

What a fucking brush-off. Interacting with Della is impossible because she's on Nico's side. She'll explain his reasoning, and somehow, make what he's doing more reasonable. Even so, I hardly know her, beyond the quickest introduction this morning.

ME

But I know you better.

ROSEN

But I'm not what you need.

My stomach lurches. He's rebuilding his walls around him, his determination to put me into a box getting annoying. Take this morning, trying to force me into the back seat. We fought over a *seating arrangement* and this family wonders why I don't want their bullshit. In a vehicle, we have a "place," and apparently, mine wasn't in the front with him.

I nearly throw my phone off to the side, frustrated, when another name pops into my head. Rafael. He wants to be the good brother; therefore, he can start now.

Opening the messaging app, I start a new thread with him.

ME

Hey.

RAFAEL

Do my eyes deceive me?

ME

Funny. Thanks for the connection to Clarisse. It's beautiful and I can't wait to meet the kids.

RAFAEL

My pleasure. Glad you enjoyed it. Hopefully it'll give you some peace away from this insanity.

ME

How do you deal with the insanity?

RAFAEL

Avoid the mansion. I'm there often for breakfast because the chefs make better food than I ever could. Or when Nico calls on me, or if I have a meeting with my soldiers. But it's why I live downtown and away from the mansion. Why I run my club. Distance.

Living away from the mansion sounds great. When do I get that option?

*Wait...*My laughter is huffed, the reminder of what I don't want crashing down on me again.

ME

Sounds like a good life. Why don't I get that option? Why does our family suck?

RAFAEL

Because they do. But I have to go. Get back to work and all that.

I wonder what running a club consists of. I imagine a lot of restocking materials and managing his staff, choosing the music, and ensuring the club is clean every night. But from a managerial level, I'm curious what he does.

ME

Bye. Thanks for the talk.

RAFAEL

No problem. I'm here, and if you need someone else, connect with Della. She's cool. Not at all like our stuffy family.

That's the second person to suggest seeing her, talking to her. The issue is she *is* my brother. Exactly like my parents are the past. Everyone here is so wrapped up in the situation, I can't separate each person from the issues they present.

Grumbling, I abandon my phone on the floor and wander toward the floor-to-ceiling windows. The curtains are still open from how I left them and the afternoon sun beats through, casting my form in warmth. A natural warmth, like a mother's hug.

Mom hasn't hugged me since she was telling me goodbye.

*Mom...*I said it. Well, I didn't *say* it, but the name replaced calling her by her title. A strange tingle courses through my arms and down my spine. She'd have a heart attack hearing it spoken aloud.

Sister Mary is encouraging a connection, but is it so easy? To go downstairs and ask her for lunch or something? Coffee even. Such mundane, simple activities, but they seem so far-fetched. Where's the manual for what I'm going through? *The How-To Guide of Returning Home to the Family Who Once Abandoned You.* If there's no book, then someone should write it.

"Ugh." My reflection moves, my hand coming down on the glass, grasping for the sun. The same sun shining over the community garden. Once again, I think about asking Rosen to take me back there. Take me anywhere at this point.

I'm fucking bored. But the moment I mention boredom, any one of the monsters below will request I spend time with them.

I exit my bedroom with my phone in my back pocket, slowly peeking out the door and down the stretch of the hall-way, finding it empty. No doubt, Nico is still in his office, and ideally, after running away from my mother, she's left, and I won't bump into her again.

Taking the risk, I tread down the hallway, straight for the staircase. At the bottom, the hallways are silent, and I take the same path Rosen led me last night, toward the back door with the small greenhouse.

He claimed my father made it for my mother. Can monsters create something so pretty?

Doubtful.

Pushing open the glass door, I'm immediately immersed into a near-silence that quells the shouting in my mind. The small stream of the fountain in the middle is the only sound my ears pick up, but it's so gentle and relaxing, it's welcoming. I stride forward, heading toward the stone's edge where I sit. The water is surprisingly warm as I dip my fingers in it, making ripples.

When the door opens, I don't look up from the water, but I know it's Rosen. The air between us becomes more electrified, the memory of his fingers around my neck returning. He remains back, his hands folding at his back.

"How'd you know where I was?" I ask without looking up.

"Do you really want to know the answer?"

I can imagine—cameras watching my every move, other staff reporting on me. "Probably not."

Finally dragging my gaze away from the ripples and toward him, I catch him leaning against the stone wall beside the door, his arms crossed over his massive chest, the leather jacket pulling tight on his arms. He's opposite of Nico in his suits, dressed more casually in cargo pants and a plain black tee with a jacket overtop. He's not smirking, his mouth flat, his eyes almost dead.

"I haven't left the house, so I'm not sure why you're here."

"Don't be cute." He nods to the door opposite where he stands. "When outside is right there."

"Very restrictive. Wonder if this is how my fiancé will be."

His shrug gives nothing away, which annoys me. How can a person's personality change so easily? He goes from angry body-guard to a void in the matter of seconds.

Aggravation coursing through me, I stand, flicking my wet fingers in his direction, even though due to my distance, water droplets fall short of hitting him. I check out the rest of the small greenhouse, still slightly amazed at the history behind this place.

Trailing my fingers over the leaves of a bush, I murmur, "How do monsters create something so beautiful?"

"They created you."

I freeze. The air grows stiff around us, tangible, and I could almost hear his mental curse.

Downplaying his statement, I flip my hair, glancing at him over my shoulder and grinning, "Wow, another compliment. First, I'm not the boring girl you expected, and now I'm beautiful."

His expression remains as flat as his reply. "You know the facts of your appearance, *princesse*, so stop."

"Aw," I pout playfully, continuing forward as I inspect the rest of the shrubbery in the greenhouse. "Did I point out your blunders and now you're trying to hide the fact you appreciate how I look?"

His eyes narrow, enough to show I've annoyed him, even when his answer is blasé, "Fishing, Aurora? New low."

"Nah, low is having my bodyguard's hands on my neck and not disliking it."

His exterior cracks again, enough that he peeks over his shoulder, ensuring we're still alone. He licks his lips once, twice before blinking longer than I've ever seen a person take. When his lids finally peel open, it's to focus on me, now only two feet away.

"You want me to keep your secrets about your Toronto excursions, then you don't breathe a word of today to anyone else."

That wasn't remotely in my plans, but with him on the topic. "Bribery."

His eyes shut again, his jaw moving with his rough swallow. His nostrils flaring remind me of when I annoyed him in the vehicle heading to Toronto Pearson. I swear a vein is about to pop on his forehead, but before it gets to that, I ease his worry.

"Relax. I'm fucking with you. You know, for a soldier with all this apparent training, you suck at keeping your emotions in check."

17
ROSEN

Only with you, princesse.

She makes it impossible to ignore her because every time I do, each time I have the intention to stand silently by her side, she speaks to me, and everything she ever does and says embeds her into my heart in every forbidden manner.

She's upset and my desire to protect her spikes.

Or she's like this—bratty, making not responding unbearable.

"And you suck at maintaining boundaries," I shoot back. Maybe if she acted like her mother, we wouldn't be in this situation.

It doesn't excuse me of pinning her to the wall.

"Hey, you're the one who stalked me out here. I was perfectly fine alone."

After the fiasco with Della, Nico had an alarm installed on this door, which informs him when it's opened. The moment his phone was alerted, it became obvious who was at fault, considering Della was with us.

"You know the rules."

"So many rules!" She throws her hands up, turning away. An act seeming dramatic and with her usual playful flair, but when she sits at the edge of the fountain, her eyes are rimmed red, a deeper emotion clouding them.

Fuck.

I suck in a deep breath and stare out the glass above her head, staring at the expanse of Corsetti land, trying to ignore her.

"Why couldn't my family be normal? Why am I bred from monsters that I want to love too?"

Don't answer. Don't respond. Don't—

"It's natural, *princesse*."

Fuck me.

"Like you said last night, making that first step is important. Going to breakfast today was wise."

"Until it wasn't." She snorts. "Until I blew up at them."

"You needed them to understand."

"Yeah," she whispers, her shoulders lowering a fraction. I'm still not looking at her, but my peripheral vision catches her every movement. "You get me so easily, Rosen. I'm sorry I keep bothering you every time someone pisses me off."

"You don't have to apologize," I say, even if she's speaking the very words she and I both need to hear, that she's respecting the boundaries placed between us.

"So," she glances up, strands of her hair blocking part of her face, "guards and the family *truly* can't be friends?"

To a point. Friendly for certain. There's a reason why only some are chosen to protect the immediate family members, why I'm here with Aurora and why my father once protected Caterina. A relationship naturally progresses between the Corsettis and those constantly around them, but it's a working friendship in which both sides understand each other's roles. There's being a friend, and then there's being friend*ly* and Aurora doesn't give the impression of understanding the differences.

But how do I deny her of a little bit of kindness?

Aurora kicks her legs out in front of her, positioning her palms on the stone's edge, looking completely at ease. So opposite from the troubling sensations rolling through my stomach.

"What's your middle name?"

"Excuse me?"

One side of her mouth pulls up. "I'm trying to be nice. Tell me about you. What's your middle name?"

Boundaries. My middle name doesn't matter to you—

"Marcus."

"Rosen Marcus Corrigan."

"My father's name."

"Any siblings?"

"One. A sister."

Aurora pushes to her feet and approaches without warning, pausing in front of me. Her eyes dance in the streaming sunlight at her back, creating a glow through the strands of her hair that my hands ache to touch. To pinch a small chunk of her hair and inspect the golden glow mingle with her natural one.

"That wasn't so bad, was it? See how a little bit of friendship goes a long way."

Basic facts don't equate to friendship, but I won't steal these small pleasures from her.

As she passes me, heading for the door back to the mansion, my eyes settle on the base of her neck, where my hands were earlier. There are no signs of marks, but it doesn't stop me from reaching for her, nudging her hair from her shoulders, so I can reveal more of her skin for inspection.

She pauses, and I know why. Hell, my head is chastising me for touching her when I could have very well asked her to move her hair, but the drive to care, to protect, to ensure I didn't harm her doesn't stop me. Touching her was one thing, but if there's marks on her, I won't hide it from Nico, for her own benefit.

"Did I hurt you earlier?"

She shakes her head.

"I shouldn't have reacted like that. I'm sorry."

"Those boundaries again, huh? Do they include touching me?"

Shit. My hand is still hovering around her shoulder, and before I do more, like stroke my fingers over her pulse again, I drop my hand to my side, curling it into a fist to ensure I don't reach for her again.

"Sorry," I mutter, my annoyance bubbling beneath my skin again. I need away from this girl as soon as possible. "Everything today was out of line, Miss Corsetti."

She frowns with the use of her name, but it's more for me— to remind myself of her and her role compared to me. As enjoyable as it is to see her free and laughing, those boundaries are becoming more important than ever.

"I didn't mind," she murmurs, almost a whisper.

That's precisely the issue.

I look away, staring over her head until she gets the hint and enters the house. Counting to ten, I ensure she's a distance away before following. When I do, I'm certain to *not* stare at her ass as she treads down the hallway. When she turns right, heading for the stairs, I go the other way, to my bedroom.

hen a text pings my phone, I almost ignore it. But there's the off chance she needs something, even if it's to return to the outdoors again.

AURORA
Thank you, friend.

For the first time in what feels like a while, I laugh. For everything we spoke about, she's fucking determined, and I appreciate that about her. How I ever imagined this woman boring and meek is another question entirely.

I shouldn't respond, but by now, she's already seen the text's status go from *delivered* to *read,* so it'd be an asshole move not to respond.

ME
You're welcome, princesse.

AURORA
Do you even know what I'm thanking you for?

ME
Not entirely.

AURORA
Every time you remind me about the boundaries between us, you still don't push me away. This isn't easy, but I'm trying. I'd like to reach out to Della in the morning and see if I can stomach being around her since Nico and my parents aren't an option. Or you apparently. But regardless, you're telling me we can't be friends in one breath and still talk to me with the next. You could ignore me and be done with me but you're not.

I could and should. Every time she opens that bratty mouth of hers, my reaction shouldn't be to react whatsoever and yet—

ME

> You're welcome. Making friends with your future sister-in-law is a good idea.

> Good night. You shouldn't be messaging me.

AURORA

Yeah, yeah. Night.

My phone thuds onto the bed beside me, and I flick it away with my fingers before I find myself compelled to continue talking to her.

If she's reaching out to Della in the morning, this is a positive thing. Another female around her age to become friends with. A person who is not involved in Aurora's past. Then, every time she wishes to comment on her hatred of her family, she can contact Della instead of me.

I'll miss her, but this is a good thing.

18

AURORA

*S*he's not going to answer. She'll ignore me. She's showing Nico my message and in moments, they'll all descend on my room and—

How do people do this friend-making stuff? No wonder I suck around Rosen. All my friends were technically forced connections. Not that the Sisters forced any one of us to be friends past the mutual respect and kindness rules they enforced, but friendship naturally developed amongst so many of us.

DELLA

I was heading down for breakfast with
Ariella soon actually. Nico left about an hour
ago, so it's only her and me. Then we're
meeting with the wedding planner.

The underlying message in her text is that breakfast won't involve any of my family, and now I understand both Rosen and Rafael's urge to get me to hang out with her.

ME

Mind if I join you?

DELLA

We'd love nothing more.

We not *I*. So far my interactions with Ariella include awkward quick glances, but maybe this can change that.

I fling the dark duvet off me and rush from my bed to the shower. For once, I'm not tempted to remain any longer beneath the water, almost, dare I say it, eager to leave my room. I brush my hair and spend an extra few minutes doing my makeup before dressing in one of the many dresses hanging in the walk-in.

When I emerge, dressed, I pass a mirror. I look different.

I *feel* different.

By the time I make it to the dining room, Ariella is already seated on the side closest to the door. She pauses from dragging a few pancakes onto her plate to nod her greeting as I cross the room to the other side.

"Where's Della?"

"Right here." Della's breezy voice comes from behind me, and she naturally takes up the end of the table between her sister and me. "Sorry, your brother ended up calling, but I told him I couldn't talk long because I was having breakfast with you."

"That must have made him thrilled." I don't bother hiding the disdain in my tone, which she goes along with.

"It did."

"Yeah, well..." My grumble trails off, unsure where I was headed with it anyway. I didn't come down here to talk about my family.

"This looks great," Della comments, reaching for the plate of pancakes after her sister is finished with them. Ariella's gaze remains on her plate as she chews, only occasionally glancing at Della. She's a strange one but reminds me of the young boy who once was at the convent. The Sisters explained he was diagnosed with autism, and experienced life a bit differently, which included his speech not developing until he was seven.

"It's a lot." The plates are piled high with both hot food and fresh fruit. There's no need for all this. Reaching for the plate of homemade waffles, I ask, "They do this every day? What if no one came down for breakfast?"

Della shrugs a shoulder, setting her plate down to reach for the syrup. "Rich people do strange things."

With my fork, I gesture between the siblings. "Yeah, so where do you two fall into all this?"

Both sisters freeze. For the first time, Ariella's eyes flash up, her cheeks puffy with food like a chipmunk. She stares at me and then her sister, obviously leaving the conversation up to her. Della slowly rests the syrup jar in front of her, her lips pressed together.

"What?"

"Not sure I should say. Nico didn't tell you for a reason."

"Seriously? Nico hasn't told me because he's being an ass. No offense." My fork gestures to the huge ring on her left hand. "I'm a Corsetti. Doesn't that give me some rights to know?"

"It's complicated." Della peeks at her sister again, who's gone back to eating. "Fine," she concludes with a sigh. "I'm sure your brother will kill me for this, but oh well. You obviously know your brother has enemies. Comes with being who he is."

I didn't precisely, but the Sisters gave me a decent idea of the lifestyle here, and what that means, so I nod, encouraging her to continue with what I suspect will be a riveting story.

"To make a very long story short, we're," she wags a finger between her and Ariella, "the stepdaughters of your brother's enemy. He's not a good person and sent me into your family's life to lure Nico to his death."

Of every possible scenario she could have tossed at me, *this* was the last one I was expecting. I look at Ariella, waiting for the punchline, who only nods, her mouth flattening in a regretful smile.

"I was blackmailed with Ariella's well-being."

"But instead, you're marrying him," I point out, my tone lined with a question. *How did you go from enemy to fiancée?*

She simply grins and focuses on her food once more as she saws into the soft pancakes. You could say I saw the error of my ways. I never wanted to harm Nico, but when someone you love is used against you...well, you'll do anything to help them."

Neither Ariella nor Della give any indication of what she means, but considering I've never heard Ariella breathe a word to anyone, and Della mentioned her "well-being," I get the sense it relates to that.

"So you're very much an outsider," I summarize, finally giving the food on my plate the attention it deserves. Given how little I've eaten since arriving here, my stomach grumbles from the mere scent.

"Like you." Della shares a meaningful look with me. "You shouldn't be, but you feel you are, correct?"

My god, am I that obvious? Between her and Rosen, nothing is sacred.

"Basically."

"Well, thanks for reaching out and joining us for breakfast. The wedding planner will be here in an," she taps her phone screen from where it rests to her right, checking the time, "hour, if you want to hang around. We're looking at venue options."

Everything to do with a wedding sounds like the worst possible activity I could ever be subjected to, but hearing Sister Mary's voice echo in my head has my response differing from the one that initially wants to be said.

"That'd be great." Not that I exactly have anything else to do anyway. I had planned on asking Rosen to take me to the garden later this afternoon, and possibly could still have time to, depending how chatty the wedding planner is, but since Della invited me, it feels wrong to back away now.

We fall silent, all focusing on our meal, until the sound of heavy steps approach the doorway, followed by the hulk of a man dressed in his typical cargo pants and black shirt. Of the three of us, his eyes sweep over me first, pausing on my face before studying the rest of me—as much as the table allows for.

My neck prickles, urging me to look away, rather than straightening in my seat. Because so far he's only seen me in a hoodie and a messy bun, or casual in jeans and a tank, I want him to see me more dressed-up. A small part of me, deep down, seeks his approval, thrilled when I get it. When his eyes turn molten and it takes Della talking to pull his attention away, shattering the spell over us.

"Hungry? Join us."

Rosen coughs, shaking his head, already backing up. "No, no, I'm good. See you later."

After he disappears, I count to ten, ensuring he's far enough away, before asking, "What's his story?"

Della pauses, food halfway to her mouth. "What do you mean?"

"I mean, what's his story? He doesn't talk much."

"Not too sure. I only know him by association with your brothers. He's close to them. High in the ranks from what I get. How's having a bodyguard all the time?"

Not bad when he's the only one who wholly understands me.

Not bad when he's the only one to be real with me.

Not bad when he gazes at me like he just did.

Not bad when he's holding my throat in his hand.

But annoying when he does his protective shit, like wanting to pull a weapon at the community garden.

Instead of answering Della's direct question, I ask one of my own. "Where's yours?"

She giggles. "Your brother is. I refused a personal bodyguard. He didn't like it but considering he and I are around one another so much, it works."

"Wait, that's an option?" I exclaim, eyes finding the doorway again. *Rosen, come back, so I can fire you and then you can become an actual friend and stop concerning yourself with boundaries.* "No one told me Rosen was optional!"

Della laughs loudly, her fork clanging against her plate. Even Ariella cracks a smile.

"Definitely not optional for you," Della replies. "Again, I have your brother. That's the compromise."

With my fork, I circle the air, indicating the mansion around us. "Where is he then?"

"Believe me, no one's getting on Corsetti land. Even I don't know everything your father has in place here."

Might explain how Rosen knew where to find me yesterday.

Finished eating, I nudge the plate away and reach for the glass of water. Ariella's done too, staring off at the far wall, her mind obviously elsewhere. The impulse to know her story grows stronger, but I'm caught midway between not wanting to come across as rude and wanting to know.

Now what?

Breakfast is one thing. I made a connection to the only non-family members in this place. The outsiders who, like me, are working to find their place. But can I sit here for the next hour with them until the wedding planner arrives and not die?

"Before I forget, Nico told you our engagement party is in a matter of days, I assume. We're going out dress shopping tomorrow and wondered if you'd like to join us?"

Shopping. The death of peace of mind. The very concept I shied away from the moment the Sisters mentioned me coming home. The whole notion of being a mafia princess, which is where my determination to get away from here and be useful to those who could use me comes from.

And Della? After everything I heard about her, she doesn't seem like the kind who would also enjoy shopping. Considering her outfit of jeans and a sweater is casual, she doesn't seem like my mother, who I've only witnessed in pantsuits and dresses so far.

"Your brother's insisting," Della adds with a shrug. "Like yours, my closet is full of new clothing, but oh no, I must spend more money." Her voice drops deep and mimicking. "'Nothing's good enough for you. Get something new.'" When she rolls her eyes, she has me sold.

"Sure," I reply through my giggles.

"Your mother's coming too."

Like that, all laughter drops. The room falls deadly silent, and I wait for a black hole to swallow us all up.

No, I can't go then. Not with *her* in attendance. Not with—

Della's palm rests over the back of my hand, breaking through the troubling thoughts. "Also, Nico's idea. He wants your mother to get to know us before the wedding, so why don't you use that as an opportunity too. It'll make everyone happy—you too, I bet. But her attention will be divided between the three of us, along with the purpose behind the trip. Consider us your referees."

I suppose that's better. Della makes a good point. If my mother's attention is split, she can't harass me. This might be the very thing needed to break through the exterior of our relationship.

Gotta try, right?

"Sounds good." My smile is tight and based on both sisters' grim looks, they see right through me.

It's okay.

We've remained in the dining room, making small talk while waiting for the wedding planner, so when a figure flies through the mansion, it drives Della into action, even if it's only Nico. He barely spares any of us a glance as Rosen approaches, and he too, continues right past Nico.

"What's going on?" Della approaches Nico, her hand going for his arm.

He's already headed back for the door, barely sparing her a long kiss. "Came for Rosen. We're headed downtown. I was notified there *may* have been a sighting of—" He cuts himself off, sharing another long look with Della before finishing. "I'm going to look over the footage because I want to see it with my own eyes."

And like that, the vibe in here changes so quickly. Ariella seems unbothered by his words, but Della's attitude completely transforms from calm and cool to rigid and concerned, her expression hardening.

They're hiding something. Whatever Nico was about to say,

he didn't want me to hear. *Me*, not Della, because based on the way Della is nodding, she's in on it.

The Sisters were *very* clear of the gender differences in mob life. How the men are the leaders, the fighters, the business dealers. They *are* the mafia. And the women remain on the outside.

It doesn't stop me from demanding, "Sighting of who, Nico?" When both he and Della look at me, like they've remembered I'm still here, I continue, "You want me part of this life, right? This family. Tell me what's going on."

"It doesn't matter, Aurora. For your safety, this is none of your business." Nico steps past us, completely disregarding me.

I follow him, keeping pace as he walks to the front door. "My safety will increase by tenfold if I'm kept in the loop. Clearly, your own fiancée knows, so why can't I?"

"Aurora." It's that warning tone again. Rosen does it too. Like all men have perfected it or something. "Drop it."

Without breaking stride, Nico walks right out the front door and shuts it in my face, leaving me seething at the wood. I could follow, but I get the sense it won't end how I want it to.

"Where's Rafael?" I ask. I have two brothers and already he's proven to be useful.

"Not here," Della answers. "He's only around when Nico is."

Tires squealing from outside make my teeth grit again, but I turn away from the door, staring at the sisters, trying to recall moments ago when we were having a pleasant time.

Della lifts her hands, palms out. "Not my business, sorry, Aurora. But hey, let's go get a drink while we wait for the planner." She offers her arm, and begrudgingly, I take it.

I'll learn the truth from someone in this place, and I know exactly who.

19

ROSEN

Without a word, Nico climbs into the passenger seat of the waiting vehicle and I take the driver's side. Sensing Nico needs to get away quickly, I immediately toss the car into drive.

"She's so frustrating," he grumbles. "She doesn't understand."

I know who "she" is without asking.

"I might have to tell her about De Falco," he muses, rubbing a hand over his head as he props his elbow on his door. "I spoke out of turn, which is my fault. We're all aware of what's happening, but I'm trying *not* to corrupt her mind."

The truth won't corrupt Aurora's mind, but I remain silent, as I weave the car through highway traffic, toward downtown, to the bar he told me we'd be headed.

"It might be the best because for her to see what we're trying to keep her safe from."

Nico makes a grunting noise. "Maybe. I'd prefer her not getting used to the freedoms this family allows. My father enjoys having Mother know all the details. I always desired a strong

165

partner by my side. I can't say the same for Erico Rossi. We give in to Aurora now, what happens when she's demanding to know the *Famiglia's* secrets?"

"They might not play nice to her demands," I finish his point, my hands tightening their hold on the wheel at the notion of any Rossi harming Aurora in any way.

Minutes later, I pull up to a Corsetti-owned club, The Elixir, and park in the back, in Nico's typical spot. He gets out and leads the way through the staff entrance, heading straight for the security room. Even way back here, when the main part of the club is many halls away, the music carries through to a gentle thumping in the background.

As I trail him, my phone vibrates.

AURORA

Please tell me what everyone is so concerned about.

Without answering, I slide the phone away. Definitely a message I'll not be responding to ever.

Nico enters the room, snapping immediately at the two security staff stationed there. He sheds being a worried brother and immediately takes on his role as underboss.

"Show me," he demands, and the men instantly get to work, their mouses flying over screens as they bring up recorded footage of the front entrance, scrolling through the timeline, until stopping at a specific spot on the recording. He leans out of the way, so Nico and I can see better.

For a few seconds, it's a normal stream showing city dwellers passing the front of the club. Cabs coming and going as they briefly stop by the curb and let the passengers out.

"Here." The staff member points to a black car pulling up in front of the club. It looks no different than every other car that had stopped there, but then, from the corner of the footage, two figures emerge. Both donning baggy clothing, both with hoods up, blocking their faces from the camera.

Nico leans forward, positioning himself against the desk like he's about to climb right through the monitor.

One figure slides into the vehicle, but the second pauses. They turn back to look toward the club, tilting their head until they're staring right into the camera. Even with their hood up, it's clear exactly who the rat-faced fucker is.

Stefano De Falco.

A weight drops into my stomach. Fuck. Fuck, fuck, fuck, he was *here*.

Stefano winks into the camera before getting into the car and disappearing from the camera's view.

"We had people immediately follow the car, sir, but they got away."

The energy in the small security room turns thunderous. Both of the security guys glance worriedly toward me when seconds pass without a noise from Nico. They don't sense what I recognize in him.

His hands curl around the table's edge and his body goes eerily still. I can't see his face from where I stand, but I can imagine his deathly expression. The frustration. A look recommending they *run for your life*.

In a blink, his energy explodes, his hands reaching for the monitor and tossing it at the far wall. It shatters into many pieces, decorating the floor with numerous sharp pieces, which are still less dangerous than Nico is.

"Where the fuck did he go? *How* was he right *here* and no one saw him?"

One of the men wisely speaks up, "Shift change, sir. For a moment, eyes are away from the monitors to complete the hand-over."

Fuck.

"Fuck," Nico voices my own thoughts. "He knows our shifts then. *Fuck!* What about the bouncers outside? Question them." He glances at me, commanding, "Get men down here to figure this the fuck out. Who is working with him? I refuse to have another rat in our midst."

"There were two of them," I comment, aiming to break Nico's rant into something more productive than anger. "You think one was his daughter?"

Nico takes in a deep breath, which then he releases through gritted teeth. "He has two daughters, so if it was, where's the other one?"

No one responds to the unanswerable question. Meanwhile, I'm mentally going through every staff member working here, thinking about any possible leads. Most of the club staff here have been with us for a while. However, money does talk and it makes people stupid—loyalties become secondary.

Nico shoves away from the desk and stalks out of the office, heading right back outside to our vehicle. He snatches the keys from my hand and takes the driver's seat this time, grumbling, "I need something to take my anger out on."

He slams into reverse, the vehicle cutting through the lot, narrowly missing a row of staff cars, before lunging into downtown traffic without checking if the path is clear. If I didn't know Nico's driving well enough, especially when he's in this kind of mood, I'd be fearful.

"Is there fucking no one I can trust?"

"We don't know it was one of our staff for certain." A voice of reason always takes Nico a few levels down. "I'll get men looking into it right away."

"Good." Nico zooms the car down the highway, weaving precariously in and out of traffic, taking us nearly thirty over the speed limit. "Almost want to postpone the wedding, until we catch him, but I won't."

"We'll find him by then," I say with conviction. "Maybe if I'm out in the city, hunting him—"

"No," Nico interrupts, "now more than ever, I want my sister protected. All of them. Get more men around my fiancée and her sister. Della was adamant about not having a personal bodyguard, but right now, she can deal with it because her safety matters more. I'll lose my fucking mind if she's harmed again."

I know. I was there the first time she nearly was, when Nico jumped into a dark house, uncaring what other dangers lurked in the shadows, his only focus was the knife at Della's throat.

"He's taunting us. He's around. I feel it. Something bad will happen, Rosen, and we all need to be prepared when it does."

20

AURORA

The next morning, I leave my room, not at all equipped for this outing. This entire charade is the representation of what my family wants me to be doing—shopping, preparing for a party. At a very tense dinner last night, with only Nico, Rafael, Della, Ariella, and me, he was thrilled to hear I'd be going out as well.

By now, I'm certain my parents were already warned. If not, my mother's about to get the surprise of her life.

I'm sure Rosen was already told about this outing, but just in case, I send him a message, first tacking on a *please*, but then grinning as I thumb the backspace six times, picturing his annoyed expression when he reads it. His skin will undoubtedly flush with that sexy shade of anger. He'll grip his phone, picturing my neck.

ME

I'm going out dress shopping. You're coming.

I stare at the screen, waiting for the bubbles to pop up when the status changes from *sent* to *read*.

The bubbles never come, but heavy steps down the hallway do. I know it's Rosen. My body recognizes the alpha energy he emits as he stomps his way to my side, stopping right beside me, glaring.

Oh, please say something. Please.

"Please," I say out loud. "I guess that would have been the polite thing to say, right?"

Annoyingly, he doesn't seem to take the bait. Not in the same way as he normally would. He glances up and down the hall before growling. "I'm not sure you know how to be polite, even if manners bit you in the ass."

"Can *you* bite my ass? Please." Gasping, I press my lips together, trying to determine where such words came from. It's one thing to have fun, but that question definitely surpasses the boundaries he's been setting. Hell, I think they even surpass the friendship boundaries.

His nostrils do this sexy flaring thing as he inhales a deep breath, his teeth clamping together. His jaw goes taut, but I know I got through to him, because his eyes subtly flick down. First to my lips, then to my chest.

Yes, please.

"If not you, my fiancé, right?"

Jealousy. That's bound to do it. That gets any man, right?

What am I doing?

Rosen blinks and a switch is flicked within him. That hardness slides off him, fading away like a past memory. He steps back, coughing once.

"Precisely, Miss Corsetti. Your fiancé." With a final glance, which I want to say is tinged with longing, but I could be making that up entirely, he continues down the hallway. "I'll go get a town car. Meet me outside when you're ready."

When he disappears, a tornado slashes through my stomach. I affect him, that much is certain. No less than he affects me. But we're both dancing on this precarious line, either one of us with the ability to win.

The question is who will break first.

After a few deep, calming breaths, even the interaction with Rosen doesn't ease the tension wrapping my every nerve as I step out into the early morning sun, spotting Rosen by a black town car with another, older man dressed similarly as him. I wonder if he's my mother's bodyguard, as I've never seen him before.

They're speaking together, not paying the group any attention from where Nico is kissing Della goodbye before she slides into the back seat, followed by Ariella.

Then my mother, who immediately spots me leaving the mansion. Her lips curl in a gentle smile and she takes a step forward, but it's Nico's hand darting out that stops her.

One more minute and we'll be trapped in a car together, so her eagerness is misplaced.

Breathe in, I remind myself, forcing the air through my lungs. There's no amount of breathing that'll make this any easier, so I push my body forward, trying my best to stare at the car rather than my mother.

Rosen, standing in the direction of the house, catches me exiting. He stops talking to the other man and his lips form a word, but I can't read them. I fucking wish I could, but it's his gaze on mine that gets me from the front steps to Nico's side, inches from where our mother stands.

"I'm happy you've agreed to come out with us."

"Yeah." I manage a tight smile. "Hi."

Mom. Say it. Mom. I can't continue calling her "my mother." Mom. Mom.

"Mom."

She lets out a small gasp, blinking rapidly as a larger smile spreads over her face. Her arms lift, her feet inching her closer—until Nico steps in front of her.

He saved me from a hug. For once, Nico *helped* me.

Miracles do exist.

He gestures for our mother—for *Mom*—to get inside the vehicle, and once she's gone, he gives me a meaningful stare. One packed with a warning, but also for once, empathy.

You can do this, he says.

Or I've lost it and he's not doing anything.

Nodding to his unspoken statement, I get into the vehicle. The seating is interesting and nothing like I'm used to. More of a limo-style seating, without the vehicle being that long. There are two seats along the driver's side, facing out toward the opposite side, and another three at the back, facing front.

Mom and Della have taken the back row, and somehow, I think this was planned, which leaves me, thankfully, beside Ariella along the bench.

I can do this.

Rosen and the other soldier get into the front, Rosen in the driver's spot. Nico barely has the car's back door shut when the separator rolls up. The dick knows exactly what he's doing too because in the last few seconds of still being able to see him, his eyes meet mine in the rearview mirror and he fucking *winks.*

I glare at it, wishing I had a superhero power or something that would allow me to laser burn it away, and then hurt him for this asshole move.

The ride begins silent, but I'm not bothered by this. Della and her sister are a blessing because it gives Mom two other people to talk to, which leaves me free to stare at the passing city and pretend I'm curious about the surroundings.

Of course, the first one to break the silence is Mom, not that I had any doubt about that presumption.

"What about lunch after shopping? There's this one restaurant I love close to where we'll be."

"I'm for it," Della answers, her attention going straight to me. I'm the one they doubt, not Ariella who hasn't spoken a single word that I've heard.

"It's about time we all get to know one another better," Mom continues. "Della and her sister are new to the family after her stepfather—" She stops abruptly, her lips folding together. "Anyway, I'd like to get to know you all."

You wouldn't have to get to know me if you did your job as a mother. The snide comment snaps in my mind, but I bite my tongue to avoid saying it out loud. It'll only hurt her feelings, which as great of a notion as that seems, it's counterproductive.

"I know about her stepfather," I explain, jerking my chin toward the sisters. "They told me yesterday."

"Oh." She refolds her hands. "Yes, well, it was a shock to your father and me. Lorenzo is still on edge about all this, but in the end, my son is happy and that's all I can ask for."

The conversation dies out again, and I return to gazing out the window as we head through the packed city, but I feel Mom watching me still.

Talk. Say something.

"You live in the mansion?" I push out.

Mom shifts, her hands twisting again. At least I'm not the only one nervous. "We keep rooms there, but we live downtown in a penthouse apartment. When your brother became underboss, your father retired from many duties. Until Nico is fit to take his position as Boss, your father holds the title, but Nico essentially runs the organization."

"Right."

Again the car falls quiet, all of us in our own reflections as we navigate the packed downtown streets of Montreal. Rosen turns at the next corner, driving up an incline. The noise of downtown slowly fades with every turn of the car's wheels, and at the top of the small hill, he takes us down another road, placing us in front of a quiet row of shops, so opposite from what is three blocks away, on Saint-Catherine Street.

These ones have an older style to them. Smaller windows with light awnings. The bricks are old and faded, but with so much character.

"We're here," Mom announces, unbuckling her belt even when Rosen hasn't parked yet. "I like these shops. More personal than the busy ones."

Rosen parks by one that is showcasing a pretty, pink dress in the window. The car stops rumbling beneath me, and the back door opens almost immediately, the older soldier there to help Mom out.

Della exits too and then Ariella, leaving only me to follow.

I glance out the window to where they're congregating on the sidewalk. Then the shop behind them.

My muscles are locked. I can't move. This is so stupid—such a basic activity to do with one's mother and soon-to-be sister-in-law, and yet...

Breathe, I remind myself, drawing my imaginary box as I breathe through the stages. When I finish the square, I manage to slide the length of the vehicle, toward the door, even as my nails curl into the leather bench, a small part of me wanting to remain in here and hide.

It's like this trip officially represents something.

My role.

My heart thumps in my chest, my throat moving with a swallow, and finally a deep breath. When did I stop breathing?

Right around the time I started holding onto the car's bench for my life, I think.

It's happening again, and this time, breathing isn't helping.

Breathing. Isn't—

"Aurora."

He murmurs it so low, so none of the others hear him. Nonetheless, I do. Every syllable weaves its way through to the base of my heart, where my nerves are fused, stabilizing me until I flatten my hand and look up at Rosen.

It's enough. Enough that I manage to take his offered hand and stand from the vehicle. Despite the crowd of four watching us, the atmosphere feels like it's only him and me here. Once I'm stable on my feet, he drops my hand, and while I want to reach for him again, I don't.

I don't because he did enough. He gave me strength in that single touch to walk across the sidewalk and join my mother.

While I think about the fact that Rosen was able to stop an anxiety attack before it took hold of me.

Again.

21

ROSEN

I didn't mean to speak with her, let alone touch her, but she required it. I don't completely know what happened, but Aurora was gone for a minute. Mentally checked-out until I called her name.

Whatever she was experiencing, I wanted to help her, no matter how much the trip to the shops had been a reminder of boundaries. As I sat in the front with another soldier, Thomas, Aurora in the back with her family, the differences in our roles couldn't be more apparent.

Thomas is the first to enter the small-ish shop that Caterina indicated, completing the initial visual sweep. He waves us all in after a second. Considering how often Caterina frequents this store, the owners are used to our ways.

Della enters behind Caterina, and then Ariella. Aurora is the last one in while I scan up and down the quiet street, seeking anyone who could be observing. When I find nothing out of the ordinary, I too head for the shop, finding Aurora propping the door open with her foot.

In a low voice, I murmur, "No need to hold the door for anyone, *princesse*," as I nudge her into the shop.

When her lips twitch into a small smile as she turns away, I know I fucked up again by using the nickname. It's becoming so natural—*too* natural.

Thomas moves to one side of the doorway while I trail behind the women, heading for the back of the store, taking position at the back, by the doorway leading to a small circular space with three changing rooms.

The owner, a stout, elderly woman rushes from the back, her cheeks red with her rush to wait on the Corsettis. Most of my time is under Rafael's leadership, so there's been very few instances I've been out shopping, which means I don't deal with shopping trips often.

"Mrs. Corsetti, we were not expecting you today. How are you, ma'am?"

Caterina gestures to the small, amassed party standing by her. Aurora's gaze roves the store from where she stands behind them all, eyes sweeping over the mannequins and rows of fancy, hung gowns. Most of which being floor-length. A shop specific to prom dresses and other elegant occasions.

"We've come to get new dresses for my future daughter-in-law's engagement party."

The woman's eager attention shifts straight to Della. She cuts in between Ariella, taking Della by the elbow and gesturing to the wall of dresses. "Congratulations, my dear. I'm sure we have something here you'll like. We stock all the best designers' clothing—Louis Vuitton, Givenchy, Balenciaga, Dior, and Prada, to name a few."

It's like an entire other language.

Even Aurora's nodding, following the woman and Della around as brands are pointed out. Dress material is fawned over.

Colours are discussed. Topics all very easy to tune out when you have no clue what half of it means.

Meanwhile, Caterina leads Ariella over to the opposite wall and starts going through gown options with her, waving her hands animatedly in the air. It leaves Aurora to wander the shop alone. Her fingers trail over a midnight blue dress, fingering the lacy sleeves.

No matter how hard I try to avoid looking at her, it's her energy. It calls to me like a bright, fucking light, lit up in a colour only I can perceive.

At some point, Aurora and Della both slip by me, each holding a small pile of material. Aurora winks as she passes and disappears into one of the three fitting rooms behind me.

Again, I try to tune out the surrounding noises as Ariella and Caterina still shop options. Silent Ariella is nodding at nearly everything Caterina tells her, but her masked expression is that of a poker player, smooth and emotionless, so I wonder what she's thinking about all this, considering her own background.

Minutes later, Della walks out with a huff. "None of them worked," she grumbles. "Never imagined I'd care that much about a damn dress, but..." She wanders away, still mumbling to herself.

Another minute passes when vibrations tickle my thigh, from where my phone is in my pocket. I pull it out, somehow *knowing*, although hoping it's Nico or Rafael.

AURORA

I need help.

ME

There's four other women here. Ask one of them.

AURORA

I need YOUR help.

ME

There's nothing you need of me.

AURORA

Please.

You get back here and I'll be good for the
rest of the day. You like when I'm good…

Fuck. Me.

No. I can't do it. There are so many reasons I should put my phone away and pretend I didn't read that latest message. For one reason, slipping away will be impossible. Then there's a matter of who she is, who she will be eventually…yet my mind can't find a way for any one reason to properly stick.

After completing another visual sweep of the store, including Thomas, who has his back to us and is watching out the window, I slink into the room behind me, until I'm in front of Aurora's dressing room: the only shut door of the three.

She must hear me coming because the lock *clinks* and the door falls open, revealing a fucking goddess.

Aurora Corsetti stands regal in a slim, silver dress with a deep V-shaped neckline, showing off her perfect round breasts. One side of the dress cuts a line up her leg, stopping inches below her hip. Two thin straps rest over her shoulders, leaving her arms bare, and so I'm able to catch the goose bumps that sprout there when she takes me in. Her teeth sink into her bottom lip, either playfully or shyly.

"I guess that answers the question," she murmurs.

I don't look away from memorizing every inch of her when I ask, "What was the question?"

"I wanted a man's opinion on this one. Too much? You've been to these things before. Will I fit in wearing this?"

Will she fit in? It's a laughable question because she'll do more than *fit in*. She'll command the room.

She's no longer the bratty, playful, and sometimes, anxious woman I've been spending time with. No, this is Aurora Corsetti, daughter to Lorenzo and Caterina Corsetti. In this, she's never looked more like the princess the organization nicknames her as: never appeared more as her namesake.

She's perfect.

Ma princesse.

Not mine. Not mine...though I'd fucking love to make her mine as she wears this dress. To grab it by the neckline and rip the silky material right to the floor until I'm able to reward her for dressing in such a way.

"You'll fit in perfectly. Your fiancé will love it."

"But do *you* love it?"

"I don't have to love it."

Her tongue flicks at her bottom lip again before she pulls it into her mouth. "What if I wanted you to love it? Then how do you feel?"

Like I need to get the fuck out of here before the others notice I'm gone from my post.

"Aurora," I warn, my voice low to ensure no one out in the main part of the shop overhears.

"C'mon, Rosen. Be honest. As a friend, I'm asking you to give me a real opinion. Look at me."

Look at her? That's all I'm doing. The vision of her in this dress will be imprinted on my mind for the rest of my fucking days. And if I keep thinking how I am—keep picturing her on her knees in that gown—I won't have many days left.

She grasps the edges of the dress and twirls around, showing off what I couldn't see before. The backless dress dips so low, it barely covers her ass. One wrong movement, and surely, it'll fall.

There's no way physics should even be allowing this dress to remain on her frame.

My gaze traces the line of her dress, over the curve of her ass. It'd be so easy to tug it down and prove my next point. "Fuck. You're showing a lot of skin." It's meant to be a statement, but given how dry my throat is at the sight of her, it comes out gravelly.

She peeks over her shoulder, her smile secretive and sexy. "You already approved of it. Said my fiancé will like it. Can't take it back now."

Hearing her mention Rossi is enough to remind me of every reason I need to get out of here—and every reason I don't. A flash of misplaced jealousy licks down my spine—a feeling I certainly *shouldn't* be having.

Our boundaries seem so far away now. Faded and unimportant. I imagine ignoring the ramifications of my actions and entering the room with her.

I'd pin her like I had at the community garden, forcing her to stare at her reflection in the dressing room mirror as I touch her. I'd command her to lift her hands above her head and keep them there, while I let my hands explore her hips, see how fragile she feels in my hold.

"Well," she twirls back around, her movements causing her bare leg to peek out from the dress's slit, which I'd delight in using to get my hand beneath the material, "I like this one, so I think I'll go with it, despite how revealing it is."

"Moderation. Can't show him everything he'll be getting before the wedding," I murmur, still stunned, unable to blink or break away to return to where I should be—out of here. My nerves feel seconds away from snapping if I don't walk away now.

Her mouth curls in that cocky way she's so good at. "Yet, you're the one staring at me."

You'll have an entire room staring at if you if you wear that.

"You brought me back here knowing full well what you'd do to me. Brat."

"*Your* brat."

She's not my anything.

No matter how fucking tempting it is.

"*Princesse.*" The word pushes through my thick throat and I'm unsure if it's a question or an impending command. "Don't."

"Don't what?"

I don't know.

I do know I should walk away from here right. Fucking. Now.

Yesterday, she was trying to be friends with me, and today… today, she's my fucking forbidden desire. The woman who continues to invade my dreams every night, no matter how much I remind myself how inappropriate it is to even be thinking like that.

"You haven't stopped staring, Rosen." She points out what we're both very aware of. "It's starting to make me self-conscious."

Like I believe that. Is it possible for this girl to get self-conscious?

"Don't be."

If she was any other woman, if I was any other man, I'd make sure she knew not to be self-conscious because when I'd have her restrained against the mirror, watching me touch her, I'd ensure she knew how fucking gorgeous she looks. How, when my hands slip over the thin material covering her breasts, I'd cause her eyes to darken with lust.

I'd make her watch and be silent, to prevent the others from hearing us, as she fell apart in my hands. I'd pinch her tight nipples before exploring the heat between her legs. She'd tell me what she likes, what she requires, and I'd revel in granting her every desire.

She's *my* every desire in this dress.

"Rosen?"

Her voice slices through the air, finally breaking my stare. Her voice—Aurora Corsetti.

Unisciti a leale. Muori leale.

It's that vow—only those words—that simple, powerful statement, reminding me of every illicit reason, whatever insanity in my mind, must remain there. A dream, a fantasy, and nothing more. Certainly, no instance of me shattering those very vows and destroying my friendship with her brothers, no matter if my dick in my pants is pleading for something else.

I manage a step backwards, my feet feeling much heavier than when I first walked back here. Her brows dip, still confused and unable to catch the torment my mind has invented. Her mouth opens to speak, but I interrupt her before she can start.

"The dress is beautiful, Miss Corsetti. Everyone at the party will love it. Yes, it'll suit the occasion."

Before the temptation to mess her up continues to get to me, I escape the fitting room, thinking up a plausible reason for why I was back there.

At the doorway, Ariella's in the process of entering the dressing room, a long, green dress in her arms. Her brows lift when she sees where I've come from, and she simply shrugs and walks into one of the other dressing rooms.

Fuck. Hopefully she won't say anything to Della, the only person she'll speak to. Based on her offhanded reaction, she doesn't seem too bothered by what she obviously pieced together.

I retake my place, hoping no one else has noticed me gone

over the few minutes I was with Aurora. A few, but it felt like mere seconds.

Within moments, Aurora exits the dressing room, that silver dress draped over one arm. She looks briefly toward me, her expression unreadable, before she lifts her chin and heads for her mother.

"I found one, and I love it."

So do I. So will Erico Rossi. And so will every red-blooded male there.

But maybe this is for the best. If she can fall in love with her future fiancé sooner, then she'll be gone, and I can move on from this and forget about her.

Even if Aurora Corsetti is the opposite of forgettable.

22

AURORA

At the restaurant after dress shopping, I sit beside Mom and across from Della and Ariella at the four-top table draped in a smooth, white table cloth that I can't stop running my hands over. The restaurant is decorated with elegance and the waitstaff all wear button-down shirts and black slacks, giving the allusion that this place is swankier than the customers seem to feel it is. I'm simply thankful not to be the only one in jeans.

Mom's in the process of ordering the table wine because she understands the strange language required to comprehend the wine list, while I couldn't begin to guess the differences between the types. The last time I had wine was at supper a few weeks ago, when the Sisters suggested I start training my taste buds to get used to the drink. Mom orders with confidence and flair as well as a smile, as she discusses the wine list with the waiter, so I won't ruin her moment by disclosing my dislike of it.

Once she finishes ordering and the waiter leaves, Mom leans over and points to a section in my menu. "The fish is really good here." Then she drags her nail to the opposite page. "The chicken too."

Beside each food item is a number, which I assume to be the price. But is it possible for chicken to cost *that* much? We were always taken out for our birthdays by the Sisters, so this isn't my first restaurant trip, but I don't recall the food ever priced this high.

"Thanks," I murmur, reading over the endless choices. It's challenging to focus on making this decision when my attention continues to drift to a table across the room.

In a less than subtle manner, Thomas and Rosen have taken a table right by the entrance, each facing a different way. Thomas watches the door as people come and go, while luck placed Rosen facing the dining room—and me. Both sip on water, looking out of place in this restaurant full of diners.

Every time Rosen's gaze passes over me, I feel it. Like my nerves are hardwired to tell he's looking at me. I never risk my glances lasting more than a second, scared to meet his eyes after what happened in the dress store.

I don't know why I bothered to call him back there. Part of what I had told him was the truth; I wanted a friend's opinion on whether the dress was too revealing or if it'd fit in. I could have asked my mother, who would have been more than happy to help, or Della, but he's who I initially thought of.

But then he looked at me. Stood in the doorway as every wall between us crumbled and there's no denying the attraction in a man's gaze.

The waiter returns with the wine, pours us each a glass, and I down mine a bit quicker than I should, suddenly needing the alcohol to kick in and wipe this day clear from my mind.

When Mom says something to Della, I return my focus to what matters—this lunch. Across from me, Ariella's watching me, the tiniest smirk on her lips as her eyes slide from me to where Rosen is, then back to her menu.

Did she just...?

The waiter returns to take our orders and I quickly request the fish, causing Mom to smile again as I accept her suggestion. Everyone else orders and the waiter leaves again with a tip of his head.

The moment he walks away, Della leans forward, her attention solely on me. "Hey, I know this might feel weird and all, since you barely know me, but I'd really like it if you could be my bridesmaid."

Della's...what? Asking me to be her bridesmaid? To stand in front of a church with all those guests who'll be observing. My plan was to hide somewhere in the back and pretend it's not happening, but she wants me involved?

Della's hand slides across the table, stopping an inch away from mine. "You don't have to, but I know Nico would really like it." She pauses, rolling her lips together. "I mean, in another life, I'd know you as well as I know Rafael, but in this life, it's unfortunately not like that. I'd like to try, and we have to start somewhere, right?"

My immediate reaction is to glance to the side and hope the three of them aren't paying attention to who I'm looking at as my breathing becomes shallower, my throat tightening as white spots mask my vision with the idea of being stared at by all the wedding guests.

Rosen's eyes pass over the crowd again before finding me. His brows scrunch together, recognizing my neediness, even from over there. An immediate look of concern fills his expression, and he rests his glass down, like he's about to get up.

He's done enough. He calmed my racing heart sufficiently to remind myself to breathe. Five breaths before the room clears again and I'm able to focus on the table.

"If you're not a bridesmaid, honey, people will talk even more." Mom lifts her wineglass and takes a small sniff, though I have no idea what for. "They will wonder. Maybe judge. People are already curious regarding your brother's bride of choice."

Ouch. Based on the offhanded way Mom said that I'm not sure if she meant it callously. Either way, Della shoots a scathing look toward her, which I appreciate all too much.

Which makes my next statement flow from my lips easier. "Absolutely, I will."

Della grins and leans away, reaching for her own glass, taking a large gulp. "That means, we'll have to plan another shopping trip for a bridesmaid gown because everyone here insists on a large wedding." Her gaze flicks to Mom and back. "Besides, I know you have good taste after today. That dress..." She whistles low. "Damn, you're gonna upstage Nico and me at the engagement party."

"I'm sorry?" I laugh, phrasing my statement as a question, gauging if she's expecting a real one.

Della waves her hands, and my worries, away. "Please take the attention. You can have it."

I laugh again, but it trails off as I glance at Rosen. This time, he has his phone out, reminding me of what started my stupid mishap in the dress store—texting him.

A mistake I won't make again.

Which is why I look away before he can catch me staring.

When Rosen pulls up to the house, this time, it's Thomas who opens the back door for us. The three of them exit first. My gaze instantly finds Rosen, who's standing by the front of the car, waiting for me.

After lunch, I requested he take me to the garden. It's criminal I haven't gone yet and being in nature and with kids is bound to ease the numerous troubling emotions this day has created.

Mom waves goodbye and immediately heads for another waiting vehicle, which I spot Dad standing nearby. They embrace each other before climbing into it, Thomas getting into the front seat.

Ariella and Della head up the mansions front steps where Nico waits in the entranceway, leaving me to wonder how choreographed our comings and goings are here, considering both Dad and Nico were waiting at the correct time.

Nico's gaze probes my back as Rosen leads me to another waiting vehicle, causing me to appreciate that he had all of this already setup, so we can leave right away. I climb right into the front seat, uncaring that my entire family is watching. The risk is worth it when Rosen's jaw clamps shut when he takes his own spot.

"Something to say?"

"Nope," he responds sharply.

He starts the car and gets us down the driveway. In the side mirrors, I watch my parents' car behind us. We turn left at the end of the road and they go right, and that's when I breathe for the first time all day.

Or, it's how it feels anyway.

"Della's nice. You're right." Anything to fill the void within this car.

Rosen doesn't respond. His hands grip the wheel a bit tighter and his focus remains on the road in front of us. Occasionally, his eyes flick to the mirrors, but never toward me. Clearly, he's setting his boundaries again.

"I think the dress will make a statement that I'm here to stay."

Nothing? I would have thought that'd do it.

"Wow, what crawled up your ass?" Kicking off my shoes, I bring my legs up around me and lean against the door.

He never answers that question. He doesn't breathe a word to me, even after he pulls up to the community garden.

Dick.

~

"You look sad, Aurora."

Children are insightful. Sometimes, I think, more so than adults. Perhaps it's one of the many reasons I enjoyed getting close to the children at school.

I focus on the child in front of me. The little girl with two pigtails and an infections grin that causes her freckles to pop in the bright afternoon sun. Amy, I believe her name is. She's one of about eight kids at the garden right now, all of who appeared to be eager to spend time with me. Clarisse said it's the price of being the new adult around and has all of them working with me on a rotation.

Amy lowers herself to her knees, but I shake off where my mind continues to go—the engagement party. Now that I have a dress for it, it seems so real. Only a day away.

Still, I haven't come here to burden children with my own issues.

"Mommy gets looks like that all the time," Amy states, patting my hand. "She says she's okay, but then I always find her crying afterwards. So I hug her and make her feel better." Amy leans into me, pressing her bare arm against mine, offering, "I can give you a hug, if you'd like?"

Is it laughable that this child seems to pick up on my emotions better than anyone else so far? Other than Rosen, at least, but I'm starting to get the idea, he's in a league of his own.

I release the shrub I'm working on replanting and lift an

arm for her to slide underneath. Her little arms wrap around my side, in the largest hug her small form can manage.

"I must say, I do feel a whole lot better," I tell her when she releases me. Her expression lights up, beaming as she gets to her feet.

"I need to go pee, but I'll be right back. Aurora, don't go anywhere, okay?"

"Okay." I chuckle, glancing around the garden, spotting where Clarisse is working with a pair of siblings on the far side.

When feet approach me, I assume it's another child who has come to take Amy's place, eager to get to know the new person here. The shadow is larger, encompassing, and I release the shrub again, leaning back on my heels, looking up.

A girl—a woman actually—stands above me. Waist long blonde hair that seems like a pain in the ass hangs down her back. I stand, studying the newcomer. She looks around my age, and she grins, stretching her hand out to me.

"Hi. I've heard we have a new volunteer. I'm Roz."

Behind her, I spot Clarisse watching us, her hand up to shield the sun from her eyes. With my attention, she shoots a thumbs up and then returns to working with the kids.

"Hey," I finally greet, taking Roz's hand in a quick shake. "Yeah. Aurora. You also a volunteer?"

"Yeah." She glances around the space. "I only started yesterday. Clarisse mentioned another new volunteer and I wanted to meet you."

Okay. Strange. I was all for meeting other volunteers too, but to go out of one's way is a bit much.

"Well, I'm she." My arms spread in a dramatic fashion. "I'll be here...whenever." Whenever I can get away.

"Same. Maybe daily. I have nothing better to do."

Amy returns then, bounding up between us, her wide eyes bouncing between Roz and me. "Whoa, Roz, you're here too!

Awesome! Have you noticed we have another new person here —Aurora? She's new like you too."

Roz chuckles, bending slightly to get to Amy's height. "Yes, and I think Aurora's a pretty cool person. Can I help you guys?"

Amy's hands clench together against her chest, her body beginning to vibrate with the excitement she's aiming to taper down. "Um, yes! That'd be awesome!" She drops to her knees and begins digging in the dirt hole she was previously working on.

"Do you mind?" Roz checks, nodding toward the child at our feet. "I'd love to hear what brought you to this little place."

Is she trying to be a friend? Or at least, friendly? A person outside my family. I can't complain about that.

Hours later, I rejoin Rosen by sliding into the car. He doesn't say anything, which I don't expect him to at this point. Exactly like the trip here, he's stoic and silent and doesn't look at me, or ask about my time with the kids.

I miss him. I miss the version of him before this morning. Whatever passed in his head broke the non-friendship we were building.

Well, fuck him then.

Over the course of the trip home, since Rosen isn't filling the silence with chatter, I'm planning my return trip to the garden. Not only for the children, but for Roz. As the children started to go home and there were less of them, she and I began talking more openly.

She knows I'm a Corsetti but doesn't seem too bothered by the fact, and that I recently moved back but didn't say from where. I told her about the kids at my old home and regaled all the comical things they did or said. I mentioned the engagement party and she suggested taking it one minute at a time, and before I knew it, the night would be over.

Roz gave fewer details, but I learned her mom died when she was younger, and she has one sister, younger by a couple years. They live with their father, and she's grown up in the city her entire life. She went to private schools, and dreams of doing "more," but never said what that consists of.

I don't tell Rosen about her. She's harmless, or else, she wouldn't be working there. He'll get weird and start demanding to run background checks or whatever it is that makes him sleep at night.

For now, she'll remain another piece of the place I escape to.

23
ROSEN

Unisciti a leale. Muori leale.

Join loyal. Die loyal.

Words I not only live by, but I'd die by. A vow taken in blood: amidst a ceremony few are aware of. A tattoo drawn as a permanent reminder.

With those vows, a promise. Any man inducted will work for the Corsetti family, serve them, protect them, die for them.

The idea of protection can look different for each person, for each family member they're referring to.

Aurora Corsetti, mafia princess, not only needs to be protected from our enemies, from anyone who'd do her harm, but also anyone who'd take advantage of her. Anyone who dares view her in any manner other than her title.

That includes me.

The second Aurora opened the dressing room door, I realized how severely I've been fucking up my vows. If I had ignored her better, been a respectable soldier around her and not ensnared by her taunts, I wouldn't have had the fantasies I had.

But fucking Christ. That silver dress she chose enhanced her already existing beauty in ways I hadn't known to be possible. The way she stood there, biting her lip, looking every bit innocent, was the second my brain memorized her every inch and locked the vision in my head.

In my mind, my loyalty won't be questioned. Aurora doesn't demand protection in my fantasies because they're simply that—imagined. Never to be played out, never to be discussed between her and me.

Illicit.

Immoral.

Mine.

Ma princesse.

In my head at least, that's what she is. *Ma princesse* to control. To peel that striking silver scrap of a dress from her body and lower her to her knees. To watch those full lips of hers, usually spewing attitude, part for me. For me to *use*.

It's that image causing the otherwise hot water penetrating my back muscles to feel cool. The shower I'm taking, standing with one arm poised against the wall, my head hung low and the waterfall above me to pour water down my head, my back, slicing between my shoulders and dripping from my face, was meant as a distractor. A place to hide away from my phone to prevent from texting her.

I fucking *miss* her and I shouldn't. She's not even mine to miss. I'm *staff* and yet, being in that car with her today was boring. Without her cocky smirks and comments, the trip to the community garden and back was incredibly dull. I'm to blame, but I had to for the sake of both our promises—mine to her family name and her to her future fiancé. Speaking to her would only allow the vision from the dress shop to return and I couldn't risk touching her. Fuck, even looking at her.

Twisting the shower's knob, I increase the water's temperature to the point of near-burning. Anything to get my cock to calm down and stop picturing her in here with us. Her in that damn dress, the water drenching it, drops framing her gorgeous face and dripping between her breasts.

"Goddamn it, stop."

My mind doesn't stop. Not sure it can.

Think about anything else. Any. Thing. Anything that isn't a blonde goddess who's about to consume an entire party's attention tomorrow when she's there with Rossi. Maybe seeing her on his arm will be enough of a reminder of who she is—of who she *will* be.

"Your brat."

Stop, get out of my head. Against the tile, my hand forms a fist, wishing my fingers could sink through the wall and the tiles could shatter, slicing up my skin, providing me pain no less than I deserve. If Nico and Rafael knew my inappropriate thoughts, I'd be in for a world of pain.

For the briefest second, I imagine they weren't a factor.

If she was in this shower with me, I'd pin her against the wall. I'd take those thin straps of the dress in my teeth and peel them down her arms. My tongue would follow the path around the top of the dress, over her breasts, now wet from the same water I barely feel. I'd chase the droplets to the valley between her breasts, and even farther. Following it down her body until it leads me to the heat between her legs.

"Fuck."

Groaning, I fist my cock. In my shower alone with fantasies in my head, I break my vows. I shatter my oaths to protect her. Instead, I dirty her up. I command her. I watch her fall apart in my arms.

"Fuck." My hand quickens, my other slamming into the white shower tile. My cock grows thick in my hand, the image of shoving it down her throat intensifying my dreams. After I punish her. How I long to punish her...To make her come over and over until she passes out from overstimulation, or to edge her so many times, she'll think twice before opening that bratty mouth again.

"Fuck. Aurora."

Aurora bent over my bed, her legs parted as I push two fingers inside her hot cunt. I'd make her beg, so when I grant her the reprieve she's dying for, her orgasm will be more intense.

"Aurora."

Aurora on her knees, staring up at me with those bold, green eyes. Her mouth full of my cock, unable to spew her attitude. Her choking as she's rewarded with my praise.

"Aurora."

Aurora poised over my mouth, drenching my face as lock my hands around her thighs and feast on her pussy.

"Aurora!"

My cock twitches the final time and cum shoots from it and all over my hand, quickly being washed away by the shower. It mingles at my feet before getting sucked down the drain, taking my secrets with it.

Orgasming to the fantasy of the Corsetti princess is everything I shouldn't be doing.

I wash my hand and shut off the blistering water, suddenly needing out here. Yanking a towel from the hook, I quickly dry my body before heading straight to the bed.

Before lying down, I tap my phone's screen, finding no message from Aurora. Disappointing, but also positive. It means she's finally understanding.

~

"E**veryone's in place?" Nico asks from where we stand at the edge of the ballroom, him fixing the sleeve of his suit jacket.

A handful of servers are across the room, pouring fresh champagne in flutes for the upcoming guests, moments away from arriving. On the opposite side, a DJ is double-checking the equipment that's been set up there, going through the streams of soft background music.

"Men are on rotation, walking the house and the ground's perimeters to ensure there's always fresh eyes," I respond, mentally ticking off everything I put into place earlier today. "A couple are monitoring the camera footage. More stationed beside all exits. No one's getting in here."

"Good. Thanks, Rosen."

I glance at my underboss, who, weeks ago, was against this very event, too busy despising his mother throwing him a party to meet anyone his parents deemed suitable. "Isn't it funny how life works out? Not long ago, we were preparing for a similar party you fought not to be a part of."

Nico whacks my arm in a friendly manner as he turns away. "Weeks ago, I hadn't known I'd meet my future. Who I must go find now. Excuse me."

As he wanders toward the stairs to go retrieve Della, I position myself on the edge of the room, taking up a wall by one of the main arches, so I can catch everyone entering and leaving.

Including Aurora. Aurora, who'll be donning that slip of a dress that hardly is worthy of the article's title. The dress that shows more skin than it covers. The dress gracing my dreams last night, making me consider the viability of taking a bullet, simply to be able to peel it slowly from her, tasting every inch of her skin I unwrap.

But that would be in a perfect world, not reality. Real life isn't the fairy tale we like to pretend it is. It's full of harsh realities and cruel heartbreaks.

Moments later, the sounds of voices begin drifting to me as all the upper-class people begin filling the room. I've seen enough of these events that I hardly spare anyone a second longer of attention. That is, until a large crowd passes by me, trailed by three particular people I recognize.

The couple enters first. The man's huge, and his chubby face shows signs of aging and a receding hairline. His energy commands the room; the man well-versed in the influence that comes with his title. By his side, his wife, no doubt. Her black hair wound up in a partial bun as narrowed eyes scan the room, calculating in her observations of every guest before her.

The *Famiglia's* Boss and his wife.

The third person follows behind them. He too walks with an authority, which I can't wait to see Nico knock down a few pegs. He steps up beside his father when his parents stop halfway to the centre of the room. He leans down to whisper something to them as he continues scanning the room, no doubt seeking the Corsettis.

Erico Rossi. Aurora's future fiancé.

And the face I'll think about the next time I'm in front of a punching bag.

As guests begin mingling, Lorenzo and Caterina enter the room, both full of measured smiles as they scan their crowd, pausing a few feet into the entryway. All conversation dies, attention swinging to the archway.

They step aside, allowing the crowd to see one of the main attractions—Nico and Della. For all his love of Della, Nico's pinched expression shows how much he's despising this. At his side, Della, dressed in a floor-length black gown, looks the ideal wife to my underboss. While she subtly steps closer to him, her determined gaze doesn't once break from the crowd.

They move deeper into the room, and people begin to wander toward them. Ariella and Rafael walk in last. Ariella goes to her sister, while Rafael pauses by where I stand, even leaning casually against the wall as he shoves his hands into pockets.

"You think everyone here is already in a relationship, or do I have a chance of getting some tonight?"

I roll my head to look at him. "That's seriously what you're asking right now?"

He shrugs the shoulder he's not leaning on. "It's that or I'm chugging as much champagne as I can to get me through this. You know how much I hate this shit."

That he does. When I spot Erico Rossi and his parents approach Nico and Della, it prompts me to ask, "Where's Aurora? Or is she getting some grand entrance?"

He chuckles, shoving off the wall to unbutton his suit, clearly not bothering with maintaining proper decorum. "Nico was tempted to. Della talked him off that ledge. Instead, she'll come down on her own, but Nico threatened to drag her from her room if it's longer than twenty minutes past the start of this thing." His attention goes to his family, still chatting with the Rossis. "There's a lot of power amongst that group. At least, he's handsome." Rafael doesn't use a name but I'm aware of who he's talking about.

"Sure," I grunt, feigning disinterest. "Go join them."

"Ah, no." His nose wrinkles with his distasteful expression. "No, thanks. I'm avoiding the Rossis, in case they find some random cousin to try to wed me to. Excuse me, I'm going to go get drunk now." He walks away, weaving between a group of guests and gets swallowed up by the crowd.

Conversations are easy to tune out when you're not in them, so that's what I do, until a nearby whisper-shout breaks it. Specifically, the words the woman speaks.

"Oh, my god, who is that? She's gorgeous. And that dress!"

There's only one person she could be speaking about like that. One person who enters the room with her head held high, despite the nerves or fear making her hands curl by her sides. One person who's so gorgeous, it makes me despise myself all over again for letting my mind go to inappropriate places last night in my shower.

Aurora almost immediately commands the room as she stands under the archway, clad in that same silver dress I dreamed of removing from her over and over yesterday. It makes me want to throw my coat over her and cover her up to keep her from everyone's roving gazes.

On one of her wrists, a delicate bangle catches in the room's lighting. The gold matches the necklace stopping barely shy of the swell of her breasts. Her hair is curled, falling down her back in a soft tumble.

Fuck, you're gorgeous. Words spoken to her in my head, my growing drive to praise her increasing every time I see her.

Aurora scans the room, taking everyone in, and I'm dying to know what she's thinking of. She finishes by finding me, only feet away from where she stands. Her lips part slightly, and I catch the subtle rise of her chest as she breathes in and out, presumably calming herself. She meets my gaze, holding it for another round of breathing.

When Nico moves through the crowd, toward his sister, Aurora's focus shatters; the fear dissipates, leaving only annoyance behind. Her gentle gaze turns unfriendly and she looks away, tipping her head in a way that leaves little room for interpretation.

Fuck you.

I deserve it. She's angry for me ignoring her yesterday, even when she attempted to strike up a conversation. It was necessary to be rude to her then.

She takes Nico's outstretched hand as he leads her to the centre of the room, toward their family and Della—and the Rossis.

I stop watching her to observe Erico's reaction. It'd be impossible not to be affected by Aurora because that's simply who she is. The moment I saw her in the garden in Toronto, she had this energy about her that intrigued me. Nothing like the woman I expected to find.

Erico stands between his parents as Nico and Aurora approach. He blatantly checks her out, from head to toe, but his closed-off expression doesn't alter. Not totally surprising since he's an underboss, trained like Nico not to reveal emotions.

Nico introduces her to the three Rossis, gesturing to Erico's parents first, and then to him. I wish I could see her expressions, but they're buried in the crowd, where, as people slowly move around, I only catch flashes of the group.

After a moment, Erico and Aurora break away from their families and head to get drinks. That's it? A quick introduction and she so easily went with him? Where's the fight? This isn't the woman screaming at Nico in his office the other day, or the one texting me her hatred of her family and this situation.

This is her Corsetti blood emerging.

It becomes easier to stare into the crowd, the far walls, or the floor by my feet to avoid watching them. I'm nothing more than the man meant to protect her, and I'll continue doing so, even from myself.

Thankfully, Nico calls the room to attention, he and Della still in the centre. Their family frames the edges of the crowd, with Aurora and Erico not far away.

"I realize this event might be considered last-minute, but your attendance is nonetheless appreciated," Nico starts, his bored tone booming over the party. "We're here to celebrate two events. First, I would like you all to welcome my baby sister home." He gestures toward where Aurora stands, her eyes getting wider with every passing second. "Aurora Corsetti has returned to us."

At first, there's absolute silence. Everyone glancing at each other and then Aurora, mouths slipping open in shock, whispers and flurried conversation as the crowd pieces together what Nico said. That the young Corsetti girl from years ago, sent away with the only explanations as rumours, is in their presence again.

No one's opinion matters more than Aurora's, so only she has my attention. Rossi doesn't even *see* what I do, and he's standing right beside her. The deep breaths she's taking while trying not to make it obvious. The constant movement of her eyes. The swaying as she shifts her weight.

Since the moment I met her, the hints were there, only getting pieced together as the days passed.

Panic attacks. Anxiety.

Nico grasps Della's hand in his, raising it to his chest as he speaks again, returning people's attention to him. "Della Lambert came into my life and stole my heart the second she tried to have it yanked from my chest."

A few nervous chuckles emit through the room, with many guests glancing at each other, unsure of the meaning behind his words. Rafael, close by the couple, lets out a loud bark of laughter.

"The day she saved my life was the day I knew this was who I wanted by my side as we lead the Corsetti family into the future. So, I ask you all to welcome my future, who I'll be thrilled to be calling my wife in two weeks."

He leans down and captures Della's mouth in a heated kiss that goes on for a while, causing a few people to whistle, breaking the pair up. As people begin moving around the room again, some outright trying to shove closer to Nico and Della, others hang back, talking amongst themselves.

"Lambert. Not a name I recognize. Corsetti's engaged to a nobody?"

"He must have gotten her pregnant."

"Who *is* she?"

The trio of women who look like they've snorted way too much Botox immediately shut up when I glare in their direction, all turning away to suck up to the couple they recently insulted.

Pushing the women from my mind, I immediately find Aurora in the crowd again. She and Erico stand off to the side, looking intimidating in their own way. People approach and Aurora smiles at every single one of them, but it's not natural. It's tight, uncomfortable, and Rossi ought to be fucking supporting her instead of shaking the men's hands.

Not my issue. Not in that regard. *Keep her safe*, that's my role.

Keep.

Her.

Safe.

Which means even from me.

I felt I was prepared for this.

I was *severely* wrong, in every way. For some reason, I pictured maybe a dozen guests, since Della reassured me it'd be a small gathering. I'm sorry, but a *few* dozen is more than what constitutes as a "small gathering." They're staring at me. First, when I entered the room, and certainly after Nico announced who I was.

Did he have to do that? Attending wasn't enough for him?

Knowing I have to go through this entire event with Rosen in the room has me in a worser mood. Countless times last night, when I was tossing and turning in bed, I reached for my phone, brought up our text conversation, and scrolled to the top, to my first night here when I struggled to fall asleep. I longed to message him again, to talk about today and the anxieties keeping me up.

Hanging out with Della was fine and all, but it's missing something. There's still an invisible barrier between us because no matter how friendly she is, she's with my brother, and discussing my fears about their engagement party isn't something she'd care to hear, I'm sure. Maybe she'd try to ease me, but it wouldn't be the same solution as talking to Rosen.

The only thing preventing me from sending the messages I typed out, deleted, and re-typed numerous times was how he ignored me on the trip to and from the garden, so I doubted he'd respond to a midnight text.

Well, fuck him. He wins. Distance and boundaries. Now that what feels like my only support in this place has abandoned me, I suppose I need to do what I've always done: plaster a fake smile on my face, hold my chin high, and focus on breathing so I don't pass out.

All under his watchful gaze.

The benefit of the continuous and overwhelming stream of people who approach me means they give me something else to focus on so I don't peek at him every three seconds.

And finally, meeting Erico Rossi. Also known as, my future fucking husband. Fiancé. Whatever—pick a term and stick it to him because I loathe them all.

He's handsome in every classical way possible. A mop of black hair, a smooth, straight face. His arms show some sign of muscle and build, but nothing close to what Rosen has. He might be okay on the eyes, but I only hope he's also nervous and that explains his dry personality.

The man's spoken a handful of words to me. He stands by my side, looking entirely bored and like he'd rather be anywhere else. Maybe he feels the same way about us as I do, in which case, this could work if neither of us are seeking more than appeasing our families, but at least for the moment, I'm *trying*. Trying to smile. Trying to respond to every question thrown my way as Erico remains a decoration by my side, chatting with the men who approach while the women bombard me with questions.

"How's it feel to be home?"

"What do you think of your brother's fiancée?"

"If you're back, what about your other brother, the one who disappeared around the same time you had?"

"When's your engagement party?"

That last one is what really hit me. What really stole my breath when the older woman looked straight at Erico, like she knew.

They all seem to know. Nico walked me straight to this man and then announced who I am. Of course, they know! Erico and I might not be officially engaged yet, but we might as well be.

Breathing gets more difficult, for every person approaching snips another string of my already-fragile nerves. And every time I attempt to suck in a deep breath, another person appears, expecting me to reply.

Erico chats easily by my side, and I look past the women surrounding me, spotting my parents and Nico in similar encounters with other people. Rafael. Where is he? So far, he's been a safe bet. I scan the room, finding him chatting with another woman, his smile flirty as he tucks strands of the girl's hair behind her ear. For fuck's sake.

I know who I *can* look at to ground me. But I refuse to.

Grabbing onto Erico's arm, I lean into him, interrupting his talk of sports cars. "Hey, um, can we go for a walk?"

"Of course, Miss Corsetti." He nods to the people around us and tucks my arm into his and then leads me away, toward the edge of the room.

I never in my wildest dreams imagined Erico the more comfortable option, but at least one-on-one, this seems a bit less hectic and even manageable.

"Thanks," I mumble. "They're a lot."

"I bet. Get used to it. Your life in New York will be similar. We're a powerful family with a lot of connections, and to maintain those, there's a social aspect to it. Why do you think your brother bothered with all this?" He gestures to the space. "It's not for him or his new wife. It's for *them*. So his guests continue honouring his family name, continue keeping their faith in his leadership abilities."

What he claims make sense, but I've kind of stopped listening after his mention of me in New York. As his wife. Doing this.

Fuck.

Breathe. In—one, two, three. Out—one, two, three.

I do it twice before most of the trepidation finds a new home on the floor rather than inside my body. With my arm in his, my body decompresses, losing some of its tautness.

"Can we walk? Standing here gives them a place to approach again, and I'd rather not."

"Of course," he replies smoothly, barely looking at me.

It's like I'm being discarded again. First by my family. Then by Rosen yesterday. And now by the man who's agreed to marry me. I shouldn't be bothered by this as much as I am. While I don't want him, maybe I simply crave someone to want *me*, and at this rate, I'll take anyone.

"If you approach them, they won't come up to you," he murmurs, leading me to a nearby elderly couple who's standing off to the side.

That option sounds terrible too, and I'm about to make that known when we walk by Rosen. His jaw is set, his eyes blazing, and when I rest my free hand onto Erico's arm, further embracing him, Rosen looks away to a far corner of the room.

What the fuck is his problem?

I'm doing what everyone here thinks I should, him included: playing my role while he remains on the outskirts.

Erico leads me to the first couple, and then another, and then another, and by the fourth, I'm trying to figure out how he knows all these people when they work with Nico, not his family. Unless this speaks to how powerful the Rossis are and why Nico is so resolute into getting involved with them.

My nerves should be calming with each person I meet, but they don't. I manage to breathe through every interaction, but my smile is completely fake. The attention I shoot at Erico also a sham.

"Aurora." Nico's penetrating, firm tone drives through my anxiety when we near him and Della. "Erico. Having a good time?"

"Peachy," I respond, plastering a sickening, sarcastic smile across my face, I'm sure Nico is smart enough to see right through.

"You're braver than me," Della comments from beside my brother, completely missing the fact I wasn't being literal. "I still haven't *looked* at half these people."

Nico wraps an arm around her waist, which drags her firmly to his side. "Fuck 'em all. They only need to know you're mine, and now that they do, I'm ready for this to be over with."

For once, I can appreciate Nico's sentiments.

"Thank you for inviting me and my family," Erico says to them. "Congrats on your engagement as well. Beautiful party. Getting to meet Aurora has been a bonus."

Ha! His words might sound nice, but they're not true. He might be by my side all evening, but he feels so distant. Even when he pays me attention, it's like he's looking through me instead. I'm a "bonus" for him, as it's part of the political game both he and my brother are navigating.

Why does that bother me so much? Considering I don't want him nor this engagement, I shouldn't care about how Erico truly feels. I peek to the side, through the crowd, seeking the only person who's ever truly looked at me. From our first interaction, he's been there for me, which perhaps is what makes yesterday's brush off that much more painful.

Nico coughs, bringing my attention back to him and Della before I could find who I was looking for. "Well, we'll leave you two alone." When they wander away, Erico pats my arm and gently steers me in another direction.

"Come. My parents would like to meet you."

His parents. My future mother and father-in-law. The Boss of the New York *Famiglia*. Nico briefly introduced me to them upon my arrival to the party, but the meeting was short-lived and most of their focus was on pushing Erico to my side before they faded into the background, leaving us to get to know one another. I barely looked at the intimidating power couple, with the firm belief if I didn't, they're not there.

Erico pulls me through a small group of people and that's when I see them, standing by my own parents. My father speaks to Erico's, while Mom gestures around the room, pointing things out to his mother.

My heels slam into the shiny floor beneath my feet and I dislodge my arm from his. Erico stops walking immediately, his brows dipping down as he finally looks at me. And he *looks* at me for once, studying my face as my mind is racing, my heart hammering. Sweat beads on the back of my neck.

I can't do this. I can't go to *them* and pretend to be enjoying their son.

"What is it?"

His tone is laced with annoyance rather than concern. He's not wondering why I'm finding it difficult to move forward, but is irritated that I've stopped walking. His gaze flicks over a few nearby people before finding me again. His hand comes up in a jerking motion, ushering me back to his side.

"Aurora," he utters in a low, warning tone. Nothing like a playful warning that makes my insides clench with the temptation to still deny his request, like what Rosen makes me feel, but instead, one that has my head shaking and my feet moving backwards.

"I-I—I need air." Spinning around, I shove between the crowd with one focus in mind—escape. Getting to the main archway we all came from. Sure, the room is filled with exits, some closer, but I want *him* to see me.

Nico catches my eye on the way past, but I spare his disapproving snarl no attention as I get to the doorway, passing Rosen. He doesn't turn his head, but I feel him watching. Without stopping, I leave, quickly turning the corner and rushing down the hall, heading for one of the few rooms I know exist in this place; the sitting room I was in with my family after first arriving.

I throw myself through the door, slamming it shut behind me, pressing my back to it to ensure no one comes in. Nico watched me leave, which means either he or Rosen will soon be here to demand I return. Or maybe it'll be my parents, embarrassed at the scene they feel I've caused.

It's not even ten seconds before the door shoves open, heaving me away from it and farther into the room. I don't look behind me as I pace forward, stopping by the nearest chair, my hands clenching the backing.

"Having a nice time, *princesse*?" The gruff voice is exactly who I expected. Of the three possibilities, I somehow knew it'd be him. Warm velvet rolls over my neck, his heat building as he approaches after shutting the door behind him.

I scoff, turning around to lean against the chair I'm standing in front of. My gaze centres on Rosen as he approaches, pure muscle and power. "Does it matter? You've made your stance very known. All that talk of boundaries." Turning my head, I aim to ignore him, while commanding,

"Leave me alone, Rosen. Do your job and tell my family I'll return in a few minutes. I needed air."

"Before you have another panic attack."

He knows. "What are you talking about?"

My peripheral vision catches him approaching, and I tense, ready to move away if he continues advancing.

"Anyone who paid you a little bit of attention could notice. In the car to the airport. Yesterday at the dress shop, when you were getting out of the car. All evening, you look on the verge of one. Between conversations, you were sucking in so many breaths, trying to calm yourself."

He pieced it together. This shouldn't make me as happy as it does, but I'm pleased in a strange way that also makes the backs of my eyes tingle with tears because *he* knows this about me, but no one else here does. Erico, my parents, my brothers, all of them saw me tonight, but none of them picked up on the fact I was minutes from a breakdown.

But Rosen did.

"I'm okay." Waving my hand in the air, I turn away, facing the windows at the opposite side of the room. It's late, so I'm unable to see much through the dark outdoors. "Go back to the party before people start wondering where we are. Tell them I'll be there soon. Erico knows I wanted air, so it's fine."

"You're a beautiful couple," he comments. "You two really look good together."

"He's got a great personality too," I sneer, sarcasm heavy in my tone. "Can't wait to move to New York and marry him."

"I'm sure you'll be very happy."

My snort can't be held in. Wandering away from the chair I was leaning on, I go toward the windows, ideally ending this conversation. I don't want to talk about Erico at all, let alone with Rosen.

Outside, the moon glows right in my face, lower than usual.

The room faces the grounds and leaning closer to the glass allows me to see toward the greenhouse, and the patch of grass I laid on the other night.

"It'll get better, Aurora. Putting on a show tonight isn't helping your case when your dislike of him is apparent. To anyone paying attention."

"You mean you?" I don't turn around to hide the fact I'm rolling my eyes. "What the fuck is wrong with you anyway? You talk about the professional working relationship between a family member and soldier, between you and me, and yet you pay me quite a bit of attention, don't you think?" Dying to see how the truth hits him, I turn, pressing my back, bare from the dress's low dip, against the cool windowpane.

He's nearer than where I left him earlier, about six feet away, his hands shoved into the pocket of his slacks. His expression is impassive, his form stiff, jaw set. Annoyance is plainly shown on his face, and normally, I'd relish in playing upon that, but my own troubling emotions take away from that kind of fun.

"My job is to protect you, which means having eyes on you the entire time."

"Yeah, and does protecting me also mean following me into dark corners of the house and pointing out my faults?"

"*Faults.*"

I'd never believe a single word could be so icy, so packed with an emotion while also being devoid of one, but he manages it.

"Panic attacks are not a goddamn fault, Aurora. There is *nothing* wrong with you."

Except for, apparently, being in the wrong for my desire to have a friendship with my bodyguard.

"Protecting you," he continues, moving past the conversation about my anxiety, "means ensuring those who'd dare harm you don't." Rosen takes a step, bringing him even closer, destroying the large bubble of air still existing between us. "It means not only making sure your life remains intact, but your body is unharmed." Another step. "Your mind unsullied by the world's darkness." Another step, leaving so little space between us, I forget how to breathe.

I tilt my chin up, putting my face in line with his while I pretend my hands aren't clenching by my side, that a pleasurable chill isn't coursing down my spine. "Then why ignore me yesterday afternoon? After the dress shop, you changed."

"Protecting you also means from myself, *princesse*."

"What does that mean?" I ask, despite my suspicions, as his gaze rakes my face, which feels hotter than before.

"It means you deserve someone who appreciates how fucking sexy you look. How, when you opened the dressing room door yesterday, I forgot how to breathe, what my own name was, the ramifications of what went through my head in that very second."

I saw it all in his eyes, but now I *need* to hear him say it.

"What was in your head?"

He lets out a low groan, his eyes shutting, head turning to the side. His walls are going back up, but before he does, I do the singlehandedly stupidest thing I ever have and delete the foot of space he's still maintaining between us. My hand lands on his jacket's lapel, my painted nails contrasting the dark article of clothing. Beneath my palm, his chest rises and falls twice before he finally answers me in a tone darker than I ever could have imagined.

"Believe me, Aurora, even thinking about it now could get me killed. Not talking to you yesterday was the only way I could keep our boundaries."

"What if, for only a moment, I asked you to ignore them? Would you tell me what was in your head? Consider it an act of friendship."

He huffs, unamused. "It goes beyond friendship." He steps back, which drops my hand limply back to my side. His eyes go over my shoulder, out the window, and in a tone I almost would like to believe is regretful, he murmurs, "Take your time in here. Come back when you're ready. I'll let people know you're okay."

He takes a step, and another, and the air between us grows cold with every inch of distance he creates. I don't know what happened, and I understand what he's concerned about, but it *can't* end like that. He'll go back to ignoring me, and I miss him.

Before he's out of reach, I grab the back of his jacket. "Rosen—"

He spins, returning to me in a blur, and the next thing I know, when my brain catches up to what's happening, he has his body against mine, pinning me to the window, the hand I reached out toward him is being held in his own, stretched above both our heads as he keeps me submissive, unable to fight back.

He's breathing hard, his exhales passing over me. His eyes more crazed than I've ever seen before. Uninhibited. Not the man I've known so far.

"You are fucking gorgeous, Aurora. You're spunky when you talk back. Resolute when you want something. Determined to get beneath my skin, and when you opened that door yesterday, I realized how much you already were." His fingers weave with mine, curling, until he's holding my hand, almost tenderly, except this position is anything but. "Watching you prance around with Rossi by your side is criminal because he hasn't looked twice at you. He doesn't appreciate what he's being freely given, simply because of his position. I can't tell you what is in my head tonight, or yesterday in the shop, or even fucking last night when I was alone in my shower because every single thought will earn me a one-way ticket to my death if anyone were to learn of them. Now, do you see the issue, *princesse?* Why I shouldn't be saying all this."

I do, but the way he's gazing at me tells me there's more between us than simple roles. He's not looking at me like a bodyguard should, but rather a way that makes flames ignite beneath my skin. For whatever reason, I'm making the walls he's built between us fragile, in the same way, he makes it impossible for me to hate him as much as I should.

But my next statement puts into words what he's been ignoring.

"You're jealous."

25
ROSEN

Jealous.

I'm not jealous because I'm not allowed to be. Aurora Corsetti is not someone for me to be jealous over. She is a Corsetti and one I've vowed to protect. She'll be wed to the very man who is permitted to be by her side, adored by all the other wealthy people in society while I wait on the edges.

She is my charge and nothing more. A job. A task, which is taking more energy than I initially believed. There's never been an issue of boundaries between a soldier and someone of the family. Everyone plays their part well, and that's all there is to it.

She's not mine to be jealous over; therefore, I am not.

I am not jealous.

I *can't* be.

Being jealous over this woman would mean—*No.* I shut the thought down before it formulates. *No, impossible.*

"No," I finally push out, "that's not it. I said nothing more than the truth: that you look beautiful tonight. That's all."

Lie.

Her lips curl in the corner, her eyes flicking up to where I'm still gripping her.

Shit. I can't be holding onto her. My body shouldn't be pressing her to the window. This is like the community garden the other day when I had her pinned by her neck. That's twice now this woman has slithered beneath my skin and stole my self-restraint.

I must release her.

Instead, my hand tightens around hers.

Her chest brushes mine with every breath she takes, but I don't look to where we're connected. I can't because it'd involve seeing her breasts and some lines can't be crossed.

"That's all, huh? For someone who's trying to push me away, you're certainly horrible at maintaining your own boundaries."

Oh, I know. "You make it fucking impossible, Aurora, and you damn well know it."

"Maybe because you're the only one who sees me, Rosen. You talk about me being on Erico's arm and the shame it is because he stares at me like I'm an item to purchase and not a person. Well, so does everyone else. They're all waiting for me to fall in line, not looking beyond the surface. But you do. You *see* me. You know, and you have from that first meeting. That's why you ignoring me yesterday hurts so fucking much."

Her hand, the one I'm not holding, lifts, about to reach for me. Once was enough. When she rested her hand over my heart earlier, I could have sworn she burned away all my clothing. When she grabbed onto me as I tried to get away, it broke me.

She's not allowed to touch me, and before she makes contact, I grab onto that one too. First her wrist, slowly lifting her other arm above her head, my eyes studying hers, seeking any hint of fear.

I *want* her fear because it'll give me a better reason to

release her. The second she seems at all uncertain, she'll be freed, and that's the promise I make to myself, as a part of protecting her.

Instead, she bites her bottom lip, and I swear to fuck, my cock feels the gentle scrape of her tongue. The corner of her lips curl up, her back arching into me. If anyone were to enter the room and see how I'm restraining her, I'd be fucked.

All reasons to release her instead of bowing my head, lining my face up with hers.

"I'm sorry. Hurting your feelings wasn't the intention."

I hurt her. That's enough to release her, right? Let her go instead of leaning into her, close enough I can see the different shades of green in her eyes. The slightest fraction of her lips parting, taking in the smoothest inhale.

She's my forbidden dream come true. Pinned to a window, a hint of what she'd look like bound to my bed. Her back arching into my chest, a tease of what she'd be doing if I had the opportunity to suck her tight, little nipples. Her slight breathy intakes, a fraction of the air I'd rob from her lungs as I keep her on edge all night long.

In another world.

"Rosen," she murmurs.

"Aurora." I swallow, although it does nothing for my dry throat. "You need to go."

To return to her future fiancé before I make the greatest mistake of my life.

Her head tips back a fraction until she looks to where I'm still holding onto her. She can't leave until I release her...but it's impossible, knowing she's returning to a man who doesn't appreciate her.

"Just kiss me already." Her eyes flick to my lips. "It's what you want."

Do I close my eyes? I might because when I reopen them,

I'll be alone in my shower, or bed, or anywhere where she isn't, suggesting something that's forbidden.

Boundaries.

"Rosen," she whispers, pulling against my hold as she tries to lean closer. "Rosen, I want you to. You want to. There's nothing else that matters."

Your family. My vows. Everything that makes what's in my head impossible. I swallow, and again, and again, hoping at some point, my head wakes up and stops remembering what I imagined last night. Stops seeing her in this very dress.

Unisciti a leale. Muori leale

Unisciti a leale. Muori leale

Unisciti a leale. Muori—

One at a time, my fingers lift from her skin, and I complete the impossible. She doesn't lower her arms right away as her gaze darkens with pain that makes my own insides clench.

I hurt her the same way she claims I had yesterday when I ignored her, but I had to. *Have* to, for both our benefits. Like last night in the shower, whatever fantasies I have about the *princesse* must remain as such and nothing more.

"I'm sorry," I whisper, self-hate driving me to turn away from her. Every instinct within my body demands otherwise, except one: common sense. The one instinct I now hate for making this possible.

Before I can turn away, she moves, pressing herself into me, her hands coming up to cup my cheeks. Her touch is soft and welcoming, but unyielding regardless. I barely understand her expression before she's lifting herself onto her toes, despite the heels making her taller than normal, and brushes those addicting, soft lips against mine.

Snap.

The line she's crossed fades away, ruptured by the shattering of my own self-restraint.

Everything I've been denying doesn't matter. The idea that Nico would have complete rights to end my life, I find myself accepting. Call it selfish, call it whatever name suitable, but in this second, stealing a taste from her before releasing her to another man, is all that matters. In a single action, I destroy my vow. The one I live my life abiding by. The one echoing in my head every time Aurora reveals a bit of her heart to me, or when she makes a snarky comment that cuts at my nerves.

Judgement—depleted.

Levelheadedness—no more.

All gone and replaced by her.

Taking her hair in my grip, I control her movements, tipping her head as I walk us to the window. She gasps into my mouth when her skin touches the cool glass again and her hands shift from my cheeks to my jacket, her fingers curling around my lapel, but that won't do.

With one hand, I manage to bind both hers and lift them above our heads again. She's not allowed to touch me because my sanity won't last if she runs her hands over me.

My tongue skates over those delicious lips of hers, the hint of champagne and cherry. She lets me, her tongue meeting mine confidently, almost like this isn't her first kiss. It *should* be her first kiss.

No. *This* shouldn't be her first kiss. This—us—shouldn't be a kiss at all. First, last, doesn't matter.

She lets out a breathy chuckle, smiling into my mouth, but this isn't a laughing matter. Disloyalty isn't amusing. She rolls her hips into mine, feeling what even my body's given up denying.

With my mouth, I break unspoken promises to Nico and his family. I fuck up a union with the Rossis. Yet, none of it matters when she doesn't fight my hold, or resist the controlling grasp I keep on her hair. She's a natural submissive and my hardening cock demands to see how far I can take this.

Coming up for air, I release her mouth but don't move away. With the hand I have in her hair, I arch her head to the side, baring her neck as my lips trace the smooth column, feeling the precise second she moans.

That moan destroys me.

"I think..." she starts, her breath catching, "I think you've been imagining this very moment."

Against her skin, I speak, so she'll forever feel the imprint of what betrayal feels like. "Have I been imagining losing every ounce of control? Yes."

"I'm glad," she whispers.

Dropping her hands, I do another stupid thing and wrap my arm around her waist, propelling her against my body. Her softness a direct contradiction to my hardness. Given the backless dress, my hand brushes her smooth, bare skin, making me to want to explore every inch and discover where else she's soft.

My hand weaves between the strands of her hair, keeping her steady rather than controlling, as I bring my lips back to her mouth, instead of doing what I crave to do.

To kiss down her body exactly how I dreamed last night. To peel this scrap of a dress from her and explore every inch with my mouth. I'd start between her legs. Right here, on one knee in front of her, her leg tossed over my shoulder, her punishment would begin. Every snarky thing she's said to me is an orgasm, and given the numerous instances worthy of punishment, I'd have her a wrought-out, sloppy mess within minutes.

With her hands free, she grips my shoulders. This should be the moment she pushes me away, when she understands the severity of what's happening, but her nails dig into my coat, clutching me tighter.

"Fuck, *princesse*. You were put into my life to tempt me."

I stroke down her side, finding the slit of her dress, slipping my hand beneath the material. My thumb drags along her upper thigh as my hand flattens, grabbing her leg to lift it so she's only standing on one leg, the other wrapping my waist.

She gasps, tightening her hold on me as I destroy her balance. With my mouth at her throat, tracing lower toward the curves of her breasts, my fingers creep up her leg, nearing her heat. My fingers ache to be inside her. To find her button and make her come over and over—or deny her multiple orgasms as punishment for her brattyness.

I *want* this. Her. Her submission, mine for the taking.

"I dreamed of this," she whispers. "Last night when I was alone in bed. I dreamed of you in ways that made me wet."

I freeze.

My lips manage to lift from her skin, my hand jerks away from her like she burned me, and I study her face. Her puffy lips, the evidence of what we did, her half-lidded eyes drawing me back to continue.

Fuck. Me. No. This isn't—this must end. My own fantasy took off and got away from me, but it's hers that must end this. If she's dreaming of me in such ways, it only solidifies the dangers we're playing in.

Boundaries.

I've shattered those boundaries already, but I'll be damned if I give her more to fill her head with at night.

I lower her leg to the floor, unable to look at her as I end the single most desired moment in my life. But fucking worse than kissing her was when my fingers traced up her thigh, heading toward the area that would damn me.

Damn me to Hell, to death for destroying her family's trust. The taste of heaven I'm positive is worth it, but I won't do that to her. For me to piss off her family is one thing, but this will also come back on her when she's branded as a whore by the traditions the mafia organizations abide by.

She recognizes the second I end the interaction that should never have been. When I rub at my face and back away, abandoning her by the window, gaining distance from her addictive scent to clear my head, to calm my dick, and to cool the fire in my veins, all while self-hate consumes me for doing this to her.

"Rosen—"

"I'm sorry, Miss Corsetti, I took that way too far."

"I started it. Don't do that, Rosen: don't start calling me by my title. You and I both know that's not me."

"It's my job to keep you safe even from me," I remind her, repeating the same statement I said earlier. "You're going to be engaged and there's a protocol in place that I just broke. We can't—"

"Because of your fucking boundaries, right?" She moves into my vision, and no matter how much I turn away from her, she's right fucking there, her hands on her hips. "That's all this is."

"That's *how* this is," I reaffirm, stepping back to gain more distance between us. My eyes remain on the ground, the couches, the moon beyond the window. Anything that isn't her. "Aurora, you're the daughter of a boss. The sister of an underboss and capo. You're going to be engaged to the underboss of another mafia family. I'm merely the soldier assigned to protect you." *Protect you from this very thing,* I think, recalling weeks ago when Nico had a meeting with Erico's father about Aurora's innocence. "This isn't for you," I murmur, my tone softer, packed with regret. "We're of different statuses, and mine isn't one you should be lowering yourself to."

"I'm not—"

"You're not what?" I cut her off, my tone turning cold. *Hate me, so you leave here and we ensure this never occurs again.* "Lowering yourself? Look again, *princesse.*" I gesture to the window to our right, indicating where I had her pinned. "If you go any lower, you'll be on your fuckin' knees."

"Rosen." It's strained with denial, like she's trying to contradict my cruel statements. "You know that's not me. Not sure if you saw me out there—which," she holds up a finger, her dramatic attitude taking over, "I know you did because you couldn't keep your eyes off me. And that's a damn fact you just said yourself, so before you deny, don't forget the conversation we had not even ten minutes ago. But I'm the girl who hangs out with children, who wants to be friends with her bodyguard, who grew up away from this bullshit life."

The thing is, she's not. She might be everything she listed, but she's also what she's running away from—her name.

My hands itch to hold her, to yank her to my chest and kiss away the pain etched on her face. The dismissal, exactly like everyone else has done to her. I despise myself for being yet another person disappointing her.

"Believe me, Aurora, this isn't because I don't want you. It's because I *do*, and now that I've tasted your lips, I ache to taste you everywhere else." *Your breasts, your pussy.* Already what I'm saying is too much. "You're a mafia princess meant to shine for everyone out there. I'll dim your light."

For a long second, she only stares at me. Her eyes convey cold hate, her lips pinched, her shoulders tight, moving with her slight breaths.

Hate me, princesse, if that's what'll make this easier on you.

"I get it," she finally says in a tone implying she doesn't. Still tense, she stalks to the other side of the room. I watch her go, her bare back slightly flushed. I long to see where that flush travels to beneath her dress.

Don't let her leave this room.

The intrusive thought is exactly that—intrusive. I have to let her return to her family and her intended, no matter how much this night has guaranteed I'll never be able to look at her the same.

For her well-being, for her budding relationship with her family...for her future.

She throws open the door, but before leaving the room, she glances back, spotting me where I stand in the exact same spot she left me. Her shoulders look lower than they were when I found her in here, and it makes me fucking sick.

"I do get it, Rosen. You're doing what you've done since day one; making restrictions you and my family feel appropriate. I'm sorry for kissing you and making you feel like you've done something you shouldn't."

Then she leaves. And I'm hollow.

Hollow and yet filled to the brim with guilt. For her, for the Corsettis.

I count to sixty before following Aurora back to the ballroom, using that much-needed time for my dick to calm down. As soon as I'm through the archway, immersed back into the conversational buzz of the elite, my eyes sweep the party to ensure she's returned.

Rossi is easy to spot where he stands beside his parents, but Aurora isn't with them. Then I catch her in the far corner next to Ariella, glaring into her champagne glass. Both women are looking in opposite directions. Aurora seemingly toward the far wall and Ariella, interestingly and oddly enough, focused on Erico.

A few minutes later, Nico announces dinner, and the entire crowd filters down the hall and into the massive dining room. Nico and Della lead them, with his parents following closely behind. Somewhere in the crowd, Rafael leads a woman forward, chatting animatedly to her. Ariella and Aurora join the crowd near the back, almost reluctantly.

I trail behind them, forcing myself to look elsewhere than at the woman mere feet in front of me. She's lost some of that confidence she exuded when first arriving, making me hate myself all over again.

All the guests take their assigned seats, matching themselves to the pre-chosen labelled spots. Aurora, of course, is near the head of the table with the rest of her family, and Erico is seated on her righthanded side. She lowers herself into her chair, throwing a sincere smile over her shoulder at Rossi, who helps tuck her in before taking his own.

Despite everything, *he* gets to make her smile. The way she props her chin up on her hand and leans into him even makes it seem genuine.

I know dozens of ways to murder another human and every single option goes through my head in that second when he rests his hand along her back.

Two servers circle the room, delivering starter salads. As one is distributing hers, she leans away from the table and her attention goes right for me, like she knew exactly where to look. She stares for a beat before turning away, the animosity in her eyes saying more than words could.

Repeating everything I've been telling her. Shouting the reasons I've been pushing her away.

Which is why, for the remainder of the evening, I don't look toward her again. I remain in the corner, in my designated spot, as Nico toasts his new fiancée and the return of his sister, making his family complete. A spot on the floor manages to hold my focus until the end of the evening when everyone leaves and Aurora escorts Rossi out before heading upstairs for bed.

It isn't until I'm finally back in my bedroom that I think of her again. When I consider marching my ass straight to Nico and admitting what happened, I don't, for her sake.

It's not the guilt over the events that keeps me up half the night.

It's the guilt for wanting to do it again. For knowing, vows aside, having her in my arms made it all feel worth it.

26

AURORA

I wake up sick.

Not *sick*, per se, but more like, sick of people. When I roll over and open my eyes, the last thing I want to do is get out of bed and go downstairs. No doubt, my mother will be there, demanding to know what I think of Erico, based on the curious, sly glances she kept sending our way at dinner last night. And then Dad and Nico might ask.

So instead of rolling out of bed, I turn over and bury my head deeper into the pillow. If I'm lucky, I'll suffocate here and will never have to leave this room. With my eyes shut and breathing hindered by the pillow, I let my mind drift to a simpler time. To mere days ago, when I wasn't lusting after my bodyguard, wasn't engaged to be officially engaged, and didn't have a swarm of people around me.

I suppose the grass isn't greener on the other side. For so long, I've wanted to come home, but I hadn't realized home would be so mentally exhausting.

My peace is quickly interrupted when there's a knock at the

door. I groan, waiting for it to open and for someone to barge in.

After a moment, no one does, so I groan again, but this time for another reason. I slide from bed, my feet landing amidst the soft, rich carpet covering my bedroom floor. Grabbing the nearest robe, I tighten it around my waist and walk toward the door.

I'm only partially surprised to find my mother on the other side. And when I say, partially, I mean not at all. Very few people would come hunting for me, and she topped that list.

"Good morning." She smiles tentatively beneath her bright red lipstick, holding a tray of food and looking entirely like someone who shouldn't be delivering food in her blue pantsuit, her hair flattened perfectly straight down her back.

The smell of fried dough and sweet maple syrup has my mouth watering with hunger, but I won't react to her pancake bribery quite yet.

"I brought you food." She states the obvious, lifting the tray up by an inch as though it'll help me to see it easier. "It's nearly ten and you haven't been down."

I shrug one shoulder, aiming to act blasé, but hunger quickly wins out and I step aside, letting her in. "Wasn't really hungry, I guess. Taking it easy today."

Her focused gaze narrows in on me as she steps into my room and rests the tray on a small table. "No garden then? I was hoping you could come with me to the hospital."

My steps falter from where I'm heading for the food, trying not to appear too eager. "Hospital?" What possible reason could she have for going there?

She clasps her hands in front of her, but the tightness of her grip doesn't get by me. She's anxious. Nodding, she replies, "Yes, that's where I volunteer. It's good for the family to garner positive press. I read and play games with the children in at the Montreal Children's Hospital, particularly those on palliative care. It was something that came to be important to me after..." Her lips roll together, and a tightness enters her shoulders. "After," she concludes, not extending the statement. "I was hoping you'd accompany me."

We're a family packed full of secrets. A family who funds community gardens for children, orphanages, and now one of the leaders spends time with sick children. It doesn't make sense, doesn't align with the image I've attached to the Corsetti name.

I don't know what to do. I'm so stuck on disliking my parents. Trapped in this deep rage I feel every time I'm reminded of them wanting to send me away again. Dress shopping was one thing, but a connection like this seems too much.

But looking at my mother's hopeful expression, I realize one thing. For all my rage, I can't deny her this.

"Only us?" I find myself asking.

"Yes. Della's with your brother. And Ariella only leaves when Della does."

"Then sure."

She tips her head in acknowledgment, but I spot the tightening in her hands as she presses them together, pinning her contentedness between them.

"And thank you for breakfast," I add, gesturing to the tray of food now likely getting cold, but certain will still taste good. "I'll get dressed after this. Let me know when you'd like to go."

"Thank you, Aurora. Why don't we leave when you're ready?" Her voice is laced with a serious amount of something that makes my insides knot with fresh, misplaced guilt. Misplaced because she deserves nothing less in my opinion.

Despite the food smelling amazing and activating every hunger response within me, once she leaves and shuts the door behind her, I pick at the food, nothing quite tasting right.

The driver pulls the car in front of the children's hospital after a semi-uncomfortable car ride packed with small talk.

"What's your favourite colour?"

A toss between blue and pink.

"Long or short dresses?"

Depends on the occasion. However, I've had little chance for either.

"Favourite hobby?"

Gardening.

"Night owl or early morning riser?"

Both.

Every single time I responded to one of Mom's questions, the distaste in my mouth grew more sour. Her inquiries are facts a mother should already know. Things that would have developed over childhood and perhaps changed, perhaps remained the same, into adulthood.

At the same time, Mom's probing questions had me relieved. She's trying, and that's all I want, I guess, deep down. If she didn't care, she wouldn't bother asking...right?

Rosen opens the door and Mom steps right out and off to the side, waiting for me to follow. I manage to suck in a quick, calming breath before sliding from the vehicle, resting my hand on Rosen's waiting one, like he did for Mom.

Our skin only touches briefly, but it doesn't stop electricity from passing from him to me. I sneak a peek up, but he's staring above my head, his expression impassive and professional.

We haven't spoken since yesterday when I left him in the sitting room, even as my head continued to replay our interaction as I readied for bed last night. My lips swollen; my body heated in ways I never considered possible. And despite his insistence to be what our roles claim we are, my hand found its way between my legs and I stroked an orgasm from my pussy, imagining the same lips that consumed me with his kisses, licking between them.

The moment I'm out of the car, I take my hand back, cutting off the burst of air his touch grants my lungs, and follow Mom through the hospital's front sliding doors. Rosen trails behind; our single bodyguard since it's only her and me.

Mom approaches the front desk, waving to the receptionist, but I stop paying attention, steps faltering halfway through the space as I take in the lobby.

Holy colours. It's like a rainbow threw up in here.

I hadn't realized bright, sun yellow was an acceptable colour for *any* place, but alas, this hospital managed to make the impossible happen and I'm assaulted with way too much of it. Every second wall is painted white, as though it's supposed to offset the yellow. But if the yellow wasn't bad enough, the entire room's trim is green.

How is this normal? Suddenly, I pity the staff working here. For their sake, I hope they go home to neutral colours and bland paint, if only to clean their visual palettes before returning to this hellhole the next day.

I scan the lobby, the blue and green chairs. The large, wooden toybox overflowing with colourful toys. Carpets that are also a combination of colours because, apparently, *nothing* can be plain in this place. They're really trying to make a statement.

"This place makes me hate every colour except black and white."

A subtle snort comes from the figure beside me, and I catch the briefest smile on Rosen's face. Shockingly, he glances toward me, making a flash of heat pool in my stomach.

The receptionist immediately jumps into action with

Mom's approach. Papers scatter over her desk as a brunette woman with too much energy comes around the side of the desk, her hand stretched for Mom to take.

"Mrs. Corsetti, we weren't sure if you'd be making it today since we've heard that your..." The bubbly woman glances past Mom, her eyes finding me, and her look manages to fill in the gap of what she was saying.

"Melissa. How are you today? This is my daughter, yes. Aurora would like to accompany me."

"O-of course, Mrs. Corsetti. I hope you don't mind, but hospital policy decrees she'll have to fill out the volunteer package. The same one you had to once." A pink lip slips beneath her teeth and she rocks back on her feet, clearly nervous to be making such demands.

Because even Mom, based on her last name, commands fear within the city.

"That won't be a problem. I understand. We haven't had a chance to get her other background checks, but I suspect that won't be an issue, right?"

Once again, our name prevails when the woman stutters her agreement.

"Y-yeah, that won't be an issue. We understand. We appreciate everything your family does here." Her gaze sweeps the three of us, but when it lands on Rosen, they widen. She scans him up and down, having *just* noticed the massive shadow hanging over all of us. I suppose, for other people, he could be good at melting into the background. While, for me, he's front and fucking centre, aggravating and hateful, sexy and breathtaking, no matter how much I pretend he isn't.

As Melissa retrieves the volunteer package, Mom turns to me. "It'll ask some basic information. Name, phone number, that sort of stuff. They track the people who come through here."

"Got it."

Melissa returns with a stack of forms stuck to a clipboard and hands them to me along with a pen. "You can take a seat, if you'd like, but the forms won't take long." Then she rubs her lips together as she glances uncertainly toward Rosen.

"He's already been cleared," Mom fills in.

"R-right." The woman nods, more of a quick bob of her head, and she retreats to her desk.

Rosen has been here before? With Mom? I assumed she came with her own bodyguard, Thomas, while Rosen was off doing whatever my brothers demanded of him.

As Mom stated, it's only basic information, a privacy statement, a few checkboxes, claiming I've brought other documentation with me—ID, police check—all things I guess Mom got them to wave off. Finally, I hand the package back to Melissa. She barely skims it before gesturing toward the attached hallway.

"You know the way, Mrs. Corsetti. They'll be so excited to meet you, Aurora. I hope you have a lovely time."

Like we're not *heading toward a ward of sick kids?*

Mom turns toward the other colourful hall Melissa pointed to. This time, the walls are white, but that grass-green trim remains. At least they had some sense before sending children down a vivid hall from hell.

"It's bright," I comment.

Mom chuckles, taking the first right, passing by a series of rooms, doctors, nurses, and medical equipment, I wouldn't know the name of if I spent all day studying them. "I had the same thought once, but the colours really amplify it for the children. They're trying to make it comfortable and less like..."

A final resting place, I mentally fill in.

"A hospital," is what I say instead.

"Precisely."

Mom leads Rosen and me toward another hallway; this time, it opens into a waiting room that's nearly as bright as the entrance. The theme seems to be more pinks and blues, and I can say with complete accuracy, this hospital has officially ruined my favourite colours.

Another woman, this one older than Melissa, but with a personality just as vivacious, is backing out of a room, her expression full of wide smiles as she jots something on a clipboard. She looks up at our entrance, that smile somehow getting larger.

"Ah, Mrs. Corsetti. Melissa messaged and said you and your daughter were on your way down. Welcome." She sticks her hand out toward me. "Nice to meet you, Aurora. The kids will be excited to have another visitor."

She glances toward Rosen and nods once with a tight smile, not questioning his presence.

But then I glance toward him, and his gaze is locked on a nearby door, a look of longing in its depths. I get the sense there's more to Rosen than he's ever let on, but before I can ask, Mom tugs me farther down the wing.

Caterina pulls Aurora down the hallway, toward the last door, as per her pattern. Usually, Caterina comes here with Thomas, but I've accompanied her frequently enough that I know her system.

Once I see them enter a room, I turn for the nearest one, opening it after a quick knock, despite already knowing what I'll find. *Who* I'll find.

My sister sits in the rocker by the window, a mystery novel in her hand. She slowly drags her gaze away from the book, hardly caring who's entering the room, given how much she's used to the various nurses and doctors completing their rounds.

Her expression brightens, and she rests the book on the table beside her, instantly rushing across the room and into my arms. "Rosen! You didn't tell me you were coming today. When you visited the other day, you made it sound like your new task would be keeping you away for a while."

Yeah, well, when the new task ends up visiting here. "I hadn't known before an hour ago."

"So, plenty of time for you to text."

I shrug, releasing her from our hug. "You know what the job's like, Poppy. Something could have changed, and I didn't want to disappoint you. Look at how frequently that happened with Dad growing up."

"Who you recently missed, by the way," she comments as I move toward the bed, and the child resting there. "He left maybe an hour ago."

I take one of the boy's hands in my own. Elliot's small five-year-old hand doesn't even fill the width of my palm, reminding me, once again, how tiny my nephew is.

"He was awake earlier for a short time," Poppy says as she comes up to the other side of the bed, standing across from me. "The treatment's really kicking his ass this week."

She acts strong, but my job involves knowing people's tells, their true emotions, and Poppy continuously pretends that after two years of dealing with her son's illness, she's fine with it.

Elliot's skin is cold and pasty, but I don't comment on it. I brush my other hand over his head—bald from the treatment— and lean down to press a kiss to his forehead. My heart feels like it's breaking all over, knowing a child, who should be experiencing kindergarten and meeting new friends and facing all the fun and thrills that accompany a child's first year of school, is instead stuck here.

"Any update?"

Poppy shakes her head, her gaze going soft as she stares at her son a beat longer before retreating to her seat. Exhaustion tears at her body and her shoulders slump, her head rolling to the side of the recliner, having no more energy to keep it upright.

Since Elliot's diagnosis a year ago, my sister practically moved in here, spending most of her time by his side. In the evening, after work, her husband, Theo, visits too before taking his wife home for a night's sleep.

Very few people know about Elliot. The Corsettis do because they've had a connection to my family for many years. First with Dad, and then me. When Poppy initially called with the news, I was out with Nico. It was then that I got another piece of the Corsettis' kindness.

They're the reason Elliot is being cared for in a private suite and Poppy and Theo have nearly twenty-four-hour access to him. When a hospital receives some of its funding from them, they have a lot of pull.

"How's your new charge?" my sister asks suddenly.

Despite Dad and I both working for the Corsettis, Poppy has always been on the outside of this life, able to live a normal one, even when Dad was bringing me to the mansion after school to train with Nico and Rafael—and once Hawke. She's never been in the dark, aware of what taking the vows truly mean, having spent time with Caterina before.

"She's fine," I manage, fighting to keep a blank expression.

She's addicting. She's sexy. She makes me want to keep her locked away. She makes me want to kill Rossi. She makes me confused, lost in a turbulent storm of maddening hate and forbidden desire.

My sister grunts, her brows lifting to her hairline. "The last time we spoke you mentioned disliking the new task."

"Still do. Your point?"

"You seem...different."

"That a bad thing?" My attention returns to Elliot and the monitor tracking his heartbeat, focusing on that instead of the truth my sister attempts to drag from me.

"It's a thing," she finally responds. "Careful, Rosen. Don't forget what she is to you."

My jaw snaps together. I don't mean it to, don't want to feel that irritation creeping up my form and wrapping my nerves, tightening them to the point they're impossible to hide. Even my fucking sister reminds me of what I already know.

I don't comment, instead dragging the nearest plastic chair closer. It squeals against the flooring before I drop into it, keeping Elliot's hand in my palm, my thumb gently stroking over his skin.

The room falls silent, and Poppy's eyes flutter shut. She sleeps so little now, and Theo's often reporting her passing out on the car ride home. My sister is drained, mentally and physically. The day Elliot's diagnosis came, I not only lost my nephew's lively attitude and energy, but my sister's too.

When the door opens, I leap to my feet, immediately on guard, even if it's only a nurse coming for their rounds. But when Aurora enters, she smirks, catching my quick movements.

"Only me," she murmurs. "Nurse said you were in here." Her gaze slowly peruses the room, landing on my nephew and then Poppy, who also stands, drifting toward the hospital bed, her hand resting over Elliot's hand in a protective manner.

I release Elliot to position myself in front of Aurora, blocking her view, even as she tries to peek around me.

"Um."

"Need something?" I keep my tone gruff, hiding the fact that my heart thumps louder having her around.

"I took a break to use the bathroom and was surprised not to find you out in the hall. I asked the nurse where you'd gone. She said you were in here, but didn't say..." Her teeth scrape over her bottom lip, her question hovering right there.

"With who." I fill in when she doesn't finish.

My family isn't a secret to hers, but this is one of many things about me I've never told Aurora. One of many things that simply haven't come up with everything else going on. After a shared agreement with Poppy, I step aside, allowing Aurora past me.

"This is Elliot. My nephew."

Her mouth slips open, her head twisting around to look at me. Clearly not the answer she was expecting.

"And my sister, Poppy."

Poppy jumps into action, and for all her reservations seconds ago, she reaches across the bed to offer her hand. Aurora takes it, but it's clear in how limp her arm is, she's still shocked.

Aurora glances from my sister, to me, and then toward the bed, her expression cracking, the true Aurora peeking out. The one I've seen in very few instances, when she's not spewing attitude to me and her family.

"Your nephew," she repeats, her statement barely audible. To him, she murmurs, "Hi, Elliot."

I share a look with my sister, but she watches on like nothing's wrong. For me, my heartbeat quickens, her empathy to speak directly to him, despite him unable to respond, chokes me up.

"Is he..." Aurora glances at Poppy, her question left unfinished.

"He's sleeping," Poppy replies. "The treatment has been rough on him lately because they're trying new things they hope will work better."

"He was diagnosed with cancer last year. He's been in care ever since," I add, explaining further.

That's all I'm planning on telling her, but my sister continues, "Your family has been very generous in helping us. They're the reason he's able to receive such great treatment here."

Aurora flinches, but it's the only sign that she's heard Poppy. She yanks her hand away and steps away from the bed. And from me.

I almost reach for her. Almost pull her back to my side, but it's the jangle of her bracelets, the shine of her skin as the dull overhead light passes over her that reminds me of the differences between us. Where she's meant to be, and who she's meant to be with. Last night crashes down on me. Kissing her seems so far in the past, especially with the knowledge it'll never happen again.

So I let her pace backward, even as her gaze gets unfocused and her throat chokes up with her rough swallows. She barely spares me another glance before escaping from the room, letting the door fall shut.

I stare after her, at the door for longer than I mean to, and when I turn back around, it's met with a disbelieving look of contempt.

"What was that?"

"I'm not sure. I don't know why she ran out like—"

"Not that," Poppy interrupts. "I mean, that little lost puppy thing you nearly did to follow her. The moment she entered this room, you gravitated toward her. There's, like, an electricity between you two." She pauses, her expression lighting up. "Oh. *Oh.*"

Fuck. Of anyone in this world, Poppy's always been able to read me well. "No, it's not like that."

"But you want it to be." She pauses again, her eyes raking the skin off my body until spotting the truth buried beneath. "No, it already is. Tell me you didn't touch her."

"Yes. No. And can you speak quieter, please?" I snap, glancing at the door again, worried Caterina is nearby and overhear. She always stops by Elliot's room last, and based on how little time we've been here, she shouldn't be around for a while, but still.

Poppy shakes her head before returning to her chair and lifting her book, ending our conversation. "I've said it once and I'll say it again. Be careful, Rosen. I know you're a part of that life, and I might not know all the fancy bullshit rules they live by, but I understand enough. She's not the kind of woman who ends up with the guard. There's always someone of rank to sweep her off her feet."

Rossi won't save her. He'll trap her. He'll force the crown on her head and drag her into a life of silent submission, breaking the fiery brat I've come to know.

Not. My. Problem.

That's what I recite in my head, anyway, but it doesn't stop my attention from drifting toward the door again, picturing Aurora beyond it.

28

AURORA

My parents are the villains.

They *have* to be.

They're the bad guys. They ruined Hawke's life. They were wed through blood, pain, and deception; a war started by my father. They sent me away, only to marry me off even before I returned.

They are *not* good. Mom doesn't volunteer to read to sick children. They deal drugs, run illegal weapons, and dabble in gambling. And fuck knows what else. They lie, steal, cheat, and murder anyone who gets in their way. They make alliances with other rich motherfucking families to ensure prosperity, to guarantee this life of crime lives on through generations.

They *don't* fund orphanages and community gardens for underprivileged children.

They *don't* pay for a bodyguard's family member's medical care. They don't.

They *can't*.

They can't be those people.

Things are black and white. Heaven and Hell, as the nuns

once put it. Good and evil. That's how it is. It's how balance exists throughout the world.

The bad guys can't *also* be good.

In a flurry of movement, I escape Elliot's room and the watchful, probing gaze of Rosen and his sister.

When I think I've caught my breath in the hallway, the crack in my heart continues, breaking yet one more piece from the organ. It falls to my feet, landing on the laminate flooring in a pile of muddled dust. It's gone, like my mind. Lost. Without direction.

With my back to the wall, my legs nearly give out, but a door opening and shutting forces my muscles to continue working for at least a bit longer. I don't glance up, but Mom's telltale heels click against the flooring as she approaches.

"There you are." She pauses, her gaze sliding to the door at my right. "You've met Elliot."

The mention of that little boy's name increases my requirement to know for sure. "Is it true?" I ask through dry, cracked lips. "You're paying for his private room?"

"Nico insisted. Your father and I didn't argue it because we agreed it's the right thing to do for Rosen's family." She pauses, her lips pressing together. "You probably don't remember, but Rosen is the same age as Hawke, so he spent a lot of time with your brothers growing up. His father, Marcus, was once my main bodyguard before he retired. Rosen trained with your brothers. When Hawke..." she trails off, pain flashing through her depths, "Rosen got closer to Nico. I think Nico started to see him as another brother in Hawke's place. He's like family."

And family cares for family.

Is that what they did for me? Sending me away for my "safety," but never bringing me home when the danger passed.

There is no grey. Black and white. That's it. That's all there can be.

"When did you start volunteering here?"

Mom looks away, shifting until her back is against the wall beside me. She inspects one of her nails, lightly, mindlessly scraping at the dark polish.

"Many years ago. I can't pinpoint the exact year, but I needed something outside of the organization to keep me busy and away from the death and grime. Something that—" She stops, swallowing. Her hands fall limply to her sides, hitting the wall beside me. "Something that reminded me of you and your brother."

What? No. My eyes become unfocused again, the feeling of tears pricking them.

"When Hawke left, he took a part of me with him. Your father and I fought viciously for allowing all the days he had to pass in which Hawke was in their captivity. Him choosing to leave us..." She sighs, heavy and drawn out. "He never hid his distaste for the mafia, but he knew what his role as first-born meant. When he left, I almost wasn't surprised. He had the prime opportunity to escape, and he took it, and I don't blame him, even when I didn't accept that I lost one of my children."

This is how the bad guys lure one in, right? They share a part of themselves to increase empathy. This isn't...*No.* Even as my stomach curdles and the demand to hold myself—and her —grows, I hold firm in my resentment.

"In the midst of your father and me fighting, there was one thing we agreed on. One stupid thing. I was terrified, even after the bastards who took Hawke were slaughtered, that they— *someone*—would return for the rest of my children."

"Which is why I was sent away," I fill in.

"Yeah. In a short time, I lost two of my children. I fell into a sense of depression in the years following. Nothing your siblings or father would do helped. Even your aunt gave up and stopped coming around, but before leaving, she suggested I fill my time by helping others in place of you." She looks toward me, eyes darkening with old regrets that cause the hate to loosen in my heart in the smallest way, despite my feeble mental attempt to still grasp onto it. "That's when I started volunteering here. Hanging out with the kids gives me a sense of...I don't know. *Not* being a horrible mother."

What do I say to that? What *can* I say to that? Deny her claim, but my thoughts align with hers—she's a bitch for abandoning me my entire life. Villains make you empathetic of their struggles and I'll continue to hold firm to that each minute of this.

Even if I feel myself losing this fight.

"I know you think badly of us, Aurora, and I don't expect anything less. I didn't bring you here to gain your forgiveness. I genuinely wanted us to do this together, but for you to also see another side of the family and who we are."

"Orphanages. Gardens. Rosen's nephew."

"Like I said, he's like a brother to Nico, so when he received the news, we simply wanted to do what we could for him and his family. We've also donated to cancer research this year, in hopes our money can help more people like Elliot."

"C-can—" *What? No.* "But death. Drugs." Do my rambles even make sense at this point?

She chuckles without humour. "Sometimes it's good to spend our money on things that mean something. Medical research in the name of helping Rosen's family is worth it."

No.

They can't.

No. *I* can't. I can't fall for this.

Mom clearly doesn't notice my mental battle when she pushes off the wall and brushes a hand down her pantsuit, turning to face the door I'm standing beside.

"I always pop in to see Elliot and spend time with Poppy.

Some adult company, which I feel she desperately deserves. You met Rosen's sister, I assume?"

I nod, still unable to manage a verbal response that doesn't involve a scream.

"Did you want to come back in with me?"

I shake my head.

"Okay." She reaches out to cup my cheek, and while I initially flinch, I don't shy away, watching her through wide eyes as she gently and briefly touches me, a sad smile gracing her lips before she steps by me and into the room.

With her gone, my legs buckle again. The nurse from earlier exits one of the other rooms and shoots me a strange look.

"Miss, why don't you sit down?" She gestures to a row of colourful chairs nearby.

Sit. She wants me to *sit*? Sitting is impossible when falling seems more probable.

Movement at all requires an energy I no longer have. Breath to keep my lungs going. Breath to reduce the anxiety attack I feel creeping up.

Somehow, I shove away from the wall, practically running down the hallway of white and bright green until I'm farther away from my mother.

Away from the truth that threatens to crawl up. Away from the grey facts of this life.

Perhaps everything isn't so black and white.

Perhaps.

29

ROSEN

She looks so broken. Lost. Unlike the girl I've come to know; the playful, sexy woman who teases me at every turn.

I approach Aurora, who's sitting at the end of the hall with her knees drawn up to her chest and her head resting on them. Her arms are tightly wrapped around her and I long to be the one to do that *for* her. For years, she's had no one to rely on. No one to fully trust, and she made it more than known yesterday that I was someone she found herself relying on, putting me in an impossible position: hurting her or supporting her.

She's exactly where the nurse indicated she had disappeared. After greeting Caterina, I excused myself on the pretense of a break. Poppy had watched me leave with that same warning glare that told me she sees right through my lie.

Aurora doesn't look up at my approach. I slide to the floor beside her, waiting a full ten seconds before I speak, when the pain of watching her silent sobs causing her body to jerk gets too much to handle.

"Princesse." The nickname slips out before I can remind myself to use her full name.

"Go away."

"Not when you're like this."

"Why not? Pretty sure a bodyguard isn't meant to comfort their charge. You've made the boundaries between us beyond clear, so," she lifts her head, looking toward me through red-rimmed eyes that send a kick to my gut, "go the fuck away, Rosen. I don't need your help."

I pull my own legs up and rest my arms over them, adopting a pose of indifference as I stare straight ahead, watching down the hall should her mother or my sister happen upon us.

"You might not need it, but I want to give it."

"Why?" she snarls. "Fuck off."

Ah, there she is. It's relieving to find a little bit of that fight remaining.

"Because I want to, Aurora. Despite all the things we can't be, I don't enjoy seeing you hurt. What happened?" I ask, continuing to talk regardless of her glare, "You ran out of Elliot's room fast."

She doesn't speak at first, but her glare does break, her stare going to a spot on the floor in front of us. I'll wait for as long as she needs. A full three minutes pass before she speaks and it's so low, my ears strain to hear her.

"For years, I've viewed this damn family—my parents, brothers, *you*—your type, anyway—as the villains. Monsters. Sending a child away are actions of bad people. But then, to hear—to *see* the evidence that they are good. Or, at least have good parts."

She's so stuck on hating her family, she's never considered they could be decent. This reminds me of when she learned about the funding behind the garden, but somehow, it's more too. Less ignorable now.

"It doesn't change the fact they *are* mobsters. They will kill to get ahead if that makes you feel better."

She snorts, shaking her head. "I wish it did, but no. Then Mom tells me why she's here. How she regrets the past and uses this place as some sort of healing method for losing both Hawke and me."

I recall the woman I knew as a kid and how Nico and I often overheard her crying. "Your mother is one to always give it to people straight. She never beats around the truth."

Aurora wipes at her face, snudging her mascara. I slide over, pressing my side to hers, granting her the small comforts I can, while resisting the craving to pull her onto my lap and hold her properly.

"Why are you being nice to me?" she asks suddenly.

"Do you not want me to?" I lean away, although I certainly have no plans to go anywhere.

"No. I mean, yesterday—"

"I was out of line, *princesse*. I'm sorry."

Aurora doesn't respond for a full minute, but when she does, it's with a slightly different topic. She pushes strands of hair away from her face, revealing a sexy, playful smirk, confirming to me she'll be all right. "It sucks to be dragged back to a place where there's systems and shit in place I'm supposed to follow, but hardly understand. To be trailed by a man who's been able to see through my façade from the very first meeting, but learn, due to protocol," she spits the term I used last night, "I can't be his friend. Sorry for the part I played yesterday. Everything you've done for me is appreciated, and I understand you're close to my family. Probably closer than I am. And you think last night broke some rule."

Don't think. I know it did. I don't say that, becoming over-whelmed by every one of my muscles tightening, but it's pure will that keeps my hands off the woman I'm moments away from dragging into a nearby closet and ensuring today ends with a smile on her face.

"This is all so fucked up. My parents are trying. Kinda." She shrugs a single shoulder. "Well, Mom is. Nico's Nico. Rafael seems too busy. Ariella and Della give the impression of trying to figure it out themselves, although they've been great. Not that I'm saying I want everyone to hover, but I'm struggling with a connection to any of them. But you…"

As much as I wish to hear her finish that statement, I play devil's advocate and suggest, "Perhaps because you're so determined to see us all as the villains, you've built a wall around yourself."

"I lumped you into that pile too."

Until I showed her kindness, which in hindsight, maybe I shouldn't have.

"Anyway," she continues, not addressing what I mentioned, "Thank you, Rosen. For being here. In general. And," she gestures between us, "now. For listening to me."

"Always," I reply, voice getting thick with an unspoken emotion.

But even as I say it, I know it's a lie. I won't always be here for her. I'm simply staff, and once she's married, she will be a Rossi. A Rossi bodyguard will be assigned to protect its new queen. I'll be here, watching from afar as she's handed to someone who won't give her the attention she craves.

Luckily, or unluckily, the door to Elliot's room opens, so I push to my feet. By the time Caterina enters the hallway, waving goodbye to my sister, I'm standing upright, offering my hand for Aurora to take.

She does, dropping it nearly right away, but in the briefest moment of our skin touching, I want to believe something passes through her to me.

Fresh understanding of one another.

30

AURORA

I t's the day after visiting the hospital, and I continue to ignore everything I learned yesterday about my family, tucking even more truths away to a place where I can pretend they don't exist, and ask Rosen to drive me to the community garden in the afternoon.

He doesn't speak to me on the trip there, but it feels like the animosity between us has lessened. The silence is natural again. Something broke and rebuilt between us all at the same time.

"I won't be long," I remark as I climb from the car before he can come around to open my door.

"No?"

"No."

Because while I'm ignoring truths and apologized to him yesterday for my behaviours, I woke this morning, with everything that happened yesterday still in my head. Everything Mom said and everyone I witnessed caring for Rosen's nephew, and I want to be a part of that in the only way I can be.

I leave him outside, finding Clarisse in the back with a single child. It's well before school ends, but I expected this, and planned for it.

Clarisse glances up from where she's working at the strawberry plants with the young boy, her head tipping in question.

As I approach, I explain, "I'm not here to stay. That rose bush I've been tending to," I gesture toward the other side of the yard, "do you mind if I take some? I know they're typically for the kids, but I'd really like to gift something I've been nurturing on my own."

"How could I say no to that? Pick whatever." After murmuring something to the boy, she stands and follows me toward the flower patches. Over her shoulder, I catch the child slip a strawberry in his mouth, his cheeks getting redder than the fruit as he spots me watching him.

I wink, turning to the rose bush, reaching for the gloves I last left there, so I can pick the thorny plant.

"I'll get you trimmers and thorn strippers."

Clarisse returns a moment later with the tools and hands me the trimmers first, so I can remove the flowers by the stem. As I cut them, she takes them from me and strips the thorns, laying them in a small pile until we have nearly a dozen.

"What's the occasion?"

"My bodyguard's sister and nephew. I'd like to do something nice for them. I suppose you can say I experienced a lot of revelations yesterday."

She makes a noise that says she's heard me but doesn't quite understand the meaning behind my words, which is fine; she doesn't have to. As I gather the bushel, she leads me to the shrub of baby's breath.

"You can't have a rose bouquet without these." She snips a few handfuls off and sticks them in between the roses, creating a lovely gathering of flowers. "They'll love it."

"I hope so." After a tight, grateful smile and a wave to the child still munching on strawberries, I return to the front of the building, announcing my arrival by opening the vehicle door and getting in.

Rosen jerks up from his phone, glancing at me and then at the flowers in my hand.

Before he can ask the question I know he's about to, I say, "Can we go back to the hospital?" Then I realize I haven't planned whatsoever. What if too much company is overstimulating for Poppy and Elliot and they don't want it?

Rosen's brows furrow, but he simply replies, "Sure," before starting the car and taking us back toward the thick of the city and to downtown, where the Montreal Children's Hospital is located.

It's not long before he's pulling into a spot in the massive parking lot. Nerves make it difficult to remain still, so the second the car is off, I hop out, careful not to shake the flowers too roughly so they don't lose any of their petals.

What if this is a bad idea? What if this is an action driven by emotion and is silly? I mean, flowers? That boy needs what my family is trying to give him, not a plant.

A rough touch glides against my right wrist, yanking me back to the present, to where I'm standing beside the massive, multi-floored complex.

"You're stressing. My sister will appreciate them."

Again, somehow he reads me. "How do you know it's for them?"

One brow lifts as he steps away, walking across the lot and leaving me to follow behind. "It's not for every other child in there or else many cars would be required to cart all the flowers here. You also wouldn't worry if it was someone else. I drew my own conclusions."

"Well, you're right," I grumble.

Thankfully, the same woman from yesterday, Melissa, is

behind the reception desk. She waves eagerly as we head in the same direction we had yesterday. A different nurse mans the desk in the wing, but the second she spots Rosen, she shifts her attention toward her tasks. Clearly, he visits enough that multiple nurses recognize him.

Rosen steps by me, entering Elliot's room first, after a quick knock.

An "Uncle Rosen!" immediately follows, and my grip tightens around the bouquet, wishing that Clarisse hadn't stripped the thorns from them, so the sharp points could make me bleed and pain would distract me.

Rosen glances over his shoulder and it's that look that encourages me to enter the room. I first focus on Poppy, who stands from where she was seated on the edge of her son's bed.

"Twice in two days?"

Rosen shrugs, moving immediately toward the bed, his attention focused on the young child, eagerly awaiting.

"Sorry," I fill in. "I wanted to…um." Shoving the bouquet at her isn't the best way I could do this, but it's what happens. "I helped grow these. Well, I guess they were there before I was, but I've spent time tending to them and—"

"They're lovely." Poppy takes them, smiling over the petals. "They'll enhance the room with some new life, thank you."

The vivid colours outlining the walls don't exactly say this place should be brighter, but the sentiment is appreciated, so with the awkward part over, I look to the bed. To the factor I hadn't considered. That Elliot might be awake for this visit.

Rosen has his large arms around the boy, swallowing him up, but the glee in Elliot's expression is so infectious, I can't help but smile too. Awake, he seems so lively, and if this is him during treatment, I can't imagine what he was like beforehand.

"Uncle Rosen, I'm so happy you're back." Through

Rosen's grip, dark eyes—exactly like Rosen's—land on me. "She's new."

Rosen releases his nephew but doesn't move away. "This is my friend, Aurora."

Mom's mentioned the numerous times she's visited Elliot and Poppy, but I wonder how much this five-year-old knows. Is he aware Mom is his uncle's boss?

Either way, I slowly approach, glancing first at Poppy to gauge her reaction. Thankfully, she tips her head to the side, granting me permission.

"Hi, Elliot. My name's Aurora, like your uncle said. I visited yesterday, but you were asleep, so I simply *had* to come back to meet you." A small, white lie, but one worth it for the grin that consumes his expression.

"How do you know my name?"

"Because your uncle told me."

Elliot shoots a dramatic, open-mouthed look toward his uncle, which makes the entire room laugh. More so when he yells, "You ruined it, Uncle Rosen! Now I can't be the one to tell her."

Oh, a five-year-old's mind. Rosen ruined nothing, considering Elliot hadn't known we'd be stopping by.

Rosen plays along and replies, "Sorry, pal. She continued to ask and ask and *ask*! I had no choice."

Elliot wrinkles his nose, but moves on from the topic, lifting his toy cars from his lap into a handful his tiny hands can't properly hold. "Come look at what I have, Aurora."

Rosen moves aside, allowing me to take his place by his nephew's side. He heads for his sister, and I hear him murmur, "If you wanted a small break, we'll be here."

"These are so cool, Elliot. Which one is your favourite?"

He seems to consider that, going through each one carefully before lifting a blue one. "This one. Wanna know why?"

"Why?"

"Because blue's my favourite colour."

"No way!" I throw my hands up dramatically, taking the car as he hands it to me. "Want to know a secret?"

"What's that?" he whisper-yells, his gaze momentarily darting to his family on the other side of the room, not wanting them to overhear the "secret."

Playing along, I lower my voice to a loud whisper too. "Blue's also my favourite colour."

"Whoa. We're like the same then. Wanna play?" He offers another car, a red one, which I take too.

Suddenly, Poppy's voice cuts through Elliot's excitement. "You know, maybe I will take that break, guys. Thank you." Her gaze lingers on me, but I pretend not to notice as I begin playing whatever game her son invented. I don't think it's a bad look she's giving, or else, I'd assume she wouldn't leave. Still, my stomach flips for unknown reasons.

When the door shuts, Elliot barely spares her a glance, but exclaims to his uncle, "Uncle Rosen, you have cool friends. Did you know, we have the same favourite colour?"

Like Rosen hadn't overheard our entire conversation. Then again, it was a "secret."

Rosen proves to be uncle of the year and responds with, "Really? That's neat."

"Guess!"

Rosen rubs at his chin, fake musing. "Hmm, red?"

"Wrong!"

"Green?"

"Wrong!"

"Purple?"

"Wrong! Want me to tell you?"

Rosen sighs dramatically, nodding. "You might have to, buddy. I'm not smart enough to guess." His eyes flick to me quickly, his lips pulling up in a smirk that tells me he knows exactly what he's doing.

"Blue!" Elliot shouts.

"Well, I was a few guesses off then." Rosen holds his hands up in a playful shrug.

Elliot, now finished with that conversation, leaps right into a long dialogue about his cars, which I devour every single word of, nodding at everything he divulges, replying when my turn, and laughing at his cute comments.

It started with flowers, but this day became more than I ever expected.

31

ROSEN

The text arrives as we exit the hospital, the sun nearly completely set now. It's been a while since I've gotten to spend that much time with Elliot and my sister, typically getting called away for work.

I tuck my phone away without answering my sister's message. I can't. Doing so puts into words what today meant. What it meant to Poppy. To Elliot. To me.

Not many people drop by to visit them. Outside of our father, me, Caterina, and occasionally Nico and Rafael—rarely —Elliot doesn't meet new people, unless new doctors and nurses freshly hired count. I knew when my sister left us alone with Elliot, it wasn't for a break. It was because the emotion clouding her eyes got to be too much. She can hide it from many people, but not me.

I've never brought someone to meet my family. Never wanted to.

Outside, when Aurora should be marching her ass across the street toward the parking lot, she turns, heading for the sidewalk. I catch up to her instantly.

"Where do you think you're going?"

"Out."

"You are out."

"No." Her arms spread wide, gesturing to the skyline above us, to the numerous skyrises outlined against the nearly dark sky. "*Out*. Rosen, out into the city."

"I can think of every reason why that's a bad idea."

"Can you?" She smiles playfully and with no warning, skips ahead, ending in a light jog until she reaches the sidewalk, spinning as her head tips back, a look of glee consuming her expression. It pains me to be the one to steal that look away when I do my job.

Nico never said where she could and couldn't go, simply that I must be with her. But downtown in the evening is when it starts to become unsafe. When the criminals come out to play and protecting her becomes more difficult.

"Get over here."

"Nope." She walks faster.

I get closer, and she again skips backwards, keeping out of reach. She'd be easy to catch, but I let her have her fun. For now.

"We're always stuck in that mansion. Are you telling me you never go out to do anything fun?"

"No. My life is my job."

She stops walking to stare meaningfully at me. "Seriously? That's depressing."

I shrug, my feet eating up much of the sidewalk to get closer to her. When she notices, she picks her pace up again.

"It is what it is. I enjoy my job. There's nothing else I want."

"A girlfriend."

Such a taboo word, considering what's transpired between us. "You think I would kiss you while I was with someone?"

"No, not now. I'm talking in the past."

"No one I ever wanted that much until now." I should have stopped the sentence two words sooner, but thankfully, she pays me no attention.

"Well, I'm getting bored in that house. If we're not there, we're at the community garden and somewhere new would be great before I die. In case you've forgotten, I didn't grow up like every other woman in this city. And my family is so overly protective, they've given me my own stalker before shipping me off to my next cage."

She's smirking as she talks, but the meaning beneath her words is weighted. She's correct in that being raised in a convent meant she missed out on many typical life experiences other women her age would already have done.

At the end of the sidewalk, we come to an intersection of one of the busier roads. The light is red, and she stops, frowning at the traffic, and then at me. "I guess back to the car then? End of the road for me. Literally."

We should. But the disappointment lowering her countenance makes my heart burn. No one from her family has messaged me, wondering where we went off to, so for now, it feels like we're free.

Tapping the crosswalk button, I signal our intent to cross. "If you want to see Montreal how the locals see it, there's no harm."

There's a ton of harm, but she doesn't have to know that.

"Seriously?"

When the crosswalk flashes with a white person walking, I start across the road, knowing she'll follow me into the thick of city life.

"I wouldn't be walking if I wasn't serious. You've lived in

Toronto, and now here, and yet, you've never experienced downtown city life." I suppose, she still won't. Not really. Being downtown at night brings forth other experiences she most definitely won't have, not with me here, but the sentiment remains.

And the way she smiles indicates she doesn't care.

Across the road, she checks up and down the sidewalk, glancing through the crowds of people. Since we're not on Saint-Catherine Street, the busiest boulevard, it's not too packed. But there's certainly enough that to keep a close watch on her and everyone around us.

"Don't do what you did earlier." Tipping my head in the way we came, I indicate my meaning. "Skipping ahead like that. We'll return to the car immediately if you don't stay close."

"*Fine*, grump." She pouts playfully, making my hand twitch with the craving to punish her for her bratty antics, and moves one step ahead. She spins, her arms lifting above her head. "Don't realize how tall the buildings are until you're beside them. It's different in a car."

I glance up the side of the nearest one, thinking how normal this all seems, considering I've spent my entire life here. Not only in the city, but *in* it.

"I'll take your word for it."

We manage another few feet. People stream around us, like she emits an invisible barrier that prevents her from walking into them. It's interesting because people here don't usually give two shits. Every man for himself kind of vibes. But the mafia princess controls the public even now.

After another block of her taking in everything, she falls into step beside me again. Unfortunate, since I was getting an extreme amount of joy in seeing her so happy. A simple thing— freedom. For her sake, I hope Erico takes her to explore the local life of New York.

"If you ever get the chance, visit Old Montreal, Chinatown, Mount Royal, and the Botanical Gardens—you'd really appreciate the Gardens, especially."

Her smile falters, both of us aware that her opportunities might be limited soon.

"Outings with your parents, perhaps," I suggest, giving her realistic options. "Or Della and Ariella, if you're interested in getting to know them better." Anyone but me.

"Yeah," she murmurs, her steps slowing for a second, "you've lived here your entire life?"

"Yes."

We reach the end of one block, which brings us to a red light. People mill around us, the crowd growing larger until, finally, the light flashes green, the cars stop, and we continue. I slow my steps and Aurora does the same, so we're at the back of the pack, rather than in the thick of the crowd, giving her the space to jump around if she wants.

"What was it like growing up with my brothers?"

I think carefully before responding. "Strange. When I got to be about twelve, I knew all about my father's life, and it appealed to me. Yours allowed me to accompany him to work, and through training with your brothers, I realized how pleasing the life was."

"At twelve."

I shrug. "Mob life is different. We're aged from childhood quicker. Your brothers already knew their futures, Hawke especially. They took me in, made me one of their own."

"Hawke," she muses. "In a way, I think you had a better relationship with him that I had, considering the age gap between him and me."

The same between her and me. Eight years. In a mild tone, I reply, "He loved you, Aurora, you know that. He might have been my fellow training companion, but he's not a sibling."

She's quiet for a moment, taking it all in. "And what about after he left, and it was the three of you?"

"The relationships altered slightly. From four down to three. Nico was most affected, being the second-born, he moved into what would be Hawke's role. Emotionally, Rafael had it the worst."

"And you?"

Hard to explain. "I missed Hawke. He and I are the same age, so it felt different with him. Easier to be friends with. A lot of our interests were the same. Nico, only being a year younger, was around often. And Rafael, given he's four years younger, and was only ten at the time Hawke left, sometimes was called away by your mother." I throw a smirk toward her. "Ten's an awkward age. Still a child but moving into where Nico and I were."

"Huh. Any regrets taking the oaths?"

"None," I reply, not missing a beat.

"Even though you're stuck with me when I know you'd rather be doing something else. What *is* that something else, by the way?"

Until Nico mentions De Falco to her, that's one truth I will not provide. It opens a world of anxieties she doesn't deserve.

"Everything," I reply in an offhanded way, hoping to break her train of thought. "Working at the clubs, guarding the house, being out with your brothers."

"Fighting enemies."

My eyes cut to her, careful in my response. "Yes."

"Well, sorry, I guess."

I nudge her shoulder with mine, aiming for playful. "Don't be. You're not so bad, *princesse.*"

She's more than "not so bad," but I don't allow the truth to infiltrate my mind.

"Hey, the clouds moved," she announces suddenly, her

hand gesturing to the sky. "Moon's already up, even while sunlight still tinges the sky. I love this time of day."

Occupied with looking up, we both miss the man walking into Aurora. He's large and consumes so much of the area, and while he quickly murmurs a "sorry" for walking into her, causing her to fall back a step, his eyes are locked on the small purse in her hand, greedy eyes devouring the rich leather.

He moves before I can react, snatching it as she yells out. The crowds around us ignore the blatant theft because while the city might be beautiful, it's also this. Dark, dismal, and packed with people who look out for only themselves.

Luckily, she doesn't need anyone else but me.

I shove between two people, snatching the man by the collar before he can make it another step. With my hand in his shirt, I risk a glance back, spotting Aurora still by the edge of the sidewalk, watching in horror.

The man tries to twist from my hold, but I throw my free hand into his face, the satisfying crunch of his nose beneath my fist. He screams out as blood drips from his nose. His hands fly to his face, and the movement loosens his hold on her purse, so I'm able to snatch it back and toss it in her direction.

"This is for stealing from her."

People around us either stop walking to watch, or continue, their feet quickening and gazes darting away as they rush by.

They don't matter as I throw hit after hit into the fucker's face. His blocks get more feeble, his hands unable to stop me as I toss him backwards, toward the nearest building. Anyone still loitering quickly rushes off, realizing this is bigger than they believed.

With his shirt in my grip, I lean over his slumped body and yank out the knife I keep in my pocket, placing it at his neck. "Your death is for daring to touch her. Think twice next time."

"H-hey, man, I know who you are." He wheezes, cold eyes glancing behind me. "And who she is. De Falco—"

Fuck, Aurora. Lost in the demand for revenge, I rip away from him, keeping my blade poised in his direction, uncaring about the numerous civilians around. I scan the street, seeking anyone watching us.

With the crowd avoiding us, the path to her is clear. She stands in the same place, her hands fisted around her purse as she watches on, shuffling from foot to foot, fear etched in her expression. I don't want to scare her, but the bastard must pay.

"Aurora." I tip my head, desiring her closer.

Instead of coming toward me, she shouts, "Rosen!" and points to the ground behind me.

Feet scrape at that exact time and I lunge for him, but his shirt slips right between my fingers, and he takes off, pushing through the crowds to get away.

"Fuck." I pace forward, the urge to follow. To catch him and kill him. He mentioned De Falco's name, which only means one thing.

Two things, actually. The second being, Aurora isn't safe out here, and while exploring downtown might be fun for her, the experience must end.

"Rosen." She approaches, hugging her purse, her attention on the man who ran away. "W-who was that?"

Huffing, I wish I could respond, but I don't. I can't tell her the truth. All I can do is something I shouldn't—reach for her.

Touch her.

This could have gone a lot worse. What was the purpose in it? If it was to take her, he wouldn't have been alone.

But at the last second, right before my arms swallow her up, enveloping her in the hug I need more than she does, I lower my arms, releasing her waist. Instead, I do a visual sweep of her features.

"You okay?"

"Are *you* okay?" she repeats. "You're the one who hit him."

"I'm fine because you are."

"Night's over, eh? Back to the car?"

"Yeah," I murmur regretfully.

"I had fun either way. Despite its ending. Thanks for this, Rosen."

It's that *thanks* that makes it all worth it.

32
AURORA

The mansion is eerily quiet. Even when arriving home last night after our outing, Rosen and I didn't run into any of my family. He dropped me off at my door before disappearing for the night.

By late the next morning, it's still that same unnerving silence. I've left my room a few times to wander around, finding myself looking for people but have seen no one. Like, literally *no one.*

Nico's off who the fuck knows where.

My parents haven't been around all day.

Rafael never popped by.

Della and Ariella both left earlier.

And Rosen, oddly enough, hasn't been in contact either, leaving me to wonder if he's with my brothers, having already told them about last night.

Maybe yesterday scared him off.

Between my breakdown in the hospital the day before, and then yesterday, visiting his nephew and exploring downtown, he's likely ensuring distance between us again.

I think about my consecutive visits to the hospital, and Elliot. How lively he was compared to the boy I first found asleep, dark shadows beneath his eyes. Little breaths making his chest rise and fall. And then yesterday, those very same lungs used only to speak in loud, animated tones.

I think about everything Mom said about using the hospital to ease her guilt, to reconnect with children who benefit from her support. I think about how my family is assisting Rosen's, simply because they care enough.

You're a part of that.

But I don't feel like I'm part of this. The visit yesterday seems trite compared to the money my family provides. It's like, I'm standing on the outside, an observer in an otherwise perfect familial connection. The intruder in their lives.

By the time night falls, I leave my bedroom for the fifth time to take another pass around the mansion, searching for any sign of life. This place seems so much larger without everyone here and it's discerning.

Is this what my life will be like when I'm wed to Erico and move to New York? I'd prefer finding work there that'll allow me to help children, but if he has an issue with it, it'll create a fight I suspect I won't be winning. He can't expect me to remain inside and wander around a house alone all day, while he goes off and does his...whatever being an underboss means.

Arranged marriages happen for one main reason: connections. But then there's the other motivation, and the realization of my future causes a new round of chills to skate over my insides, bringing me to a halt, hand bracing on the nearest wall.

Heirs.

My free hand lowers to my stomach as bile fills my throat. *I'm* barely an adult. Most of my life has been spent locked away. I can barely manage to *attend* a party, let alone run one. Let alone birth another life. He can't expect a child for years.

But he does. Does and will. On our wedding night, consummating the marriage will be his first attempt. Which means within the year, my stomach could be expanding with life.

"Oh, god."

How did I not think about any of this before now? How did this not *dawn* on me until this instance?

Children. Babies. Marriage. They're all connected. Erico will want his heir because in the grim obscurity of this life, nothing's certain. Definitely not his own safety and his position requires future leadership.

I can't be a mother. For all Mom's explanations yesterday, it doesn't change the fact I hardly had my own mother's influence. What does it look like to *be* one?

I don't realize I'm hyperventilating until a hand lands on my shoulder and I gasp, gaining more air in that breath. Spinning, I find Nico looking down at me, his dark brows furrowed.

"You okay? You don't look well."

"I-I'm fine." Straightening from my slouch, I use the wall to stand upright again.

Although Nico conveys concern, I can't tell him what's in my head. He'll brush me off because that's essentially all he's done since I arrived.

Still, he watches me skeptically as I step away. "Okay," he murmurs finally, his eyes narrowing as if he knows there's more to my comment. "Rosen told me you met his nephew yesterday."

My feet stall, my breath too, as I'm faced with yet another mention of the ulterior motives behind this family's actions.

"And Mom told me you're helping him," I reply carefully.

Nico crosses his arms, becoming larger, as though still insisting to reflect the darkness within, even to me. "It was an agreement amongst all of us and one that took no deliberation.

Rosen's like family, therefore his family is too. That little boy never asked for any of this."

His words smash right into my heart, tightening his unforgiving grip around it. Not that I despise his mention of Rosen being like family, but it's another reference of what I'm *not*.

"That's kind," I manage. "Seeing him when I visited with Mom was a bit of a surprise since Rosen never mentioned him."

Nico blinks, one brow arching. "And you and Rosen frequently have conversations in which his personal life gets brought up?"

Fuck.

I'm not doing anything wrong by being friendly with my bodyguard. Nico simply can't know *how* friendly we've been.

"He and I spend so much time together, I've asked him questions, yes." My hands go to my hips as my back straightens beneath the weight of his probing gaze. There's *nothing* wrong with what I'm admitting. "If someone is going to be around all the time, I should know about him, right? You disagree? He's your friend."

"He's staff," Nico snaps, but his rough, argumentative tone fades with his blink and a hint of a smile graces his mouth, even if he'll never admit it. The ringing of his cell drags his gaze away for a moment and he backs up, the device already rising to his ear. "I have to go. We'll talk later."

With that unpleasant conversation finished, I escape back to my room, so I can finish my earlier meltdown in privacy, without anyone's probing attention. Walking to the large window across from the bed, looking out into the lands beyond, I drop my head to the pane, sighing and watching my breath momentarily fog the glass.

There has to be more to this life. Volunteering with kids keeps some of my days busy, but if life consists of being a princess, I won't make it a year. Mom managed, and Della agreed to this. Even her sister, Ariella, moved into the mansion.

Or is it me? Is it because I grew up hearing about the kinds of things I'd be doing rather than experiencing it? I had freedom, to a point. My classes and gardening. But nothing typical of someone my age. Outside of champagne and wine, I've never tasted hard alcohol. I've watched movies where the characters got to experience clubs—the drinking, the music, the social aspect, and it's always made me curious of what that would be like. Certainly, the Sisters wouldn't have allowed me to go.

Rafael runs a club, Eden. Nico couldn't find issue with me dropping in on a family-owned club.

So many life experiences have passed me by. Petty friendships, school-aged crushes, clubbing on my eighteenth birthday, post-secondary schooling. Those things weren't allowed at the convent, and the social differences didn't seem to exist to our made-out-of-necessity family.

University could keep me busy for a few years, which makes it a viable possibility, even if I end up not using the degree after graduation. Erico might have an issue with it, but one I could convince him otherwise of. Anything to give me purpose is worth it.

Perhaps I can have this conversation with Mom or Della. I'm sure my mother would appreciate me reaching out, but Della might be able to provide a different take.

I find my phone and instead open my most recent text thread, opting to speak with the person who'll understand better than anyone else.

ME
I need you.

Okay, so did I type a message that he can take in multiple ways? Yes, I did.

ROSEN

Princesse.

ME

Please. I want out of here.

I don't know where those words came from, but the sudden demand to have Rosen take me away, to *be* elsewhere for a while, consumes me. To have a repeat of yesterday. To feel freedom again, in the short bits I'm able to steal it and not sit inside this mansion, hating myself and my impending future.

ROSEN

It's late.

ME

And? I'm not asking to prowl the underbelly
of the city. Merely a drive.

ROSEN

Where to?

ME

Anywhere.

ROSEN

Meet me downstairs in a few minutes. I'll get
a car.

Thrilled, I slip on my Toms shoes and, for half a second, debate changing from the sundress I put on this morning, but opt not to. I rush from the room and down the hallway until I get to the main floor.

I find Rosen already leaning on the front doorway, his phone in his hand and his thumb scrolling in a downward motion. The sleeves of his shirt are rolled up, revealing the arms that once held me when he ignited flames within my body I still feel. The nighttime behind him casts his form into darkness, with his foot crooked, resting on the door jamb.

He's so sexy, it physically hurts my core.

"Hey," I call out, approaching.

He glances up, scanning me up and down, taking in the casual sundress I put on this morning. He tucks his phone away, kicking off the doorframe at the same time. "Hey. We can go."

A black car is waiting, and he pulls open the front passenger door, no longer pointlessly fighting over a seating arrangement. Once I'm in, he takes his place behind the wheel and immediately gets us off Corsetti property and headed toward the city in no time, weaving in and out of the streets. It isn't until he gets closer to downtown that he speaks.

"What triggered the outing, *princesse*?"

"I realized what this life truly means."

His eyes cut to me. "Is this an extension of yesterday?"

"No. Yes." *I don't know.* "I guess thinking about the past two days is what initiated my reflections. Then I got thinking about the after."

"After?"

"Erico," I tack on, letting him infer my thoughts.

He's silent for a minute, but I spot the whitening of his knuckles as he clenches the wheel a bit tighter than normal.

"After you're wed, you think your life will change." It's not a question.

"Won't it?" I ask harshly. Pulling my legs up, I manage to turn as much as the seat belt allows for, hugging my body. "Once I'm his wife, who the fuck knows what I'll be. *Who* I'll be." My breathing comes harsher, air getting more and more difficult to drink in. I pause, sucking in sharp bursts of air, rushing to speak again. "Returning here's been—well, you know. My entire life, I've been forced to live as *they* want me to. And when I think I'm starting to get it, they'll ship me off, forcing me to re-learn it again."

"You'll be all right, Aurora," he says, his tone hard, despite his attempt at softening it.

"Stop placating me because you and I both know that's not the case. The *Famiglia* will expect *things* from me."

"*Princesse—*"

"No," I cut him off, my hand slicing the air and my mind rolling to new places. "No, stop, Rosen. I asked you to get me away from home for a reason. Do you realize that I could never have this conversation with my parents? With Nico? Even with Rafael, because despite his easy nature, he's still a part of this."

"As I am."

"But it's different with you." I bring my arms around my body, imagining it's his instead.

When we approach a red light, his braking is too hard; it's more of a stomp, jerking me forward. With the momentary pause in driving, he looks at me. "Aurora, it's a damn honour to be the one for you. You have no fuckin' idea. But again, you have walls built. Let them crumble. Let your siblings in. Your mother. They can become for you what I'm not allowed to be."

Wiping away the frustrated tears before they begin fully forming, I continue, "I don't want to be a mother."

The light turns green, but before he drives again, I catch his flash of empathy. "Ah," he finally murmurs.

"That's what these unions are for, aren't they? A bridge to New York on the deal I become *his*. His to fucking reproduce with. His to *breed*," I spit out the now-tainted word. "He'll force motherhood on me because that's what his family requires of us, and once he's done, once there's an heir, I'll be left to raise it."

Rosen presses his lips together, but a muscle in his cheek twitches. His arms get more corded as they form fists around the wheel. "You might come to care for him, Aurora."

"But I might not," I counter. "I might hate him. The man

by my side at Nico's engagement, you said so yourself, hardly looked twice at me. *That's* my future, Rosen. That'll be the father of my future children, which, at the fucking moment, I can't even think about."

Rosen abruptly pulls over to the side of the street, parallel parking in a manner quicker than I ever believed possible then shuts the vehicle off. His arms drop into his lap, and he stares straight out the windshield, his nostrils flaring with every heavy breath he takes.

"Aurora, it pains me to know this is hurting you. I miss the woman you were days ago. You're sad now and I want to help you, but I'm not allowed to."

His admittance makes the pain in my chest ease up a fraction. Seeking more, I admit, "You helped me at the hospital, when you came to find me in the hallway. I just...I don't know. Wanted someone to hear me out, and you've always been the best."

He doesn't respond. He opens his door and effectively stops whatever else we each might have said, coming around the vehicle and opening mine. I unfold my body, turning to watch what he does as he leans past me and unbuckles my seat belt.

"What—"

Rosen's arms slide beneath my legs, bare from the thigh-length dress. This touch heats my skin but it doesn't last for long when he somehow manages to turn us both around and replacing himself where I was, this time, with me over his lap. His legs rest on the ground outside the vehicle, while mine dangle over his. The dress hikes a bit higher than it normally would be, but the position is too comfortable to be concerned with my outfit.

His body is warm and hard; his arms firm around my waist. Safe. I feel so much smaller having him hold me. His other hand cups my neck, stroking the base. I shut my eyes, allowing myself to enjoy his touch while I can, before he remembers the boundaries he spouts all the time and robs me of this feeling.

"I can't make these ideas go away, *ma princesse*, no matter how much I wish to. You have no fucking idea how difficult it is to see you like this. I want to help you, but the only way I can will start a war your family won't win."

"I hate my life. If I wasn't a Corsetti, I wouldn't be shoved into this union. Wouldn't be feeling everything I am now." I drag my hand up his chest, resting it over his heart. "My *friend* hugging me wouldn't be an illicit act."

Reinforcing my words, his arms tighten, reminding me of every reason he's the one I reached out to first.

"Rosen—"

Vvvvvvvvvvvvvvv. The sound fills the car, cutting me off. With a quick maneuver, Rosen manages to shift me enough to retrieve his phone from his jeans. Right before he answers the call, I spot the name flashing on the screen.

Rafael.

"Capo," Rosen greets, his body stiffening beneath mine.

I can't fully hear what Rafael says, but there's a few *mmhmm*s and *yes*es from Rosen before he hangs up and tosses the phone into the center console with a clatter.

"Your brother needs me. We've got to go."

33
ROSEN

I maneuver the car into the spot closest to the staff entrance, ensuring Aurora is cast in the shadows and safety of Lotus, a Corsetti-owned nightclub. Leaving her alone is a stupid decision but bringing her inside might prove more work than it's worth. By the time I track down a bouncer to stand with her, Rafael could be finished with me.

His phone call's timing had me cursing the entire short ride over, but it was probably for the best. I shouldn't have held her the way I did. Shouldn't have allowed myself to get sucked in by her emotions. She'll definitely have to adapt to survive Rossi.

"Stay here, 'kay?" I get out of the car, but before shutting the door, I lean down, catching her attentive gaze. "I mean it, Aurora. I'll be a few minutes. I'll lock the doors behind me."

She twists her hands together, glancing toward the painted black door I'm parked beside. Then she scans the side of the building, which is a nondescript painted black brick with no windows.

"Sketchy place. Come here often?"

"Your family owns it, so yes."

"Eden?"

Rafael… "It almost doesn't surprise me he's mentioned that place to you," I mutter, my tone deepening into a gruff. "But no. This is a nightclub."

"And Eden is…not a nightclub?"

Clearly, Rafael didn't tell her everything. "It's a sex club."

Her mouth slips open. Of everything I could have said, that wasn't something she was expecting.

"Stay," I reaffirm, holding my palm out in a stopping motion. "I'll be right back."

"Got it." She nods, settling back in the seat as she puts her feet onto the dash. I'm skeptical she'll remain patient for long, which is even more of a reason I should send someone out, but hopefully, I can be in and out before her interests get piqued.

Before I think too long on this and *do* make her impatient, I lock the car doors and enter the club, passing the storage containers and cleaning supplies kept in the back, through the service hallway and toward the surveillance room, where Rafael directed me.

We're far enough away, the music is only a minor thumping in the background.

In the surveillance room, I find one staff member seated in front of numerous monitors, each showing a different angle of the club's interior and exterior. Rafael, the normally relaxed Corsetti, leans over him, one arm propped on the table, holding his weight, while his other is shoved in his hair.

This is a disturbing amount of déjà vu, taking me days ago when Nico had me join him at The Elixir for a similar reason.

"Hey," I announce my arrival. "What's going on? I can't stay long." *Because I have your sister waiting outside.*

"Hey. Look at this." He gestures to the paused video stream on the nearest monitor. Taking that as a signal, the staff member taps the space bar on the keyboard and starts the feed. "I wanted your opinion first because the last time Nico found evidence of De Falco's presence, he went apeshit. His wedding is approaching and he's getting more agitated."

The feed is of the camera by the front door, put there for the club's safety. It's angled in a way to catch little of the surrounding area. After a moment of nothing, a figure dressed in all black approaches the door. There's movement as they lay something on the ground before straightening. Then, knowing precisely where the camera is, the figure tips their head back, smiling into the lens.

"Is that...? Rewind."

The feed is rewound about ten seconds until we're all rewatching the item being laid at the door. This time, knowing they will be revealing their face, I lean over, reaching for the keyboard, reading to slap the space bar at the same time they look up.

It's blurry, but clear enough to catch the face of a woman with long, light hair but no telling features.

Reaching into his back pocket, Rafael pulls out a ripped sheet of paper and hands it to me.

Watch yourself, Corsettis. We're everywhere. You can look, but you won't find what's right beneath your noses.

No signature, but it's obvious who it's from.

"De Falco." I growl. My feet inch back, instinct suddenly driving me to return to outside, to Aurora. If De Falco had people here and if they were to return now, while she's unprotected...

"You think that's his daughter? One of them, anyway."

"Too quick of a flash to get the details but who else would it be? She knew exactly where the camera was."

"They're taunting us." Rafael snatches the note back. "Fuck, they're enjoying this! Nico's gonna flip if he were to learn of this."

If? "You have to tell him."

He curses, his fist also thumping on top of the note. "I fucking know. I don't want to make him angrier than he's been. Maybe I'll find Della first. She can use whatever magic spell she cast on him to make that cranky ass fall for her to calm him down afterwards."

Despite the dark topic, Rafael's casual nature causes me to chuckle. "Good luck with that then. I'll be chasing your sister around in the meantime."

He straightens, slapping the man on his back. "Thanks for calling me and not Nico. I'll deal with it." To me, he asks, "How's she managing?"

So many answers I could give him, including the truth, that it hasn't been well. Between her future, her past, her family not being as bad as she thinks them to be, she's all over the place.

I shrug, keeping my response casual. "She seems well. The hospital visits were good."

"She met Elliot, I assume."

"And was surprised at learning all your family is doing to help him."

Rafael moves toward the door as I talk, gathering the note, his phone, and his keys. Slapping my arm on the way by, he chuckles. "I'm sure she has her reservations that we're all knocking down bit by bit. Didn't I say you'd have your work cut out with her?"

"Essentially," I agree.

Rafael accepts that final response and exits his office, leaving the door open for me to follow. I've been gone no more than five minutes, so I better find her in my car, or—or nothing, I suppose. Can't do any of the things to her I crave to.

As I turn away from the multiple cameras, I catch the distinct flash of a face. It better be my imagination, but as I peer closer to the monitor, I recognize the woman who's singlehandedly starring in my dreams. The woman whose casual light blue dress is a field of flowers amongst the glitter, leather, and micro-outfits of the other women. The woman who should be in my motherfucking car.

She's on the edge of the dance floor, staring into the thick crowd. I'm caught halfway between wanting to get to her right away and watching to see what she does. Other people would shy away at certain experiences, but not this woman. She does every fucking thing to grate my nerves down until they're a thin strip of nothing, and when she steps into the mass, I picture wringing her neck—and not in a way that'll be enjoyable.

"Fucking Christ!"

Pushing out the door, I jog down the length of the hallway. Waitresses and other staff members linger by the edge of the bar, right by the entrance to this back hallway, but they quickly move out of the way when they see me barrel their way.

People are everywhere, reminding me why I hate clubs. The bar to my right is packed with clubbers clamouring to spend their money on overpriced drinks. Couples and friend groups shout into each other's ears to be heard over the pounding music. The very music I'll feel in my bones even tomorrow because nothing less than deafening is appropriate in such a place.

Shoving by everyone in my path, my gaze is locked on one place only: the dance floor.

I don't see her through the crowd, but she better be there and not escaping to anywhere else.

The *princesse* will pay for ignoring my single request.

34
AURORA

Obviously, I didn't listen to Rosen.

He leaves me alone outside a club, the very thing I'd been curious about experiencing. Having seen them on TV, but never getting the traditional eighteenth birthday other people my age would have.

Ten seconds after he left, I followed. First, glancing down the attached hallway, seeking anywhere he could be. One room I passed had me quickening my steps when I heard both Rosen and Rafael talking, and while I, for a beat, debated listening into what was so important to cause Rosen to rush here, I knew this opportunity would *not* come again.

So away I went.

Exiting the service hallway was a process, involving a high chin and resolute attitude that I belonged. None of the staff gave me a second glance, causing me to wonder if they know who I am. That thought alone made me move even faster before they could recall all the reasons they would probably know my face, Nico's warning to them no doubt.

I'm only guessing, but after the short duration of being home, my speculation is likely correct.

Holy fuck. It's not the first time that thought has passed through my head since entering. It's not even the tenth.

This is *life*. Vibrancy. Connection. A place for every one of my senses to bloom.

Amidst the dark, flashing lights passing over the crowds. The colourful drinks people chug. The multitude of colours the patrons dress in.

With the packed crowd, the scent of alcohol and sweat, as well as severely lowered inhibitions. The impossible thumping of club music at decibels louder than I ever believed my ears could handle.

Simply put: people enjoying their lives. No one here is trapped by a family, forced to live one way while being kept from another.

The sticky air brushing over my skin. The bumping of people as they move around the club, stumbling from the alcohol, or simply from the crowded space.

And when I part my lips, breathing in, I taste the difference between this life and my own. The intense flavour, driving me to step into the chaos of the dance floor and *become*. Become average. Free.

The music swallows me up, my limbs naturally moving to the bouncy pace. While none of the faces around me are familiar, the people who meet my curious gazes, grin. A girl stretches her hands toward me, grasping one of mine and leads me into her group of four—two guys and another girl.

I don't know how the hell to dance to this music, but that's the thing about clubs, I'm realizing. It doesn't matter. People are either too drunk to care or simply do not care because they're not here to judge, only to have fun.

The girl releases my hand when she notices me dancing and

turns to the guy at her back, wrapping her arms around his neck.

So natural. So free. They don't care who's watching.

The guy she's left me beside me grins, nodding as his eyes rake over me. Even amidst the passing lights, I spot his appreciation, which is nice, considering I'm dressed more casually than everyone else's tiny dresses or halter tops and tight pants.

He moves closer until I feel the roughness of his jeans against my hip. I don't know how to do this, but when I curl my body into his, moving my hips as my hands weave between my hair, lifting it to be weightless, it's obvious he doesn't care about my lack of skill.

And then the air shifts and my skin prickles the precise second I know my night's about to end.

The same second the guy's smile falters and his brows dip as he takes in the shadow at my back. Annoyance quickly has his mouth opening, to argue, but the growl in my ear dissipates everything else.

"What the fuck do you think you're doing in here?" A thick arm wraps around my waist, propelling me away from the stranger and into his own chest.

The guy I was dancing with immediately follows, his hand reaching for where Rosen holds me. "Hey, man—"

If the club ignited my senses, it's nothing compared to the way Rosen's response does. Death has a sound—a tone. A feeling as it rolls over my neck and straight to the heat between my legs.

"If you don't back the fuck up and keep your hands to yourself, you will lose them. They will be placed in a box and mailed to your mother, your intestines as the motherfucking bow."

"Possessive much." He holds up his hands but doesn't back away, asking for death at this point.

"I know twenty ways to kill a man and how to prolong torture until you beg me to execute any one of them. Leave."

This time the guy listens, his face paler than usual, and it has nothing to do with the lighting.

I spin, Rosen's arm remaining around my waist, and tip my head back to better see the wrath darkening his expression. "You didn't have to scare him like that. That was..." *Terrifying. Intense. Hot.* "A bit much."

Rosen lowers his head to the crook of my neck, his cheek brushing mine, and he speaks into my ear, so I can hear him over the deafening music. "You seem to forget my job means protecting you, *princesse*. Which you make fucking impossible." He grasps the back of my neck, holding me still, reminding me how much of my body is in his control. Very little space is between us. "I'll ask again: what the fuck are you doing in here?"

Breaking all your rules. Breaking you *because you look on the verge of that happening.*

My arms stretch over my head, waving around the club. "Living, Rosen. If you get that stick you have shoved so far up your ass removed, you'll know how to do it too."

His jaw tics in every sexy way possible. For all our interactions, I don't recognize this Rosen, having only witnessed hints of it.

"You lived yesterday when you dragged me through downtown and almost got your purse stolen, or have you already forgotten that?"

"That was a hint of what I could be doing." My palms come to rest on his shoulders, stroking down until I reach his rolled-up cuffs. "You and I both know, I didn't get a typical life, and before I'm shoved into some box and forgotten in New York, I need this." Lifting on my toes, I get as close as humanly possible without kissing him and repeat, "I *need* this."

His huff causes me to think I'm winning. But when he drops his hand and yanks on my wrist, I've lost. "We have to get out of here, Aurora."

Although I'm nothing to his strength, I still try, digging my heels into the sticky ground. "Rosen—"

Over his shoulder, he tosses a cold stare. "Don't make me throw you over my shoulder and carry you out."

Instead of fighting, I go for another tactic and step in front of him, blocking him with my body, my palms landing on his chest. Thankfully, he stops walking, even as dancers around him keep moving.

"Three dances only."

"This isn't a fuckin' negotiation. Zero."

"That's not how compromise works. Three."

"Zero."

"Three. You can't use the excuse I'm not safe when you're literally right here." And when—*when*, not if—I win, he won't be going anywhere.

His eyes narrow the slightest fraction. "Fine. One dance."

"Two. And a shot."

His brows spike, amusement curling his lips, but I think it's partially exaggerated. "Now you're asking for alcohol. Hint, *princesse*, win one battle before beginning another."

"Come on. Besides wine and champagne, I've never tasted hard liquor. It's criminal."

His fingers tighten around my wrist, reminding me of the hold he still maintains. "Then we should keep it that way."

"Rosen," I add a whine to my tone, "*please.* For me."

When he looks away, toward the bar, I know I've won, and I have to press my lips together to keep from showing my excitement and him robbing me of the experience. His eyes shut and he groans low enough I shouldn't hear him over the music, but I swear, I feel it.

"One dance. One shot. That's the deal. Take it or leave it."

In response, I bring my arms over his shoulder and rock my body against his, exactly like I saw the girl do to her guy earlier. I finally stop hiding my grin and in the massive, packed room, with the music swirling around us, I dance.

And then his hands clamp my hips and when I think he'll push me away, he turns me around, my back to his front, his hands controlling my every movement. Even when he dances, he dominates, so I let him and as my head falls back against his shoulder, I use one arm to cover his and then wrap my other one around his neck from behind.

"Holy shit, he dances. So you do know how to have fun."

His rumble in my ear makes goose bumps spread over my neck. "I took a sexy woman's advice and took the stick out of my ass in order to do so, but yes."

Am I still breathing? I have no idea at this point.

Either way, I no longer question myself. Rosen controls my body and our movements. The music drives us toward each other, and we fit perfectly together, if it wasn't for that pesky wall still between us. Although, it's growing more fragile and one wrong movement and it'll tumble.

We feel intimate. His face in the curve of my neck, his breath blowing over the top of my chest, coercing warm air down my dress. His hands heavy on my hips, his chest against my back.

One song melds into another and I soon learn how exhausting dancing like this truly is. The overstimulation of the loud voices around us, the bodies moving to their own rhythm. But I wouldn't trade this moment for anything. This is...freeing. Rosen and me, locked in a world only we have the key to.

After the second song, despite his instance for only one, Rosen tugs me to the edge of the dance floor, and when I'm about to complain, he turns toward the bar.

Oh, this is acceptable.

The bar is packed with people, but Rosen doesn't seem bothered by this fact. He drops my wrist a short distance away, his finger coming up in a firm motion.

"Stay."

Like I'd go anywhere now when I'm getting what I want.

"Yes, sir."

With a final heated look, he heads for the side of the bar, leaning over the counter to speak with the nearest bartender. They share a manshake-hand slap thing and Rosen walks away shortly after, holding a small shot glass filled with clear liquid and a water bottle.

Of course, he knows the staff here and gets special attention. I can't be surprised by this.

He hands me the glass, commenting, "Tequila. I promise it'll be the final sip of hard liquor you ever take, *princesse.*"

Challenge accepted.

Jerking my chin toward the water bottle, I demand, "Where's yours? Don't tell me water is your drink of choice?"

"You being here is bad enough," he shouts over the music. "I'm not drinking when your safety is on the line."

My safety? Making a production, I slowly glance around. "In a club my family owns. Pretty sure they know better than to fuck with me."

"The staff might. They," he jerks his head toward the dance floor, "don't."

Rolling my eyes, I try a different tactic. "You're so much of a lightweight one shot will affect you? Give me a break."

"Anything taking away my absolute focus will affect me."

"Rosen, I'm not going anywhere. One shot was the deal, and I insist you take one too. Consider it a command by a Corsetti."

With his next sharp breath, his nostrils flare, his jaw ticking.

He mumbles something as he turns away, but I catch none of it over the music. Rosen heads back for the bar, speaks with the same bartender, and returns with a clear shot for himself.

"You drive me fucking insane, Aurora," he says right before placing the glass to his lips. Tipping his head back, he swallows it in one go, his expression not faltering whatsoever at the flavour.

Must not be too bad. Mimicking his motions, I do the same. Over the rim, I catch his smirk right as the cool liquid pours between my parted lips and down my throat.

Holy fuck, I drank fire. Coughs wrack my body, the glass nearly slipping from my hand as I shove it into his chest. My lips form a small o, and I attempt to push out breaths, trying to cool the burn in my throat.

Okay, I see what he meant now.

"What the hell was that?"

"Tequila," he repeats what I already know before shoving the bottle of water toward me. "Here. Hydrate."

The point of alcohol is to let it consume me, not to chug water and wash it down away. I block him, shoving the water away. "Thanks, but no."

And then, I flit away, throwing myself into the crowd before his sheer size and speed catch me and haul me away from the club. The deal has been met already. One dance—we had two, technically—and one shot.

But I don't want to leave.

I get myself to the centre of the floor and spin, immersing myself with the others, who are lulled by the music and the numerous shots they likely took. For their sake, I hope it wasn't tequila.

Rosen doesn't let time pass before following, not that I expected him to. He's by my side quickly, his arm hauling me to his chest as the water is lifted between us. I'm about to brush it away again when he unscrews the top.

His gaze entraps me, his brow hiking the slightest fraction with his point.

The point I expect doesn't come as he takes a large sip of the water. A snarky comment, which I *know* he'll love, is on the tip of my tongue when Rosen grasps my jaw between his thumb and forefinger. His hold is firm, and I don't fight him, not that I think I'd want to.

His fingers slide up my cheek a fraction, and then he pinches, forcing my lips open. He leans down, his lips brushing against mine before parting.

Warm water trickles from his mouth into mine.

"I said, hydrate."

35
ROSEN

I've lost my damn mind. There's no other plausible reason for everything I've done since spotting Aurora on the camera feed. Allowing her to remain in a club, to have her first drink, to dance with her all feels so prohibited.

Nico didn't present me options of what's acceptable, but I know him well enough that allowing Aurora in a nightclub doesn't fall on his approved list of activities. Neither does supplying her with alcohol, even if it brought me gratification to be another one of her firsts.

But if all that wasn't bad enough, I should have remained off to the side and observed, rather than dancing with her. I told myself it was so I could remain close and protect her, but protecting her doesn't involve holding her intimately, brushing her ass against my cock, and breathing in the scent of her skin, now glistening with sweat. I longed to lap it up, to imagine her sweating for different reasons.

Worse than dancing with her was what I just did. Passing water from my mouth to hers to force her to hydrate after the shot. It's doubtful the single shot would affect her, but water will help ensure it doesn't at all.

If she were mine, she'd pay for what she pulled, pushing away the bottle and taking off through the crowd.

Aurora stares up at me, her wet lips parted from where I'm still gripping her, seconds away from pouring water down her damn throat if she doesn't start obeying. She's panting, her chest rising and falling in her light blue sundress, meant for daytime use and not dancing in a club. Nonetheless, she commands my attention—and not for the purpose she should, such as my job.

We're at an impasse as we stare at one another, both breathing heavily but for different reasons. As much as I hate myself for it, my fingers release her one at a time, freeing her jaw as I push the bottle into her hand.

Eyes still on mine, she takes a small sip—smaller than I'd prefer, but acceptable—and hands it back for me to screw the lid on. Her throat moves with her swallow and her tongue dabs at her wet lips.

"Atta girl. It's time to go now." I reach for her, and surprisingly, she doesn't fight as I bring her closer.

Her hands go to my chest, sliding up to the sides of my neck. "Must we? Admit it, Rosen, you're having as much fun as I am."

Am I having fun witnessing complete glee on her face and being aware that I'm behind some of it when I didn't carry her away from here, but should have? Yes.

But approved fun would be to return her to her bedroom and avoid her and lock this night into being yet another fantasy. Pretending it didn't happen will be best to ensure I fix the boundaries I'm one breath away from rupturing.

Except, I don't stop her as she lifts onto her toes, her damp lips inches from mine. Or when she wraps her hands around my neck, like we're the only two in the room, living for the sounds of our heartbeats as outlawed feelings creep up again.

"Tell me the truth," she demands, and fuck me for not pushing her away.

"Anything that makes you smile is worth it, *princesse*. If that means driving you to spend time with children, letting you roam Montreal streets late at night, or being here, seeing you take your first shot and dance like there's no greater worries, then yes, I'm having fun."

Her fingers play with the hair at the base of my neck, while mine grips the water bottle so tightly, it's seconds away from exploding. Better it than her.

"So we don't have to leave. No one's looking for us. You clearly don't have enough fun and I'll have limited chances after this, so for both of us, let's just stay."

Why—how—this girl— I growl, my thoughts so unfocused, nothing is making sense anymore.

The bottle slips from my hand as I haul her hips against me, pressing her to my body the same way she had earlier. Every action since spotting her on the camera feed has been the opposite of what I ought to be doing.

She grins, biting her bottom lip as she, yet again, wins her argument.

"You have me wrapped around your finger."

Now that I'm done fighting, for now, she begins moving, her arms tightening around my neck, our dance way too intimate for even this environment. Still, I don't push her away because at this point...can I?

My insanity must be coming from the single shot she convinced me to take. It *must* be, even while I know that's not at all the case. It's not the alcohol; it's *her*.

She's dancing against me in a way meant to entice, to tease, hugging me close to her. I allow her the control, unlike earlier when I took over because, this time, if I were to touch her more than I am, I'm not sure I'd stop.

Her hips rock against mine, brushing against my cock every few seconds. She licks her lips, her gaze lowering between us, aware of the effect she's having on me. It's impossible to calm my body down when her skin is inches from my mouth, so readily available to be devoured.

"Princesse."

Her lashes flutter not-so-innocently. "What?"

"You know what you're doing."

"Do I?" Grinning, she turns, giving me her back while continuing her arduous torture.

My fingers tighten on her hips to prevent them from moving downwards, to the bottom of her dress and exploring beneath.

"You're being a brat again."

Her hair flicks me in the face as she turns her head, smirking. "Coming from the man who wants nothing to do with me."

With that hair, I dominate her movements, wrapping it around my fist and keeping her still as I pin her to my body. My lips trail over her sweaty skin, in the space beneath her ear, tasting the sin, imprinting the truth onto her.

"I want nothing to do with you because I want *everything* to do with you."

Her dancing stops, a tenseness knotting her shoulders. Her chest stops rising as she stalls breathing altogether, and when I think I severely fucked up, when I attempt to straighten and get away, obviously having taken this too far, she turns again to face me.

"So do it, Rosen. I want to. You want to. We're already apparently doing everything we shouldn't be, so what's the difference?"

Oh, princesse, there are so many differences. Bringing her to a club entices Nico's anger. What she's offering can start a war with the Rossis.

Aurora lifts on her toes and brushes her lips against mine, offering, "Tell me no and I'll back up."

No.

I can't. The words don't formulate on my lips. Even when my mouth parts, attempting to say it—I can't.

My hand slides from her hip down her leg, fingering the bottom of her dress. I shouldn't be touching her. I can't be. Not only for the Corsettis and Rossis, but for her. Aurora must stay the perfect princess they all demand her to be and not get sullied by her bodyguard's touch.

"I like to claim my women, Aurora. I don't enjoy when other men play with them. And for a soon-to-be engaged woman, do you see the issue?"

Her only response is to repeat, "Then tell me no."

I can't.

Gripping onto her dress with one hand, her neck with the other, I back her through the crowd. Drunk patrons stumble out of the way, some uncaring as I direct a woman through them; some watching intently, which means getting her out of the spotlight becomes increasingly important.

"You make me want to return to the bar and down an entire bottle of their strongest liquor."

Amongst the excitement, her brows drop a fraction with her question.

"You make me want to return to the bar and down an entire bottle of their strongest liquor, so I don't have to feel guilty about what's next."

I don't know why. Maybe this is the cost of my sanity being gone. There is no reason for anything anymore. Nothing beyond her.

I walk us to the nearest dark corner of the club, praying the camera feeds haven't recognized us and that the staff isn't calling Nico. Her back hits the wall, sparking a gasp from her lips, which I'm seconds away from devouring.

"Last chance, Aurora. End this, because I'm not strong enough to avoid you any longer." Even as I say it, my hands tighten in her hair, around her hip, ensuring she can't escape.

"Don't."

When small hands wrap the back of my head, I know we're fucked. *I'm* fucked when she lifts on her toes and pulls me down, taking my mouth with hers, granting me permission, the understanding that while I've already done more than I should have, this is it.

This.

Is.

It.

Snap. There it is. The sound of my self-control. Of years of training. Of endless service to the family I've taken oaths for.

She might have initiated the kiss, but I quickly take over. My lips against hers, my tongue darting through her mouth, so there's not a part of her that forgets who's holding her. My arms come up beneath her thighs and I lift her, keeping her all for me.

Kissing her is the last thing I should be doing, but *fuck*. She made me want this, to crave it as much as I need my next breath. *Her* next breath, so I can rob her of it when I grant her only pleasure.

"Seeing you unravel is fucking hot."

Unravel. Oh, I'm no longer unravelling. Rather, I've snapped. Broken. Shattered. Gone.

My hands inch up her thighs, fingers finding the edge of her panties. With my body, I block her from anyone who could be watching, the shadows assisting, because I'll be damned if we're interrupted before I feel her pussy. All more reason to get away from the club, but backing away now ends this, and unless she instructs me to...I can't.

My finger slips beneath the edge of her panties and I pet her pussy, feeling her shudder into my mouth. Male pride bursts through me with the knowledge I'm the first man to touch her. So many first I shouldn't be, so many firsts I'm robbing another man of and risking my own life for, but every passing second with her makes those details matter less.

I pet her cunt, stroking my fingers up and down through her slit, feeling as her clit grows more swollen with every pass. Her kisses get more winded, her breathless moans consuming me. With two fingers, I spread her lips, dipping a third inside her core, pausing as she adjusts. I've never been with a virgin, that I know of, and it's only care for her own comfort preventing me from roughly taking her before reality crashes around me and steals this opportunity.

"You okay?"

She nods, so I sink my finger in deeper until her head falls back against the wall. Her eyes flutter shut, and I inspect her for any sign of pain, adding another upon finding none.

"Tell me if it hurts."

My palm rocks against her swollen clit, enticing a moan from her I'll hear long into my death if Nico learns of this.

"I command control, Aurora." Not sure if I'm warning her or me, or simply giving her a final reason to end this. "You're going to learn the art of obeying me. When I say come, you come, and not a moment before. That's the price for being a brat. Next time, think before you open your mouth."

"*Yes.*"

Doubtful she comprehends my meaning, I explain, "Your orgasms are *mine* to dole out as you deserve."

Her head lifts from the wall, and when I think she'll push

me away, that I've gone too far and my preferences don't align with hers, she nods, biting her bottom lip. With her silent permission, I push my finger in as deep as I can, pulling out halfway before pushing in harder, curling against her inner walls.

"I should punish you for taunting me on the dance floor. You did this. Made me lose my mind."

"The same way you're stealing mine," she murmurs, "so I'd say we're even."

We're nowhere close to even.

Her hands grip my shoulders, her hips rocking into my touch. I long to deny her first orgasm, while the craving to see her fall apart grows.

"Rosen," she gasps after another intense moment, "Rosen, I'm going to come."

Dragging my lips up her neck, I like the fact she told me. Like she was asking for permission. I should reward her for that alone, but she's done me wrong more instances than not.

I tug my fingers from her, cutting off her building orgasm, and lift my hand between us. With the roving lights, I wait for one to pass over us, catching the gleam she's coated me with. She'll come soon because where we are doesn't allow me to do all I want to, but first, I taste her.

I dip my fingers inside my mouth, groaning as I lap the sweet flavour. She watches me as I finish cleaning her from myself and then stroke between us again, petting her soaking pussy, inches from my cock, blocked by our clothing.

"Taste good?" she asks, breathless.

"Good is too simple of a word, *princesse*. Nothing else compares."

I take her mouth again, pushing my tongue against hers, sharing her flavour as my fingers sink back inside her wet cunt. She accepts me easily, groaning in my mouth as I spread my fingers and I find that spot she won't be able to ignore for long. Her hand clamps harder on my shoulder, her head lolling back, breaking our kiss.

"Rosen," she gasps.

"I love the sound of my name on your lips, especially as you beg. Be aware of whose fingers are inside you."

"Rosen, p-please."

And I'm dying to see her orgasm, even once. If we were anywhere else, I'd drag this on for so much longer because untouched woman or not, Aurora is everything I crave. Every desire I've spent years understanding. A natural submissive who revels in the game when she's being a brat. Who had numerous opportunities to end this and to demand an interaction more typical but continued to play. When I stop petting her insides and circle her clit with my thumb, she groans again.

"Please what, Aurora? Say the words."

"Rosen, please let me come."

I pinch her clit at the same time my fingers increase their pace. My head drops into her throat, the urge to bite her, to mark her, to claim her like an animal, increasing with every pump, but there's every reason why I shouldn't, can't, and won't.

Rewarding her, I say, "You can come now."

Her nails dig through my shirt, nearly stabbing my skin with the orgasm that consumes her. Her legs tighten around my waist, keeping my hand locked between us. I take her lips again, to prevent her from crying out and alerting others, even over the impossibly loud music. Normally, I wouldn't fuck around with a woman in public; exhibitionism isn't my thing, but here, with Aurora, it's worth it for this experience.

When the pulsing of her pussy slows and her breathing becomes panted, I break from her mouth, tracing the column of her throat. I should release her. Pull my hand away, fix her dress, and put her back to her feet, but I can't let go of her yet.

"You're fucking sexy, Aurora. Like something I've dreamt up."

"I'm real, Rosen.

She's as real as the taste on my tongue—*her*. After a long moment, I remove my fingers and lick her juices again. This isn't enough. This is a mere appetizer for the real thing and I long to drop to my knees and have her riding my face, drinking her second, third, and fourth orgasms, everyone else be damned.

Her hands cup my face and when she looks at me, the entire club falls away.

"Rosen, I want you to fuck me."

If I was a stronger man, I'd let her beg.

If I was a stronger man, I'd release her.

But I can't do either.

36
AURORA

If anyone told me how this day would end, in my wildest imagination, I wouldn't have believed it be this way.

We're back in the car, after an amazing night, driving home. Rosen never said yes to my request for sex, but he didn't deny me either.

His response: "Not here."

His hand remains on my thigh, his fingers mindlessly tracing a line up and down. With every pass, my dress is pushed higher.

Rosen parks the car on the side of the house, in front of an entrance I've never seen before. Wordlessly, he removes his hand, exits the vehicle, and comes around the other side, helping me from the front seat, exactly how he has time and time again. This time feels more, and the differences between our stations, less.

Rosen ushers me through the single door and into the dark attached hallway. By the time my night vision kicks in and I make out rows of doors on either side of the hallway, he's nudging me through the first one on our right.

A queen-sized bed takes up most of the room, against the far wall in the centre. Beside it is a single nightstand with a lamp and a charging cord waiting its partner. There's a dresser against the far wall and a smaller door to the left with a small bathroom through it.

His room.

It's about the size of my entire bathroom, but I love it. It reminds me of my bedroom at the convent.

Except for the main striking difference: the convent didn't have my bodyguard in it.

My bodyguard who had his fingers inside me. Who gave me the only orgasm I haven't given myself. Who commanded my body in a way I wasn't sure I'd appreciate but now understand. His dominance is masked beneath his entire exterior, hints peeking out every time I ignored him. And now, I'll be so deliciously fucked when his control is solely focused on me.

As I wander through his bedroom, Rosen stays by the door, watching me, expressionless. This is it, no doubt. He'll deny me, claim the club was a huge mistake, and everything he told me in there will no longer matter.

"Last chance, Aurora. Leave because I'm not strong enough to avoid you any longer."

"Rosen," I start, turning for him.

"I don't know how to go there," he says in a pained tone, but providing no explanation for his words.

"How to fuck?" Doubtful. Big-dick energy is what I initially thought about him and based on what I felt between my legs earlier, that's exactly what's in his pants.

"How to fuck a virgin."

"The same way you would any other woman."

Unamused, he swallows. Once, and then again before responding, "I'm a dominant, Aurora. What you experienced in the club is only a mere preview. Denying your orgasms, having you pinned against the wall. I don't know how to be what you deserve when my every desire is to punish you for being such a damn brat since the first day I met you."

I go for him, lifting onto my toes. "That's seriously what you're concerned about? How about I reassure you and say that was the best experience I've ever had. If I didn't enjoy it, I would have pushed you away. Do I look like someone who is interested in gentle?"

His eyes shut briefly and when they reopen, the argument is gone. "No."

Sliding my hands up his chest, I ask, "What's one fantasy you've had about me? Let's make it happen. Please, I *want* this."

He doesn't respond. He stares at me. But I study him back, searching for the guilt that's undoubtedly there, the argument he's putting up—anything I'll need to defend myself against.

"I'm already damned," he whispers, but I think it's more to himself than me.

In a flash, he changes. He's no longer my protector, but rather, my destroyer.

He spins us around, pressing my front to the door, his movements quick and rough, as he yanks the dress over my head and then onto the floor at our feet. I watch it go, watch as with that action, he unleashes his own bounds.

He snatches my wrists and, locking them into one of his hands, lifts them over my head, forcing my back to arch into him as his free hand comes around to my front and teasingly strokes the skin. Between my breasts and down to the edge of my panties.

"You came in here wanting to play...so let's play."

Oh my god. His voice, coated in his unbridled desire, wraps around the room, locking inside my body. In my core. My knees shift apart, pushing my aching centre against the door, brushing my panties, damp from the club, along the seam, seeking relief.

He notices, or feels me pulling from him, and yanks me away from the door, my ass to his body. "You don't get to find your own pleasure. You're *mine.* It was my rules you chose to disobey and it's my punishment you'll receive."

Punishment. I long to know what that means, and if it's anything like the club, I'll happily take it. All I know is Rosen won't hurt me, so with that trust, my lips press together, remaining silent.

His hand skates over my panties and it's impossible to think that a mere hour ago, he had his fingers inside me because he creates distance, not going beneath the damp material, even as a beg works its way up my throat. His fingers travel up my stomach, over my ribs, to the point it tickles the edge of my breasts. He traces the curve, fingering my bra.

He moves his hand away from my wrists, but instead of lowering them, I leave them where they are, invisibly restrained by his influence. He grasps my chin and turns my head until I'm able to see him.

"This can stop, Aurora," he states in a near-whisper. "At any point, you can withdraw your consent and we end this, no questions asked. I'm not going to hurt you. That's not my game, not what I enjoy. We're playing."

Is it possible for this man to creep more inside me than he already has? I suppose so because I melt with his words.

I nod, trying my best to convey how much I'm in this with him. How I'd rather die than refuse his pleasure.

"Then before we continue, pick a safe word."

"A safe word?"

"A word that when spoken ends this all."

"But you said you won't hurt me." Why would I require a

word to end this if it's not painful? *Why* would I want to end something giving me immense pleasure?

"It doesn't mean there might not be a time you want to pull back, if it gets too intense."

I still don't see how it could, but I shrug and murmur the first thing that comes to mind, "Flower."

"Good." He releases my jaw and backs away from me entirely, robbing me of his every touch. I don't move, waiting for his command, and receive a low, pleased sound when I don't. "*God*, how are you so fucking perfect?" With that question, the caring Rosen demanding my safe word is gone again, the dark one in his place. "Undress yourself. I want to see every inch of your body before I fuck it."

I turn around like I'm about to follow his instruction but instead ask, "Aren't you going to do that? Or are you too much of a pussy to touch me yourself?" Even knowing I'm playing with fire—with a man who looks seconds away from losing it— I don't bother hiding the snark in my tone.

A coldness enters his expression, his brow hiking is the only signal of how my words affect him. With a cruel smile, he says, "Keep stacking your punishments, Aurora. You're only stretching this night out longer."

Then I'll continue, as he worded it, "stacking" my punishments, so we'll never be done.

Like he knows what I'm thinking, he shakes his head, his thumb coming down on my lip with force. "That's not necessarily a good thing. I'll have you so wrought out by the end of the night, the only word you'll know how to say is my name."

"Don't tempt me." But I follow his earlier instructions and unsnap my bra before sliding my panties off. I've never been naked in front of another person, but Rosen pausing from unbuttoning his own shirt tells me him being my first is the best decision I ever could have made.

His eyes languidly devour every inch of me, pausing at my breasts, and then the space between my legs. One word formulates: "Fuck," before he snaps back and finishes undressing himself.

He removes his clothing, tossing them all to the side. His cock is erect, a vein running down the length, making my mouth instantly water. The Sisters, having to teach us about sex education, didn't exactly have every website blocked when they should have, which means Rosen isn't the first cock I've seen... but he's certainly the only one that matters and the only live one.

He cups himself and I lick my lips. I've never sucked someone before...but I want to do that for him.

"Come over here."

I obey, stopping right in front of him, beside the bed. My body hums, leaning into him.

He cups the back of my neck and brings me closer until he's touching me *everywhere*. Not with his hands; besides the one controlling my head. But his very being controls my breath, my reaction, my own hands, which itch to touch him, but instead, I cross them behind my back.

Rosen's tongue flicks against mine, controlling our kiss and me, and I allow him to. He kisses hard, and no doubt, he fucks like it too.

"There's so much I crave doing to you. So much I *can* do to you," he whispers, ending the kiss.

"Anything." This man can literally do anything to me, and I won't walk away. Not this time. Not after today. Not while we're wrapped up in another world, in another place.

He releases me and gestures to the bed. "Lie down."

Oh, my god, is this really going to...?

I don't know, but I won't allow my psyche to question what easily might be the best day of my life. The most unusual day.

His bed is tall and requires a small leap up. Once I'm seated, I push myself backwards, toward the pillows.

Rosen heads for the drawer unit across the room, crouching until pulling open the bottom one. I watch, impatience making me shift over the dark comforter until he straightens, holding a long string of red rope. Trepidation runs through me. Not because I think he would harm me, but because I don't know what to expect with something as mild as rope.

"W-what will that be for?" I swallow, disliking the fact that I stuttered through my question.

"I will tie you to the bed, which will amplify the experience for you. And me."

I glance at the rope and then the wooden footboards. "No pain?"

"Oh no," he replies in an almost purr. He reaches out and gently pushes on my shoulder, urging me down. "No, no, my little brat. You'll be punished for disobeying, but like I said, there will be no physical pain brought to your skin."

My little brat. Those words imbed in my heart, standing out from his other carefully planned words, which imply more. They don't matter, not when *my little brat* continues to replay in my mind, even replacing his other nickname for me.

"Since the first day we met, you've been a brat, and this has been my fantasy. Having you all to myself like this."

Yet...he doesn't move. He stands by the end of the bed, his gaze lost somewhere between guilt and second-guessing himself *again*. For a second, it feels like we're going backwards, and while I despise with my every being, the words that leave my mouth, I know him well enough that jealousy will activate and rid the guilt or whatever other dark emotion is passing through him.

"If you're going to stand there, I might have to find someone else to do what you're hesitating to."

In a flash, he's over me, his hands pinning mine above my head, the rope forgotten between us. He looks so crazed, so fucking sexy, and I'll continue saying whatever, if it means he'll react like this.

"You forget who I am, *princesse*. I'm a fucking killer, and unless you want a man's death on your conscience, you might want to shut your spoiled, little mouth and learn some patience. No one else will give you what you need. How," he rolls his hips, digging his hard erection into me, "to give your pussy what it's craving."

I can't help but smile, so I do, believing his insanity for a brief second. We both know it's false; eventually, there will be someone else who'll touch me, who he'll be unable to murder, no matter how tempting it might be.

He rolls to his feet again, grasping the rope between two fingers. It drags along my skin, between my breasts, as he takes it toward the footboard where he grabs my ankle and props it up, looping the rope around me and then the bedframe's posts. When he moves to do the same with the other, I pull on my ankle, testing his restraint. They're tight and dig into my skin, proving I won't be escaping.

Then he comes up to the side of the bed and silently works, tying each wrist to a separate post. With him bent over me, his bare chest is inches from my face. I manage to lift my head and lick a small line up his chest, pulling a grunt from him.

When I'm tied, he grasps my chin, re-angling my head. "I have fucking news for you, *princesse*, you're not in control here, so give up."

He gives me his back again, returning to the dresser. I strain to see what he pulls from the drawer, but my angle blocks my view. Instead, I study him. His powerful back, following the lines of muscle toward his hips and an ass that makes me jealous of my lack of one.

He returns and holds up a feather. A feather? My punishment is a feather? I definitely don't see how this is safe-word worthy at all.

"Ready to begin, *princesse*?"

37
ROSEN

Forbidden has never looked more delectable than when I have her tied to my bed.

A feather is my first tool, to ease her into more. To show her all the ways I can lull her senses through a gentle approach.

"A feather?" she questions, her brows rising in disbelief.

"Patience. This doesn't start until you're silent."

Her lips press together, and she smiles through it. I'm almost disappointed she didn't say more.

Starting at her neck, I trail the large feather through the valley between her breasts. Her breath hikes as the tool meant for arousal continues down her body, toward her stomach.

"It kinda tickles," she whispers. Her stomach caves in, arching away from the feather. Frustration comes over her expression, and it's like she second-guesses herself and stops shying away from its touch.

When I reach her hips, she arches her back, lifting into it. If she assumes the feather will be brushing her pussy, she'll be disappointed. At her hip, I take a sharp right, trailing it along her thighs. I do the same to her other side, before moving it down her leg.

It reaches her knee when she murmurs my name. Already wanting more. Confused I'm not doing what she expects.

At her feet, I tickle them. Her legs kick out from the hold my restraints have her in, resulting in gentle grunts when recalling she can't escape.

Her arms and legs are bound, making her body into an X over the bed. Her bright gaze continues to watch me, wide and trusting while also being so vulnerable. There's not an inch of her hidden from me, and by the end of the night, there won't be an inch of her I haven't tasted.

After a few seconds, when I feel she's had enough, I glide the feather back up her leg, over her hip, and pause right below the curve of her breasts, which rise rapidly with her shallow breaths.

"Do you see now, Aurora?"

"See what?"

"How I can control so much of you. You expected me to touch your cunt, and yet..."

"Maybe you don't know how to touch me." She smirks playfully. "Maybe you think you do, but you continue to pull back when it matters."

She's seeking a rise out of me, but she won't get one. Not yet.

"And here I was about to take the feather to where you desire it, but now I won't. Your taunts won't be rewarded." Then I drop the feather onto the bed beside her.

She realizes I'm not playing and any sign of this being a game slips from her expression. Her mouth forms an O, and her eyes widen and look frazzled. She jerks in her bonds, trying to reach for me. "No, Rosen, wait. What—?"

We've hardly begun and she's already dying for more. As long as I'm careful and don't bring her to the point of using her safe word. If I even hear the murmured beginning of that F-word, I'll stop immediately, but I really don't want this to end that way. Aurora doesn't seem like someone who'll give in easily. Her own determination will take her as far as she can.

"You continuously taunt me, Aurora. Even when you're bound and under *my* control, you still think you're in charge." I lean over and grasp her chin, bending to brush my lips over hers, tasting her. "If you play nice, we'll continue."

"Please," she gasps when I pull back.

"Say it again."

"Please."

"Hm." I pause, pretending to debate her request before lifting the feather and bringing it back to her body. I move it in a circle over her stomach, watching as her eyes flutter shut, her teeth biting down on her bottom lip.

I slide it up her chest, circling each breast, watching as her lips curl, teeth still biting into the bottom one. She rolls her shoulders into the motion, arching those budded nipples into my touch. I give her what she craves, because *I* need her reaction, and I trail the tip of the feather over each nipple.

She gasps, her eyes flying open. "I-I didn't realize how sensitive they could be."

"It'll get better from here, I promise."

I move the feather around each nipple in a few circles, enough that she begins to be desensitized by it before changing course and progressing down her body, pausing right over the hood of her clit.

"Rosen." Her legs twitch as she tries to move her body, urging me where she needs the pressure. "Rosen, please."

Oh, how I want to. Instead, to make my point, I toss the feather away, flicking it to the floor. She follows its trajectory until it's beyond her sight on the floor. Her head whips to face me, flashing red with anger.

"See how you asked so nicely, but I didn't listen? Remember that the next time I ask you to stay in the car. Or not to run ahead downtown. Or any other command I've ever given you."

"But—"

"But nothing," I interrupt. "For everything your pretty little mouth begs for, it's one more thing I'll deny you."

"What does that mean?"

I smile. *Perfect.* If she doesn't understand my words, then this is about to get even more delicious.

Walking around the bed, I return to the dresser to retrieve something else, hesitating only when it's in hand. It's so easy to get wrapped up in Aurora, like I did at the club. Allowing my desires to consume me makes the fact of her innocence even more striking.

First, I fold a condom in my palm. Then, taking the wand vibrator from the drawer, I don't bother hiding it as I return to Aurora.

"What—"

I climb on the bed, crouching between her legs, her swollen slit begging for attention. Lifting the wand, I allow her to inspect it from afar.

"Tell me, *princesse*, have you ever used a vibrator before?"

"No," she replies right away. "I didn't exactly have access to one."

Another first I shouldn't be sharing with her, but here we are.

"What's your safe word, Aurora?"

"Flower."

"If this gets too intense and you think you can't handle it, I want you to use it. Most people think a vibrator is a method to bring oneself pleasure, but it's more than that. It can be a form of very enjoyable punishment."

Then, before she can ask any questions, I press the button on the wand, feeling my hand quivering beneath the strength of the rubber. The *vvvvvv* sound fills the otherwise silent room, but it quickly becomes muffled by her cries.

I place it over her clit, and hedonism wracks her form almost immediately. Her body arches, restrained by the ties around her ankles. One little, brief touch and she's already losing her mind. She's fucking gorgeous.

"Look how you're responding, *princesse.*" I move the wand up and down her clit, dipping low to her core and then back to her most sensitive parts, listening to how her pants change based on the vibrator's location and memorizing every single one. "Look how your body reacts to a simple touch."

I glide it up and down her clit, her body responding so naturally. Her pussy lips get puffy and that ball of muscle gets swollen, peeking out from her folds. Her hands, tied above her head, punch into the pillow as her hips try to chase the direction of the vibrator.

"Rosen," she pants, her tone low and wanting. She's so close now. Her sweet, delicious scent makes the room heady. I want to see her come.

But when her legs try to clench again and her body jerks with the beginning of an orgasm, I yank the vibrator away, stealing away the possibility.

She lets out a sound that's almost a scream, almost a groan and packed with frustrated wildness. "What the f—"

I lean over her, pressing a finger to her mouth to shut her up. Her brows lift in an *are you serious* expression, but I shake my head, reminding her to keep silent. "*This* is your punishment. I will have you on the edge so many times, you will be begging me for it."

Her eyes widen and beneath the weight of my finger, she mumbles, "That's what you meant by not physically harming me."

"Precisely." With the vibrating wand in hand, I shift it between our bodies, right over her clit again. She's sensitive, so I won't be there for long, just enough to remind her of it. "Don't come before I allow you to, Aurora."

"Or?" she challenges. But when the vibrations pass over her clit and she twitches, arching her hips beneath me, her defiant tone grows weaker.

"You don't want to find out."

Repositioning myself at the end of bed, I move the vibrator toward her clit, while one of my fingers dip inside her, checking her before my next act. She's soaked.

"Tell me if this hurts."

Replacing my fingers with the vibrator, I feel her tense. It remains still, vibrating against her core until the muscles in her legs become looser.

"Atta girl. Breathe. I'm...bigger than the vibrator. This will help prepare you."

Watching her expression for any sign of pain, I slowly push the vibrator inside her, only an inch before pulling it back, coating it with her cum before replacing it inside her. She shows no sign of discomfort, just unbridled pleasure as she bites her lip and shuts her eyes, her movements slowing as she adjusts to the stretch.

"So pretty, Aurora," I praise, watching how her pussy tightens around the vibrator with my words. I manage to push two inches in then pause, not wanting to hurt her. I continue slowly, teasing her G-spot, but not pushing against it, aware her body won't be able to help itself if I do.

With every pass, she makes a noise. Her body shudders in its bounds. Her pussy is soaked now and my mouth waters with the demand to taste. The little bit I'd gotten from her in the club wasn't nearly enough. So I bend over and take her clit in my mouth, biting it lightly.

"Holy fuck!" she screeches.

The vibrator fucks her slowly as my tongue flicks back and forth, feeling the moment she's brought to the edge, when more of her juices seep between my hand and the bed. She's sweet; her taste something I'll happily die to receive again.

Before she orgasms, I pull away, removing the vibrator entirely and switching it off.

She lifts her head. "You're...really..."

"Really not allowing you to come?" I assume the rest of her sentence. "That was only two. You have a lot more to go."

In truth, as much as I'd love to keep her on the edge all night. Fuck—to strap the vibrator to her pussy and watch from afar as she fights to obey me, she won't make it. And that's okay. This is Aurora's first experience, and I have to maneuver carefully, maybe eventually putting aside the play for her needs.

But for now...

I crouch over her, my legs between hers as I take her budded nipples into my mouth. With my hand, I strum between her legs, feeling her sopping pussy. It's easy to dip two fingers in, and if I really wanted to, I have little doubt I could fit three.

"Tell me how much you want to come," I mumble into her skin as I work my way down. I want to hear her tell me, and then to explain why she can't.

When I curl my fingers against that highly sensitive spot inside her, she pushes out, "So much, Rosen. So...fucking... much."

"Hm." My thumb circles her clit as I lightly fuck her with my fingers. "And why can't you?"

"Because you told me not to."

I press once hard against her G-spot in warning, causing her voice to let out a half-shriek, half-moan. "Tell me why you really can't come."

"Because I don't listen to you."

"Mhm." I trail my lips down her stomach to her hipbone, stopping right above her pussy. When I speak, I blow cool air over her, knowing she feels it more intensely, given how wet she is.

"I don't see you complaining."

Ignoring her jab, I move my mouth over her clit, fucking it in tandem to my fingers inside her. Seconds later, her core clenches, her body beginning to twitch with the beginnings of another one.

So I lift my mouth, and when her breathing evens out again —kind of—and her movements slow, I curl my fingers against her G-spot, petting the spot until her orgasm returns to the top, and her whimpers fill the room.

I pull my fingers out, stealing yet another one. I place them against her lips, tapping once, and when her lips part, obeying my silent request, I grin. My fingers slip between her lips, tracing her bottom one, and her tongue darts out to lick.

"What do you taste, Aurora?"

"My desire."

When I'm satisfied she's had enough, I return to her pussy, taking what I'm really dying for. With my hands gripping her thighs, I push my tongue inside her tight hole, fucking her.

"Fuck...fuck."

She quivers beneath my touch, and with her response, I know she's finally getting it. The shaking, the noises, the *need*.

Which means, she's nearly where I desire her to be.

I cycle through licking her, petting her, and fucking her with my fingers, taking her to the edge so many times before pulling back. She thrashes in her restraints, makes ungodly noises I never believed a person to be capable of, and begs.

In her movements.

In her cries.

She begs *me*.

38

AURORA

The bed beneath me is soaked and I haven't even orgasmed yet. I didn't know it was possible to be *this* wet without coming. It's been, what, six...seven... times now? I don't know. I lost count, not that I'm exactly keeping track.

Rosen's doing things to my body I hadn't known it was capable of. I'm reacting in ways I never assumed I would. I'm fucking *crying*. Begging him so much, tears have formed, my body sobbing—pleading—demanding release. My breaths are shallow and rough and the rope he placed on my body feels more constricting with every missed orgasm.

One word could end this all.

Yet, I wouldn't stop this for anything.

I *have* had enough, but I'm not ending this. I'd rather die than finish early. He'll see I'm strong enough to withstand what he's calling torture. Beautiful, delicious, forbidden torture.

He must realize I'm sobbing the same time I do, for his fingers pause inside me and he leans over. I almost expect him to stop entirely, but instead, he watches me, his lips curling up in the corners in a smirk so devious, I nearly don't recognize the man attached to it any longer.

"Your tears are beautiful. Your pussy is a mess. Your hair is dishevelled. Your makeup smudged. But you've never looked more perfect than you do right this instance."

Maybe it's the look in his eyes. Maybe it's his praise. But he causes me to enjoy something I shouldn't be.

"*This* is what I wanted, *princesse*. To see you a mess. To *make* you a mess."

I don't know where these words come from, but they slip out, mixing into everything illicit we're doing. Words I wish could be true. "*Your* mess."

When he pulls back, I curse myself for saying that. But then I hear the rip of a package and watch as he quickly rolls a condom on.

When he catches me watching, he murmurs, "I assume you're not on birth control and while I'd enjoy nothing more than the feel of you bare—"

"I get it." He can't. Everything we're doing here is prohibited, but if I were to end up pregnant with a child that isn't Rossi's, it could earn both our deaths.

He reaches out for my chin, angling my head to brush his lips over mine. Soft, but as claiming as it would be with force.

His erect cock brushes my core, and when I think he's about to readjust and merely tease, he slowly pushes the head inside. He might have had the vibrator inside me, but now I see what he was talking about. A burn erupts through my insides, my hands curling above my head.

"Breathe, Aurora."

My eyes squeeze shut, and he reaches between us, petting my clit. He gathers some of the liquid and strokes himself with it before placing his cock back inside me. First the inch he already gained, and then another, pausing yet again.

"Why are you so fucking big?" I hiss, although I'd change nothing of this interaction because there is no better feeling in the world than Rosen inside me.

Another inch and he reaches above me and undoes one of my wrists, taking my hand in his. It feels...intimate to have him hold my hand, his eyes on mine as he fucks himself inside me. It's his gaze that ensures I don't shut my eyes again.

"You're doing amazing, Aurora."

His praise spreads my thighs wider, accepting him deeper into me until the pain begins to fade.

"It doesn't hurt anymore. I just feel...stretched."

With a tightening grip, Rosen sinks deeper, until I feel him *everywhere*...until he's nowhere, pulling out of me and panting.

"Are you sure? Do not lie to me about your feelings, Aurora, or else this next part might hurt."

"I'm not, I swear." It's the truth, but I'm also curious about the meaning behind his words.

He drags his cock up and down my pussy, gathering more of my desire before he thrusts inside me, all of him entering me at once.

All our banter, my teasing, his determination combined into a single thrust.

This is so wrong. Yet so right.

I won't get enough. This can never end. This forbidden moment in time needs to pause, so we can lose ourselves forever.

My body stretches to accommodate his welcoming length. My head tips into the pillow, unable to keep his gaze any longer, as pleasure sweeps over me, making me question if the discomfort from minutes ago was present at all or if it was all in my head.

And then he moves his hips, once, twice, and that orgasm returns yet again. But if he's inside me, he won't deny me, right? After all, that's what this is. Officially having sex means his punishment is over and I made it through to the other side.

His hips pound against mine as he pushes unforgivingly inside me. His previous worries float through my mind, when he was concerned about my well-being, and I get it now. Rosen doesn't fuck gentle, but I wouldn't want it any other way. He takes my face again, angling my head toward his, so when my eyes beg for release, he can see it for himself.

"This is…this is so…"

He lifts onto his knees and his cock slips out of me, leaving my core empty.

"Too much," I pant through sobs. Every muscle in my body is alive; every nerve hardwired to respond. I can't concentrate. Even with my ankles bound, I manage to dig my feet into the bed and push up, arching my hips toward him.

"Please…Rosen, please."

"Begging, Aurora. So fucking perfect, my little brat. *Ma princesse.*"

That name. I swear I could come from that alone. From him growling it in my ear in his low, sexy, possessive tone.

In one thrust, he pushes inside me again. My wet core accommodates him without effort, now used to him. This time, I will remain silent. He won't get a warning. My abs tighten, the force to keep myself still and unresponsive, to not give it away when I—

His cock disappears and I groan in dismay.

He takes my chin again. With his thumb, he gathers a tear and I watch in unbridled fascination as he licks it, shutting his eyes with his low moan.

"The taste of your desire. It's fucking sweet. Your tears can single-handedly feed me."

"They will, if I can't come." I'll likely pay for that one, but what does he expect?

"Soon," he promises. "You've taken your punishment almost flawlessly, but I should remind you, the next time you piss me off, your penalty will be double this."

Double? I'm hardly making it through this time, and he's threatening *double?*

I can't think about that yet. Not with my mind blank, all other instincts and necessities secondary to one thing only: the demand to come. The building orgasm wanting to burst free.

Rosen enters me again, but this time, it feels different. *He* feels different.

Forgiving.

He reaches behind him and undoes my ankles, one at a time, and my legs happily fold around his thighs, wrapping his waist to lock him inside me.

"I want to feel you touching me."

Then he reaches above my head and undoes my other wrist. I roll them quickly, getting feeling back into them before holding onto him. I nearly sink my nails into his arms, ensuring he can't go anywhere, but I keep my fingers relaxed and don't mark up his skin, fearful of his reaction when I'm so fucking close to getting what I want.

His arm wraps around one of my thighs, removing it from his hip, and lifts it up, bending me nearly in half. His cock gets deeper, pressing into another part of me that makes me lose my mind, blinded by ultimate longing.

When my core tightens, the orgasm *right there*, I nearly allow myself to, but instead, his earlier words ring in my mind.

"Can I come?"

He smiles, almost proud, and his thrusts quicken, a silent *yes*, but I wait for his verbal permission before releasing. "Yes."

No orgasm has ever felt so right, so extraordinary, as a turbulent wave sucks me under. Every nerve, every muscle, every fibre of my being lets go with it. I think I scream, but I don't know. The pleasure is blinding and my senses only narrow into one thing—relief.

"You feel fucking amazing, *princesse*."

I come again with his use of that nickname. Or, maybe I never stopped orgasming the first time, and it stretched into one long one. Either way, bliss coats my body and I want to sleep, but I also don't want to let go. Letting go means this night is over and I don't want it to be.

"Say my name as you orgasm, Aurora. Let me hear you."

For once, an easy request. *"Rosen."*

When my continuous orgasm slows and I feel my soul returning to my body, Rosen buries his head into my neck and groans. His noises bring a smile to my face. He unleashes everything he's been holding back in his strokes. His lips skate the skin of my neck, strangely intimate for what just happened.

My weak and useless arms slide from his body, landing limply on the bed. Rosen lowers his body onto mine, distributing his weight to his knees. Contentedness fills the room, both of us silent in our head.

What does this mean? Every encounter between us ended so differently, he's bound to push me away again. Tonight felt *right*. Final. Official. Like we can ignore the other facts hanging over us—Erico, my family, his job.

As if his thoughts go to the same place, Rosen lifts his head. His dark eyes meet mine and emotion passes through them. An emotion I don't want to name yet.

"For now, you're mine, *princesse*. You're worth the cost of betraying everything."

～

I doze. Or we doze, but I'm awakened with a wet cloth between my legs. The bed beneath me is still soaked, so there's no point in cleaning me, but through a sleep-fog, I manage to spread my legs.

Until that cloth passes over my thighs, I hadn't realized how sore my muscles are. The heat of the cloth pokes at my nerves, making me sigh and shut my eyes again as sleep steals me.

"Go back to sleep, Aurora. I'll take care of you."

I know you will.

I've just ensured I'll never be able to sleep in my bedroom again after her. Because the sight of Aurora there makes something shift inside me. Not in an uncomfortable manner, but rather, different. Something making me rub at my chest, right over my tattoo.

How can one woman cause me to break my vows to my boss, all while driving life into my very being?

After my clean-up, I couldn't release her back to her room. Not yet. Coming here at all with her is on the verge of idiotic. The mansion's walls are thick, but a woman's loud cries can still be heard through them. I know because of the women sometimes brought to the other soldiers' rooms who are around mine.

After untying the red rope from the bedframe and returning it to my bottom drawer, along with the vibrator after washing it, I'm reminded why I made the choice I did. Having Aurora tied to *my* bed became my every living fantasy.

After cleaning what I could and laying a couple towels over the soaked sheets, so she has somewhere slightly more comfortable to rest, I slide beside her, wrapping my arm around her waist. She's so small, I'm able to fit her into my chest easily. She sighs happily and wiggles her ass in her sleep against my cock. It settles when she returns to her deep slumber, this time practically hugging my arm.

Continuing to shove aside all the *should*s in my life, I sleep with Aurora Corsetti, Montreal's mafia *princesse,* in my arms.

~

How does the steaming water of a shower make one's outlook so different? It washes away the moronic choices, clears the head, and makes apprehension creep up again.

Not regret. Not guilt.

And that's probably what makes it the fucking worst.

Beneath the spray, I lean, my hands positioned on the wall in front of me as I stare at the water swirling at my feet.

I fucked up. I didn't only sleep with my boss's daughter, but I took her virginity. And while my stupid male pride is thrilled, the reality of the situation is grim if anyone were to learn.

These reflections bring to light the other thing making me sick—that Aurora has gotten under my skin and I'd love nothing more than putting a gun to Erico Rossi's head and enticing a war.

Small hands glide up my back, tugging me from my musings. I hadn't heard her enter the shower and it's not until she wraps her arms me that I turn to face her.

"Your thoughts are so loud, they woke me up."

"Sorry," I mumble.

Taking the loofah, I pour a healthy amount of soap onto it and make it sudsy before washing her. My movements are methodical, focused, as I stroke it over every inch of her skin.

Her arms, her hands, even between her fingers. I circle her breasts without lingering, move up to her neck and then her back before washing each leg, spending extra time at her feet. Lastly, I lightly wash between her legs.

"Sore?"

"More like sensitive in a good way."

Good.

"Is this the part you kick me out of your room because you've remembered all of the rules and you regret last night and now we'll go back to being non-friends?"

I flinch, her recollection of the night I kissed her the only example of her expectations. I haven't been the most welcoming since she's joined me in the shower, so dropping the loofah at our feet, I show her, apologizing for now and conveying the meaning behind my final statement to her last night.

Cupping her cheeks, I bring her face to mine for a heady, possessive kiss. "It's your decision if this continues. I meant what I said last night. We absolutely shouldn't be doing this, but I'm done fighting. You're worth everything."

Words spoken with absolute certainty. She *is* worth everything, even if I don't quite understand why or how this tiny woman removes the influence of my oaths. *She's* becoming my oath instead. If this was ever to be discovered, I'd take the entire fall, if it means protecting her from their wrath.

"But what happens if we *are* figured out? I'll fight my family for your life, but what if—

I press my finger against her lips, quieting her. "Your concern is everything, Aurora, but that's only *if*. Right now, I'm focused on us."

"Us," she repeats. "You called yourself something last night. Something with a D..."

"Dominant."

"And what does that make me?"

"Mine."

She's not yours. She's owned by another man. She will be owned by another man but—

She's mine. For as long as she's willing, I'm done with fighting what's between us.

"If you want," I add.

She rubs her hand in a small circle around my chest. "That consists of punishing me then?"

"That consists of being who we want to be. You like to be praised, and I enjoy doling it out. You don't listen to me; I will remind you of all the reasons that's a bad idea."

"Like last night?" she checks.

"There's other methods." Letting my eyes trail over her pale skin, I imagine all the ways I could show my brat why she ought to listen. She's done great with orgasm denial, but continuous orgasms are another intense method.

"Last night didn't hurt," she tells me. "I mean, I guess my abs now feel like I exercised, but considering it was my first time, I think it went well." She shrugs, downplaying how great she did.

I chuckle, lowering my left hand to her hip, splaying over a piece of her stomach, right atop the muscles she speaks of. "That's normal. Your body was trying to grab onto that orgasm so many times."

"Where do we go from here? I don't want to stop but..."

But this is not allowed, I imagine her unspoken words being, or something of that likeness.

"It can't be forever."

The stakes are high, because while I want to tie her to my bed and not let Rossi anywhere near her, I know the reality is that, one day, I'll be forced to watch her walk down the aisle to another man. With his ring on her finger. He'll get her smiles every day. Her bratty attitude when she's in a mood.

Every single concept in that notion makes me want to go hunt his ass down, but I keep my emotions in check, my expression smooth, not to alarm her.

"When the engagement is officially made, you'll have more attention on you, so it might be best to end this then."

The words scrape at my throat, but I hold firm, so Aurora feels okay going forward, even when my own instincts demand me to remove Erico Rossi from the equation. So that I'll never have to give her up.

"Okay," she agrees, her eyes distracted. "Only if I don't have to obey you suddenly."

"You'll be rewarded when you do."

"And when I don't, I get a duplicate of last night." Playfully, she rolls her eyes, grinning. "Oh, the horror! Believe me, I enjoyed that way too much to start listening to you all the time."

"I approve."

Her hands slide down my wet body, over my abs. Her touch avoids my tattoo this time, as she traces my hip, heading straight for my cock, which begins thickening with her gentle hands.

"I didn't get to fully explore you last night," she murmurs. One hand cups my balls, while her other strokes me, my body responding easily to her touch. "I want to...I want..." Her eyes flash up and she dabs a tongue at her bottom lip. "I want—"

"Want what, Aurora?" Thumb smoothing her lip, I add, "Use this pretty mouth and tell me what you want." I have an idea, and while I long to put her on her knees, I want her verbal consent first.

"To...to lick you. To take you in my mouth."

My body burns to have her do precisely that. To come down her throat and be another first for her.

Her face is framed by wet hair. Droplets catch in the strands, making her look like a water goddess. Even the look of her—so beautiful and perfect— has my throat catching when I command, "Get on your knees. You came in here wanting to see my cock. You're about to get a very intimate tour."

Her lips part, water beads kissing between them, and I vow to soon chase them. To lick every dewdrop from her skin as I make her come on my mouth. The ultimate fantasy.

Aurora lowers herself to her knees and a million dreams come true with that little action. She keeps her gaze trained on me, blinking often when water bounces off my body and into her eyes. They scatter over her eyelashes, dampening the black lines. Still, she never shies away.

"Safe word?"

"Flower."

"Use it if you want me to stop."

I cup her chin, tipping her face up, committing every second of this to memory so I have something to recall in the final moments of life before Nico sticks a gun to my head and pulls the trigger.

"Out there, you might be their princess, but in here, you're mine."

"Rosen..." she whispers, my name on her lips trailing into a low moan as I release her chin and stroke my cock, inches from her face.

"Well, what are you waiting for? A hard cock in front of your face and a mouth that should stop spewing attitude. I think you can figure it out. This is what your teasing has done, brat. It's time to pay up."

"Yes, sir." She grins wickedly.

"*Princesse.*"

Her hand reaches for me, wrapping around my cock. How can betrayal and illicit feel so fucking good? She strokes me once, twice, her thumb brushing over the head of my cock, but still, she doesn't take me in her mouth, and it's then, the realization hits me, making me feel like a complete asshole.

Reaching down, I cup her cheek, angling her head up until she's forced to look at me again. "You've never—" She better have not, but my question presents her a chance to reveal if she had.

"No," she interrupts, her cheeks flushing in a way that has nothing to do with the hot water. She nibbles on her bottom lip before murmuring, "Can you show me?"

Fuck. Me. The little mafia *princesse* wants to be trained how to please a man with her mouth. Shoving aside the dark thoughts of where these skills will eventually be used for the longing wrapping my every nerve, I command, "Keep your hand around me, exactly like you have. When you're ready, put your lips around my head."

She leans forward almost immediately, sliding the tip of my cock between her lips, keeping her lips shaped like an O, all without direction. I groan, slamming a fist into the tile releasing the surge of energy that will prevent me from shoving carelessly down her throat. I want to prove to her how good of a girl she can be, how deep her throat can take me.

"Good," I praise, resting my hand over her head, petting her hair. "If you need to stop, tap the back of my legs. For now, let me show you how I like it."

With my hand over her head, I lightly guide her forward, forcing her to take more of me into her mouth. "Keep your lips tight. I enjoy the pressure. If you can't swallow all of me, it's okay. Use your hand."

Her mouth glides over me, her tongue teasing my underside, like she's unsure what to do with it. That'll come next. Her hand holds me gentler than I typically prefer but I'll let her finish exploring before I teach her more. My cock hits the back of her throat before she pulls back a half-inch.

"That's it."

Vibrations from her responding moan coast the underside of my cock and straight into my balls. My hips jerk unintentionally, forcing more of me down her throat, causing a shocked noise to come from Aurora.

"Shit, sorry. You're doing so good. Move your mouth up and down. Explore with your tongue and your hands. You can't do anything wrong." She's so far from doing this incorrectly.

Her lips drag along my underside until she releases me entirely, her tongue wrapping my cockhead. Her eyes dart up the length of my body, meeting mine, and she grins, completely aware of how she's seconds away from making me lose my mind.

I grasp the strands of her hair, forcing her head back until she releases to avoid the pain. "Did you lie when you said this was your first time at oral?"

"N-no."

Her stutter tells me she's being truthful, so for that, I let her go, and she immediately takes me in her mouth again, this time lightly dragging her teeth along my length.

Tapping the back of her head, I grit, "Careful, *princesse*. You bite, I punish."

Her tongue flicks at that sensitive spot connecting my head to my shaft and I see white. My hands grip her shoulders to keep me steady as she swallows me as deep as she can, her nails dragging up my calves.

Holy fuck, this girl.

"I have the *princesse* on her knees when I should be the one there for her." I cup her cheek. "You look so lovely with my cock down your throat."

She takes me so fucking perfectly that when her hands continue up my legs, stopping between them to fondle my balls, every muscle in my form tightens with a demanding throb. I feel my release there, so close. I need—

She releases me with a *pop*, licking my precum from her lips and pulling a frustrated groan from me.

Gripping her hair, I move her mouth back toward me. "You forget who's in charge. Your name may carry weight outside this room, but in here, you're under my control."

I thrust into her mouth, keeping a hold on her head, muscles tense, should I feel her gag reflex requiring me to get her off me. Rather, she swallows me easily, dragging her nails down the back of my legs, on the verge of playing another dangerous game.

"Tap if this gets too intense," is my only warning before I fuck her face. Her tongue slides along my base, her pressure ideal, and her throat so full, I won't be able to last long. Seeing her swallow might be a dream come true, but I give her the option: "Tap once if you want to swallow. Twice if you don't."

Tap.

With her silent permission, I continue thrusting, my cock swells nearly instantly, the heat running down my spine.

"Coming," is my single warning before my cum shoots straight into her mouth. I release her hair, clutching both my hands on the sides of the shower to keep me upright and steady as she sucks the remainder of my cum.

Once emptied, she pulls her mouth off me, grinning as she takes my offered hand. Her tongue flicks out and takes in a dab of cum on the side of her mouth. "Not bad."

I kiss her, taking her face in my hands and thanking her for what she did. My tongue strokes over hers, possessiveness making every second passing more and more difficult to release her when I taste myself on her.

"That was fucking hot," I whisper, pulling away. "You've drained me. Worked up a hunger only your pussy can satisfy."

Reaching behind me, I switch off the shower and grab a towel on the nearest hook and wrap her in it. Once she's out of the shower, I follow, quickly wiping the water from my body.

"If we don't get you back to your room soon, people will begin wondering." If they haven't already.

She glances over her shoulder, pouting with that same expression she used in the club last night. "But you're hungry. Five minutes."

Tempting. But to get more time with her later, she should go now. "We shouldn't."

She drops the towel and climbs back onto my bed, spreading her legs with a coy smirk as she crooks a finger toward me. "Five minutes won't change anything."

"Do it in two and we have a deal."

"That depends on your performance."

"Brat."

But like the club last night, she wins the compromise.

40

AURORA

Turns out, fucking around with Rosen becomes more difficult than I ever imagined. Despite his job of constantly being around, it's like we're never left alone for long. I've managed to sneak to his room once, two days after the club, and him to mine, but it's precarious.

With Nico and Della's wedding coming up soon, the family's been more active as well. Della and her sister have been in and out shopping with the wedding planner for the ceremony because although she's made it known she couldn't care less about its grandeur, Mom is insistent for a wedding she believes suitable for a Corsetti.

The sisters often offer me to tag along, and I've agreed a couple times, but not always. Sometimes, I visit the community garden and pretend to have a simpler life when I'm with the kids and laughing with Roz, who has become a friend. When I'm not doing that, I'm with Rosen.

This time, I must attend the dress store because Della spoke specific terms: bridesmaid dress.

Which is how I end up exiting the individual changing

room, heading into the circular room of mirrors, and standing in front of Della and Mom, both of whose expressions brightens as they take in the pastel blue dress.

Amidst their *ooh*ing and *ahh*ing, I study my reflection. The girl I'm staring at doesn't even look like me, but Della has chosen well. The off-shoulder dress cuts into a V, dipping right into my breasts. Its sleeves, if the chiffon curtain-like drapes by my side can be called that, are soft and a nice addition.

"Wow," Mom breathes, lifting to her feet. "Honey, you're beautiful."

Della also stands, and Ariella exits the room beside mine. Their attention goes straight to her for another round of admiration.

Awareness slithers down my spine and I glance to the right, out of the dressing area and toward the front of the private wedding dress shop, where Rosen and Thomas guard the door.

His reaction is subtle, but powerful nonetheless. His shoulders shift the slightest fraction; an amount one wouldn't notice unless they were so attuned to him. By his side, his hands curl into fists.

Before anyone notices me staring, I look away from him and back toward my reflection, which seems like it fits into this life. Like I belong.

I look like a princess.

~

"You sure you don't want to come for lunch?" Mom stares warily, her hand poised on the top of the vehicle's door. Della and Ariella are already inside, preparing to head for the restaurant they've all chosen for a late lunch after dress shopping.

The very dresses now getting final alterations in the expensive shop behind us.

I give Mom a fake apologetic look, consisting of lowering brows and a half-smile. "Sorry, today's the day I visit the garden, and I don't enjoy breaking promises."

Thankfully, I made this decision known earlier to Rosen. I need the peace helping children brings to my mind, which is why we travelled in two vehicles; that way, he and I can head in the other direction after shopping.

While I might be getting a fraction more comfortable in accepting my life as the days pass, they signify something else too. That as the wedding approaches, I will be seeing my fiancé again, which frightens me.

And what happens when you're officially engaged to Erico? How do Rosen and I end something neither of us want to?

"I understand." Mom speaking pauses my depressing considerations and takes me back to the present.

"I'll see you all later." I stride toward the SUV behind the town car, where Rosen is leaning against the front grill, looking too delicious to ignore.

My feet want to quicken, but I keep my steps measured as I pass him, his eyes tracking me beneath his sunglasses.

Keeping my voice low enough so no one else but Rosen can hear me, I state, "You're not gonna get my door? That's your job, isn't it?"

I'm playing with fire as I can't see his expression through his glasses. Biting back my grin, because Mom is still observing, I duck my head, using my hair as a shield as I lower myself into the passenger seat.

Once the other vehicle pulls away, Rosen kicks off the front and comes around to the driver's side, sliding in, his hand immediately heavy and possessive as it comes down on my thigh.

"My *job* is to give you pleasure, *princesse*, but you make it fucking impossible when you open this mouth." He flicks his thumb along my bottom lip, lingering for a beat longer. "If you're not careful, I might have to put it to better use."

"Not out here, you wouldn't." He wouldn't chance being seen.

His fingers curl into my thigh, to the point of near pain. My breath catches as I bite back a reaction. "Careful how much you threaten me, Aurora. I can put you on your knees right here and you'd fucking love it."

I'm nearly disappointed when he starts the car and pulls away, breaking the moment entirely. He pulls into traffic, and once we're settled on the road, he replaces his hand on my thigh.

Such a simple touch. As each day passes, I grow more comfortable with Rosen, even when this is a limited thing. Eventually, we'll be forced to stop. For now, I pretend Rosen and I are a normal couple out for an afternoon drive.

"The wedding's in a matter of days," I comment.

His mouth presses into a flat line and he seems suddenly hyper-focused on the road. In a gruff tone, he responds, "You'll have a good time, Aurora. Nico has a surprise for you. And you're sexy in that gown."

There's so much of that sentence I want to unpack, starting with the surprise comment, but I stupidly go with, "If only we could dance together at the reception."

Rosen doesn't respond, making me want to sink deeper into the seat. I wish this moment could pass—or go backwards, and I could not say what I had. Of course, Rosen isn't where I am; he's understanding of this forbidden romance, but my stupid heart is getting way too attached.

"We technically could," he mutters. "I'll be attending as a guest."

A guest? Mom once said Rosen took the place of Hawke in

my brothers' minds, so is this an example of that? If he's a guest, it would be natural to dance with him and my family shouldn't see an issue with it.

"But we shouldn't," he continues, shattering my positive feeling, "I'm there as a guest with an insider's focus." His gaze slides to me, silently conveying his meaning.

Me.

"They might think it's strange if we were to dance."

"Would it be weird? Considering how much time we spend with each other."

"Yeah," he answers, his tone getting weighed down with regret. "Yes, because they'd expect differently from the both of us."

Somehow, I know that to be true. The Sisters were very clear in my role; the system the family has. And how Rosen's place isn't in my arms.

Slumping into the seat, I stare out the window, tuning everything else out while I, once again, curse the absurdity of this life.

"You seem distracted," a small voice shouts, its loud chime pulling me from my thoughts, which are a jumbled mess of confused emotions, stuck on a path they don't want to be.

"I guess I am," I muse, glancing up from the rose bush I'm working on with Amy. "A lot on my mind."

"Your brother's wedding, you mean?" Her cheeks bloom pink. "I overheard you talking to Roz the other day. That's mighty exciting, and I bet you'll look like a princess, all dressed up! I enjoy dressing up sometimes. When my mommy takes me to the community centre, they have costumes I sometimes put on."

"I'm sure you look amazing," I respond, trying my hardest to remain focused on her words. It isn't easy because what I'm going through isn't something I can share with a six-year-old child. Amy's excited by the prospect of dressing up, while this wedding will signal something for me.

Will *represent* something. My own wedding.

Maybe if Erico wasn't there, I could enjoy the ceremony.

I stand from the rose bush and pace away, removing my gardening gloves and brushing the dirt from my jeans. Wandering to the edge of the garden, I catch the front of the vehicle. No doubt, Rosen's leaning somewhere on that SUV, looking completely delectable, or waiting inside. I imagine his fingers drumming along the wheel as he waits.

"Looking for your sexy bodyguard?"

Roz's voice snaps me out of my daze. That's twice now within minutes of each other, my mind has wandered away from where it should be, and it took other people to bring me back.

"Just thinking about this week."

"You mean your brother's wedding?"

"Jeez." I roll my eyes, turning around. Roz's waist-long blonde hair is mussed, likely from being pushed away from her face one too many times as she bends over the plants. "Does everyone know about it?"

"I mean," she shrugs a shoulder, pursing her lips, "your family's kinda big, right? Even people on the outside know to stay away from them. So, yeah, anyone who's anyone knows about this wedding."

"What's that mean? People on the outside."

Instead of answering, she reaches into her pocket and pulls out something small. Her hand remains in a ball, and I can't see what she has. "I find these help sometimes. I have bad anxiety and taking one usually eases my mood."

Stepping closer, she unfurls her hand at the same time she reaches for my wrist, bringing my hand to hers, where she pushes the item into my palm. I glance around, making sure no one's paying us any attention, and then at the plastic baggy of small, coloured gummies she's given me. There's only a couple. Four, if that.

Candy?

"Edibles," Roz murmurs.

"Like...drugs?"

She shrugs again. "They're legal. Cannabis. You've never tried them?"

I'm sure the Sisters would have a coronary if I took drugs while in their care.

"Well, I've already chopped them in half, so don't worry about dosage. Before walking down the aisle, take one. They calm your body and mind and will make your worries a bit less pressing."

She's suggesting I swallow drugs to get me through the ceremony? I never believed I'd ever consider drugs, despite what my family may have dealings in, but if they're as effective as Roz's claiming them to be...

"I take them all the time," she adds, speaking more offhandedly. "I get bad in social situations, like large events. Hell, some days, even grocery shopping overwhelms me. I eat one before leaving the house and it helps me manage."

"No long-lasting effects?"

"None. They're about a half-hour to kick in, so be aware of that. You'll probably be tired by the time night hits, but once you wake up, you'll be back to normal."

They sound harmless and might not be a bad idea. Perhaps, it'll make Erico a bit more manageable. Besides, I could always change my mind. Roz was nice enough to consider me, so I tuck the baggy into my pocket.

"Thanks. They could be good to have."

She smiles and lifts onto her toes in a movement of excitement. "Great. I'm sure it'll help you a lot." She peeks behind her, at the bush she left two kids by. They're watching us, their wide, patient eyes waiting for her to return. "I should head back," she says, waving as she wanders back across the space.

Before returning to my own task at the rose bush, I peek at Rosen's vehicle again. What would he say about me carrying edibles? I get the sense this breaks some unspoken rule, so before I create unnecessary drama, I decide not to say anything.

Beside me, Rafael rubs his hands together and then against his thighs. He shifts once, twice, three times, and then a fourth, for good measure. His shoulders lift nearly to his ears before dropping back down with a heavy, long breath. Then his hands ball by his side and his leg bounces.

I'm seconds away from reaching out and demanding he remain still for longer than two fucking seconds, because his bristling energy is exhausting to even stand beside, when Nico, apparently sharing the same thoughts, reacts. His arm flings out to the side, whacking his brother in the middle of the chest.

"Will you fucking stop?" Nico shouts, his words getting drowned out by the whirling of the Corsetti jet as it slows to a stop.

Even as we stand a ways back, it's noisy on the private airstrip. In a moment, the door will open, the stairs will be lowered, and Hawke and his girlfriend will be here.

"Easy for you to say," Rafael mutters. "You've seen him before. Think how I feel."

"Think how *he* feels," I point out.

Hawke Corsetti is home. Back for only the day, only for the ceremony, and will be returning to the plane during the reception. The plane will also be on standby, in case Hawke demands escape sooner.

I look toward my underboss. He's leaning on the SUV beside Rafael, but I spot the strain in his arms, the stiffness in his shoulders. Nico has few tells, but that's some of them. He's anxious about how today will go, and it has nothing to do with his wedding, which begins in a matter of hours.

The three of us have come to pick Hawke up while Aurora, Della, and Ariella prepare for the ceremony. Coming here with Nico and Rafael is a perfect distraction to the shitshow that's about to take place. Not the wedding, but in my head. My mind.

Rafael bounces on his feet again as the plane's steps unfold. "It's happening."

A figure gets to the top of the stairs and Rafael curses. Beside him, another one appears. Smaller. Her blonde hair draped over her shoulders, halfway down her back as her arm reaches for Hawke's. She's dressed in a short, black dress, already prepared for the event. The two descend the steps together, Hawke angling himself in front of her.

Black, shaggy hair hangs over his face, which he flicks away as he paces warily toward us. The sun catches on his piercings. One in his lip, which are formed in a small sneer, and one in his nose. He's much more filled out than the fourteen-year-old who had left us all those years ago, but nonetheless he still looks as deadly. His black dress shirt, his black slacks, his tattoos peeking out from an open collar all scream Corsetti.

I glance to my right, toward both his brothers, dressed in their suits. So opposite from their older brother, who's adopted a gothic style.

"Holy fuck," Rafael breathes.

Nico shoves off the SUV and treads closer, taking one step for every three of Hawke's, even now, careful to let Hawke remain in control.

"Hawke," he greets. Shifting his attention to the tiny woman past Hawke's shoulder, he adds, "Hi again."

Hawke's sneer expands, his arm coming around the girl, even as she tries to peek over his shoulder. He shifts so he's blocking her completely, and when I think he's gotten his way, he staggers from the shove she's given him.

"Will you fucking relax?"

Nico throws a look toward Rafael and me, his brows raised.

"Willow." Hawke bares his teeth at the three of us, warning us away, even when no one's moved.

She pushes against his arm and side-steps at the same time, her hand stretching toward Nico, who, smirks and takes it, much to the chagrin of Hawke. Red climbs out of Hawke's black shirt, fury rolling off him in thick waves. So thick, he's yet to pay a moment of attention toward his other brother. By my side, Rafael shifts again, stuck between caution and his own impatience.

"Hi. Nice to officially meet you," she says, shaking Nico's hand. "I'm the girl who stood on the step when you were at the house the other month. I guess I owe you thanks for..." She trails off. "Either way, before Hawke spends the next twelve hours trying to put me in his pocket, we should go."

Nico smirks again and releases Willow. "I get the sense you're the reason you two have come, so I feel like *I* should be the one to thank you."

Hawke's gaze stalks her until she comes back to his side, grinning up at him with a brimming smirk. Not-so-subtly, she tips her head toward Rafael, her hand coming up to rest on Hawke's back, nudging him forward.

After a final glare, Hawke finally looks at his brother. And for once, really *looks*.

Rafael, he mouths. His expression pinches, but he doesn't move.

No one moves. Not even the wind. Stagnant as it waits for Hawke's reaction.

"Hawke," Rafael murmurs. He leans off the SUV, his anxiety dragging his feet forward a step. But then he stops, glancing to the right, to me, and then to Nico, who observes with his typical blank expression.

"You've grown," Hawke says finally.

"Right back at you."

Then Hawke glances at me, his widening another fraction. "Rosen. Following your father's footsteps, I see."

"Essentially." I tip my head in hello, right as Hawke shifts his attention back to Nico.

"I'm here. Get us to wherever this wedding is taking place so we can go home."

Willow smacks her hand against his shoulder, shooting him a long glare before an easy expression replaces it when she glances to Rafael, and then me, nodding her head in hello.

"He means, we know you have a wedding to get to," she revises. "Congrats, by the way."

Once again, Nico smirks at the girl and gestures to the vehicle behind him, opening the door for her. "Of course. We can head for the church right away."

She walks to the car, so trusting to get into a car full of killers. Hawke, of course, reacts, and yanks her back to his side, approaching the vehicle with her. He glares into the dark as if it's about to do something to him. Once he's appeased, he releases her to slide in.

"Right to the church," he repeats.

Once Hawke's settled, Nico gets in after them, leaving

Rafael to take the front seat beside me. He pouts for a second, obviously annoyed by Nico's seating arrangements, before climbing into the passenger side.

I get in too and start the car, pulling away from the airfield before Hawke can change his mind. For long moments, there's only tense silence. In the rearview mirror, I occasionally catch Hawke staring straight, glaring out the front windshield. His arm is stretched over Willow's lap protectively.

Of all people to break through the thick fog of silence, I'm unsurprised it's Rafael who speaks first. "Way to go, Nico. Of course, your wedding ceremony won't be an easy one."

"This family has no one to blame but yourselves," Hawke shoots back.

"*Father* is to blame." Rafael turns in his spot, hooking his arm over the back of my chair to position himself so he can see into the backseat.

"We will be seated far away from our parents," Hawke declares. "I don't care where, Nico, but the only reason I've agreed to come today is this woman right here," he pats Willow's knee, "because she has a fucking heart of gold. I'm here for *you* and that's it. I don't want to even look at them."

I share a look with Rafael, who wears an identical expression of interest. Hawke agreeing to come for Nico is a positive step in the right direction. It means, he's able to separate the event and his hatred from his siblings.

"Of course," Nico replies smoothly. "I promised you in my letter, there will be no fighting. Not even from them. In case you've all forgotten, it's *my* wedding day. The day I get to ensure my little mouse never runs from me again. Everything else is secondary."

It's a good outlook, I mentally agree. Nico's wedding day should only be about him, but unfortunately, every prominent family in Canada and in the US has been invited today, which means Hawke won't be hidden for long, no matter how much he tries.

"We're not staying for the reception," Hawke continues.

"You've already said," Nico replies. "In your response to my letter."

"Speaking of, your letter mentioned something about," he pauses, and in the reflection, I catch him swallowing before he tries again, "about Aurora."

Nico, trained well in the art of delivering news, merely shrugs a shoulder. "She's returned after some time away. After you left, our parents got paranoid—"

Hawke scoffs, breaking his stare with Nico and glancing at the woman beside him again, shaking his head slowly, already doubting Nico's next words.

"—And they sent Aurora away."

"Away?" he echoes. "What, for, like, a couple months?"

"Listen again, brother, when I say she's just returned. Very recently, I might add. Two weeks ago."

There's a beat of silence, only the sound of the engine underfoot, as I turn into a small, but rich neighbourhood where the church is located.

"Aurora grew up away from the family."

"In Toronto, to be exact, yes. They broke all connection with her until recently, which means, she's still adjusting as well. It was my fiancée's idea to move our wedding up so soon, to help Aurora get immersed into her new/old life."

"Aurora grew up away from the family," Hawke repeats, his gaze sliding away from Willow. "You all abandoned her."

"Which is why you'll be good for her, Hawke. She'll bond with you over any of us, I bet."

A flash of misplaced jealousy courses through me, making my hands clench tighter around the wheel. She's his sister, but still, they'll share a secondary connection now; one I never will.

Aurora will always lump me into the crime life, and rightly so, but Hawke represents her past—her childhood and the sense of freedom she had weeks ago.

I peek into the rearview mirror toward Hawke, and for once, he doesn't look angry, or even fierce in his expression. Instead, his shoulders lower a fraction, and his gaze seems to go unfocused as he stares down at his feet.

Family.

It's an interesting notion. In one second, we can hate them, curse them to the ends of the earth, and refuse all contact. And in the same breath, they affect us, break us down and open us up.

And it's Hawke who's realized he's not the only one affected by their parents' decisions.

42

AURORA

Della warned me. Mom warned me. They all warned me.

I hadn't realized the extent they were right until now, when I'm standing beyond the double, wooden doors that are cracked an inch, enough that I see through them. Enough that the church *packed* of people shoots chills of unease through me. My hands tighten around the flower bouquet of calla lilies in my grip, thankful I'll have them to hold onto.

"I tried," Della murmurs, leaning in beside me to peek out at the crowd too. "I agreed to a wedding of this style, for Nico, but I really tried not to invite the world. Your parents wouldn't hear otherwise. And considering what I did..." She trails off, straightening and shooting me a wry smile. "Well, I'm not in a place to fight the larger institution at play."

"I get the sense, war wouldn't have even stopped all these people from being invited," I reply with a shake of my head. "Very impersonal."

"I agree," Della replies, brushing her hand down the front

of her wedding dress. It draws my attention to the quivers beginning to wrack her body.

I've only seen Della dressed in casual clothes, other than the dress she wore for her engagement party, but today, she's transformed into someone else entirely. Her slim dress is classic and plain, until you get to the sweetheart neckline, which is lined in diamonds. It's strapless, showing all the goose bumps sprouting over her shoulders.

I reach out for her arm, stopping her jitters. "You'll be okay. It'll go quick. Ignore everyone. You know who's at the end of the aisle, and he's all who matters."

Beside us, Ariella approaches and rests her head briefly on her sister's shoulder, silently giving her own support.

Della nods, sucking in a deep breath through pursed, red-painted lips. "I know. I guess, it's just, I never put any stock into marriage. To be here and doing this and not have our mother with us sucks."

The moment becomes somber very quickly and I don't know how to respond. I might not have grown up knowing my own, but at least she's now around.

"Hey," I stroke my hand up her bare arm, trying to soothe her in the only way I can, "she's happy for you, Della, and she's here in spirit."

"I know," she replies. Pulling her arm free, she carefully pats a finger beneath the eyeliner circling her eye. "I can't cry. Not now. This is a happy day."

"Exactly."

At that moment, the chipper wedding planner comes out from the hall, her hands dancing through the air as she scans the clipboard in her hand, directing us to stand in front of the door. "Okay, all of you line up. The processional music is slated to begin in a minute."

Like that, I'm going to complete a death march. No, that's

too bold to think. I'm going to *practice* for my own death march to Erico Rossi, whenever they're forcing that on me.

Music starts up then, filling the small lobby we wait in. The lyric-less tune of "Can't Help Falling In Love," which was pre-chosen by the planner, drifts toward us.

"Aurora, you first," she instructs, even though she drilled this into us a few times already yesterday, during the rehearsal. It was easy to pretend this was a game then, but in the blue brides-maid gown, not so much.

I wish I wasn't first, but Ariella is Della's maid-of-honour, which means she goes before the bride. Since I'm the only other bridesmaid, it has to be me, unfortunately.

The double doors open before I can fully take another breath, revealing what I've only seen a hint of. Most of the church's pews are full, making me wonder how many of these strangers want to be here, versus how many simply wish to remain on the right side of the Corsettis. As one, all some hundreds-of-strangers twist to watch me.

One step.

I take it, placing one heel in front of the other, leaving the safety of the back room. I practiced this yesterday; I counted how many steps it would take me at this agonizingly slow pace to reach the end.

Twenty.

Only twenty. Doable.

I'm already five in. As I pass people, they turn to face the front, to stalk me the rest of the way down the aisle.

I lock my gaze where Nico waits. Even from my distance, I catch his subtle nod as he encourages me forward. Beside him is Rafael, who also shoots me a reassuring smile. Beside him, is a cousin of ours. Julio, I think his name is. When Della asked me to walk in the ceremony, Nico needed another groomsmen, and to my understanding, there might be other people Nico would prefer to have stand up with him, something about family and the politics of this life demanded he have a relative up there. And since Della has no male relatives she knows, it came down to his own blood.

Halfway there. This is getting easier. With each step, the crowd becomes simpler to block out and pretend they don't exist.

All except one man, who sits at the end of the aisle, probably placed there on purpose to get a better view. Erico Rossi looks on, his eyes briefly going down the length of my body. Like the first time I met him, he doesn't seem particularly thrilled, and while that should annoy me, it doesn't.

Two more steps and then I find the man I was subconsciously searching for. Rosen is one row from the front, right at the end of the aisle, exactly where he said he'd be, seated as a guest to enjoy the show, while still being available should anything dangerous occur.

Unlike Erico, Rosen doesn't scan me. He doesn't look away from my face, one side of his mouth hiking into a barely-there smile. His eyes say everything he's unable to, but I can't focus on him for as long as I'd like, with the crowd of onlookers, including my brothers.

It takes effort to tear my gaze away, but the sooner I do, the sooner I reach the end and the sooner this whole day will go by. Sighing, I glance toward the first row, to my parents. Mom's seated right at the end; her hands held by Dad's. Unlike Rosen, she isn't hiding her huge smile, her eyes shining with nothing but pride. But this is it. I've become the mafia princess my role demands of me, complete with the pretty gown. Dad, like Nico, has a more controlled expression, but he nods his head.

Finally, I'm at the end, and I lift myself up the two small steps, onto the dais overlooking the entire crowd. I find the small mark on the floor the wedding planner trained me to look for yesterday and position myself there, relaxing my arms for the first time. My eyes pass over Rosen on their way toward the back of the church, to where Ariella is now a third of the way down the aisle.

It's easier to watch someone else walk, even if it's paced and slow, like mine was. I count her steps too, for something to focus on, until she takes her own place on the dais beside me. He shoulders lower an inch with her own deep breath, which eases me to know I wasn't the only one nervous.

I suppose, everything I'm feeling, Ariella and Della are as well. Over the days with Rosen, he's given me the background on them, more than what Della told me. They may have had a slight taste of the lifestyle with their stepfather, but it doesn't sound like what they're experiencing with the Corsettis. In my opinion, Ariella has it worse because she's chosen to remain with her sister. Her sister picked this life when she agreed to marry Nico.

Choices. An interesting thing. One can claim to have a choice but is it actually a choice when its options are limited? I've chosen to remain with my family and take my place, but did I, really? I certainly didn't agree to a union. My position came with it, and I've been forced to follow my duty.

The music in the church shifts into the traditional wedding march song, signalling Della's arrival. As one, the crowd stands, but although my position on the dais makes it so I can see right over all their heads, I don't look toward them.

I've seen Della already, was with her as she prepared this morning. Watched the makeup artist and hairdresser work their magic, curling her hair into an updo and creating a smoky makeup look that reminds me of a midnight sky. Hints of blue were mixed into her eyeshadow, matching the glimmering, blue filigree her train is mingled with.

Instead, I observe my brother. As Nico readjusts his footing and peace overtakes his expression. In the short time I've gotten to know him, I've seen him angry, annoyed, and impassive, but not this.

In love.

Rosen may have shared further details of their story, but I'm witnessing it on Nico's face. She lied to him, deceived him, stabbed him in the back, and yet, they fell in love. Her strength, her compassion to protect her sister—I don't know; something drew him in, and whatever it was, I can't imagine my brother standing at the end of this aisle for anyone else.

He'll kill for her. She'll die for him. Amid hundreds of allies, who, any one of them could easily become an enemy, he's revealing his weakness. Her.

When Della makes it to the end, Nico breaks all appropriateness and reaches for her wrist, hauling her to his side, making the crowd chuckle. He mumbles something to her, which I can't catch from here, but whatever it is has her blushing.

The ceremony passes quickly. I mainly watch the couple, but occasionally, my gaze travels to Rosen. It never lingers, even if no one would likely notice, given all their attention is on the front. Every time I find him in the crowd, he smiles, even if his gaze remains on the couple.

The vows Della and Nico tell each other have me feeling all sorts of soft emotions I can't identify. Once again, the evidence of their love—of each of their weaknesses—becomes apparent with those few statements, and when Nico grasps her face, he's not gentle in claiming her mouth, breaking typical wedding decorum.

This time, when he speaks, it's certainly loud enough for me to hear. He grasps her hand, his fingers holding tightly to her new wedding band. "I fucking dare you to run now, *petite souris*. With my ring on your finger, I've marked you in the most permanent manner."

Ariella chuckles, as do some of the front rows. I don't find his declaration amusing, but rather sentimental. To have someone love you that much…Marrying her wasn't a chore, wasn't a pre-arranged agreement. It's because they both wanted it. To have a man lay such a claim, not because he's controlling but because he refuses to live without you.

When the priest calls the wedding to a close, Della and Nico begin their walk back down the aisle. Ariella takes Rafael's arm, and they follow. Then it's time for me to grab Julio's arm. He's cold and barely looks present.

When I pass Rosen, I don't look at him. I can't see what's in his eyes.

That possessiveness creeping into them.

Because we can't be Nico and Della.

And when I pass Erico, I'm struck with the realization that the next time I walk down a church aisle, it'll be for my own wedding.

43
ROSEN

I hate weddings. I've decided that. The next wedding, I better be working it. It's so much simpler to stand against a wall or patrol a building than be involved in the festivities. Even if it speaks to Nico's honour of our friendship by inviting me.

A wedding planner was tasked with throwing a party fit to appease all the guests, and it's beyond obvious. Nico couldn't care less about anything after getting his wedding band on Della's finger. Della's remained by his side the entire night, her gaze never going to anyone beyond those she's already familiar with.

I sat at the table nearest the main table with Nico's parents, who struck up small talk about Elliot's well-being. Aurora stared at her plate most of the night, taking small nibbles of her food, and looking completely miserable. She sat beside Ariella, who I know wouldn't speak to her, due to her own traumatic past.

The meal thankfully passed quickly, and then Nico and

Della took to the floor for their first dance as husband and wife. The rest of the wedding party joined them, and Aurora danced with their cousin, Julio, who had to take the groomsman position, much to Nico's distaste. His father demanded it, to show good faith to the rest of the family. Something about a compromise since Nico wasn't marrying for connections.

After that mandatory dance, Aurora floated back to the table, and I've been debating how to get to her. It'd be normal for a man, who's with her nearly all the time, to talk with her, right?

Fuck it.

I stand and march my way over to the head table, passing Nico and Della still on the dance floor. I walk by Rafael, who's speaking with some woman, his flirty grin making it clear how he's hoping to conclude the night.

When I get to Aurora's side, she doesn't look up until I speak. "Dance?"

Her head jerks toward me, her wide eyes spotting her parents in the crowd, then Nico, before finding mine again. "Um. But—"

"Fuck them. We're dancing. I'm here as a guest, so I'm going to dance with the woman I'm around all the time. If anyone later questions me, I'll say I was making sure you're okay since you look miserable." *Truth.*

Her eyes complete another scan before that determination I love about her replaces any previous nerves. She grins and hops to her feet, laying her palm in mine.

"You're right. Fuck them all. Nothing wrong with a dance."

As long as my hands remain in the proper places and not where I want to put them.

I lead her to the dance floor, before swinging her in front of me. She adopts the correct position too, almost instantly, sparking a question.

"School teach you to dance?"

She nods as we spin. "And you?"

"My mother."

She's silent as we take another turn. I catch Nico's gaze over her head, but we move too quick for me to catch his expression.

"Where's your parents, Rosen? You never talk about them. All I know is your dad used to work for my family, and he visited your nephew right before we did the other day."

"Mom passed when I was a teenager. Dad retired around the time Nico became underboss. As leadership began passing hands, he decided to step down so I could have his position. Your parents agreed it was best. He certainly put in his time." A vision of him returning one day with his arm bleeding fills my head.

"What does that mean?"

"*Unisciti a leale. Muori leale.* I'm sure you've heard it before."

"Join loyal. Die loyal," she correctly recites. "It was taught to me."

I tip my head, hoping she picks up on the meaning. "He served loyally, but there were a few near misses in his final years. Age was catching up with him, and he felt like he couldn't protect your mother as well anymore."

"My mother." Her brows dip. "Wait, you're saying he almost died for Mom?"

"Of course. We take our oaths very seriously, Aurora. Soldiers are here to protect your family."

"I knew that. You told me so, but I guess thinking about it in plain terms is different. So, you'd die for Nico?"

I hesitate. For the first fucking time *ever*, I waver, and I know exactly the reason—the person—behind that hesitation, even if I'll never put it into words.

"Yes," I finally push out between my dry lips.

"Which means, you'd die for me too?"

In a heartbeat. And it has nothing to do with any oaths I've taken to your family name.

Bending my head, I lower it into the crook of her neck, forgetting the role I should be playing. The scent of her skin has my mouth watering to lay my claim on her, right here, for all to witness. To understand.

"I'd *kill* for you."

She gasps, tipping her head to catch my gaze. She searches my eyes, likely looking for some sense of an exaggeration, but finds none. And that's because I spoke the truth.

"Everyone will be drunk later," she murmurs, her hand tightening into my coat lapel. "I want to come to your room tonight. Or you come to mine."

"Only if you follow one simple rule for the rest of the night. Disobey me and..." I trail off, shrugging my response, silently hinting toward what she *won't* be receiving if she does.

"I won't." Her blue-painted nails scrape against my chest, grabbing at my coat, bringing herself nearer. We're skirting the edge of inappropriateness now. "I'll do anything."

"Like my good girl," I whisper. "I know you will, Aurora. No more drinking for the remainder of the night. I want you sober for all the things I plan on doing later."

She nods, almost animatedly, flipping her curled hair from her shoulder. "Too easy. Done."

Tightening my hand around hers, I take a final turn. The song's going to end soon, and we can't risk a second dance. That *will* raise curious looks, more than I'm already getting. Giving her up for the remainder of the evening to have her during the night is a simple trade-off.

Dancing us to the edge of the floor, I lower my voice away from any listeners. "Keep that promise, *princesse*, because I plan on tying you to the bed and will have you coming so many times, you'll forget every syllable of the English language, except those that make up my name. This fucking dress won't make it two minutes when we're alone."

Her lips part, her response right there, but a two-fingered tap on my shoulder breaks the spell. Instead of speaking, her eyes narrow on the person beside us.

It's not Nico and Rafael. Having trained with them for so many years, I've come to know their steps, how they approach a situation. This person clamps over, hateful pride rolling pungently off him, making me tighten my hold on Aurora, aware that in a mere second, I'll be forced to release her to the man who'll one day get to keep her as his.

I want to kill him for that alone.

"Excuse me. May I cut in for this next dance?"

Clamping my teeth shut is the best way I can respond with the answer I have to give, rather than the one I want. "Of course," I grit, releasing Aurora.

Erico fucking Rossi steps into my place and takes her hip and hand in his, barely sparing me another glance. Aurora does, which makes me feel a bit better. Her mouth opens, about to deny him, but I shake my head and back up, off the dance floor. She watches me go, her eyes lowering, tinged with a sadness I despise.

But this is how it must be.

The first time I saw her in his arms, I hated being jealous. Things have changed since then. They shouldn't have, but they have, and it's not minor, passing fleets of jealousy when I watch him twirl her around the dance floor.

It's deadly.

Fatal and vengeful. It'd be so easy to spark a war right here.

I can't, I remind myself, forcing air down my lungs in heavy gulps. *I can't. I can't. Don't do it. Don't—*

My phone vibrates, breaking my attention in a much-welcome distraction. I pull it out, glancing at the name attached to the message, feeling my stomach drop upon reading it.

NICO

Get to the front. Hawke is here.

44
AURORA

he temptation to pull away from Erico is so strong.
After all, I'm not a player in this game yet. Until
we're engaged, I'm a free woman, and can dance with
whoever I want.

"You look beautiful," Erico remarks, his words obviously
meant to lull me into a sense of security.

"Thanks," I mutter, forcing politeness when I'm feeling
anything but.

Over his shoulder, I search for anyone who can help me. At
this point, I'll even take Dad. My brothers, ideally, but now that
I think about it, I don't see Nico, Rafael, or Della. And Rosen
took off a moment ago, acting like something was chasing him.

Which seems like the ideal excuse to follow him because
where he's headed, I bet I'll find my brothers. I'm loosening my
hold on Erico when he says something that has my insides
numbing. My body freezing, so my fingers are unable to release
his coat. A mix of chilling shock and bitter hate mingle within
me, neither emotion winning nor losing against the other.

"My father has spoken with yours about moving up our

engagement. Your parents feel today has proven how well you've adjusted. In one more month, we will announce our engagement. We'll be wed by fall."

A month.

Three until I have to walk down the aisle.

A fucking *month*. Thirty more days until this man's engagement ring traps me and no one fucking *thought* to inform me in a method different than *this*?

A scream is at the edge of my throat. At him. At Nico. At my father. To this fucking *life* for making me choose. No, not choose. It's an impossible stipulation. Wanting to be with my family somehow means also giving them up and being shipped off to this near stranger.

This is fucking bullshit. This is—

"Holy shit."

That about says it, yes.

However, Erico isn't looking at me. He's staring over my head toward the hall's main entrance. In fact, as I scan around us, most people are gaping that way. Using the distraction as an excuse, I release Erico and escape, nudging through the dance floor until I have a clear line of sight to the front door.

Nico stands with his arm around Della's waist. Rafael and Rosen are also there, standing to the right of another guy. A stranger who has his hand in a woman's. The two of them scan the room, the girl inching closer to him.

I pace nearer, eyes narrowing at the sense of *familiarity* I'm having toward the newcomer. I shouldn't. There's nowhere I would know this gothic-styled guy from. With his black bangs tucked behind his ears, his bold eyes scanning the room.

My eyes.

My father's eyes.

His gaze lands on me, halting and he mouths one thing: *Aurora.*

He knows me.

Of course, he knows me. When those very arms once held me after I tripped on the front step and skinned my knee. Those eyes peering at me between the slightly cracked door before he shut it, so he could fight with our father without me overhearing.

Hawke.

Impossible. Hawke is gone. He left. He left *us* and sparked years and years of loneliness when our parents sent me away, fearing a similar outcome for me. Me, a young girl at the time.

I take a step, only to be stopped by a sound halfway between a scream and a sob. Mom pushes through every person in her path, all sense of decorum and politeness gone. One girl even stumbles into a nearby server, nearly dropping the tray of empty champagne glasses he has. Dad trails behind too, both stopping at the edge of the room, mere feet from where Hawke stands.

Everyone goes still. No one can move. No one knows what to do.

Even me, still a way's away from them, struggling to bring myself closer.

Mom drops to her knees, uncaring that she's dirtying a dress that cost more than some people's yearly income. She reaches for Hawke, but her arms quickly fall limp to her side. "Son…"

Hawke blinks, looking from me to his parents. I can't imagine what's going through his mind right now, because mine is too full of the impossible.

My feet bring me closer. People shift out of my way without question, and I stop beside Dad, managing to look away from Hawke for the briefest second. To catch Nico's gaze, and then Rafael, both who don't seem at all surprised to find their *long-lost brother* standing beside them.

Neither does Rosen. He watches me, only me, for once

uncaring in who might be paying us attention because let's be honest—no one is. No one's attention is anywhere else but on Hawke Corsetti's arrival.

Rosen knew about Hawke. They all did. No one told me. I don't have time to focus on the betrayal because when Dad steps forward, Hawke's laser-focused gaze halts him in his tracks.

"No closer."

"My boy," Mom whispers, her hand covering her mouth. "You sound so…"

"Older," Hawke fills in, sneering. "That's what happens when one avoids their family for fifteen years."

"You're back," Dad breathes.

"For Nico," Hawke states coldly. "And for my siblings. I'm here for them. Don't think this is anything more. I can't even— I can't. Get out of my sight, both of you."

"Hawke." Mom lifts to her feet, taking a step closer, which sparks Hawke's arm to shoot out, blocking the woman at his side.

His action pulls their attention from him to the woman, who watches on, her eyes on Hawke's face. Her love for him isn't hidden, but based on the dip in her brows, she's concerned too. Her free hand strokes calmingly up and down his arm, but I don't think it's having the desired effect.

"You brought someone," Dad states, a question present in his tone. The same question I also have too. Who is she?

Hawke's lips lift, baring his teeth, and he shifts his body in front of her, partially blocking her. "She doesn't matter to you. You will never know her name, so don't bother trying."

Perhaps it was his words, his actions, or something I'm not entirely certain of, but Hawke's reaction draws Nico to release Della and step between Dad and Hawke, his palms out.

So low, he murmurs to my parents in a tone I only hear

because I'm right there. "You might be Boss, Father, but right now, unless you want to see him shed blood, back the fuck up. Take Mother and go elsewhere. You want your son to return? Go."

Although a flash of anger has Dad's mouth opening, an argument brewing, he quickly clamps it shut and nods. Looking past Nico and toward Hawke, pain flashes in his gaze, but he takes Mom's hand and propels her out the doorway, past them. Hawke stalks them until they're gone from sight.

"Play the music again," Nico commands to the DJ across the way. "You either continue with the celebration or you leave."

The DJ starts up the music and people begin conversing amongst themselves again. I don't look behind me to know a lot of their attention is still on us.

"Way to draw a crowd," Rafael jokes, crossing his arms from where he stands beside Hawke.

"I shouldn't have come," Hawke mutters. "I knew this was a fucking mistake."

It's not a mistake. That's what I want to say, but I still can't decipher how I'm handling this.

The girl strokes her hand up and down his arm again. "You know why you came, and I'm proud of you."

Hawke's attention goes from her to me again, and some of that rage cracks a fraction. Enough, a small break between us opens, and I take another step, uncertain how close he wants me to come. How close *I* want to come.

"Hawke." I think I say it out loud. Maybe I don't.

I must because Hawke lowers his arms from the girl at his side and murmurs, "Hi, Aurora. You look so grown up."

He spoke. To me. He spoke to me.

"R-right back at you."

My breaths come more shallow. Impossible to catch. Impossible to trap in my lungs.

It hurts. Like a hand is reaching inside my chest and squeezing around my heart. It steals it, yanking it from my skin, leaving me to clutch my chest. My throat. My heart.

I can't breathe.

I can't even recall my own breathing techniques. Nothing can break through the cloud over my head.

Steps come to my side and the voice that speaks is one who'll become part of my fucking nightmares soon. "Hawke Corsetti. Your name is legendary."

Erico thinks he has a right to be here? What, because we'll be fucking engaged in a *month*, he thinks he has a right to be involved in family situations? Especially one as precarious, as this. He has *no* right.

No right to me. To my family.

Yet. Fucking yet. The power of that goddamned word.

My breaths come out more shallow, my lips trying to suck in any air I can. No one can see my pain because it's invisible. Imaginary, brought on my shock and panic.

What is happening to me?

Before my vision blurs and things get unfocused, there's two sets of eyes that capture my notice for different reasons. Rosen watches on, concerned. Of course, he's detecting my breakdown.

And the girl at Hawke's side. As she peers around him, her brows furrow, and she's about to speak. She knows. I get the sense she *recognizes* it.

I can't breathe.

Everything is too much—an engagement to Erico Rossi. Losing Rosen soon. My parents—are they the villains or the good guys? Nico, Rafael, Della, Ariella—so many people new to my life. All with their roles to play. All to impose *my* role.

My role.

My role of a mafia princess, slated to wed the New York crime family's underboss.

Hawke. Hawke is back and I don't know what it means.

I can't breathe.

I must get out of here. Away from all of this.

I shove through the small gap between Rafael and Hawke and out into the attached hall, running blindly down it until I find somewhere that heals the pain in my chest, the hole that's letting all my breath seep out.

My first instinct is to follow Aurora.

My second is to look toward Nico and Rafael for my orders, like the trained soldier I am.

I want to break rank and go find her. To hold her. To heal her. A fucking anxiety attack that I wish I spotted happening sooner than I had. It was so close when speaking with Hawke, but she was still in control. And then fucking Rossi came up beside her, like he has any business in this and that's when it hit her. That's when the deadly demand to kill him continued to grow.

Rafael and Hawke stare at the doorway she disappeared through. Nico's watching me, so I glower back.

He breaks his stare to flick his fingers at Rossi. "Leave." He does, with no argument.

Della, chewing on her lip, rests her hand on her new husband's chest. "I could go after her. You should go find your parents."

"No," Hawke cuts in, turning around. "I'll go. No one here understands what she requires."

I do, I want to argue, but Hawke's correct. This started when they spoke to each other. As past and present collide, neither I nor her brothers have any place in that.

Hawke shoots me a long stare, pointing to Willow. "If she loses even a fucking single hair on her head while I'm gone—"

"She'll be safe," Nico cuts in. "Rosen won't let anyone near her."

Once Hawke seems satisfied with that answer, he briefly but tenderly touches Willow's neck and then disappears into the hallway, turning left, in the direction Aurora disappeared to minutes ago.

Nico fills the air with a long, dragged-out sigh. He leans forward and presses a kiss to Della's head. "I'm sorry, *petite souris,* that this is happening, but I'm going to find my parents."

Della rests her hand on his cheek. "Go. It's okay. You forget who urged you to invite him."

After a long look toward me again, he tips his head at his brother and the two leave, turning right, the opposite way from Hawke and Aurora.

With all the Corsettis gone, other than the newest to take the name, the crackling aura finally shatters and breathing becomes less precarious. Della breathes deeper than anyone and it ends on a gentle chuckle.

"I'm sorry," Willow murmurs, glancing between us both. "I was the one who pleaded with him to come today, but Hawke was adamant to only stay for the ceremony. On the way back to the plane, he continued to talk about Aurora, so I was the one who, again, encouraged him to return, to see her." She pauses. "It was a lovely ceremony."

"Please don't apologize." Della steps closer. "Nico's happy you're both here. As for coming back to the reception, I mean, all this had to happen eventually, right?" Della shrugs one shoulder.

"Did it?" Willow muses. "Before your letter, Hawke was adamant about having no connection with any of you. In fact, before me, he never contacted them at all."

It's funny how some people can affect others so much. For Hawke, this girl claims to be the one who got him here, but based on what I saw, Hawke isn't one someone can push around easily. Standing up to his parents was further evidence of it. Yet, this woman can.

Nico. Underboss. Killer. Leader. I've never witnessed him grant mercy, yet for his now-wife, he did. Even when she betrayed him, she had already captured him in an entirely different way.

And Aurora. Forbidden. Brat. Despite all the reasons I shouldn't be the one to dominate her, I am. She's caught me, like the thorn on a rose bush, trapping me until my insides are sliced up.

"I believe everything will work out," Della continues. "I'm happy to meet you, Willow. Nico's told me a bit. Do you want a drink?" She waves her hand to the nearest server, who instantly approaches, tray held out. "Or food? To dance?"

Willow shakes her head. "Oh, no thanks. I'm sure if I move even a fraction, Hawke will lose his ever-loving shit. And while I love fucking with him, here isn't the place for that." She glances at me, amusement making her eyes brighter. "And I don't want to see you hurt," she teases.

"Appreciate it," I reply.

Despite Della being the bride, she doesn't leave Willow's side either, watching on as the other partygoers become less obvious in their curious glances. Willow takes it all, standing there, rocking slightly on her heels, the only sign of her agitation.

After a long while, Hawke returns, rubbing his hand over his hair. He wraps an arm around Willow immediately, pulling her face into his neck, her body into his arms. In the briefest second I was able to see his face, I caught the red around his eyes.

If he's emotional, I need Aurora. I *need* to make sure she's okay.

I quickly slip out of the room to do just that.

46

AURORA

ir no longer graces my lungs.

My vision is a combination of white and dark spots.

My body feels like it's about to collapse.

I have no idea how long I've been running or how far I've gotten from the reception hall. I could be inches away from the door, or a whole hall away; I have no idea.

Nonetheless, wherever I am now is where my body stops working, and I slump against the nearest wall, sliding to the floor and pulling my knees to my chest. The blue dress, a sign of a celebration, now holds only disdain for the memories of this day it'll forever hold, and I itch to rip it from my body.

My chest clenches in pain. I don't know how to fix this. How can I practice breathing when there's no more air for me to take in?

Gummies.

I wasn't going to bring them, but a small voice in my head recommended I do, just in case. Roz encouraged taking one if things got too much, and a panic attack seems like an ideal time, and I pray it does something to help.

Reaching into the bosom of my dress, where I've balled up the baggy, I remove a red one, squishing it between my fingers before popping it in my mouth, chewing slowly as I take it all in. It tastes almost normal. Like a gummy with a slightly off flavour. Nothing bad, but nothing great either.

Feet echo through the hallway but turning my head requires strength I no longer have, even if the urge to see who followed me is strong. Rosen, perhaps. Nico, most likely. As long as it's not Erico, I don't really care.

"Aurora."

I know that voice. It's not one I *know*, but rather I've recently become familiar with it. A voice having come into my life again.

Hawke.

He lowers himself beside me, adopting a very similar position with his legs drawn up, his hands hanging between his knees.

"It got too overwhelming."

"Yeah." At least he understands.

"I'm sorry I surprised you today. I didn't know how else to do it."

"Then showing up at the reception and shocking every-one?" I'm sure there's a million other ways.

"I was at the church too, in the back, hiding from anyone who'd recognize me."

Huh. I hadn't noticed him, but I suppose I was too focused on the front. If he was there, then his presence was pre-planned, which explains my brothers' and Rosen's non-reaction to his arrival.

"Della encouraged Nico to invite me. I agreed to attend the

ceremony only, but on the way back to the plane, I realized I had to come back."

"Why?" I scoff, shaking my head lightly. "You got in and out unnoticed. Why return?"

"To see you."

What? "What?"

"I couldn't leave without meeting you. This morning, Nico told me what our parents had done. Sending you away, but now you've been brought back. I guess, I relate to you, and I'm not mad at you. Or our brothers. None of it was their fault."

Not Nico or Rafael's fault. I guess not. My situation too was caused by my parents. But with Nico's position now, he's also making choices I hate him for, like an engagement.

"Simply what they represent."

"Precisely," he agrees. His head falls against the wall with a heavy sigh. "This is so fucking surreal, Aurora, and I'm sorry to have caused you stress. I'm sorry for what our parents did to you. That was all because of what happened to me."

He's apologizing for getting— "Hawke, that also wasn't your doing. Neither of our lives can be blamed on the other. Intermingled. A domino effect, maybe, but I don't attribute being sent away to you. You didn't make that decision. Our parents suck."

"Do they?"

He's not agreeing with me? I nearly get whiplash with how fast my head spins. "You don't think so? I mean, you certainly acted like you do."

"Oh," he smirks, his lip ring becoming more obvious, "I definitely agree, but I've had a long time to contemplate it. Once, I promised myself to never come back. Never to contact them. Nico found me a while ago, and I shoved him away until I required his assistance with a situation regarding Willow."

"A situation?" I phrase it as a question.

"A long situation," is all he responds with. "Somehow, that opened up the floodgates for all this." He waves his hand. "It was Willow who made a point that caused me to change my mind about coming. She sees a therapist regularly for her own traumas and mentioned something about letting go of the past to further process my own."

"Is that what you were doing then when you yelled at our parents?" I ask, but his words lodge into my mind.

Trauma.

Trauma is, like, a serious thing. Is abandonment the same as trauma? A type of trauma?

"I've been bonding with them," I tell him. "Well, Mom, mainly. I guess I haven't spent much time with our father. I was young, but I remember them being the reason you left, and then they sent me away, and I made them to be the villains." I sigh because while I state that, I think about everything I've learned about them too. "But they're not bad people either."

"It's the life," he fills in. "It twists them to do evil things, even when the people themselves aren't evil."

Is that what is happening with Nico? He's not a villain, but he's marrying me off the first chance he gets. Becoming underboss has twisted his morals and now he's turning into our father.

"That's why you never came back."

"That's one reason," he agrees. "There's a few other now."

There's a beat of silence and my heartbeat slows. Perhaps that edible is beginning to kick in, although I've yet to feel any different.

"How do I prevent that?"

"What do you mean?"

"My entire life, all I've wanted was to come home and be with our brothers, our parents. And now, they're trying to wed me off for some connection. For all their niceties, I'm only a chess piece to them in their political game."

His mouth breaks into an *Ah* motion. His eyes roll back, and he curses. "They're all dicks. Aurora, we all have our own path to forge. Mine should have been in line to be Boss, but situations happen, and here we are. Nico's path was to replace me, and I'm okay with that. Rafael gets to be the backup. Dad has to be a leader. Mom by his side. But you..." He reaches for me, slowly laying his palm over mine. "Like me, your life changed based on a single situation. Growing up away from here meant you had time to form your own opinions and dreams. You weren't trained by our parents."

"That's the thing, I kind of was. For years, I've been taught what my role means."

"Hearing it is different than experiencing it. You got to be *you* and now being tossed into the politics of this life is different." Hawke pauses, his bright eyes searching mine, seeing right through me. "Who is he?"

"Excuse me?"

"I'm a lawyer, Aurora. I know when people are hiding something. There's another reason you're feeling like this. I saw it the moment that guy walked up behind you. He's not who you want."

"Erico Rossi," I fill in. "My future fiancé. Nico told me it would be a year until I'm married, but minutes before you showed up, Erico told me the agreement had been changed to a month." My head slumps, chin landing on my arm. "I-I can't do this, Hawke. I hoped I could, but to be miserable for the rest of my life..." *No.* "But I don't want to leave because for all their faults and shitty decisions, I love our parents. I've never wanted to go. I didn't choose to."

As I speak, Hawke nods slowly, pressing his lips together. "So don't do it. Choose to be with who you want."

That's the second implication of him being aware there's more, so I sigh and reply with, "Rosen."

His brows lift nearly to his hairline. "Rosen. The same Rosen?" He blows out a long breath, smirking toward the end. "Okay, wow, didn't see that coming."

"We didn't at first. It was a slow build-up. Today, I realized the next wedding I'll be attending is my own, and then I was in Rosen's arms, and it felt right. And then Erico bombarded me with the news. *Apparently,*" I don't hide the disdain in my voice, "I'm adjusting so well, they think moving up the timeline is fine. Fucking bullshit."

Hawke makes a noise in the back of his throat. "Again, don't."

"Don't what?" I ask glumly, without looking up from staring at a spot on the floor.

"Don't marry him. What will they do? Throw you out? I doubt our parents would want that. Between you and me, I think they might be learning their lessons."

He's nuts. Being away from the family has understandably made him lose his knowledge of this life.

"Right." I roll my eyes. "Like it'd be that easy. What can they do?" I echo his question. "They could tie me to the altar. Force me to speak the vows."

"Or they won't. Aurora, you can do what you want, but if earlier was any indication of how you'll handle marriage to that tool, you need to truly think about what you want. It's one thing for them to have forced you to grow up away from here, but it's a whole other to toss you into an alliance. Women in this life don't stand up for themselves. It's expected everyone play their part, whether that's wife, mother, Capo, or Boss. But what if it's time for a change?"

"Della's a change," I muse, feeling like I'm finally *hearing*

Hawke. "She was part of a plot to get Nico killed, but they fell in love."

Hawke shoots a *See?* look, seemingly unbothered by the fact that his younger brother married a traitor. "Bet he pissed off our parents doing that too. Yet, he's still an underboss. See how little that affected him overall?"

"Because he's a man," I point out. "We all know the gender differences here."

"Della was welcomed into the family, nonetheless. Nico could have kept his status while Father put a bullet between her eyes. But they didn't."

"Likely because Nico would lose his shit."

Hawke shrugs again. "Or because they respected his decisions. Aurora, if you let them marry you off, you risk leading an unhappy life. I don't want that for you. Not when seeing you like *this*," he waves his hand, "this broken, sad woman, pains me. You lose nothing by standing up to them, but you could gain everything. A life you want. The man you love. Their respect."

Respect. A life I want. It all sounds so easy hearing Hawke say it, but the reality is so much different.

What if it's not?

My heart begins to beat fast again. Those old feelings resurfacing with something else with them. Hope.

Hope and...*What is happening to me?* I hold my chest again, confused as a different kind of pain makes my form tingle.

"Are you okay to return to the party? I don't want to leave Willow for too long."

I nod, even if I didn't completely hear him. His voice becomes muted, and when he uses the wall to push to his feet, I try to follow.

I think I move.

Maybe I don't because my viewpoint hasn't changed at all.

"You coming?"

"Yeah, one more moment."

Hawke's steps take him away and I wait for his blurry form to disappear around the corner before I stagger to my feet. Hand on the wall, first to my knees, then to my feet. My heels wobble and for a moment, I'm concerned with rolling my ankle, but right now, removing them seems like it'll require more effort.

What is happening? I was fine. Then I wasn't.

My chest doesn't hurt. I'm not breathing heavy.

I'm cold. I touch my neck. Clammy. Bile climbs my throat, twisting my stomach at the same time. I feel sick.

I manage a step in the direction of the reception.

I need...

I need Rosen. And to talk to Nico. To talk with him while Hawke is here to back me up.

I try to move again, but my feet are weighed down. A wave of dizziness drowns me, and suddenly, the wall isn't right way up any longer.

I'm no longer right way up.

Am I on the floor?

That wave returns for another swell of—of something.

Of something that makes everything go dark. Black.

I'm gone.

47
ROSEN

I retrace the same direction Hawke came from, my feet eating up much of the floor in a rush to get to Aurora. At the first hall, I turn, thankful the building is shaped in such a way it'd be impossible to get lost.

A flash of blonde hair is all I see before the rest of the image of Aurora's body on the ground throws me into action. I'm by her side in an instant, rolling her onto her back, two fingers at her pulse point.

"Aurora!"

Thump. Thump.

With its gentle response, relief is instant, but also fleeting because breathing or not, she's unresponsive.

I move clumps of her hair away from her face, my hands going to her shoulders to shake her, but there's no sign of her hearing me. "Aurora, fucking wake up!"

She's gone. Not dead. But gone.

"Help!"

Not dead. But not here. Not throwing flirty smiles my way. Not laughing. Not doing any of the things she should be doing.

And that's when I feel it.

Snap.

Snap.

Snap.

My sanity. My rationality. Everything. Nothing matters but Aurora opening her big, beautiful fucking eyes.

One arm at her back and the other beneath her knees, I lift to my feet, lunging toward the reception hall.

"Help! Fucking someone!"

Finally, I'm heard, and at the same time Della, Hawke, and Willow appear in one doorway, Rafael and Nico appear from down the hall, where they had gone earlier.

"What the fuck?" Nico bellows, running at me, stopping short of where I stand with his sister in my arms.

"She's alive," I tell him through panted breaths. "But she's not...She's alive," I repeat instead, my mind unable to come up with more suitable words.

She's alive. That's what I echo in my head, holding onto that fragile statement.

The Corsetti name carries a lot of influence, which is why when we slam our way into Montreal General Hospital, it takes a mere three minutes until I'm ushered into a private room and instructed to lay Aurora on the hospital bed.

I haven't let go of her. Not as Nico and Rafael took the front of the limo, which was originally designated to drive Nico and Della away after the reception. Della, in her wedding dress, followed by Hawke and Willow, who climbed into the back with us.

Nico didn't think twice before hopping into the driver's

seat and maneuvering the long vehicle through downtown traffic. Similarly, I didn't think twice every time I stroked Aurora's pulse again, using its gentle beat to remind myself that whatever happened to her is secondary to the fact she's still alive. I didn't hide my touching from Hawke or Della, who both watched with a brow raised in a knowing manner.

Placing her on the hospital bed leaves my arms empty, when all I want to do is protect her, but the only way to get Aurora back is to let the medical staff, who trail closely behind me, do their thing.

Behind the staff, Della and Nico stand by the door with Rafael, looking entirely out of place. Through the glass window that makes up one wall, Hawke and Willow watch, right as their parents rush by everyone and into the room, closely followed by Ariella, who had later left the reception with them when Rafael phoned from the vehicle.

"Oh, my baby girl!" Caterina yells, lunging for the bed, only for Nico to throw his arm out and block his mother's path.

Two nurses flit around the room, preparing trays of items, including a needle and an IV bag as a doctor also enters, barely sparing any of us a glance.

"There are too many people in here. Out."

When no one moves, the doctor turns his head, finding Nico, obviously aware of which family he's dealing with.

"I have to figure out what has her like this. We're going to draw blood. But first, there are too many people in here and we can't move around as we require. All of you, leave."

Della wanders to the door with Rafael, pausing to wait for her husband. Nico stares long at the doctor, his mouth pressed together in a firm line before he finally nods and ushers his parents out too.

I don't move.

They can work around me.

I can't leave until I know why she's like this. Until there's answers.

When everyone's gone from the room and watching through the window, Nico jerks his head. "Let's go, Rosen."

I don't move. I watch my *princesse*'s chest as it barely rises, willing her eyes to open. Pleading with whatever energy exists in this world for her to wake up.

"Rosen," my underboss snaps. He rushes near me, grasping my suit jacket in one fist, roughly jerking me. "What the fuck, man?" But even as he speaks, his expression dawns.

Maybe it's what he spots on my face. Maybe it's something I've stopped hiding.

Either way, he shoves me out the door and into the hall, sparking loud gasps from nearby nurses. Nico doesn't care, an unbridled look in his eyes as he leaps on me, his fist heading straight for my face.

Knowing Nico and his fighting style, he's easy to block. In the same instance, I roll, getting to my feet and backing up, palms up in defense.

"Boss."

"Don't fucking 'boss' me." He growls, striding closer.

Down the hall, two nurses approach, one reaching for her phone. Another doctor at the counter puts his arm out, stopping her otherwise stupid action, and only when she does, does he begin to approach.

"This isn't the place, Nico."

"You should have fucking thought of that before. My goddamn *sister*."

Rafael steps between us, a place he's often found himself in during training. His arms stretch, one toward each of our chests, while his head turns back and forth. "What the fuck is wrong with you both? Aurora is passed out and you two are playing battle royale in the middle of a hospital."

"He's *fucking* our sister. That's what's wrong." With a loud shout, Nico shoves past his brother, throwing his body into mine.

I go down with a hard thump to the laminate flooring but manage to block his pending hit again.

"My sister, Rosen. *You.* I fucking trusted you. You *know* the severity of what this means."

I buck him off me, throwing my arm out in a shove rather than a punch. Behind him, Della unwisely approaches, her hands reaching for her husband. I've seen the woman literally jump in front of a bullet, so I'm not surprised that a bit of fighting isn't bothering her. Behind her, Hawke watches on, smirking, and somehow, I *know* Aurora talked with him about us.

Lorenzo Corsetti shoves between us this time, his pure domineering presence making us all back down. He stands between his sons, his hand at his waist with the threat of pulling his gun out.

My Boss, Underboss, and Capo glare at me. Me, a soldier, whose only care right now is for the woman lying in the bed inside the room behind us. The tattoo over my heart burns with every reason these people should never have known the truth.

I shattered their loyalty and corrupted their virgin mafia princess before her wedding. I wrecked possible alliances. They have rights to kill me, but I won't let it happen until I see Aurora open her eyes.

The doctor emerges from her room at that moment and Hawke announces it, breaking up the tension. "Ah, doc, right on time, believe me."

Nico returns to Della's side and pulls her toward the doctor. The grey-haired man scans the group, pausing on both Nico and me, who's breathing heavier after the small fight. With a countenance of slight impatience, he holds up a baggy of coloured candies.

Candy?

"My nurses removed her dress so we could better examine her body for any other indicative signs of what happened. We found this in her bosom."

Nico snatches the bag, voicing my same question. "Candy?" He opens it, sniffing them, catching nothing identifiable before handing them to Rafael, who pulls out one and inspects it closer.

"These were cut. Why would she cut bite-sized candies into smaller pieces?"

"And have them on her during the wedding?" Della finishes.

"In any case, we've already drawn a vial of her blood and sent it straight to the lab," the doctor continues. "A rush order, and we should have it in minutes, Mr. Corsetti. We understand how troubling this must be on your wedding day." His eyes shift to Della, whose white dress is beyond obvious.

Troubling. He calls Aurora being unconscious as fucking *troubling*?

I don't realize I'm making noises until Hawke glances at me again, lifting his hand in a small wave up and down, to indicate I take a deep breath. A deep breath. A fucking deep breath is what he wants from me?

"Can we see her while we wait for the results?"

As one, every person turns to look at me. Everyone except Hawke, who's instead still staring at the bag of gummies in Rafael's grip, his teeth chewing on his lip ring.

"They're edibles," he states quietly. Still loud enough, it takes all the attention from me. "Weed."

Where would she have gotten edibles from? She certainly was never around anyone outside this circle.

Nico whirls around, death shadowing his face as he zeroes

in on me. This time, for a better reason. I was charged with protecting her, and somehow, she got drugs.

Where would she have gotten them? *Who* would have given her them? The soldiers around the mansion could be a possibility, but any of them would risk the wrath of their Capo, Underboss, and Boss for doing so. If not them, then who?

A nurse comes jogging down the hallway, pushing through us until reaching the doctor's side. She waves a paper in the air, handing it to him before rushing off, likely to complete one of the many other tasks she has.

The doctor scans it, much slower than my sanity can handle, before he announces, "There's traces of Fentanyl and THC in her bloodstream. Based on that, my hypothesis is she's overdosed on the drugs, placing her in a coma-like state."

Overdosed.

Drugged.

Coma.

"We'll pump her stomach," he continues. "Then it's a matter of her waking up."

I stagger back a foot, my gaze going through the glass window to the girl inside. She looks so tiny in the hospital bed. So unlike the flurry of energy I've come to know. To care for.

She overdosed on my watch. Why? How? Nothing makes sense.

Stopping by the window, I lean forward, nearly to the point my forehead rests on the glass. By my side, her parents stand, and on my other is Hawke and Willow. Nico's glare penetrates my back, probably imagining the number of knives he can stab into it.

She's always been in my sight. The few times she isn't, she's with her family and other soldiers. She wasn't alone long enough in the club to have been able to complete a drug deal. We drive everywhere together. Drugs are kept away from the mansion for this reason, so where could she have gotten it from?

Then it hits. *Fuck.*

The community garden. It's the only place, the only time, she's *ever* out of my sight.

"Holy fuck," I breathe, my breath making a momentary spot of fog on the window. *Fuck, I am at fault.*

Finding her on the floor at the reception ripped a hole in my chest, and my realization only tears it open wider.

My arm whirls, fist slamming into the window, aware that any hit could shatter the glass. My anger must be released somehow.

I should *never* have let her go alone. She fought me and I let her win. A place where there's children should never have drugs, but here we are.

Without a word, I turn and stomp down the length of the hallway, straight for the elevator. I punch the button, to take me down, and before the doors slide closed, a hand shoves between them, forcing them to reopen. Rafael and Nico enter the elevator, their expressions grim.

"You know," Nico states.

"I suspect."

"Then let's fucking go."

48

AURORA

Lights.
Shadows.
Voices.

Yelling.

Crying.

Sleep.

Oh, delicious sleep.

Sleep filled with pink and blue light bursts. Of wedding dresses and the clinking of glasses. Of me walking the aisle, toward the only man to ever fill my dreams.

Rosen.

I'm so close to him now. Removing one hand from the bouquet of red roses, I stretch it toward him. He reaches for me too, but as my foot touches the step to take me to his level, I stagger. The ground beneath my feet goes black, the dais disappearing and leaving Rosen hanging in mid-air.

Still, I reach for him. Now more than ever, I want his hand. To hold me and never let go.

Our hands miss, and I fall straight down into the black hole.
Into nothing.

49
ROSEN

"I know Clarisse," Rafael comments as I park the limo in front of her house. "She wouldn't have done this. That's not her game."

"No," I agree, getting out of the vehicle, thinking of the elderly woman I met. "But this is our only lead. She might not have known what was happening."

Nico steps in front of me, leading the path to the door, where he bangs his fist into it. "She has two minutes before I'm breaking in."

"It's one in the morning," Rafael continues playing devil's advocate. "She's probably asleep."

"Then she'll wake up." Nico growls, hammering on the door again, this time with more force.

After another moment, feet scrape the other side of the door and it slowly opens, dark, sleepy eyes peering through the crack, only opening when she spots me and Rafael.

"Mr. Corsetti. Rosen. What are you...?" She trails off, scanning over our heads.

I shove past Nico and into the house, no longer caring

396

Clarisse isn't behind this, but requiring some sort of an answer that makes sense.

"Where the fuck did she get the drugs from?"

"D-drugs?" Her gaze goes behind me again, toward Nico and Rafael, her brows dipping in confusion. "What is going on? Is this about Aurora?"

Hearing Aurora's name sparks a new wave of urgency. I have to fix this. My hands tighten by my side, so they don't end up around the old woman's neck.

"Who. Else. Comes. Here." Every word is punched, emphasized with rage. "Besides the kids." I certainly fucking hope any of the children aren't drug runners. "How many volunteers do you have?"

"A-a few. She was only ever around one of them."

"Names," I demand, hating, once again, how much I allowed Aurora to walk over me. She didn't understand why she shouldn't be around other people. This entire time she was hanging around another person, and never mentioned anything.

"I'll get you a list."

Clarisse scrambles down the short hall, which we closely follow behind. I stand in the doorway, the vision of the last time I was in here making me weak. When my attraction to Aurora initially took over and I had her pinned to the door, her gentle neck moving beneath my palm.

Clarisse returns holding a sheet of paper, which Nico snatches. His eyes scan it, and I catch the moment he determines who's at fault because his expression turns deadly. His eyes becoming frozen and empty, his mouth flattening, and he crumples the paper before shoving it at my chest.

It takes me a second to find what he had.

Rozelyn De Falco.

"De Falco." Of fucking course. How did none of us see this?

"His fucking daughter," Nico curses, spinning on his heel, heading for the exit.

Without a word to Clarisse, we return to the car. Nico takes his place in the front seat, and I get into the driver's side again. When Rafael climbs in the back, the tires peel with urgency to get away, to go find the De Falcos before they can do any more harm.

"It's risky to use her real name." Rafael rests an arm on the back of our seats.

"Not risky," Nico responds. "Purposeful. She placed herself in Aurora's life and chose a spot we wouldn't be able to watch them talk. We know about his vendetta against this family, but to use his own daughter is terrible."

"He used his stepdaughter," Rafael points out, gesturing to the gold band on Nico's hand. "I suspect he doesn't see much of a difference in using his own blood."

"Except it wasn't Aurora who paid the price that time."

My hands tighten around the wheel, recalling her in the hospital bed. This wasn't how the night was supposed to end for any of us. Nico should be enjoying his wedding night; Rafael with whichever woman he chose; and me tying Aurora to my bed.

"I'll find that bitch and she will pay for what she's done to Aurora. I'll drop you both at the hospital and then I'll gather men."

In my peripheral vision, I catch them sharing a look before Nico curses, "Fuck that. You forget, she's *our* sister."

"And you left your brand-new bride in the middle of Montreal General at nearly two in the morning after a long-ass day. She deserves to rest because sitting in that hospital room won't change anything. Add in the fact that Hawke and Willow are here still, with your parents in that small area. So before war breaks out in that hospital, you need to take care of your family. I'll assemble the men at the mansion, and we can plan once you get everyone settled."

"Man has a point," Rafael murmurs. "If Hawke wants to stay in town, I'll give them my condo and keys to my car. It'll solve the parental issue."

"Fine," Nico agrees, "gather everyone in my office."

~

2 Days Later

My hands curl around the large, printed map stretched out over the table. It's been full of useless trails, based on the amount of marker etched on it, as we cross off every suspected area in the city.

My muscles refuse to unlock. My breaths are shallow. Crinkling the paper only satisfies a small part of me while also wanting to break something—some*one*. To make them bleed. Rozelyn or Stefano, it doesn't matter, but I crave stabbing a knife into one of them and watching a De Falco cry out in pain.

With a guttural roar, I rip the map in two, throwing the pieces behind me. They hit the men that stand by the door of the spare room in one of the casinos we've been using.

They've disappeared. There is no sign of any De Falco in this fucking city. Nico called on his connections at the RCMP and they've been scouring the country for any sign of them. The local police forces are searching. Every Corsetti soldier. The Canada Border Services Agency is ensuring they don't pass over to the US.

I feel like I've scoured every inch of the city with my bare hands. Two days have passed since Nico's wedding and I'm no

399

closer to finding Rozelyn than when we discovered she's at fault.

In those two days, I haven't been to the hospital. Not because her brothers have been preventing me, but because finding the De Falco bitch has been more pressing than sitting by Aurora's bedside, who's had her mother, Della, Ariella, and Willow with her.

When I slam my fists in frustration into the table that used to house the map, it wobbles. I'm seconds away from breaking it too if someone doesn't get me a damn location.

Rubbing a hand over my face, I slap my cheek, trying to clear the fog from my eyes. Exhaustion is a cruel monster hanging onto my back, but I refuse to let it take me down. I won't stop until this is finished.

"Everyone out," Rafael suddenly commands his men. "Everyone except you, Rosen."

Without question, the dozen men filter out. Nico steps up beside Rafael. At the desk behind them, Lorenzo glances up from the computer he's been using to get to Corsetti contacts. Against the far wall, Hawke crosses his arms.

He chose to stay in the city, though he hasn't paid either of his parents any attention. *For Aurora*, he had said, making me like Hawke more than I already had.

My lip curls. "Gonna finally kill me? I know you've all been imagining it since the hospital."

Aurora's brothers and I have made an unspoken agreement, in which, for now, Rozelyn's involvement matters more than my relationship with their sister. Perhaps after two days, they've grown impatient and wish to end me.

"You haven't slept, have you?" Rafael mutters. "You're a fucking mess."

I shove off the table, more and more of my energy waning every passing minute I don't move. It's how I've kept going for two days. Adrenaline, constant movement, caffeine, and picturing Aurora's eyes opening.

"No, and you know that, so stop asking stupid questions. I will once we've captured De Falco."

"You won't be effective for her," he continues, every word grating on my nerves.

Fists form by my sides. "What are you trying to say, Capo, because we're wasting time in this conversation?"

"Holy fuck, I see it." Rafael breathes, throwing an elbow into his brother's stomach. "Nic, that face right there," he gestures, "is the exact expression you had the day Della saved you, but you said she was leaving, so I called you a moron for nearly allowing it. Remember that?"

"Vividly," Nico replies, his voice flat, unamused.

"You didn't just fuck our sister," Rafael declares. "You *love* her."

I stop. Everyone stops. Lorenzo's fingers stop moving over the keys. They all wait for my response.

Love? I mean, I care for her, sure. More than I believed I would. It was supposed to be forbidden fun before she got married.

Do I love her? I suppose, I wouldn't stay awake for anyone. While the other men have worked on shifts, I haven't stopped, and I won't because picturing my *princesse* in that hospital bed drives me to continue.

I open my mouth to respond but the chime of Nico's phone fills the small room. I've never been so fucking happy to be interrupted.

"Corsetti here," he responds, placing the phone by his ear. After a nod and a *mmhmm* as well as a "We'll be right there," he hangs up. A sick smile spreads over his mouth, promising death. "They found her. Let's go."

50
AURORA

"She'll wake up."

"I feel like I've hardly gotten her back. Now, to nearly lose her..."

Mom?

Wait—why is Mom upset I'm leaving for my marriage when it hasn't happened yet? Why is she having this conversation while I'm asleep?

Why am I asleep?

Because it's nice in the dark. In the blackness with my pink and blue stars dancing behind my eyelids, it's easy to forget the dramatic shitshow my life has become.

51

ROSEN

I've never tortured a woman.

Hell, most of the torturing goes to Flynn, our enforcer. He waits nearby, leaning against the far wall of the mansion's basement with a knife in his hand, picking at dirt beneath his fingernails as he watches.

This one's mine. He'll get his chance when I'm done.

Behind me Nico and Rafael loom, both watching, neither acting. Hawke observes from the base of the staircase, his requisite for barriers still here, while fighting his desire to be involved for Aurora.

No matter. Because the only thing that does is the fact that we have Rozelyn De Falco in hand. It's a fucking payday.

I hold up a knife in one hand, letting it catch on the bulb above her head as I lean over the girl, tied to the metal chair, drilled into the cement ground. She tips her head back lazily, her long hair nearly brushing against the dirty ground.

"You're going to answer some fucking questions for us, bitch."

"And if I don't." Her brow hikes, smiling through the dirt

smudges on her face. "You won't kill me because you want information about my father, and whether I hand it over or not doesn't change the status of my life. You won't get rid of the only person who could potentially provide those answers."

She thinks she's cunning, but she's simply irritating. Her attitude isn't cute like Aurora's.

"That's where the knife comes in." I bring it closer, resting it right at the base of her neck, ready to dig it in, should she force me to. "Why did you drug Aurora?"

"Aw," she pouts, "did I do that?"

"Why?" I repeat, teeth baring.

She only grins and I press the blade into her collar bone, watching as a small dot of blood beads.

"You could have killed her."

"One Corsetti down. That doesn't sound like such a bad thing."

It's not the sight of the dot of blood on her neck, but red fills my vision and I swing my hand down, stabbing the knife into the fleshy part of her thigh. She screams out, her eyes bulging wide, clearly having not expected me to injure her.

I didn't expect to.

"Rosen," Nico warns.

He wants me to stop? His sister is in the hospital because of this cunt.

Her breaths come out sharper, her attention on the knife sticking out of her leg. She whimpers, her head lolling to the side.

I press my weight onto it, revelling when she flinches, her clamped jaw fighting not to scream again. "Answer me or I will pull this out and we can watch as you bleed to death. Then it'll really hurt."

She better call my bluff because Rozelyn already guessed it;

we can't kill her because she has information we require and removing the blade will be fatal.

Between clamped teeth, a heavy breath, and a cold glare, she grits, "For this. To be—here."

To be here? Like, *here*, captured?

Behind me, Nico snaps his fingers. "Flynn, get Dr. Shappo. We'll bandage her up."

Ignoring him, I demand, "What does that mean?"

Rozelyn doesn't answer, but when her eyes flick past my shoulder, they provide me a two-second warning before Nico grasps my arms, propelling me away. "You're done. Before you kill the girl, you're finished."

I shove out of his hold, whirling on him, as Rafael, once again, steps between us, his back to his brother, clearly taking his side.

"You're so sleep-deprived and rage-filled, you're not thinking rationally. Flynn will take over." Nico points to the staircase by Hawke, silently commanding me up them.

For the millionth time since meeting Aurora, I debate disobeying him.

"We have her now," he continues. "She's not going anywhere, which means you can sleep. And eat. Shower."

Flynn steps forward, his lips curling into his psychopathic grin. The man has this job for a specific reason—his unbridled lust for blood and pain. He ambles toward Rozelyn, whose head is still flopped to the side, the pain quickly knocking her out.

"Fine."

Spinning on my heel, I tread up the stairs, closely followed by Hawke, Nico, and Rafael. At the top, I don't stop, but continue straight to my bedroom, and fall into bed, sleep devouring me instantly.

～

It's the next morning when I finally wake, the previous days catching up to me quickly. Returning to the basement to continue what I began with Rozelyn is tempting, but I'd prefer focusing on Aurora.

My shower is refreshing and so is clean clothes, throwing the suit I had worn to the wedding in the laundry. At some point, I lost the jacket, and the white shirt is caked with dirt and blood. Once I don't look like I dined with death, I drive to the hospital.

Inside Aurora's room, I expect to find it full, like usual. Instead, there's a single person, like he knew this is the first place I'd be today.

Nico.

He leans against the far wall, watching his sister sleep, but the moment I step through the door, I gain his complete attention. "You have some nerve coming here."

"Yes."

"I should kill you."

Rolling my lips together, I sneak a peek at Aurora, quickly scanning her form. "So do it. I deserve nothing less." I know that. I broke his trust the moment I even thought of her that way.

"At least you recognize that." Frowning, he tips his head toward the bed. "Clarify one fact for me: you *did* fuck her, right?"

"You already established I had sex with her."

"So, you ruined her? You wrecked possible unions because you couldn't keep your dick in your pants."

This time, my hand goes to my waist, a silent threat to my underboss. Another action directly opposing previous vows I've made to him. He spots the threat and a single brow lifts.

"And now, you threaten me?"

"I didn't *ruin* her. Your sister isn't someone who can be ruined."

"Hm." Nico pauses, rocking back on his heels before he takes a single step. I don't move, don't back down. He takes another, and then another, until he walks right by me, snarling, "We're not done here."

The moment he leaves me alone with Aurora, I shut the room's door, falling against it as my lungs fill with new air. Seeing her, wanting to be beside her, urges me to the plastic chair that's been dragged by her bedside. Before sitting, I lean over and stroke the top of her head.

"Holy fuck, Aurora. Come back to me. I need you to wake up."

Shadows decorate beneath her eyes, which have been wiped clean from the makeup she had on at the wedding. Her gown has been replaced with hospital clothing. Her arms rest by her side, an IV in one. Her cheeks are still full of colour, giving me hope. The machine beeps, monitoring her ongoing heartbeats, and there's no sound more comforting.

Taking the hand closest to me, the one without an IV in it, I grip it as I fall into the plastic chair. Despite my long sleep, I'm tired again, this time for another reason.

My insides are tired. Tired of denying something we clearly all already know; something I've more than proven in the previous days.

"I love you, Aurora Corsetti. *Princesse,* you got to return to me."

~

2 Days Later

When someone enters the room again, I don't look up. I've stopped jumping, thinking everyone entering is a threat to an already-precarious situation, when it's typically a doctor or nurse checking vitals. If it's not medical staff, it's her family. Della and Caterina frequent here. Della makes small talk with me while Caterina stares blankly at her daughter until Lorenzo pulls her away, sending me a glare every single time. Sometimes, it's Hawke and Willow who visit.

"Thought you'd have taken off by now," I had said to him the other night.

He simply shrugged and settled deeper into his spot by the door. "She's my sister. I won't abandon her."

So when this person enters, I assume it's one of them, until a small hand rests on my shoulder, pulling my attention away, finding my sister and father both standing behind me.

Poppy frowns, her eyes studying my messy hair and two-day old clothing. "Rosen, you're a mess."

"So everyone keeps saying. What are you doing here?"

Dad speaks up, his attention going to Aurora in the bed as he talks. "Well, imagine my surprise when Nico Corsetti himself called me. Said you could use some company. My god, she's so much older than the child I remember."

Poppy rubs at her forehead, still frowning. "If you're by Aurora Corsetti's bedside, you didn't take the conversation we had at all seriously, did you?"

Dad mirrors her expression, resting his hand on my shoulder again. "Son, what did you do?"

I shoulder away his touch. Their reprimands over something I'm clearly aware of are pointless. "I knew how dangerous it was even before you said anything. Trust me," I scoff, crossing my arms, "I knew."

Poppy walks around to Aurora's other side, where a chair is

situated for someone else to occupy it. She takes it, saying nothing more on the subject. Father remains behind me, silently offering support.

"You've always been horrible at hiding your emotions," Poppy remarks after a few minutes. "Now is no different. You really care for her."

"Yes." There's no sense in hiding it. It seems like everyone is aware at this point.

"Idiot. Before her family kills you, would you mind coming to say goodbye to me?" There's amusement in her tone, but she could be correct. Nico will still want the connection to the New York *Familgia*, now more than ever, given what's happening with De Falco. If he's smart, he'll hide the lack of Aurora's virginity to ensure the wedding to Rossi goes forward.

There's a difference this time. Nico will have to kill me before I let her walk down the aisle to another man. This isn't a game any longer and losing her to this coma—to not knowing what was happening to her when I discovered her passed out during the reception—made me realize what my heart was already aware of.

For the remainder of the hour, my sister and father stay, not saying anything further. Before they leave, Poppy presses a kiss to my forehead and a quick pat on the back of my hand.

Minutes after they go, I stand to stretch, wandering toward the window, catching the mid-afternoon sun shining over the hospital parking lot below. City noises and honks filter in through the window pane; noises that have been easy to block out in the days I've been here. Everything seems to have been put on pause since I started sitting with Aurora.

I've been reading a lot about coma patients and learned talking with them helps. That even while they're asleep, they can hear things. It's been difficult to do so because, while I want to make promises of life after this, I can't.

I want to promise to hold her, to be with her, but minutes after she awakens, I could find myself at the other end of Nico's gun, breaking that promise.

"You've had so many people abandon you when you were a child. So many times, you were forced to find comforts where you could. I don't want to be yet another person who does that to you." I wander over toward her, dragging my fingertips up the stretch of her arm, toward her collar bone, and then cupping her face. "I want to make you every promise you deserve, but when you wake up and your family decides my fate, I'll be breaking that promise. Abandoning you in all the things I claimed I'd provide. It kills me not to, Aurora, so the only thing I have is to promise to love you." Leaning down, I gently press a kiss to her lips—the first I've given her since she's been here. "I love you, Aurora. Please wake up so I can tell you that in person."

"Ahem." A cough-grunt mix jerks me upright, my attention flying to the door where Lorenzo and Caterina stand, their expressions indescribable as they catch me with their daughter.

I yank my hand away from her, but don't move from where I stand.

Lorenzo enters. "We'd like some time alone with her, Rosen."

Rubbing my lips together, I leave Aurora's bedside for the first time in days, stopping outside the room, feeling at a loss. There's a demand to remain and wait for her parents to finish, but away from her, my head clears. The fog of broken emotions tapes me up, even temporarily, and I realize what everyone, even Poppy, has been alluding to.

I can't make any promises to Aurora Corsetti, even the promise to love her.

It'll be yet another one I break when the Corsettis make me uphold my oaths.

52
AURORA

Something cool traces my lips. A barely-there touch, but it ignites an energy inside me I hadn't known to exist. With that brief touch, it wipes away everything black. Everything pink and blue I've been seeing.

Am I awake?

My eyes won't open. Hints of that darkness still coat the edges, locking me in this lull.

"I love you, Aurora. Please wake up so I can tell you that in person."

He loves me?

I love him too, even if I'm not allowed to.

"Please wake up so I can tell you that in person."

Okay, Rosen. I'll try. I want him to say that to my face.

"Ahem." That's a new voice. "We'd like some time alone with her, Rosen."

Alone? Rosen's leaving. I try to follow, but my body is too weighed down. Without my sight, my hearing is sharper, so I know the exact stride Rosen takes when he leaves, and the air around me get chillier in his absence.

Who's here now?

A heavy sigh accompanies the sound of a door shutting. Based on the footsteps, there's multiple people. They split, and I hear them go to either side of where I lie.

"I've never been good with words, Aurora, and I know I'm taking the coward's way out by saying this to you as you sleep and are unable to hear me."

Dad?

He thinks I can't hear him, but I can.

A colder, thin hand rests over mine. Mom? Somehow, I know it's her. I think about moving my hand, about responding to her touch, but I can't.

"What happened to Hawke was the first time I questioned myself and my role. I was terrified of doing wrong by the family, and those fuckers only wanted the power I held. They captured your brother to use him for blackmail and I didn't respond how I should have."

I know this already. Well, I know the concept of what happened, from a six-year-old's understanding as well as over-hearing where I could.

"That was mistake number one. The second was when we made the call to send you away. Even after those horrid men had been dealt with, your brother left us, and your mother didn't sleep for over a week, terrified to shut her eyes."

"None of you know this, but I took turns sitting in all your rooms, each night," she murmurs, her soft touch rubbing the back of my hand. "I had three soldiers stationed at you and your brothers' doors, and I spent a few hours there. I *needed* to make sure you weren't taken from your beds."

"There's only so much pain a person can handle, Aurora," Dad continues. "I forced more training onto your brothers. My way of coping, I suppose, but we couldn't do that with you. And you were so young. A girl."

A girl. Helpless. Because that's what this life assumes. That's what *they* assumed. What would have happened if I stayed, and they trained me like Nico and Rafael? Rosen had told me about Della and how she saved Nico from getting shot, so they can't claim women are not fighters, when she's proven otherwise.

"We felt the only way to keep you safe and protected, and allow you some semblance of a life, was to send you away where few people would know where you were."

What were they smoking back then?

"You were so young, so confused. Bringing you home for holidays would have been hard on you."

"And me," Mom cuts in. "I think if you came back, I wouldn't have let you go again. For weeks after you left, I still didn't sleep, for an entirely other reason this time."

I guess that makes sense in a fucked-up kind of way.

"So we never did," Dad continues. "That was error number three on our parts. As months and years passed, it got easier. Like Hawke, you were a person of our past, as heartless as that may sound, but it was the truth. It hurt less to mourn you both together."

But you had no consideration for me and what being aban-doned would do, I want to yell, but my lips are too heavy.

"As more time went on, I suppose we were scared. Bringing back our now-adult daughter was a lot of pressure. It was only when Nico was promoted to underboss, that he insisted it was time. Trust me," his tone lightens, "your brother had a lot of unsavoury words he finally got off his chest in regard to not bringing you home sooner."

He did? He doesn't give that impression, considering he's trying to send me off again.

"We haven't had this conversation yet, Aurora, and appar-ently we're still cowards for doing this while you can't respond, but I wonder if we'll ever get a chance to. I feel like every time we turn around, we're losing you."

And you will continue to when I march down the aisle in a *month*.

Mom sighs. "Baby girl, I'm sorry I ruined your life. I'm trying to do right by you now."

Are you?

"You're very missed," she goes on. "By a certain soldier especially. That was an unwelcome surprise we'll discuss when you wake up."

Rosen. I want Rosen back. Where had he gone?

"For now, we'll leave you be."

There's silence for a moment, and then a rustle. Mom stands from the chair and they both exit the room, shutting the door behind them.

I'm alone.

Once again, I'm alone.

My eyes flutter open.

Wandering aimlessly around hospital hallways while Lorenzo and Caterina are with Aurora only lasts about two minutes when the text message comes through.

RAFAEL

Meet me at the pin.

Quickly following that message is a pinned location on a map. Then he attaches a screenshot in a separate message, showing a text thread between him and another one of the soldiers, Maurice. An older man, close to retirement, having served the family for a long time. He was placed in Rafael's regiment last year for his experience.

ME

On my way.

Within twenty minutes, I arrive at the designated area, finding Rafael already there, leaning against his sports car. He jerks his chin in greeting.

"I'm surprised you want me here."

Rafael rolls his head around, lazily glancing at me with his usual carelessness. "What, because of recent revelations? I mean, sure, you're scum and all," he grins, breaking the heaviness of his statement, "but you're still one of the best." Lower, he adds, "And a friend. Nico won't kill you, you know?"

"Wanna bet?"

He shakes his head, about to respond with something else, but another car rolling up stops him. The older Toyota Corolla stops beside my car and Maurice stands, his eyes darting around the open area.

He stops two feet away from us, scanning the surroundings still. Rafael glances at me, mirroring my own *what the fuck* expression. My own eyes take a slow graze around the area, peeking through the afternoon sun into the treeline and the neighboring streets.

"You wanted to talk, Maurice," Rafael starts, pulling the old man's attention toward us. "Very strange circumstances, I must say."

He jerks his head into a nod and shifts his feet, pressing his lips together, making me feel even more confused. Maurice has never been one to visibly show nerves. Given his experience, we often have him training newer soldiers.

"The entire family has been hunting for De Falco."

Rafael straightens from his slouch. "You have news?"

The man rubs a hand down his face, drawing my attention to his features. The crazed, red-rimmed eyes, cracked lips, and blatant fear. He's scared of something. But not us, I think, or else he wouldn't be here.

"I-I do. I know where he is. But..."

"But?" Rafael prompts, taking a step closer to Maurice. "But what, Maurice? Where is he? What do you know?"

The man's breathing increases, his head lowering to the

point I'd believe his body could sink into the ground. He shudders, wiping at his face again, at the tears that well in the base of his eyes.

"I-I'm sorry, Capo. I-I h-had to protect her and—"

"Who?" I demand.

"My daughter."

He has a child? In all the years I've known Maurice, he's never shared his family situation, and I've long assumed he's been a single man, dedicating his whole life to service.

I glance at Rafael. Curious if this is news to him too, or if he's aware, but his taken-back expression provides the answer.

"Stefano De Falco is—" Maurice stops, swallowing. "You must help me protect her. De Falco is—"

This time, when Maurice's speech cuts off, it's with a gurgle and a spurt of blood that dribbles to the space between our feet. His eyes bulge and he stumbles forward, his hand flying to his bleeding neck.

I lunge, reaching my arms out, and he falls right into them, but there's nothing left. The gunshot wound to his throat has quickly taken his life, hitting an artery.

"Get down!" Rafael yanks at my arm, causing me to misstep and drop Maurice as he pulls me to the side of his vehicle.

"We can't leave him!"

"We have to get out of here. Standing could mean death. We'll come back for his body, but our lives matter more." He crawls toward his driver's side door, opening it, while I make it to the back door, each of us sliding safely into the vehicle.

The moment I'm inside, Rafael punches the gas pedal, throwing us forward and away.

～

"**A**re you fucking kidding me?" Nico booms, punching his desk after hearing what we've reported. "I can't fucking keep up. Our own soldier knew something! Gets shot by someone who clearly fucking knew he was about to squeal. *Goddamn it!*" He stabs his finger at me. "Tell Flynn. Get the fucking truth from his cunt of a daughter *now*."

Rafael speaks up, interrupting a potentially longer rant. "Why did we not know about his daughter? If Maurice has been hiding a family from us, but he's been sworn in for decades, what are some of the newer ones keeping?"

Everyone gets extensive background checks, but clearly, someone slipped up somewhere.

"This daughter might know something too," Rafael continues. "At the very least, find her and inform her that her father is dead." He sighs, rubbing the back of his neck. "He's in my regiment, so I should be the one to that. I'll pull his address from our files and hopefully find her there."

"And if you don't?" Nico asks.

He shrugs. "Then I keep looking. Someone wanted Maurice to remain silent, which means, it's possible she knows what he does. Which makes her valuable."

Nico nods, and the tight muscles in his arms loosen a fraction. Enough he's able to release the desk and he falls into his office chair, cursing. "I feel like we're mice in a wheel. Continuing to go around in circles, never quite able to catch up. De Falco is playing with us and—"

His cell phone ringing interrupts him and Nico lifts it to his ear, listening briefly but not saying anything. When he hangs up, there's a tangible, positive energy in the room.

"Aurora's awake."

~

When we arrive at the hospital, everyone else is already there. Through the window of her room, I spot her parents by her bedside, her mother clutching her hand. Against the far wall, in their usual place, are Willow and Hawke. Della and Ariella are there too, having been driven in by Nico's parents.

There's one person I focus on. One light that makes the past week worth it—the hunting, the sleepless nights, the pacing by her bedside. One light with the brightest smile as she scans all the people who care about her.

Despite witnessing Aurora awake, instead of pacifying pleasure, a weight drops into my stomach. Nico allowed me to sit by her bedside and has brought me with him after receiving the call, but what now?

When Rafael marches right into her room, movement by the door catches my attention. An obnoxiously large bouquet of mixed flowers enters, carried by the man who'll one day get to claim her. He smiles tentatively being thrown into the mix of Corsettis and lingers awkwardly by the door.

Erico Rossi.

Nico pauses. "Upon his father's recommendation, he remained in the city until she woke up."

His father's recommendation. He stayed because he was *ordered* to, while I hunted the person who dared harm her. I didn't sleep, eat, or shower in those days. I stayed by her bedside, increasing my boss's wrath every moment I remained. Rossi didn't visit once. Didn't *care* enough to check on her. With her awake, he'll likely be on the first flight back to New York.

"He'll be her fiancé in a month, Rosen."

A month. Trapped air chokes my lungs. A fucking month, not a year. When had that changed?

Without air to breathe, my heart stops pounding, watching

as Rossi slowly crosses the room, laying his bouquet on the far windowsill. He belongs there because other than the vows they've yet to take, her family has already declared them as married.

"He might find it strange when her bodyguard is in the room."

I've never wanted to slaughter Nico more than I do at this moment. He's reminding me of my place.

I don't respond because I can't. There's nothing more to say, not when he's being so fucking clear.

Instead, I turn on my heel and exit the hospital.

54
AURORA

Since the moment I opened my eyes, there's been people around. First, the nurses and doctors, checking my vitals and explaining what had happened. Something about overdosing on the gummies I swallowed because they were laced with Fentanyl. I've barely processed that fact before my family was getting called and my parents were there, along with Della and her sister, and Hawke and his girlfriend, which has been another thing for my slow-ass, foggy brain to process.

Rafael enters the room, making a very loud exclamation I don't quite catch, but his entrance pulls my attention toward the door, to the large bouquet of flowers carried by a man I certainly don't wish to see.

Erico's presence emphasizes who's missing. Nico and Rosen. While Nico's probably doing his million and one tasks, who I really want is Rosen.

He was here. I heard him. I think I did anyway. He told me he loved me, or did I dream that?

Of course, he wouldn't be here. Our romance was a secret. Hell, even dancing at the wedding reception meant being cautious, so he wouldn't have been able to sit by my bedside and tell me all those wonderful truths.

A flash of black in the corner of my eye draws my focus toward the window, showing the hallway beyond. Nico's there, backing up from a figure.

I lean forward, but the figure's gone and Nico enters my room, his gaze drilling into me. I blink, throwing a smile toward Mom, pretending like my attention wasn't elsewhere.

"We're so pleased you're okay," she murmurs, her eyes misting as she leans forward and kisses me on the forehead. "I was terrified of losing you, honey."

"I know," I murmur, glancing from her to Dad. "I heard you both earlier. I...I think I was awake for it. Kinda."

Dad slowly reaches toward my other hand but doesn't take it.

I glance toward Hawke, the only person who understands the power in what I'm about to do. The small piece of tape I'm placing on my relationship with our parents.

I take Dad's hand, squeezing it as much as my strength allows for. *It's okay,* I tell him with that action.

What he had done will never be *okay*. Will never be right or anything I'll ever stand behind, but they're not bad people. They made stupid decisions. Decisions, that, ultimately shaped me to be who I am, but I'm starting to see the positives in that. Hawke became his own person, one who can deem his own future, because of their choices.

I had to, too, to an extent. Raised under the influence of the Corsetti name, but not as one of them. Raised to be told what I would be doing, but not practiced. Not under the belief that, as a woman, I have one role only. My eyes shift to Della, the example of what mafia women *can* be, with a little bit of push-back.

What I strive to be.

Not a political chess piece.

The conversation Hawke and I had in the hallway returns to my mind, tightening my hold on both our parents. Something about letting go of the past to process the trauma. Or for me, my abandonment. What they did occurred, but it's what will happen next that changes everything.

When Hawke nods his head, it's a subtle motion. One that shows he agrees with my actions.

Everyone's waiting, bated breaths, for me to do something. There are too many people in here and my gaze can't settle on any one person.

Somehow, silent Ariella recognizes my struggle and tips her head to the side, nudging Della's arm. She throws a small smile over her shoulder and then leaves, enticing action from the others.

Dad releases me, clearing his throat with a rough motion. "I'm going to speak to the doctor about discharging you sooner than they'd like. We have Dr. Shappo who can visit you daily at home. I'm sure you'd prefer that?"

"I'd love that," I reply. "Thanks, Dad."

He pauses in his tracks, glancing back at me with eyes packed with emotion before clearing his throat again and exiting the room. Mom pats my hand and follows him.

Now that they're significantly less people in the room, I can breathe normally. But there's still a person hovering in here who doesn't belong. Who I don't *want* to belong. At some point, he's moved to the opposite side of the room, laying the bouquet on the windowsill by Hawke.

"Can you guys give me a minute with Erico please?"

Rafael moves first, approaching the bed, giving me a one-armed hug. "I have something I need to do anyway. Glad you're okay, sis. You really scared us." He leaves, followed by Hawke and Willow who both wave, and then Nico, until finally, it's only Erico remaining.

He slowly approaches, gesturing to the bouquet and stating the obvious. "I got you flowers."

Duh. Pushing my hands into the mattress, I lift myself off the mountain of pillows the nurses, for some reason, assumed would be a good idea, so I can better brace for this conversation.

"Do you even want our union?"

Erico hesitates, his lips parting a fraction. By the time he answers, "Of course," in a smooth tone, it's too late. His hesitation said it all.

"You don't."

He blinks, nodding once, his gaze diving to the floor. An inner conversation seems to occur because when he looks at me again, he seems different. Reserved again, like the first time I met him.

"It's a wise move for both organizations. Our families are prominent in their own countries, and it's a great move to become allies. That was once the plan, long before either of us was born, and now we can make it happen." He pauses, quickly dampening his lips. "That's how most marriages go, Aurora. I understand, growing up away from the life, you were able to read fairy tales that filled your head with notions about love, but that's not how the world works."

It wasn't books that filled my head. It was Rosen. Witnessing Della and Nico. My parents. Examples of non-connections gone right.

"You'll be cared for and will want for nothing," he continues.

Except love. That small piece I've always missed. Growing up without a family's love. Marrying a man who won't give it.

No. I won't accept that. Maybe it was my extended, drug-induced nap. Maybe it was believing Rosen told me he loves me.

Maybe it was my parents' truths—whatever caused this awakening is relieving, and I grasp what Hawke was talking about.

Erico coughs when I don't reply. Apparently, he takes my silence as an agreement for he rubs a hand down his suit jacket and steps toward the door. "Right then, I must return to New York for business, but I'm pleased you are awake. I will be in contact with your brother regarding our engagement. For now, see you soon."

When he goes, I'm left trying to process what occurred and the assumptions that dick took with my silence. To admit he won't love me but believes I'll agree to marrying him.

The door opens again, and I swear to fuck, if he's returned, I'll—

"Hey." Hawke pokes his head in the room. "Figured it was safe to enter."

Willow approaches my bedside, her eyes scanning the machines around me. "Glad you're awake."

When Hawke steps beside her, I reach for his hand, taking the strength of his presence. "Thank you, Hawke, for the conversation we had before I...well."

"Don't let them push you around, Aurora. Like you said, they make shit decisions and Erico Rossi is yet another one being thrown your way."

"I don't want that. To be wed and shipped off for a *connection*. Bullshit. Nico gets his happily-ever-after, while I don't."

What does my happily-ever-after look like? Rosen's clearly not here, so what does that mean?

"You've been awake for all of an hour," he starts, amusement tinging his tone, "and you've made peace with our parents and, judging by Rossi's face as he passed us, made your stance known there. You seem like you're already halfway, Aurora. You have our father and Nico to get through since they're the ones who hold the metaphorical reins over this family, but you control your own future, and don't let them think otherwise." He pauses, glancing at the plastic chair by my bedside. "He didn't stop looking for the culprit, Aurora. I know because I was with him and our brothers. Rosen scoured every inch of this city for days. Didn't sleep. Didn't do anything else but obsess. Then he stayed by your bedside until this morning."

So he *was* here? I didn't imagine what I heard.

"Nico knows," Hawke adds, "about you and him. The moment Rosen found you in the hallway at their reception, it was obvious. Once Nico actually took two minutes to examine the situation, he figured it out."

Shit. So this whole time, as everyone stood here, Nico knew? "Mom and Dad too?"

"Everyone."

"He's not..." I trail off, wondering if what I'm about to whine about is stupid. *He's not here.*

Willow speaks up. "Sometimes, people require a kick in the ass." She smiles fondly at Hawke. "I think we all do."

Hawke reaches into his pocket and pulls out a folded-up piece of paper, pushing it into my hand. "When they annoy you and you want a break, this is my number. Please don't share this."

This day continues to stun me, but this action most of all. I unfold the paper, reading over the digits. Over and over, trying to commit this to memory, in case something happens to this paper before I can get the number programmed into my phone. These are the most valuable ten digits I'll ever read.

"Thank you." This was a huge step for Hawke, and no words are good enough for what this means to me. "You're still here. I would have thought you'd be gone already."

"Now that you're awake, we'll go back home. My partner's been holding our law firm afloat in my absence."

I search through the dyed hair, the piercings, and find the

fourteen-year-old brother who had walked out on us so many years ago. A brother I share a strange connection to now, one the others will never understand.

"I want you here with us, Hawke. I miss you."

His expression pinches, like he's in pain, and he crouches so his face is lined up with mine. "You know why I can't. You've forgiven our parents, but I haven't, and I'm not sure I ever will. Besides, I have a life back home. Work. Friends. I can't leave them, nor do I want to, not to live here. But," he pauses, his lips curling, "I'm not going anywhere."

Words that's sound contradictory. That he's going home and isn't coming back, but he's also not going anywhere. But I understand the meaning behind them. He's here still, for me, for Nico and Rafael, and now that he's visited once, he won't cut us out of his life.

"Now that I've met you again, I can't go years without you, Hawke."

"You won't," he promises, wrapping his arm around my neck.

He pulls me into the longest, most-needed hug I've ever gotten, and I think I ever will. A hug filled with his strength, which pulls out my own. A true older sibling, who is the example of who I should be, not what Nico and Rafael embody —what they *want* me to be. When he pulls back, I feel it enter me—feel it strengthen me in a way that'll allow me to battle our brother and father and win.

"Besides, you should come visit my neck of the woods some time."

"I'd love that."

"Once you figure out your place here." With a final brief touch to my face, he steps back, taking Willow's hand in his own. "Find your happiness, Aurora. Text me when you do." At the door, he peeks back at me, winking. "If you're anything like me, and I'm starting to think you are, I'll be receiving that text in a week."

When he leaves, I make a silent promise to him.

I'll find my happiness, Hawke. I'll take it for myself. I'll be my own person.

And that starts now.

55
ROSEN

She's safe and alive. That's what I continue to remind myself as I lie in bed the same evening.

The world is playing some cruel trick, in which everything I desire continues to be out of reach. After leaving the hospital, I tried to push my way into the basement since Flynn's made no progress with Rozelyn, and I'd hoped it would give me something to do, something to feel, in the absence of not being able to see Aurora.

But Flynn kicked me out before I made it three steps down. Asshole.

Aurora's safe and alive. That's all that matters. In a month, things will return to normal. She'll be married off to Rossi and will move to New York and my life will return to where it was before her arrival. That was always the plan, anyway. I never should have touched her, let alone fell in love with her. Distance will be beneficial. She'll live out her future and I'll be a fling from her past. The pain will fade, and I can make up for my disloyalty to her family.

When the doorknob to my room twists, I curse myself for

forgetting to lock it. It's likely Nico, come to deliver more news I could deal without.

Instead, it's a flash of blonde curls, followed by the face I continue to see in my mind. Her skin is paler than usual, exhaustion drawing her into my room, slamming the door and pressing her back against it, her breaths shallow and heavy, her hand going to her chest.

I blink. I can't possibly be seeing what I am.

Aurora in my room, dressed in sweats.

"Hi."

No, I wouldn't have imagined that. I leap to my feet, approaching to convince myself she's here.

"You should be in the hospital."

She lifts a finger, signalling for me to wait, while she continues to take in heavy gulps. "I discharged myself. After my parents spoke to them, they agreed to let me go in the morning. When my parents left, I fought with the doctors, declaring twelve hours wouldn't make much of a difference. Besides, it's against the law to hold me there involuntarily. Then I hailed a cab here. It's amazing what happens when you throw your name around. Stuff becomes free."

My mind is still replaying the start of that speech, about discharging herself, not even able to focus on the fact that she travelled in a cab alone, in the middle of the night. And that she's *here*, in my room.

Half of me wants to kiss her, to hold her, to never let her go, while the rest of me wants to strangle her for placing herself in so much danger when she left the hospital against doctor's orders and without calling anyone.

I'm torn between what I crave and what I should be doing. The desire to keep her with me, while the reality is I should call Nico. Instead, I awkwardly stand there, never feeling more emotionally torn than I do in this moment.

"Why didn't you come to see me today?" she asks in a low, dejected tone that nearly brings me to my knees.

There's the truth, and then there's the answer I'm forced to give. The one that pours from my mouth: "You have your family. You and I aren't anyth—"

"Bullshit," she cuts me off. "I heard you by my bedside."

Deny. Aurora will be wed soon so there's little point in being truthful.

"You were in a coma. You don't know what you heard."

"Stop lying, Rosen. Hawke told me what you did."

Fucker.

"How you worked for days to find who drugged me. How you sat by my bedside until this morning."

The truth can't be denied any longer, but speech also evades me.

Aurora takes a step closer, her feet staggering, her skin growing paler. My arm darts out, catching her before she can fall. I hold her for a beat longer than I should, the feel of her body against mine healing days of heartache.

She huffs a small laugh. "I guess lying in a bed for days really fucks with a person's strength."

"Come sit." I lead her to the end of my bed, the exact opposite direction I should be pushing her. Controlling her body, I pull her down, and then move her farther onto the bed, until she's nearly in the middle.

Her lips curl, watching as I care for her, likely for the final time. "Strange actions of a man who claims we're nothing. Like we're falling right back into old behaviours, where you take care of me, even when reminding us both of those damn boundaries."

Because I want to be that for you. Instead, I turn away, heading for the bathroom, returning with a small cup of water. "Drink."

"Yes, sir," she replies, taking the cup and swallowing a healthy swig, pretending to be unaware of the effect her words have on me.

"Aurora," I warn, voice hardening.

"There's the man I missed."

I swipe a hand down my face, heading away from her before I do something stupid. This time, I aim for the complete and devastating truth. "There's nothing here anymore, *princesse*. We knew going into this, it'd be a limited time. In a month, you'll be engaged, so anything said tonight is irrelevant."

"Look at me when you say that."

I can't. But I do, steeling my expression to lie. A well-practiced behaviour, assisted by training to keep up appearances when necessary.

Aurora stands from the bed, placing herself in front of me. Her head comes up to my chest and she has to tip her head back to look me in the eyes, but somehow, when she does, it's like she's looking down on me. She rests her hand over my heart, right over the tattoo I once had etched there to signal my loyalty to her family.

"You're fighting our relationship again."

Her other hand comes up, wrapping around my neck. If I was wise, this is where I'd push her away, but I don't because I don't want to.

"I challenged you then, and I challenge you now. For both of us, tell me the truth, Rosen. Do you love me?"

Yes.

"*Princesse...*"

"That tone says it all."

"Don't," I tell her through a thick throat. My stupid, betraying hands come up to her hips, holding her. I know I've lost, even before the next words come from my mouth. Before I seal my death.

It'll be worth it. A final taste of her in exchange for an eternity beneath the ground.

My mouth crashes into hers and I walk her backwards, to the nearest wall, taking her mouth in a vicious kiss—a battle of emotions. Of what's right and what's wrong.

"Yes," I admit between kisses.

"Say the words."

Wrapping my arms beneath her thighs, I lift her, lining her core up with my cock, which almost immediately jumps to attention beneath my shorts, having missed her. With my hand on her neck, I reclaim control of her body—control I've fucking missed having.

She entered my room thinking she's in command, but I'll remind her who has the reins.

Lie, my mind instructs. Lie because she's still in control. She has my heart in her hand and it's her next actions that'll deem if she crushes it or not.

"If I do, I won't let you go."

I won't be able to. Nico will kill me before I let her walk down the aisle to another man. This is it—this is why I *can't* admit these words because I won't be in control of my next actions.

"That's the point." She smiles into my mouth, her fingers weaving with my hair. "I don't want you to let me go."

What we want and what must happen are very different realities of this life.

I pull back, to look her in the face before I speak words that'll change everything. Words already spoken to her sleeping, unresponsive form but when she opens her mouth first, I'm a fucking goner.

"I want to be yours, Rosen. I want to marry you one day. To *be* with you. Always. I don't know when it happened, but it did. I love you."

"I love you."

"I love you."

"I love you."

Her words embed themselves in my heart, and it's official, Nico *will* have to kill me now because I'll slaughter Rossi before he takes Aurora from me.

"I love you too, *princesse.*"

"Take me as yours then. Make this happen, Rosen."

Using the wall as leverage, I rip her sweatshirt with my hands, baring her breasts to me. Her sweater lands at my feet, right alongside my loyalty.

"It was very dangerous for you to come here. That's punishment number one."

Playing along, she holds up one finger. "You list 'em, and I'll count them."

"You left the hospital when you should be getting better."

She lifts another finger, rolling her eyes. "I'm fine. It was a long, deep nap."

"You were drugged." *Under my watch.* A fact still tearing me up. I lower her feet to the ground, hooking my fingers into her sweatpants, dragging them to her ankles. Skating a finger up her leg, I stop short of her pussy. "Number three: I haven't had you in days."

"Does that constitute as a reason for punishment?" she asks, her tone amused.

I stand, showing her there's no joke in this. Scooping her into my arms bridal-style, I lay her on the bed, her head on my pillow. As much as I'd love to take her against the wall, I can't tonight. She's too weak for a rough fuck.

"Everything over these days have been punishment," I tell her, honesty weaving through my words. "You have no idea what went through my head when I found you on the floor, passed out."

"You found me?" No one told me that part. In fact, no one's told me much of anything, including who the culprit is, although I've drawn my own conclusions when the doctors mentioned the drug-laced gummies.

Roz gave those to me, and now, I have so many questions regarding them and her. For tomorrow.

"Yeah. After Hawke left you at the reception, I went to make sure you were okay. There you were, on the ground. I didn't know if you were alive still or..." I trail off, pressing my lips together, unable to say the word. Crouching down to my knees, I line my face up with hers, so she can see this isn't a game. Not for me. I push through a tormented, rough tone to admit, "You fucking terrified me, *princesse*. I held you the entire drive to the hospital, only releasing you so the doctors could care for you because I didn't know what the fuck happened."

She sits up, crossing her legs as she cups my face, tilting it up. "Hawke said it was at the hospital when Nico learned about us."

"I wish I could have better controlled myself, but seeing you like that." A flash of her passed-out rushes through my mind, causing me to shudder. "Then, learning the De Falcos were behind it, when they drugged you, I wanted vengeance. *Needed* retribution. Needed them to pay, as if you'd wake up by me getting it. You didn't and I waited for days, determined to see your eyes open again. To know you're all right."

"I'm okay," she whispers. "I'm better than okay because I'm here with you. When everyone was in my hospital room, there was only one person I wanted to see, but he wasn't there." She lifts a single brow, shooting me a pointed look.

I want to ask about Rossi's presence and what that meant, but it doesn't matter. Not now. Not while I make promises to her that I'll die trying to keep.

I lift to my feet, stripping my shorts, revelling in the way her eyes go straight to my cock. She reaches for me, but I swat her hand away. "I didn't give you permission to touch."

"But I missed you," she whines, reaching again.

Instead of hitting her hand, I grasp her wrist, twisting her body in one quick movement until I have her on her back and I'm climbing over her.

"Are we going to play?" Her eyes sparkle in the low light of my bedside lamp.

"Not today. Tonight, I'm claiming you, Aurora, but I refuse to exhaust your body. When the doctor clears you, then we'll play. Your punishments will be on pause until then."

She pouts, which looks entirely too adorable. It's almost tempting to grant her the night we spoke about while dancing days ago, but I'll stick to my word about her health being a priority.

After retrieving a condom from the bedside table and putting it on, I weave my fingers in between hers as my cock drags over her pussy, making her wet. My mouth claims hers, my tongue licking hers, demanding she grant me what I crave.

Her.

The day's frustrations come out in my kiss, the constant reminder not to hurt her coursing through my mind.

She makes a low sound in the back of her throat and her hips move with me, her heels digging into the bed as she begs, "Rosen, inside me."

Locking my eyes onto hers, I instruct, "Use your safe word if this gets too much. Your body is still weak and we're not testing your limits tonight." With my free hand, I grasp my cock and line it up with her centre and slowly push inside her.

In an inch, out a fraction, in two inches. Over and over until I'm bottomed out inside her, and her moans fill the room, a sound I was certain I wouldn't ever be hearing again. Her hand tightens in mine, clutching as she rocks her hips off the bed.

"You okay?"

"I'm perfect, Rosen. I'm not fragile."

I know she isn't. From day one, this woman's been tough, unforgiving in her drive, and that's why I fucking love her.

Wrapping my hand around her leg, I push it up, stretching her open. I kiss her again, swallowing her moans as she orgasms, to hear her accept my claiming, to feel her pussy tightening around my cock.

To know she's fucking *mine*.

"Don't prolong this," she pleads against my lips. "I'm dying to feel you."

Enforcing her words, I thrust into her again, faster this time, my pace quickening when she shows no sign of pain. Her moans get louder, her hold on me firmer, her eyes squeezing shut as she arches.

I lean down, taking one of her budded nipples between my teeth, lightly sucking as her first orgasm wracks her body. I don't slow my thrusts, releasing her nipple to drag my tongue up her chest and to the base of her neck.

"You still okay?"

"Yes, Rosen," she responds, with a slight gasp. "Fuck, I'm fine."

"Careful," I mumble into her neck. "Wouldn't want to give attitude and risk what I'll do."

"Except you won't be too intense tonight, which means anything I say goes unpunished." She grins wickedly, being the brat I love.

Making my point, I pull my cock from her, instead dragging it along her wet, sensitive folds. "That might be true, but I'm keeping track for when you can handle more."

"Promises." She rolls her eyes, still grinning.

Another tick. Normally, I wouldn't reward her for the comments she makes, but tonight isn't about that.

As her heat envelopes me again, I thrust back inside her, her smirk quickly wiped away for a moan, her head falling back onto the bed.

"So good at taking me, *princesse.*"

"*Your princesse.*"

"Fuckin' right." This time, they're not only words. They're a promise; an agreement we're both making.

I grasp her ankles and position them over my arms, lifting her legs higher, gaining another inch inside her. She gasps, her attention locking where we're connected.

"Atta girl. Watch how your pussy takes me. How it knows who it wants, who it needs most."

It's only a moment before her eyes are squeezing shut, her hands fisting in the blanket at her side, her pussy tightening around me, her orgasm right there.

"Can I come?"

If I didn't already know she was so perfect for me, this would have secured it. She asks for permission, like the perfect, little sub.

I reach down, stroking my fingers between her clit, petting her swollen bud. "Because you asked so nicely, yes."

Her orgasm ripples through her pussy, head shoving into my pillow as she cries out at a volume I wouldn't doubt my neighbours, soldiers living in the rooms around us, could hear. It no longer matters. Only death will end this moment.

"Let me hear you. I fucking love the noises you make."

"The noises *you* cause me to make," she murmurs between heavy breaths. Her legs go limp against my body, sliding from my arms, exhaustion catching up to her.

"One more. Give me one more. You can do it."

The small amount of praise is all it takes for her to light

right up. Her heels dig into the mattress, her hips meeting my thrusts.

"That's my good girl."

"And your brat," she whispers.

"And my *princesse*."

I lower her legs back to the bed and reposition myself over her. Cupping the back of her neck, I hold her gaze as my thrusts speed up. When my body feels the familiar pleasure tightening my abs, making my legs weaker, I claim her mouth, tasting her as my orgasm hits.

Her nails scrape at my back, her orgasm instantly following mine. She moans into the kiss, her legs locking around mine until we become one. There's not a fraction of space between us, exactly how I prefer it.

"I fucking love you, my little brat."

"I love you too, dick." And then she laughs, thrilled with the snarky nickname she used all those times before.

"Laugh all you want. Because soon, you'll be paying for that."

She grins but buries her head into my neck. Her lips brush my skin, imprinting her own claim on me.

"Can't wait," she murmurs, right before she curls into my arms and sleep takes us both.

56

AURORA

When morning comes, I dress in the same sweatpants the hospital gave me and one of Rosen's shirts, since he ripped mine. Getting to wear my own clothes again will be great, but this will do for now.

I find Nico in his usual spot: his office.

Without knocking, I stride in, stopping on the other side of his desk. He must know I've entered because his lips purse, and without looking away from his laptop, he mutters, "The hospital called, warning me."

"Based on that tone, you're not worried. I should be upset."

His eyes slowly drag from the laptop, landing right on my shirt. His gaze hardens, his mouth flattening. "Somehow, I knew that's where you'd be. You must think I'm stupid, Aurora, but you forget what my position means. You asked to speak with Rossi alone, and then Hawke visited right after. Then that night, you escape, and the hospital's camera footage has you getting into a taxi. Our own footage has you arriving from that same taxi. It doesn't take a genius to figure it out."

"Except we snuck around for days without you noticing."

The shadow passing over his face tells me it was the wrong thing to say.

"Well," he leans back, folding his hands over his stomach, "you're in my office, dressed in the shirt of one of my soldiers. Demand what you've come here to do. And if it's what I think it is, you should know, our parents have already given their opinion on the matter and so has my wife. I stand alone in my beliefs, it seems."

Our parents are with me? Perhaps they're trying to remain on my good side.

"Can we all agree our parents made a stupid decision in keeping me away for so long? Don't lie because I know I only returned because you insisted after becoming underboss."

"I do."

"Good. You've witnessed Hawke's hatred for our parents. Do you want me to feel the same about you?"

His eyes narrow. "Stop beating around what you've come to demand and just say it. Actually," he picks up his phone, "wait. There's another party involved in this. Let's bring him in."

He quickly taps on his phone then sets it down, levelling his stare with me as we wait for the door to open and shut, neither of us glancing as Rosen treads through Nico's office. He stops a couple feet away.

"Go on." Nico gestures. "Get back to threatening me."

His off-handed behaviour is disrespectful, and my jaw tightens, clamping down on the annoyance, so I can make my points in a rational manner. "This isn't a fucking game, Nico. No more. I've played by this family's rules my entire life. Our parents sent me away and somehow, fucking forgot about me, not considering what being abandoned would do to my mental well-being. Then you, big brother, bring me home. Fantastic, but at first chance, I'm a tool. For a marriage that, by the way,

Rossi doesn't really want either. A connection between families. Politics. That's all it will ever be." Stabbing a finger onto his desk, I lean closer. "But *I'm* not politics. I'm not putting up with this. I want to be here with you, with Rafael, with our parents, but being back in this life doesn't mean being used that way."

Nico's expression only breaks when I finish speaking and he stands, towering over me. "You're asking me to break an alliance. What, to be with a soldier?" He jerks his head toward Rosen.

"Rosen isn't a part of my request." *Not completely.* "This is about me, Nico. Me and my life. You married a woman who deceived you," I throw my hands up, "but I can't be with a man you literally trust with your life? With *my* life."

"It's not that simple."

"Then please, enlighten me. Why is the connection to New York so important?"

Nico's jaw rolls as he builds his response carefully. "With the De Falco issue, they're not only influential to have on our side, but they're also smart business. Having a connection to their family is huge."

"At the price of my happiness," I conclude.

"It's your role, Aurora."

"That's the issue, Nico. You want us all to fall in line with how you think things should be, but you forget, we're human. You and our parents lost all right to using me as a pawn the *second* you sent me away and never brought me home."

I think I've won because for a long minute, Nico doesn't speak. Doesn't blink. Only stares at me. His one and only movement, finally, is to glance at Rosen. "Years before any of us were born, this family did wrong by New York. We have the chance to fix it."

I lean closer, not letting up on my stance. Not until I walk away the victor. Baring my teeth, I reply, "Not at the expense of me, you don't."

"That's what being in the mafia is about," he says, his tone less harsh now. "We're a unit. Loyal." His gaze flicks to Rosen with that last word, his jaw clamping tighter. "Loyalty means working for the family. I lead it. You help foster connections."

"Then I want no part of it. I'll leave."

Nico explodes, his fist coming down on his desk. "Aurora, what you're asking for could start a war. This would be the second time we've duped the Rossi family, and right now, a feud with New York is the last thing we need."

"That sounds like your problem. The last thing *I* needed was to be alone growing up."

He pretends my words have no effect, but they do, because more of his resolve cracks and he glances at Rosen. "Your take? You've already shattered allegiance by not keeping your hands to yourself. Do I grant Aurora the freedom she's asking and risk a war?"

"There will be a battle regardless of the decisions you make, sir. If she walks down the aisle to any man but me, I'll slaughter them."

Precarious words. Except...no. Instead of showing any anger whatsoever, Nico lifts back to his feet and paces around his desk. He stops in front of me, his eyes still locked on Rosen.

"You have no fucking idea the impossible situation you've placed me in."

"Except there is no decision, Nico," I tell him, drawing his attention back to me. "You seem to think I'm asking, but I'm not. Call this an impasse and if you want to kick me out because of it, save yourself the breath because I'll start packing."

I angle away, only partially meaning my words. Partially, because, if Della and our parents already stood against him on this, I don't imagine him making the decision he's determined to do so.

In one swift movement, he yanks me tightly to his chest for a hug, conveying physical emotion. "Proud of you, sis," he mumbles into my hair.

"What?" I go completely still, more so when he releases me, unable to move or do anything but watch and wait for the punchline. Agreeing is one thing, but pride is something entirely different.

"You didn't take the easy path. And I have no fucking idea what I'll do about New York, but that's a later problem. You might have been raised without the Corsetti influence, Aurora, but you're more like us than you know." He pauses, his lips curling in the corners. "We don't grow weak women here. Our mother withstood everything Father threw at her. Della duped me, and still made me fall for her. Mother and Della both get involved in the family in ways women from other crime families aren't. With you, it's clear, you're not the princess we all assumed you'd be, but rather, an individual. You're a Corsetti, Aurora, and to force you down the aisle would be an insult to our name. You win. You're out of the engagement. Because you're right: I did lose all rights to using you as a pawn." He shifts his attention to Rosen, his mouth flattening. "As for you, I'm completely within my rights to kill you. My father is leaving your fate in my hands, but unfortunately, you're too much like a brother to me. You are the most loyal soldier I have and the moment you looked twice at Aurora, I already lost, even if no one knew it at the time. When it mattered, you stepped up. You drove yourself to near-death trying to get Rozelyn. You sat by Aurora's bedside for days. When she came to you last night, you kept her with you instead of sending her to me." He holds up his hands in submission, falling back against his desk. "And now you talk of starting a war to keep her for yourself. How I see it, I already lost. Now go, both of you, I have to call Rafael and get this figured out."

I don't bother hiding my grin, spurred with a new focus to find my cell phone and input Hawke's number so I can message him the updates, as he requested.

At the doorway, Nico calls Rosen's name. "You hurt her; I kill you."

"Pretty sure she'll hurt me herself," Rosen replies with a smirk, before pulling me out of the office and shutting the door.

He immediately swings me around, slamming my back against the wall and crowding me. "You, *princesse*, fucking terrify me sometimes."

I giggle, resting my hand over his chest. "Like you wouldn't have done the same. I'm happy it's over with. Fuck." I push out a long breath. "I swear, even my insides were quivering. My brother is petrifying. Kudos to Della for once doing what she had to."

"Well, you looked like a goddamned queen standing up for yourself. I'm not sure if I could love you any more than I already do." His expression quickly changes to a somber one, and his fingers play in my hair, his eyes locked on my neck rather than my face when he speaks. "I won't be able to offer you that, you know."

I scoff. "Rosen, you know I don't—"

"It's everything, Aurora. I live on a soldier's salary. I mean, it's a hefty amount because your family is generous, but not as much as you could have gotten with Rossi. I'll provide for you in any way you want, but I can't make you the queen of any mafia. I'm merely a soldier and—"

This time, I cut him off by shoving my hand against his mouth. "You think I care about that? Why are you second-guessing us when we've won?" I drop my hand so he can respond, but the break in speech reminds me we're still outside

Nico's office, so I duck under his arm, taking his hand in mine as I tug him down the hall toward the stairs and up to my bedroom.

Once we're through the door, I usher him in and position my back against it, to ensure he can't escape until we've talked. Rosen takes the same seat he had when he taught me to use my phone. His arms stretch out over the backing and levelling his gaze on me, he crooks two fingers in my direction, silently commanding me forward.

I obey because the rewards are worth it. I almost skip forward, stopping right in front of him. He tips his chin toward his lap, which I happily submit, sitting and drawing my legs up, using the space between his own to steady me.

"Are you going to talk to me?" I murmur.

"I'm not second-guessing you," he responds to my earlier question. "But you must understand this isn't a game. You're it for me. But this means your life will be whatever *we* make it, not your brother. I'm not an underboss; I'm a soldier."

"Good. I don't know if you've noticed, but that life isn't what I want."

I think back to the other day when Rosen held me in a similar position inside his car during a mental breakdown when considering my future, and what I was thinking about before even leaving the house, wondering if Rossi would approve of me working with children, or earning a degree, or anything to keep me occupied.

"I can't work at the garden forever, I know that, but would you care if I did something else with my time? Something like…" I press my lips together, suddenly feeling silly for even asking this. "Would you care if I got a degree? Maybe something that could get me working with children. You heard Nico; even Mom and Della work within the family, but there's nothing here I want to help with when all my enjoyment relates to making children's lives better. Maybe something in child and youth care, or a teacher, or," I shrug a shoulder, frowning at my own directionless rambles, "I don't know, something."

Cupping my cheek, he brings his mouth to mine. "I think that's an amazing idea, Aurora. You can do whatever the hell you want, *princesse*. Your future is yours."

"It's ours," I correct. There were other realizations I had that day, and other things he talked with me about. Things that weren't pertinent to his life back then. "Do you want kids?"

He blinks, taken aback, and his focus shifts to the side of the room, like he's really considering. "I don't know," he finally responds. "I never gave relationships much consideration, so I hadn't contemplated anything further. Maybe. I don't know." He rubs circles on my back. "If you want to be a mother, Aurora, then I'll be honoured to raise a child with you."

His response is positive, considering where my own feelings are. "I mean," I bite down on my bottom lip, weakly shrugging again. "I don't know. Right now...no. The future? Maybe. I don't really want to think about all that now. Like I said in the past, I feel like *I'm* barely an adult, and thinking about caring for a child feels so far out of reach."

"That's perfect. You were raised to feel everything must happen now, but you and me, we don't have to be rushed. We can table this conversation for another day. Another year."

This time, I initiate the kiss, grateful. "Thanks for understanding. Also, I do want to marry you, Rosen, but maybe not right away. With everything that's recently happened," I shudder, "I think a break from weddings will be good."

He chuckles, his warm breath mingling with the strands of my hair. "As long as I get to call you my wife, you pick the time and place." He grabs my hand, resting it over his heart. "*Princesse,* this right here—my heart—it's fuckin' yours now. What you do with it is completely in your control."

57
ROSEN

3 Days Later

"I'll admit this isn't exactly the future I had planned for my daughter, but I'm not completely disappointed either." Lorenzo Corsetti pours three glasses of scotch and carries them toward Nico's desk, resting them on the edge for all of us to take one. "With you, at least she'll remain in the city."

Had he never agreed to a union with the Rossis, she could have always remained here. But it's a thought I bite my tongue on, taking the offered glass and raising it in a small toast.

Nico swipes the third, chugging it down in one gulp. "When's the wedding?"

"When she wants there to be one." I'll admit, I'd love to put a ring on her finger sooner than later and officially make her mine, to change her name from Corsetti to Corrigan, but so much of Aurora's life has been decided for her and if she needs a few extra months, or years, before she's willing to take that leap, so be it.

Nico's brows rise over the rim of his glass. "For fuck's sake, you two don't make it easy. Wed because then the Rossis won't have a leg to stand on."

I shrug, wanting him off the topic of my nuptials. "Maybe."

"What did you wish to speak about?" Lorenzo asks, leaning against Nico's desk.

"Moving out. I thank you for the room, but I've opted to get an apartment downtown. Rafael said there's a condo a few floors down from his available, so I'll be moving there."

Even amidst his drama in dealing with Maurice's daughter, he still managed to find time to help me out with this.

"With my sister, you mean." Nico's lips flatten, unimpressed.

"Coming from the same person who was asking about a wedding. Surprised Raf didn't mention it."

"You two can stay here," my underboss commands with finality.

I could, but here doesn't provide the privacy my *princesse* and I require. I'd rather Nico not overhear her wild cries as I dish both rewards and punishments.

"No thanks." I down the rest of my drink before placing the glass on his desk. "You seem to think I've come here asking permission. If you didn't want her with me, I'd be dead already. I've bought the condo and now it's up to Aurora to choose to move in with me or remain here, but I'll provide for her, and living inside this mansion isn't what she deserves."

Lorenzo lets out a bark of laughter and takes his glass back to the sidebar, pouring a greater amount than before. "I've always liked you, Rosen. You have your father's humour."

Nico merely shakes his head. "I'm really glad it's you, Rosen. Rossi seemed too weak to handle Aurora. She has you wrapped around her finger."

Essentially. I stand, dismissing myself. "If you'll excuse me,

I'm going to pack up my room and pick up my keys from Rafael."

~

I wait a week before bringing Aurora downtown because, as much as I hate it, I'm nervous. She's going from living in a mansion to a condo, and while I know she's not the kind of woman who cares about that, I want to do right by her and that means providing her with everything.

"What are we doing here?" she asks, clutching my hand in the elevator as it climbs the numerous floors until dinging with our stop. "We visiting someone?"

The doors chime, sliding open to reveal an ornate hallway, lined with small overhead chandeliers. I direct Aurora about halfway down before stopping in front of a door.

"Not exactly," I respond to her earlier question as I reach inside my pocket and pull out the set of keys Rafael gave me a few days ago. "Less visiting and more staying for a while."

"What?" she squeaks, staring open-mouthed at the door I unlock and open. "What did you do, Rosen?"

"Go in and check it out."

She does, slowly passing over the doorframe, pausing in the entranceway, scanning the bachelor-style, split-level apartment. The living room on a lower level, the kitchen a few steps up, a dining-room platform attached. To the right, a short hallway leading toward the bedroom.

"I bought furniture, but I wanted to leave decorating to you."

Aurora wanders deeper into the condo. "You bought us a place?"

"Yes. This is Raf's building, and he mentioned an opening

when he knew I was searching. You deserve a place *you* choose to make a home out of."

"But you live at the mansion."

"For simplicity. I had no one to come home to, so it was easier to live where my job is."

Aurora spins slowly, her eyes wide and brimming with excitement. In the next instant, she's bounding over the small space and throwing herself into my arms. Her legs and arms wind around my waist and neck and I walk forward, shutting the door before carrying her through the condo.

She peppers kisses along the length of my jaw until taking my mouth in a heated kiss. "I fucking love you, Rosen. You got us a house! This is amazing!"

"I got us a house so we can live without your brother breathing over our shoulders. So I can fuck you for hours on end without anyone overhearing. Our space. *Your* space, Aurora. If you want it."

"A million times, yes, Rosen!"

"Good. Now, do you want to look around or can I show you the best part?"

Aurora's fingers wind into the hair at the base of my neck. She leans into me, pressing her breasts against my chest. "I think you know the answer to that."

"Good," I repeat, positioning my hands beneath her ass to ensure she doesn't slip from my hold as I walk the length of the hallway toward our bedroom. It's only been outfitted with a bed so far, but right now, that's all I need.

A bed and one gift for her.

In the bedroom, I lower her to her feet. She clings to me for a second longer, making a whining noise in the back of her throat, but eventually does release me to study the expansive bedroom. The wall of floor-to-ceiling windows, the door opposite from the bed, boasting a large walk-in closet, and in the centre—a king-sized bed. An unmade bed, as I wanted her to choose the bedding.

She wanders closer, her eyes going to the rings I've had installed on each post. Slowly, she reaches out to touch one. "Are these—?"

"Yes. I told you once, if I had you, I'd tie you to my bed and never let you go." I nuzzle her neck, my tongue darting out to feel the thump of her pulse. She shivers, turning away from the bed and into my arms. "Therefore, now that I have you, I'm keeping that promise."

She bounces on her toes. "Tonight?"

Yes. "If you're good. If you go to your bedside table and look inside."

Her brows dive downward, wiping away her excitement. She does as I request and heads in the necessary direction. opening the drawer, and finding what I placed there this morning.

A small, black box—a necklace-sized jewellery box.

Aurora might not want to think about marriage yet, which I respect, but a pre-engagement gift for her to wear was something I indulged in. Now, I'd love to know what's in her mind as she opens it.

"Rosen..." She turns as her finger hooks around the simple gold necklace with a diamond rose pendant and lifts it from the case. "This is beautiful. But expe—"

"Yours," I inturrupt. "You won't let me get you a ring yet, but you deserve something regardless."

"It's beautiful. I won't ever take this off."

She presses the chain into my hand, her touch lingering for a second. "Could you put it on?" She whirls around and gathers her hair, moving it to the side, so I can gain easier access to her neck.

Once it's clasped, Aurora turns to face me again, her fingers stroking over the rose pendant. I've never bought a woman a gift before but seeing the chain around her neck makes my insides heat.

I toss her onto the bed behind us, immediately climbing over her. A savage sensation slices open my heart and demands I fuck her until she can think of nothing else. Stretching, I reach for one of the side tables, and gather the rope I placed there.

"We're going to make a mess of the bed. There's no sheets."

I lay the rope around one of her wrists, tying it methodically before stretching the same arm to the corresponding loop. "Then I'll buy another one. In case you've forgotten, you still owe me for risking your life when you discharged yourself from the hospital." I work on her other wrist. "And seeing that necklace around your neck is making me absolutely feral, *princesse*, so believe me, a fucking bed isn't changing anything."

"I'm still dressed," she points out, voice boarding on breathless, and we haven't even begun yet.

"That so, hmm." Trailing my finger over her check, I linger around the pendant, before tracing the dip of her breasts, where her shirt begins. Grasping the material, I quickly rid her of it.

She watches as I toss it to the side and get to work on her bra too. Once I have it removed, she murmurs, "You rip my clothes, I'll have nothing to wear when we leave."

"Leave?" Humoured, I grab her chin, forcing her eyes on me. "Oh, you're not leaving, *princesse*. Not ever."

"Never's a long time."

Brushing my lips over hers, I repeat, "Never, Aurora. Fucking never. I love you and this is where you're meant to be."

Her lips part, but my brat quickly returns, smirking at me through a much more devious expression. "Prove it."

Fucking happily.

Thank you for reading! Continue the series with The Beauty in Scars (Fractured Ever Afters #3), a Beauty and the Beast inspired forced proximity romance.

Shop signed books by scanning the code below:

ALSO BY M.L. PHILPITT

Fractured Ever Afters

A 6-book (& 2 novellas) mafia romance series of interconnected standalones based on fairytales, featuring the Montreal mafia and the New York Famiglia.

The Desire in Deception (Prequel Novella)

The Hunt in Elusion

The Craving in Slumber

The Beauty in Scars

The Freedom in Captivity

The Sound in Silencea

The Obscurity in Wishing

The Bonds in Christmas (Epilogue Novella)

The Bratva's Elite

A 4-book mafia series of interconnected standalones featuring the Russian Bratva.

Merciless Queen

Deadly Knight

Defensive Rook

Violent Pawn

Captive Writings

A new adult suspenseful romance series that progressively gets darker with each book

Ruthless Letters

Obsessive Messages

Vicious Texts

Burning Notes

Twisted Holidays

A series of dark romance holiday novellas

Silent Night

Egg Hunt

Fright Night

Be Mine

Midnight Kiss

Lucky Clover

Black Magick

A 5-book paranormal romance series of interconnected standalones featuring witches, vampires, shifters, mortals, and demons.

Dark Flame

Dark Mist

Dark Storm

Standalones

A Vampire for Christmas

Audiobooks

Silent Night

ACKNOWLEDGMENTS

First and foremost, thank you to YOU - my readers.

The biggest shout out goes to Rebecca Barney from Fairest Reviews Editing Services who worked diligently on multiple drafts and versions of this book. There is no word good enough to describe my gratitude.

To Megan for being there through the tears and voice messages and working through it all with me.

Colleen, thank you for being a wonderful beta and answering my billion questions.

Thank you to The Next Step PR. Colleen, Megan, Anna, and of course, Kiki - you're all amazing. Thank you for everything you do. You're the best team to have!

Thank you to Cat Imb of TRC Designs for creating the prettiest cover ever for Aurora and Rosen.

Thank you to Karina (@id_rather.be.the.moon) for double checking my French.

Thank you to all the bloggers, booktokers, and

bookstagrammers who helped with the release of this book. Your help doesn't go unnoticed!

ABOUT THE AUTHOR

USA Today Bestselling author M.L. Philpitt writes both dark romance and paranormal romance. When she's not writing made-up realities, she's reading them. She lives in Canada with her four pets and survives life with coffee and an obsession with fictional characters, especially the morally grey kind. By day, she masks as a therapist.

WARNINGS

- Explicit sexual content
- Mention of cancer
- Depiction of a child illness
- Physical violence
- Drugs
- Degregation
- Orgasm denial